THE GOLDEN ORANGE

Books by Joseph Wambaugh

Fiction
THE NEW CENTURIONS
THE BLUE KNIGHT
THE CHOIRBOYS
THE BLACK MARBLE
THE GLITTER DOME
THE DELTA STAR
THE SECRETS OF HARRY BRIGHT

Nonfiction
THE ONION FIELD
LINES AND SHADOWS
ECHOES IN THE DARKNESS
THE BLOODING

THE GOLDEN ORANGE

Joseph Wambaugh

BANTAM BOOKS
TORONTO · NEW YORK · LONDON · SYDNEY · AUCKLAND

THE GOLDEN ORANGE
A BANTAM BOOK 0 553 40255 2

*All of the characters in this book are fictitious, and any
resemblance to actual persons, living or dead, is purely
coincidental.*

Originally published in Great Britain by Bantam Press,
a division of Transworld Publishers Ltd.

PRINTING HISTORY
Bantam Press edition published 1990
Bantam Books edition published 1991

This book is set in 10/13pt Plantin by
County Typesetters, Margate, Kent

Bantam Books are published by Transworld Publishers Ltd.,
61–63 Uxbridge Road, Ealing, London W5 5SA, in Australia
by Transworld Publishers (Australia) Pty. Ltd., 15–23 Helles
Avenue, Moorebank, NSW 2170, and in New Zealand by
Transworld Publishers (N.Z.) Ltd., Cnr. Moselie and
Waipareira Avenues, Henderson, Auckland.

Printed and bound in Great Britain by
Cox & Wyman Ltd, Reading

For my son, David

ACKNOWLEDGMENTS

My thanks go to the officers of the Newport Beach Police Department, present and former, who treated me to terrific cop talk

and

to the many friends in and near the splendid bay of Newport who provided much of the atmosphere

and

to David Pillsbury, stalwart sailor of The Golden Orange

THE GOLDEN ORANGE

1: *The Drinker's Hour*

'*Welcome to The Drinker's Hour!*'

That's how they introduced their 3.00 a.m. show, those doom jockeys.

Still, sometimes they didn't arrive exactly on time. Sometimes they wouldn't perch on the foot of his bed until 3.30 or so, and once they even showed at 4.15. But more often than not, they were ready to open their act within ten minutes, either way, of 3.00 a.m. The Drinker's Hour.

Winnie Farlowe's twin phantoms needed about three hours, after which he could once again fall unconscious until mid-morning, thereby screwing up his entire day, making himself feel so rotten he'd start drinking a bit earlier in the afternoon to 'right' himself. After which the cycle would repeat.

He had dubbed them 'Fear' and 'Remorse', those winged apparitions, and imagined them as turkey buzzards, black ones with hooked bony beaks, and necks like Ronald Reagan. He'd learned at an AA meeting (which his lawyer had *forced* him to attend) that lots of drinkers had horrific night visitations not connected with d.t.'s. This, after the drinkers were jolted awake by a drop in blood sugar, or by withdrawal syndrome. The tormentors could take any gruesome form: bat, snake, rodent, spider, pit bull, lawyer. Often they appeared as ex-wives or husbands, parents, children living or dead – dead ones made

11

memorable visits – or as Memories of Youth. And, of course, as Lost Promise. Winnie's night sweats, all that dog-paddling in the flotsam and jetsam of life, were partly brought about by his fortieth birthday. The Death of Youth.

After the wake-up call Winnie's buzzards took turns crawling all over his besotted steaming flesh – cackling, snuffling, growling. There was no point fighting them and lights didn't scare them. It was usually the bigger one, Remorse, that did more damage. Winnie would close his eyes and feel the stinking smothering wings pinning him, while the bloody beak dipped into his palpitating heart.

Once he'd made the mistake of describing his 3.00 a.m. horrors to the various saloon psychologists at Spoon's Landing, his favorite waterfront gin mill. He got what he deserved.

'Winnie,' a beached sea poet clucked, 'you're just another sad clown playing a nightly gig under the boozer's big top. Under a circus canopy of putrid buzzard wings.'

Spoon himself was more prosaic and even less sympathetic. 'You gotta learn to ignore whiskey goblins,' the saloonkeeper told Winnie. 'Things that go bump in the night? That's just the other drunk that lives upstairs.'

But this night Fear was the most ravenous. Smaller but relentless, the feathered demon went straight for Winnie's guts, tearing at viscera, rooting for the swollen slab (It must be swollen by now!) of heaving quivering liver. Remorse gripped him with iron talons but Fear ate him alive.

Winnie's awful memories of the Yuletide evening were vague. He'd been drinking more than usual at the time, predictable during the holiday season (again according to the AA speaker). It was a week when Remorse was supposedly the hungriest. Winnie's sharpest memories of that terrible evening were all sensuous, beginning with the smell of hot rum, a Christmas season specialty at Spoon's Landing.

'You're listing to starboard,' one of the hull scrapers from Cap'n Cook's Boatyard had warned while Winnie sat at the bar topping off his giant thermos with Spoon's hot rum. 'Maybe you shouldn't go to work tonight.'

Winnie could not remember riding his beach bike from Spoon's Landing to the ferry. Nor had he any memory whatsoever of taking over the boat from a blond, permanently tanned summertime ferry pilot who was home for the Christmas holidays from Harvard where he pursued an MBA that would, the kid claimed, be followed by a Beemer, a condo not farther than three hundred feet from the water, and a membership in *the* yacht club. Winnie could not remotely remember the first several ferry crossings that he apparently navigated without a hitch. He could vaguely remember a group of youngsters singing Christmas carols on Balboa Island.

People on Orange County's Gold Coast loved the Balboa Island ferry. The one-way, two-minute, one-thousand-foot crossing from Balboa Island to the Balboa peninsula and back was still only 20 cents for pedestrians and 55 cents for a car and driver. Residents of The Golden Orange say that the toot of the ferry whistles is as reassuring as high tide, and for tourists it's the hottest ticket in town. There's the panorama from the deck: the old Balboa Pavilion, the sleek Newport Center skyline on the distant hills, the channels teeming with nine thousand boats, the waterfront homes with multiple boat slips and just enough land to make you stretch a bit when you lean

13

toward your neighbor to borrow a jar of yuppie mustard.

The Newport Harbor Christmas Boat Parade was probably the most festive event of the year on the Orange County Gold Coast, Newport Bay being one of the largest residential harbors in the world, and probably the wealthiest in median income. All three ferryboats were in service during the holidays, and on every crossing carried three cars and as many as fifty passengers. Many of the ferry pilots were young men who'd gotten their Coast Guard licenses after a college boating program. For them it was a temporary or part-time job, and a better way to meet girls than being a lifeguard.

Winnie Farlowe was not a typical ferry pilot, but he had been taken on temporarily upon the recommendation of his former boss, a Newport Beach police captain, who, thinking Winnie needed a break, had encouraged him to get his license to operate a passenger vessel.

The police department's reconstruction of that evening – written by a merciless female cop – alleged that Winnie Farlowe had, in the middle of a ferry crossing, emerged from the little pilothouse clad in deck shoes, blue jeans, and a Hobie Cat sweatshirt and yelled at the astonished passengers as the ferry immediately veered to starboard: 'You people are just as good as all the rich assholes in this harbor! You're gonna be in the boat parade!'

Then, according to witnesses, the pilot reentered the pilothouse, turned hard to port, and powered into the queue of two hundred boats motoring down the channel, two hundred floating Christmas parties ablaze with twinkling colored lights, awash with festive decorations, and brimming with good cheer.

Winnie somehow remembered gazing at the Balboa

14

Pavilion that night. He always found the old Victorian edifice nostalgic and lovely, its observation platform and cupola studded with permanent white lights. He may have been looking aft toward the pavilion when he rammed a fifty-eight-foot motor yacht, sending its giant necklace of five hundred Christmas lights whiplashing from the fly bridge and crashing to the deck in a series of pops that reminded him of an AR-15 in the boonies of Nam.

Then, again according to witnesses, there was lots of screaming and yelling when the ferry passengers panicked. And dozens of parade boats – sloops, ketches, motor yachts, runabouts, boats of every stripe – began to scatter, their skippers grabbing radio dials to summon the Harbor Patrol.

Within three minutes of the first ramming, Winnie Farlowe had donned a Santa hat he'd borrowed from a wooden mermaid at Spoon's Landing and screamed, 'You're all my prisoners!'

It was then that a beach volleyball star aboard the ferry – a guy much bigger and fifteen years younger than Winnie – decided to impress a volley dolly cuddled next to him in his mom's Mercedes.

He leaped from the Mercedes on to the deck, yelling, 'OK, you drunk! Outta that cabin!'

Which caused Winnie to reply, 'I was gonna shoot myself. But now I think I'll shoot *you*, you yuppie son of a bitch.'

The reference to a gun caused police divers to drag the channel for two days before they finally concluded that there was not, and never had been, a firearm in Winnie Farlowe's possession.

Nevertheless, the volleyballer retreated to his mom's

15

Mercedes, where the volley dolly screamed, 'Chill out, dude! Chill out!' to Winnie Farlowe.

Her boyfriend leaped from the car once again after Winnie reemerged from the pilothouse babbling something about his ex-wife and threatening to shoot all adult *female* passengers starting with the male volleyballer, whom Winnie called 'the biggest pussy on this boat'.

Which caused the volleyballer to abandon the blonde, the Benz and the ferry itself. He dove over the rail into the frigid, silt-clouded water of Newport Bay and swam the first thirty yards underwater to elude nonexistent gunfire before he was hauled out by two teens in a Boston Whaler.

The pirated ferry had reached the tip of Bayshores, only sixty feet from the former home of John Wayne (on offer for a quick sale at a reduced price of $6,500,000), when the renegade ferry was overtaken by two boats, filled with gun-toting sheriff's deputies and backed by a Newport Beach Police Department chopper hovering overhead and lighting everything in the channel with blinding spotlights, including Winnie Farlow who was urging terrified tourists to sing 'Jingle Bells'.

When Winnie was released on bail the following day, and visited his lawyer, Chip Simon – who'd handled Winnie's recent divorce – the former ferry pilot claimed to remember clearly a Grand Banks 42, lit by green and red laser lights, towing a helium-filled, thirty-foot Dopey the dwarf in a Santa beard. Except that while Winnie was plumbing his spotty memory, he was informed by his lawyer that the law firm's own Bertram 46 was decorated with the parade's biggest Christmas figure, which was not Dopey but Rudolph the Reindeer. And that there was *no* Dopey in that parade, except for his client. The suggestion was made then and there to plea *nolo contendere* and pray for probation.

Three months later, Chip Simon hadn't changed his mind. And he'd gotten all the continuances he could. He sat quietly while Winnie sweated his way through a reading of the lurid police report.

Finally the lawyer asked, 'Did you ever read *Moby Dick*, Winnie?'

'No, Chip, but I'm sure you have,' Winnie replied.

'There was the great whale, powering along like a floating island,' explained the lawyer, 'carrying all sorts of land life with him. Just like you taking all those people and cars right into the boat parade. People screaming and boats crashing out of your way. *Moby Dick* revisited!'

'Now I know why I hired you, Chip,' said Winnie. 'You've got such a heartwarming, bright and optimistic way about you. You light up a room. Like a frigging electric chair.'

'Could've been worse,' Chip Simon said. 'You could've sunk a couple of boats out there instead of only banging into a few. You could've drowned a few . . .'

'Please, Chip, I got a headache already.'

'It's the story of your . . .'

'Night. It's one goddamn night in my life! What about the fifteen years I gave to police work? What about the three years in the marines? I'm a Nam vet, for chrissake!' Then Winnie remembered something he'd heard from the beached poet at Spoon's Landing. Winnie said, 'I take a few drinks so the turbulent waters of life can glass out and let me trim the sails and cruise for a few hours.'

'The judge will be made aware of all that, Winnie,' the lawyer said, writing: *Life's turbulent waters. Trim the sails.*

17

All the time he was talking to Winnie, Chip Simon was toying with a crystal paperweight that was the latest hot toy among Gold Coast executives. It was a Testarossa, a car coveted by Newport Beach yuppies. Nobody *ever* called it a Ferrari. If you didn't know what a Testarossa was . . .

'I think it's partly a midlife crises,' Winnie said. 'I turned forty a couple weeks ago. I got a midlife crisis so real you could put a coat a paint on it. Wait'll it happens to you in ten years.'

'Eleven.'

'Eleven. Or maybe it was the divorce. I always tried to do the decent thing with that man-eater.'

'How well I remember her during the hearing for spousal support,' Chip Simon said cheerfully.

'I could never decide which one a her twins was more horrible,' Winnie said. 'They were both clones of their mother. When I met her second ex-husband one time I asked him which twin was meaner and he said to me, "Win, it's a jump ball." Still I *adopted* those monsters! The judge should be told what a decent guy I really am. Legally adopting her brats!'

'Some people might say that such a rash decision is proof of your . . .'

'I'm *not* an alcoholic! I jist shouldn't drink rum!'

'. . . drinking problem, I was going to say.'

'It was the Christmas season and I couldn't stop thinking about how she savaged me with the child support for my *adopted* kids. How she even took away my sailboat. I earned that sailboat with my insurance payoff when I got hurt.'

'Yes, it's very sad,' the lawyer agreed, running over a

18

bent paper clip, a make-believe pedestrian, with the Testarossa.

'I'd still be a cop today,' Winnie said, 'if I hadn't hurt my back chasing a boat burglar all over that yacht club. Getting knocked down the companionway of some millionaire's seventy-five-footer that never leaves the dock except to get hauled out for inspection every year or so. Jist a place for him and his cronies and bimbos to get drunk on. Might as well be set in concrete right there in front a the club for all the good it does. Kind of guys that put shoe trees in their Top-Siders. And here I am, unemployed with a bad back and that barracuda chewing up my balls and pirating my sailboat and leaving me beached and broke. The only person in town that watches a TV without a remote control. I shoulda bought a copy of *Soldier of Fortune* and hired me somebody like Ollie North to snuff that man-eater. So why don't you tell *that* to the judge, Chip?'

'I'll tell him everything positive that's relevant, Winnie,' Chip Simon said, smoothing back his fresh haircut, causing Winnie to observe that ever since Michael Douglas made that *Wall Street* movie, every yuppie in The Golden Orange had his hair Dippity-do'ed. And Chip wore silk suspenders decorated with little water-skiers.

'And I'll certainly point out that a pensioned, fifteen-year veteran of the Newport Beach Police Department is not just some *ordinary* unemployed beach rat,' Chip added.

'They're treating this like piracy, for chrissake! It was nothing more than joyriding, is all!'

'Except that the joyriding took place not in a car but on a ferryboat, Winnie. Not on a public highway, but in the bay of Newport. In the midst of the Christmas boat parade when the harbor was alive with boats and twinkling lights. And the smell of hot rum filled the air and filled the defendant's belly. That's what my learned opponent, the assistant district attorney, will say.'

'So nobody's gonna care that I actually did my best to continue on active police duty with a herniated disk I got when a boatyard burglar coldcocked me with a length of anchor chain knocking me down into the galley of a booze cruiser they shoulda hauled out for bottom paint and it wouldn't of been there in the first place!'

Writing once again, Chip said, 'Judge Singleton is impressed with a good clean job history, Winnie. Give me yours *before* the police work.'

'Lifeguard, US marine, street cop. That's it,' said Winnie. 'Three jobs in my whole life. None of which am I now young enough or fit enough to perform.'

'The judge will be impressed, I hope, by the fact that you're voluntarily attending AA meetings,' the lawyer said.

'Because a *your* insistence. I'm not one a *them*.'

'Tell me, how many meetings have you attended since the ferryboat incident?'

'Four, I think,' Winnie lied. 'Altogether. More or less.'

Chip Simon wrote: *Has attended at least four meetings a week for past three months. At same time he looks for work.* Then the lawyer wrote in caps: BAD BACK PREVENTS EMPLOYMENT.

'Before Tammy's ambulance-chasing shyster crucified me with the spousal support and shanghaied my sailboat I had hopes of hiring on as a fishing boat skipper,' Winnie reminded him. 'Put *that* down.'

'I suggest we forget that divorce,' Chip said.

'Maybe if she hadn't been born in the Debbie Reynolds era she wouldn't be such a pitiless crocodile. I never met a broad yet named Tammy wasn't a nut cracker.'

'It would help if you could get a job, *any* job.'

'We're going to court next Monday, Chip.'

'Any job or even a prospect of a job. I can't paint a complete portrait of Winston Farlowe without the materials. And I can't introduce irrelevant information. By the way, did you know that lots of American baby boomers like you are named Winston? For Churchill, of course.'

'What the hell's relevant about that, Chip?'

'Just an interesting aside.'

'Is it *relevant* that I thought Tammy and me were happily married when in fact she was in the process of silkworming our *Loveboat* cruise and leaving me dead in the water?'

The lawyer didn't answer but wrote: *Ship of Fools*.

'Is it *relevant* that she dumped me for the owner of a dental clinic who started out exploring her root canal and just kept moving south?'

'Very little about your failed marriage is relevant. Now tell me, Win, have you reached the stage of drinking wherein you're cold sober until a given drink? You know, the tenth, fifteenth or twenty-fifth, whatever? You know, when you never know *which* drink will turn off the torment and shut down the stress factor and give you alcoholic bliss?'

At that moment, Winnie Farlowe knew that he *hated* his lawyer, Chip Simon. So while Chip gave his writing hand a rest to rev up the Testarossa, Winnie said, 'If nothing I

21

can say is relevant and if the judge decides to fire a broadside, what would he give me? Realistically? Me. An ex-cop. A person with a clean record. Only mistake I made was drinking rum!'

'Judge Singleton despises drunk drivers and, by inference, will hate a drunk ferry pilot even more. I wouldn't be shocked if he gave you three months in the county jail.' Chip was still revving the Testarossa.

Just like that. Three months.

Winnie nearly had his first midday visitation from the winged scavengers who ate his guts. Three months! The Orange County Jail! One of the most overcrowded lockups in California! A jail so jammed with the scum of the coast, not to mention inland Orange County, that the sheriff had actually been instructed by a US District Court judge not to incarcerate more prisoners in the dangerously overcrowded facility. Three months!

'I can't do three months in jail, Chip!' Winnie said. 'I can't do three *days*!'

The lawyer propped up a paper clip again, shook his head sadly, ran it down with his Testarossa and said, 'Yes, life truly *is* unfair, isn't it.'

Then Winnie watched as Chip aimed the Testarossa at the pathetic kneeling wire man and squashed it flat.

Reliving that meeting with Chip Simon brought forth a dive-bombing attack from one of the winged scavengers. Fear plummeted straight for his guts. Winnie cried out and bolted upright in bed. The huge turkey buzzard retreated and grinned like a gargoyle, a coil of Winnie's large intestine dangling and dancing from that horrible leering rictus.

22

2: *The Ghetto*

Tess Binder secretly hated the ocean because she feared infinity. Of course, the water in Newport Harbor is usually placid, particularly in the summer, but it *is* seawater, even though at night the harbor sometimes reminded her of lily pads and frogs. The water never reassured her, not like the water of Lake Arrowhead where she'd summered as a girl.

Tess liked to pretend that it didn't chase the moon and tide, this normally placid water outside her home on Linda Isle, but it certainly did impose definite limits in her life: north to Dover Shores in upper Newport Bay, so-called because of the white cliffs, then south to the Balboa peninsula, west to Balboa Coves, and east . . . She didn't like to think of east. East was the harbor jetty and beyond. There *her* water turned into the vast bleak ocean. Infinity.

It wasn't only infinity that frightened Tess Binder. Since her latest divorce she had discovered that she was afraid of crowds, sagging triceps, AIDS, herpes, being single, trying to survive on her last $50,000.

Tess Binder was forty-three years old, and had been searching with growing despair for another husband, one who would *not* insist on a prenuptial agreement. But there were very few of those around The Golden Orange these days.

Tess opened the balcony door of the master bedroom

23

and put on her round tortoiseshell *serious* glasses to look west toward Bayshores. But she didn't have a main channel view. She was forced to face Pacific Coast Highway and to endure traffic noise. Once, at a party on Spyglass Hill, she heard her side of the island called 'the ghetto' by a Linda Isle neighbor on the other side.

She had made the mistake of starting the day by going grocery shopping in the market she'd used during her short marriage to Ralph Cunningham: one of those where white eggplant, apple pears, elephant garlic, and Maui onions are individually wrapped in little nets. And the long-stemmed strawberries are so big that only eight of them fit in a basket, and Pepino melons go for nearly ten dollars a pound, ditto for Holland purple bell peppers. She *did* note that soft-shell crab was on sale at thirty bucks. And white truffles were being 'offered' at sixteen hundred dollars a kilo. In short, a week's shopping could overdraw a plumber's Visa card.

Just shopping there made it impossible *not* to think of her present state of affairs. She was surrounded in the store by people she knew casually, people who could still afford to buy anything they wanted. She saw the *parvenue* wife of a Costa Mesa car dealer, buying slabs of abalone like it was lunch meat, at forty dollars per pound. That was when a panic attack struck Tess Binder, the first since Ralph Cunningham left her. She had to get *out* of that place in a hurry. She had to go to the beach.

When she reached her five-year-old Mercedes (the one Ralph Cunningham let his office help use to run errands), she discovered with amazement that she was holding an empty banana skin! She'd been compulsively eating a banana while she was in the store and hadn't even realized

24

it. When she got in the car she almost wept. Tess Binder wasn't just an abandoned woman. She was a goddamn thief.

The Easter season had brought with it Santa Ana winds from the desert. It was 85 degrees Fahrenheit on the sand at her club, and the club's hot mommas were white-hot on that Saturday afternoon. There was a tanker load of Bain de Soleil sliding over a thousand square yards of winter-white, health-club – firm, middleaged female flesh on the tiny beach.

Some of the women chose to wear the dated string-bikinis instead of the newer French-cut. This by way of proclaiming that there were no irreparable stretch marks. No hip scars from liposuction, at least none you could notice. Most of the hot mommas were no younger than Cher and no older than Jane Fonda. Many could rival either when it came to body sculpting. It was astonishing what the Nautilus, the knife, and single-minded dedication had accomplished in The Golden Orange.

Tess Binder arrived on the beach that afternoon wearing tinted prescription glasses with white plastic frames. She nodded to the other hot mommas, acknowledged a few panther smiles and found a suitable place on the sand away from the others but close enough not to *seem* aloof. She sensed whispering, actually heard a few giggles, and imagined she heard a few clucks of sympathy. Which were about as genuine as those heard when Vilma Draper, former queen of the hot mommas, had experienced silicone-curdle and sued Dr Max Jenner (Max the Knife), a swashbuckling surgeon whose work was on carnal display in the club lounge one afternoon a week, when the price of booze was reduced and free food was offered.

As she was applying the lotion to her arms Tess got more depressed. There was no doubt about it, her triceps *were* sagging! Tomorrow she'd do at least three hundred tricep extensions.

Corky Peebles was smiling at Tess as though she was about to join her. Corky was at *least* forty-two years old, though she swore she was thirty-eight – one year younger than Tess claimed *she* was. Corky's triceps were firm and smooth, and there wasn't a dimple on her thighs, not one. She *must* have had a tummy tuck, but Tess couldn't see the goddamn scar. The fact is, her skin and mucle were twenty-five years old, the bone and viscera, forty-two.

The summerlike weather had brought hordes of outsiders to the club that weekend, including the Reverend Wilbur Matlock, a television celebrity who'd spent the last ten years pursuing evangelical work for the Cathedral of Heavenly Bliss. Tess watched as Reverend Matlock and two acolytes in blue satin cassocks stood solemnly on the yacht-lined docks just below the ramp leading down from the cocktail lounge. Reverend Matlock faced a resplendent yacht and raised his arms to the heavens, and prayed.

He said, 'May He who guides us on our voyage to eternity, keep this ship and this glorious crew safe from all harm!'

A few people sitting on the patio mumbled 'Amen' into their mai tais and piña coladas, and two of them started applauding but got shushed by the sober ones.

The 'ship' was the seventy-foot custom yacht *Ecstasy*. And 'this glorious crew' were Beverly Hills caterers hired for the day. It would *perhaps* voyage to Avalon Harbor on Santa Catalina Island once or twice a year, less than thirty miles from its slip at the club. The boat's owner, Jeb Driscoll, was busy with three commercial real estate developments in San Diego and L.A., and rarely saw his boat. Like the other seven-figure yachts docked at the club it was a condo-on-the-water, a *pied-à-mer*, so to speak.

Driscoll was single once again and had been definitely targeted by the hot mommas. But Tess Binder felt that she had no chance whatsoever with Jeb Driscoll, having blown her opportunity by foolishly accepting a marriage proposal from Ralph Cunningham, one of the biggest developers in Orange County, and the 303rd wealthiest man in America, according to *Forbes* magazine. Ralph had never become quite as popular as she'd hoped, in that he'd declined to join 'Team 100', along with the dozen or so Golden Orange donors who each gave $100,000 to the presidential campaign of George Bush. After multiple solicitations he did manage to step up with a $50,000 check, but it was too late, coming as it did after Bush was well into his insurmountable lead.

And then, long before George Bush was inaugurated, Ralph had played a game of singles at the John Wayne Tennis Club with a thirty-year-old manicurist who had a hell of a backhand and a tongue like fibrillating paddles. The manicurist and Ralph moved in together, and Tess was suddenly living alone in the ghetto, in a home she bought from him during the divorce with a minimum down payment and monthly payments that were exhausting what was left of her family trust. Her third marriage had lasted seventeen months from honeymoon to final decree.

Tess Binder had never thought for a minute that she couldn't persuade Ralph to abrogate the prenuptial agreement. If she'd known how heartless he was she'd

27

never have invested a chunk of her inheritance in gold certificates at exactly the wrong time with exactly the wrong swarm of goldbugs.

Lying on the hot sand, Tess suddenly felt a shadow cross. She looked up to find Corky Peebles in her ultrarevealing jet-black bikini, with a jet-black power bob like silent film star Louise Brooks. Tess was sure that Corky dyed her hair. Nobody's was *that* lustrously black, but she hadn't been able to prove it. And Tess hadn't had a real conversation with her since Corky had returned from a six-month cruise with the 342nd richest man in America who decided not to marry her after all.

'You should be visiting the tanning salon at least twice a week,' Corky said, kneeling in the sand, her fingernails studded with ersatz gems, à la Olympian Florence Griffith-Joyner.

'I think a natural tan might be less damaging than your . . . *unnatural* salon tan,' Tess said, forced to note that the goddamn powerhouse Lulu bob looked smashing on Corky.

'There's a great deal of research being done these days on the effects of ultra violets,' Corky said, peering across the dock at Reverend Matlock, who was being congratulated by several landlocked yachtsmen wearing blazers and a gin flush at eleven o'clock in the morning.

'Ultra Violet was the playmate of Andy Warhol,' Tess said dryly.

'Who?'

'Never mind.' Artsy allusions didn't register around these parts, but an obscure reference to Donald Trump or *any* billionaire west of Suez could get you an instant grin of recognition.

28

'Has Jeb invited you to tour his new boat?' Corky asked, sure that he had not. So far, only half a dozen locals had been aboard the yacht since its delivery, and Corky was one of them. Everyone knew that she'd slept with Driscoll on land and sea, and once, it was said, during a flight to Tahoe in his jet.

'I guess I'm just not interested in boats,' Tess said. Then she added, 'How much did it cost?'

'I've heard three-point-five,' Corky said. 'Sam Sloan's cost four, you know. Four-point-two-million to be exact.'

'He's still married, isn't he?' Tess asked, since Corky obviously wasn't ready to leave without finding out whatever she'd come to find out.

'Sam? Barely.'

'He must be sixty-five.'

'A vigorous sixty-five.'

'You should know,' Tess said, relishing a microline that slashed its way across Corky's golden forehead.

'I should, but I *don't*. I've only *heard*. Vigorous does not always mean what you think it does.'

Tess kept smiling but turned her face to the sun.

Then Corky said, 'He's dating Vera. If he marries her he'll need to mortgage the boat to pay for her prescriptions. She uses more drugs than a Bulgarian weight lifter.'

Tess turned a hip ever so slightly away from Corky, but instantly regretted it. There was a trace of cellulite forming on her thigh and Corky wouldn't miss it!

'She'll end up regretting it more than he does,' Corky continued. 'He has a dry day about as often as Joan Collins irons her sheets. He'll have the prenuptial put on a granite slab and she'll have to chisel her signature on to the goddamn thing. Speaking of prenuptials, I wanted to tell you how sorry I was to hear that after Ralph left, you ended up with zilch, yes? I mean, living on Linda Isle isn't zilch, but you know what I mean. Leased land? Facing the highway? A huge mortgage? He could at least have bought you a house outright where you wouldn't be making land-lease payments as *well* as mortgage payments. Yes?'

'I'll get along,' Tess said, the sweat boiling and beading through the lotion.

But Corky was relentless. 'And when your father passed away. I mean, I was more shocked than you were when I heard he left his desert estate to his old . . . *pal* in La Quinta. Yes?'

Tess felt faint. She kept smiling, but her upper lip stuck to her teeth.

Corky tossed her head and her power bob bobbed powerfully. Three men sipping long drinks in the beach-hut bar whispered and nodded in her direction. She sucked in her tummy and arched her back, causing her breasts to balloon. 'Let's have something cool, yes?' Corky had eyes like a seagull. She looked toward the three guys without turning her head an inch. 'Maybe a Ramos fizz.' She dropped her gaze toward Tess's hips and said, 'Or something with fewer calories?'

'I don't think so, Corky,' Tess said, finally summoning the courage to abandon her horrible smile. 'I'm not feeling well. Cramps.'

'Well, it won't be long before that too shall pass. Permanently. Cramps, I mean. Yes?'

Corky stood up suddenly, no-hands, pirouetted, sashaying back toward the other hot mommas. Causing the three guys in the beach-hut bar to start pumping the bartender, who referred to Corky's little patch of sand as The Kill Zone.

Relieved to be alone, Tess opened her beach bag, took out a copy of the local newspaper and turned to the inside page, scanning a story about the ex-ferryboat pilot who was being sentenced today. She looked at the photo of forty-year-old Winston Farlowe, taken back in December when he'd been bailed out of jail by his lawyer. There was another photo of Winnie beside the sad jail shot – an old one of him in a police uniform. The article said that Winnie had been a detective for most of his fifteen years of police service.

A forelock tumbled across his brow, and he had a little boy's cowlick. He looked like a strapping man who was going to fat, probably from booze. The journalist wrote that Winnie was well known at Spoon's Landing, a waterfront saloon where millionaires and yuppies often went for 'atmosphere'. Sort of the white Republican equivalent of Harlem slumming in the thirties.

Corky Peebles must've learned something about the guys at the beach-hut bar. Tess saw her moseying in that direction, looking at her watch, as though she was expecting someone. Actually, she'd caught the scent.

The French *parfumeries* say that there are a few 'noses' in the world – most of them from Grasse – that can correctly identify a scent across a crowded bistro with one sniff. At her club Tess Binder knew at *least* a dozen hot mommas who could correctly identify a Dun and Bradstreet with half a sniff. The presence at the club of one of the country's fifty-two billionaires was like a visit from the Pope. The noses of Grasse had *nothing* on the hot mommas.

31

Tess Binder read the story of the Christmas boat parade. Then she put the paper down, faced the heavens and tried not to think about potential skin damage: keratosis, basal-cell and squamous-cell carcinoma. Not to mention melanoma! Then she sat up.

Tess looked at Winnie Farlowe's photo again. She was suddenly feeling some very strange emotions. The eyes were soft and vulnerable, the eyes of this problem drinker. The eyes of a lost little lad.

First Tess felt a growing excitement. Then she felt something else – *fear*.

3: *The Virgin*

It wasn't as though he was facing a felony, he told himself. Technically, it was only a violation of Section 655 of the Harbors and Navigational Code, pertaining to reckless or negligent operation of a vessel while under the influence of alcohol or drugs. But it wasn't often that such a colorful breach of the code was brought before a judge in Orange County. The local newspapers in and around The Golden Orange were still having fun with imaginative references to the hijacking. But in that the groaning wheels of American justice haven't received a dollop of grease in this century, it was a fairly easy matter for Chip Simon to have his client's sentencing postponed until local interest had waned.

The Honorable Jesse W. Singleton looked like a graying Mike Tyson on steroids. He weighed just less than a tuna ship anchor, had been a college football player in the late forties, and a cop for five years, before completing his law degree and leaving police work for the DA's office. Because he was smart, and because he was black when tokenism paid dividends, he had been appointed to the bench by a liberal Democratic governor. After which, Judge Singleton had disappointed that governor and tickled the hell out of the next one, a conservative Republican, by being the hanging judge that Republican Orange County had come to love.

Unfortunately for Winnie Farlowe, Judge Singleton despised drunk drivers even more than he hated short-eyed pedophiles. He often jailed first offenders for drunk driving and *always* jailed a 'deuce' with a prior. And especially unfortunate for Winnie was the fact that the Christmas joyride had resulted in a disruption of the Newport Harbor Christmas Boat Parade on the very night that Judge Singleton was an honored guest of the parade committee.

Chip Simon was halfway through his eloquent plea for leniency in Harbor Court that April morning when Judge Singleton interrupted him.

'Let's take a short recess, counsel,' he said abruptly, glowering at Winnie with luminous black eyes. 'I'd like to see the defendant in chambers.'

The request was so unusual that both the prosecutor and Chip Simon followed the judge into his office, seeking an explanation. Judge Singleton poured a cup of Evian water, sat in his red leather throne-on-casters, and with his robe billowing like a black spinnaker, or maybe the wings of a nightmare bat, said, 'I want to see the defendant. *Alone.*'

'Judge,' said the prosecutor, 'is there something I can . . .'

'No,' said the judge. 'You're excused.'

'Your Honor,' said Chip Simon, 'I think if you wish to see my client privately I ought to . . .'

'No you ought *not* to,' said the judge. 'If I were you I'd ask my client to step in here and then I'd go outside and have a soda pop until you're called. *That's* what I'd do if I were you.'

The lawyer weighed it. If he challenged the hanging

judge, Winnie was going to the slam without a doubt. If he let the judge indulge his eccentricity . . .

Ninety seconds later Winnie Farlowe stood alone and silent before Judge Singleton. The judge downed another glass of Evian, and finally, with a look that could've opened a safe, he said, 'Do you know what they say in county jail when somebody farts and the other prisoners hear it?'

'Excuse me, Your Honor?'

'Do you know anything about me?'

'A little, Your Honor.' Winnie suddenly went damp all over. He'd sprung a leak from last night's vodka binge, and a gremlin golfer was taking divots from his brain.

'Do you know I *enjoy* putting deuces in jail?'

'Your Honor, I wasn't driving a car. Why, I'd *never* drive when . . .'

'You happened to be at the wheel of a ferryboat, but you've no doubt driven a car lots of times when you were drunk. All alcoholics do.'

'Your Honor, I assure you I haven't. And I don't know where you got the idea that I'm an . . .'

'Alcoholic.'

'I don't think I'm an . . .'

'What kind of car do you drive?'

'A five-year-old VW, Your Honor.'

'How often do you drive it with a BA reading of point-two-oh, or higher?'

'Your Honor, I don't . . .'

'Do you have any memory whatsoever of making a citizen, in effect, walk the plank and nearly drown in that cold black water?'

'It's the newspapers, Your Honor!' And now Winnie

was sweating buckets. 'Walk the plank? *What* plank? Your Honor knows there's no plank on the ferry!'

'You told the passenger you were going to shoot him.'

'My old service revolver was at home, Judge! I didn't *have* a gun on that boat!'

'But he believed you. And he jumped into that cold black water.'

'He panicked, Your Honor!'

'People were screaming for help. Other people were threatening to jump into the cold black water rather than ride it out with an alcoholic at the wheel of the boat. A dangerous drunk who really doesn't remember what happened that night. Do you have blackouts?'

'Blackouts?'

'Never mind. Of course you do. You're an alcoholic. I read the probation report.'

'That guy from the probation department jumped to conclusions, Your Honor!'

Then Judge Singleton said casually, 'I'd decided to send you to jail. For six months.'

Winnie went as silent as a barnacle on a keel. His skull was on fire. The Evian looked like a tall cool sweating vodka in the meaty paw of Judge Singleton.

Winnie could hear the ice cubes clinking against the judge's teeth. Winnie's own mouth seemed full of beach sand. The judge's stare was a prison searchlight.

'I wouldn't be helped in jail, Your Honor,' he finally croaked.

'Helped? Do you think I'm interested in *helping* the people I send to jail? Boy, I'm a warehouse specialist! I put lawbreakers on the shelf so the people of this county can have a break for a while. And I'm also here to provide a little revenge and retribution. Oh yes! People *need* revenge. Just ask the family of someone *killed* by a drunk driver. Just ask the family sometime.'

'Judge, please! I'm not a . . .'

'How long did you serve with the Newport Beach Police Department? Fourteen years?'

'Fifteen years.'

'Fifteen years. And then what?'

'I'd still be there except some disks blew when a burglar kicked me down the companionway of a boat. My back locks up on me maybe three days a week. Can't hardly sit. Can't ever lie on my stomach. I paid for the boat parade damage, Judge!'

Winnie Farlowe was drowning in vodka ferment. He couldn't think. He tried to recall some of the commendations he'd been awarded as a cop, but strangely, all he could think of was his late father. Winnie was a little boy again, facing this terror not at The Drinker's Hour, but in broad daylight. And he wanted a father to save him. He felt like weeping.

'I was in law enforcement myself,' said Judge Singleton.

Prepared to *grovel*. 'I know, Your Honor!'

'Sheriff's Department. I worked at the county jail when you were a baby.'

'Yes, sir.'

'I know what can happen to ex-cops when they do jail time. Do you know what can happen to ex-cops in jail? When the inmates get hold of him?'

A gulp. 'I got a pretty good idea, Judge.'

'I remember once when I was a young deputy. We had this policeman in jail awaiting trial. Lived in Orange, I think it was. Maybe Tustin. Anyway, he shot his wife in a drunken rage one night. We isolated him, of course, but somebody screwed up on the graveyard shift. He was taken in for a morning shower with the other court transfers. The inmates knew the guy was a cop and they got to him in the showers. Know what they did to him before anyone could stop them?'

'I got a pretty good idea,' Winnie repeated, wishing the judge would *stop*!

'Well, I guess I never forgot how he looked on that shower room floor. Bleeding like a pig and crying like a woman.'

Winnie's instincts told him to keep his mouth shut and let this man have his say. He *thought* he saw a glimmer of mercy in those ferocious black eyes.

'I'm going to give you five days and suspend it. You'll pay a fine of close to a thousand bucks and be placed on probation. That means you better not operate a boat if you've even walked *past* a saloon. And you *better* not appear in public in a drunken condition.' He took a sip of Evian and said, 'Don't thank me. I don't like to be thanked.'

Another croak. 'No, sir!'

'Lucky you're white. If you were black I'd catch hell for giving you a break, wouldn't I? You treated Christmas like a seagoing Scrooge, didn't you? With *contempt*.'

'I guess so, Your Honor.'

'If you get picked up for anything, anything at all related to drunkenness, you'll do time. Do you understand me, boy?'

'Yes, Your Honor.'

'OK, get outta here and tell your lawyer to can that boring speech.'

'Yes, Your Honor,' Winnie said, walking shakily to the door.

'One more thing,' said the judge, stopping Winnie in his tracks.

'Sir?'

The judge grinned. A chilling grin. Chocolate ice. 'Do you know what they say in county jail when somebody farts and the other prisoners hear it?'

'No, Your Honor.'

'They say, 'Still a virgin, huh?' So every time you're tempted to booze it up you think about how nice it is to *hear* yourself fart. Do you understand me, boy?'

'Yes, Your Honor.'

Winnie's sweaty fingers slipped right off the brass doorknob on the first try. A hairy shudder sidled up his spine like a tarantula. *Still a virgin, huh?*

4: *Dream Vision*

It was still warm and balmy at five o'clock in the afternoon. That's when Winnie got to his apartment on the Balboa peninsula, wanting a drink more than he'd ever wanted one in his life. Wanting it all the more when he pictured Judge Singleton with his James Earl Jones Voice of God, and eyes like a defendant's bad dream.

Winnie's brand-new pinpoint Oxford shirt looked like a bar rag from Spoon's Landing. He stripped it off and tossed it on the floor with the rest of the week's laundry. He put on his old baggy Hang Tens, opened two beers, drank the first without stopping and took the other with him out on the porch, where he sniffed the brisk salt air over the peninsula. He gulped down the second beer, shivering when he thought about psychopathic inmates and soundless farts.

Winnie shook it off, trotted down the steps to the alley behind the apartment house, then jogged barefoot across Balboa Boulevard to the beach, one block away. That block saved him about $300 a month in rent for a cramped 'studio' with a daybed.

He sprinted across the warm white sand and hit the surf without much of a shock. He figured he was greenhousing: Sheer terror followed by utter relief equals one hot body. The ocean felt like Hawaii water to him, not the cold surf of Southern California.

Winnie plunged through the breakers, enjoying the sting as they slapped against his chest like a wooden mallet smacking fresh squid into tender steaks.

He knew it was risky to swim out. He'd lived near the beach all his life and understood riptides and undertow, yet he was swimming right toward trouble. Daring the rip? Some surfers two hundred yards down the beach yelled 'Dumb shit!' at him, but he swam past the rip and beyond. He swam out perhaps five hundred yards before the juices started draining.

The undertow was much stronger than he'd thought, and the sun was dropping fast. Winnie treaded water and looked toward the sunset, knowing that before he swam much farther *against* this tide, the fireball would melt into the sea.

He began stroking desperately. As a young lifeguard, he had patrolled this beach, notching his jeep with esoteric little rabbits to record the heads (tails actually) of all the surf bunnies he'd collected. But this was no time for surf bunnies. Winnie Farlowe was in trouble!

Too macho to call for help from the teenage surfers who straddled their boards less than a hundred yards away, he continued to stroke. He couldn't bring himself to do it, not at ex-lifeguard/marine/policeman. But at last he hollered: 'Here!'

Here? The surfers knew he was here. There, actually. There in the surf, churning back and forth in the undertow.

Winnie finally screamed: 'HELP ME!'

The kid who paddled toward him, and towed him from the skeg of his board, was wearing a wet suit with a yellow stripe. The kid was blond, of course, about sixteen years old. He bitched about missing some rad tubes and said that old dorks shouldn't be anywhere near a rip, even a baby rip. That was the gist of the conversation, as much as Winnie could understand, in that he was gagging on the last rad tube that whacked him in the back of the skull while the kid's powerful strokes dragged him through the foam.

When Winnie's feet touched sand and he turned to thank the surfer, the kid was already submarining through the nearest breaker, heading back toward the school of others lying still on the blue-black ocean, awaiting nirvana. The Perfect Wave.

A violent coughing fit struck Winnie when he reached the back stairs leading up to his apartment. By the time he got inside, he was shivering and queasy, tasting brine from his mouth to his belly. A cold beer made him feel better. A shot of Polish vodka helped even more. Another beer and Winnie was half-convinced he could've managed just fine without that little son of a bitch. He might even go for a swim tomorrow, rips or no rips, just to prove a thing or two. After all, a former lifeguard never really loses it.

By eight o'clock, Winnie had devoured a pot of clams at Digger's Hot Pot, where he 'dined' four nights a week. By 8.10 he entered Spoon's Landing ready to tell everybody how he'd toughed it out in court. How the hanging judge just had to watch helplessly as Winnie slid out of his clutches, like an eel through a gill net.

He found Spoon glaring at Bilge O'Toole, who was racing his turtle, Irma, across the bar against one owned by a commercial fisherman they called Carlos Tuna, a turtle wrangler who amazed Gold Coast millionaires with

42

the outrageous story that his turtle, Regis, was one hundred years old.

Bilge O'Toole was already weepy drunk, which was as predictable as investment swindles around these parts, and Spoon was telling him he should take his Irma and go on home. Five young off-duty cops were shooting snooker in the adjoining room, and bitching about the yesteryear music on the jukebox.

At the other end of the bar, Guppy Stover was sighing mournfully, but everyone ignored her. They knew that to say 'What's the matter?' would get them gaffed for half an hour, during which they'd hear about the US Navy boatswain's mate who wooed her but left her on the beach when he found a Waikiki grass widow on a refueling stop during his last cruise. Which was in 1945, but seemed like yesterday to Guppy, who still wore her mass of gray hair in the Second World War, Andrews Sisters shoulder-length style.

There were about four or five others at the bar, three of them strangers to Winnie, everybody looked exceedingly miserable, which was normal on Tuesday nights for some reason. Winnie walked to the bar and nodded at Spoon, who poured him a draft and a double shot of Polish vodka.

Spoon's navy cap dipped twice, which was Spoon's way of asking, 'Well, what happened?'

'This place is about as cheery as the Gaza Strip,' Winnie said, sipping the vodka and chasing it with two big gulps of draft.

Spoon's navy cap – according to a has-been movie star who left it in the bar during those days when John Wayne was The Golden Orange's greatest living celebrity – was the cap James Cagney wore in *Mister Roberts*. Even though it perfectly fit Spoon, who had a head like a beer keg, twice the size of Cagney's.

It was almost impossible to exaggerate the impact of John Wayne. Everybody knew he didn't *really* win The Big War and settle The West, and yet . . . And yet as far as Orange County was concerned, the Duke could replace Kennedy and Roosevelt on US coins any old day. But why stop there? Why *not* the Duke on a fifty-dollar bill? In an era when heroes were routinely demolished, his icon hung everywhere. He was clearly the patron saint of The Golden Orange.

There's an annual softball event in a Southland beach city wherein dozens of teams enter a three-day elimination event, mainly just to drink and party. Entrants are encouraged to pick imaginative names for the teams, and crassness is not discouraged. For example, one team composed of police detectives called itself 'The Swinging Dicks'. And yet, the *only* caveat insofar as picking a team name is that no entrant can, in any way, denigrate the United States of America, or John Wayne. *That* is how profanity gets defined in *these* parts.

Spoon had acquired his sobriquet back in The Big War because of his incredible ability to rap out the beat of any popular song with a pair of inverted tablespoons. He still won lots of bets by playing identifiable melodies with the rat-a-tat-tat on the hopelessly battered bartop.

'We gonna have to visit you every other Saturday or what?' Spoon finally asked. His voice was a drone, usually. Everyone said Spoon could put you to sleep yelling 'Fire!'

'Probation,' said Winnie. 'They didn't wanna go and

persecute a guy that's served his country and his community as many years as I did.'

Guppy Stover said, 'I figured that big spade'd put you on ice, Winnie.'

Which won her a nod from Winnie to Spoon. She chose an Alabama slammer since Winnie was buying. Straight up.

There wasn't much more to talk about. By 9.30 p.m. Bilge O'Toole's patchy gray hair was standing up in sweaty tufts. He obsessively twisted and pulled it when he was loaded, and the booze had raised his temperature till the veins were popping, not just on his blood-bucket nose but on his chin and dumpling cheeks as well. Another six fingers of Spoon's bar whiskey and they could grow orchids in the clumps protruding from his ears. He had a plaster cast on his wrist, but few even questioned it. The answer was obvious: Drunks fall down.

Bilge was getting weepy, *very* weepy. Winnie hoped that he wouldn't sing 'Too Ra Loo Ra Loo Ra', but when there wasn't a single sporting event on the big screen TV, anything could happen.

Suddenly Bilge looked at Winnie and said, 'I'm getting away from the ocean. I'm moving inland. Maybe out to Riverside or San Bernardino. I'm sick a tasting salt every time I lick my lips.'

'That's from the tequila,' Guppy offered, amazing everyone because she wasn't comatose yet. 'You always got tequila salt stuck to your chin. That's what the problem is.'

Bilge said to Winnie, 'I knew I'd been around the ocean too long when I saw one a Spoon's cockroaches hanging sixteen on a swizzle stick.'

'I think I'll go home,' Winnie said. 'This place is too zany and full a fun. Like an East German embassy.'

'I used to *have* a home,' Guppy offered, tucking half a bale of gray under her red velvet hair ribbon, 'before Franklin dumped me for that hog in Honolulu back in forty-five.'

Winnie found a quarter and walked to the old Wurlitzer jukebox in self-defense. He had to choose between Sinatra, Tony Bennett, Mel Torme, Peggy Lee or Bobby Darin. Spoon considered them to be the great saloon singers of our time and was convinced that any song written after the fifties was bad for business. Spoon liked old songs with ocean water in them, like 'Red Sails in the Sunset'. Winnie punched Peggy Lee's 'Fever'.

When he got back to the bar there was a blonde in an ivory cardigan, with navy blue and ivory striped pants, sitting at the bar. She wore a funnel-necked navy pullover under the cardigan. The outfit looked nautical without any of those corny little anchors.

Winnie tried not to stare. Her boyfriend or husband might be in the john. Another wealthy couple out slumming, probably. He figured her for the old yacht club. She was understated but elegant. Tiny ear studs and a platinum wristwatch with art deco dials, that was it for the jewelry. Not even rings on those long elegant pampered fingers. Not even a wedding ring!

Winnie sipped his brew and looked toward the door to the men's room. One of the painters from the boatyard got up from the bar and staggered in. A minute later he staggered out. Still no boyfriend or husband! She wore those round, no bullshit, yuppie eyeglasses. Winnie *loved* glasses on classy women like this one.

46

Her hair was the color of melted butterscotch, streaked with golden highlights, like that last halo before sunrise he used to see from his boat when he was bobbing level with the horizon. Before that bitch Tammy took his sloop and anything else with a salvage value.

The woman at the bar might as well have been wrapped in razor wire, she looked so unapproachable. She smoked, and sipped something that looked like an Americano. Winnie knew he was blasted when he heard himself blurt, 'I used to have a twenty-nine-foot sloop. She was Danish, a double-ender with a canoe stern. A production boat, glass, but sweet. Once I was sitting in her cockpit at four a.m. And . . . Do you know that water boils at a higher temperature at sea level?'

'I only know about water in my kitchen,' she said. Smiling!

'Anyways,' Winnie continued, 'the coffee was very hot. The sun was beyond the curvature of the earth but getting ready to rise at the stern. I put my coffee down and watched this light start at the horizon. And there were these cottonball clouds so heavy you couldn't star-sight. The clouds were so full in that breeze, well, the fan spread and it sorta backlit the clouds. That's the way it *must* a looked before there were continents. The light, it was something like . . . it was like the color a your hair. Well, I jist wanted to tell you that.'

She was *really* smiling now, not the way a beautiful woman usually smiles at a drunk. He had lots of experience in such matters. She smiled like she meant it, with those wide vermilion lips of hers!

'My name's Tess Binder.' She held out her hand and he took it. She was strong.

47

'I'm a sucker for women that shake hands like a man,' he said.

She chuckled. Like wind chimes! She said, 'That's flattering. I guess.'

'I don't know why I said all that. I don't know why I told you about the sun backlighting the clouds. It's like when you've seen something like that, you can't take life's other crap too seriously. And I took a lot of it today.'

She was looking him over, but subtly. Still, she *was* looking at him. Winnie was dressed better than usual: A Reyn Spooner aloha shirt designed inside out for that faded look, Levi jeans bleached nearly white, Sperry Top-Siders. Suddenly, he wished he was wearing socks. Were his ankles cruddy?

'Is it something you'd like to talk about?' she asked, causing Winnie to nod to the ever-alert saloonkeeper, who fixed two drinks before they could change their minds.

'I went to court today,' Winnie said.

'And what happened?'

That was strange. She didn't say, 'Traffic Court?' or 'Divorce Court?' She was looking at him like she *knew*.

'I'm the guy that hijacked the ferry,' Winnie said.

'Did he mind?'

'F-E-R-R-Y. The boat.'

Wind chimes again! 'I knew what you were talking about,' she confessed. 'I get silly when I drink these.'

'You knew? How?'

'I saw your picture in the paper. You're the ferryboat skipper. So what did you get from the judge?'

'You saw my picture? You a reporter?'

'I came here partly because of the article. This is a place

48

I've been wanting to see. Everyone I know's been here once or twice.'

'Probation. I got probation. You read about me, huh?' They were quiet for a moment. Then he said, 'Yacht club. You belong to the yacht club, I bet.' He moved his leg until the knee of his jeans was just touching her pants.

'Wrong. The other club.'

He was disappointed. She looked like *old* money. Then she pleased him by saying, 'My grandfather was commodore at the yacht club many years ago. I grew up there but I've always *hated* boats. I joined my club because nobody cares about boats. They just own them. Huge ones.'

'Whadda they do at your club?'

She shrugged. 'Aerobics class. Dinner sometimes. Lie on the beach. Gossip. Drink.'

He'd never seen a serious drinker order Americanos. Campari reminded him of the cough medicine he got drunk on in Nam when it was all he could get.

'So you read about me and you came here to have a look?'

'I admit I'm curious about you, Mister Farlowe, and . . .'

'Win.'

'. . . and you seem an extraordinarily colorful character. I *hoped* I might see you. I like unusual people.'

She hadn't said, 'You seemed *like* a colorful character.' She talked the way they did on *Masterpiece Theater*! With an English accent, she could be called Beryl or Elspeth! Winnie felt deboned. This woman was turning him to jelly. But she'd probably call it jam or marmalade. *Masterpiece Theater!*

'Whatever your reason,' Winnie said, 'I'm jist glad you

came. You look like a Daphne or Sybil, but I like Tess. In fact, I'm crazy about the name.'

Tess Binder took a cigarette from her purse, and Winnie searched the bartop for a match. She lit it with a gold lighter.

Winnie looked apologetically at the wormy ship timbers holding up the oppressively low ceiling. The walls were padded from the floor at least six feet up so the drunks didn't get hurt when they stumbled against (or were knocked against) the bulkheads. A post in the middle of the room was wrapped by three-strand hemp. There were obligatory nautical maps on the walls, and nets, and wooden blocks and ship lanterns. A huge outrigger hung from the ceiling, and someone had stuck a bobble-head doll at the prow. The doll wore an L.A. Dodgers baseball cap.

Life preservers bearing the names of the Second World War fighting ships hung on the walls, as did an old Mae West, supposedly retrieved from the USS *Arizona* when Spoon was transported to a hospital after being wounded during the surprise attack on Pearl Harbor.

In short, it was the kind of waterfront saloon where members of yacht clubs might drink or shoot snooker with dory fishermen and boatyard roustabouts. The bumper sticker over the bar alluded to the kind of rogue Republicanism practiced by the Orange County working class. They were pro-choice all right. In fact, they favored free abortions for every welfare mother in the country. The bumper sticker said: ABORT A FETUS, KILL A DEMO-CRAT.

'What're you going to do now?' Tess asked. 'Got another job?'

'Oh, that ferry gig was jist part time. I have a Coast Guard license and they needed somebody during the holidays, so . . .'

Her teeth were the most perfect he'd ever seen up close. Rich people's teeth. And she had those cheekbones. Did rich women get them the same way they got those teeth? he thought boozily.

'The newspaper said you're an ex-policeman.'

'Medical retirement. Bad back. Fifteen a my best years I gave them.'

'The pension isn't enough to live on, is it?'

'I gotta work. Besides, I *wanna* work. I'm still young.'

'Forty,' she said. 'The article was *very* revealing.'

This woman was interested in him! He felt his goddamn pump starting to miss beats again. The scary heart business had started when he was just weeks from facing the hanging judge: two beats off every sixty.

'I think I gotta cut down on my worries,' he said, massaging his chest.

'You feeling OK?'

'The court appearance. It was . . . stressful.'

He could feel the sweat break out on his forehead. He really *wasn't* feeling that well. Tonight of all nights, when his miserable luck was changing for the better!

'Perhaps you ought to get a good night's sleep.' Tess Binder said, snuffing out her cigarette. 'After what you've been through.'

She was leaving! And now his pump was firing on every fourth stroke, and there was a fire in the engine room!

'I like this place,' she said. 'I'll be back.' She smiled for the last time and floated away from him. He thought he heard wind chimes as she drifted through the doorway.

Winnie remembered a photo he'd once seen of a blond model with twin Borzois on a double leash: elegant leggy animals with long aristocratic Balkan noses. The dogs looked like Marlene Dietrich, and the woman was like this one. He took a quarter off the bar to play Tony Bennett's version of 'Sophisticated Lady'.

A roar went up as Carlos Tuna's turtle, Regis, got cheered on by a small group at the other end of the bar. The reptile had stopped racing and had mounted Bilge O'Toole's Irma. Regis was gasping open-mouthed and struggling to find his way inside Irma's armor plate.

Bilge was in the corner crying in his beer with a rich guy from Bay Island who *never* should have said, 'What's wrong tonight, Bilge?'

Bilge didn't know about the ravishing of Irma until the cheering started. When he saw it he roared like a sea lion, and Spoon had to scramble over the bar to break up a brawl.

Winnie got up, staggered to the men's room, splashed cold water on his face, but felt no better. By the time he got back to the stool, Bilge was drinking alone, twisting his patchy hair into dreadlocks, wailing, 'You OK, Irma?' to the turtle, who was sound asleep in a puddle of spilled beer.

'What's wrong with *you*?' Spoon mumbled to Winnie, who paid his tab and listed unsteadily, still rubbing his chest.

'I don't feel so good. My pump. It's like, missing beats!' Winnie said. 'That's scarier than Dan Quayle!'

'Well, I can't help you with that,' Spoon said, droning. 'I'm busy as the beach master on D-Day. I can't be worryin about turtles gettin boffed and I can't fix bum tickers, OK? Do you understand what I'm sayin?'

Guppy, whom one of the snooker-playing cops had outlined in chalk while she snoozed on the bartop, suddenly lifted her head from her arms and cried: 'Of *course* there's something wrong, Winnie! You're *drunk*, you dummy!'

Spoon decided to pop for a musical freebie and actually put a quarter of his own into the ancient Wurlitzer, beating out a spoon-fed accompaniment to Bobby Darin's 'Beyond the Sea'.

When Winnie lurched out of the saloon that night, he heard Guppy cry out to the sleeping she-turtle: 'I got boffed and left on the beach! I know what it's like! How was it for you? Did the earth move or what? *Did* it, Irma?'

5: *Star-crossed Lovers*

The invitation to 'The Champagne Brunch and Fashion Show' carried a suggestion of 'Big Apple attire'. The Big Apple had come to The Golden Orange! Which meant that there were a lot of women wearing red or black, and everybody hoped to be described as either chic or sophisticated, this on the southwestern edge of North America, where, despite some of the most expensive residential property in the nation, only a few of the most chic and sophisticated restaurants *suggested* jackets for gentlemen. At its *most* formal, The Golden Orange dress code mirrored the Costa del Sol in summer, but ordinarily, Pago Pago casual was OK. The gentlemen's dress code just about anyplace on the Gold Coast was: shoes, and a shirt with a collar. The salespeople in shops and department stores pay no attention whatsoever to how a customer is dressed. But they can spot a $10,000 Swiss watch faster than anyone this side of Zurich. They address themselves to a customer's wrist.

The afternoon fund-raiser suggesting the Big Apple duds had Tess Binder agonizing, but she settled on a persimmon and white nautical jacket with braided trim and brass buttons, over a white skirt. She'd worn the outfit two or three times and hoped anyone who'd be there wouldn't have seen her in it. She couldn't remember where she'd worn it last and worried that it made her look heavier. Tess wore only a size six, but there was a time when she wore a four. The years were tumbling by so fast, Tess couldn't even remember when the hell it was that she *went* to a six! She'd begun perspiring even before putting on the jacket. Oddly enough, when she thought of Win Farlowe it calmed her.

Tess got stuck in a traffic jam on MacArthur Boulevard, caused by a two-car fender bender. Traffic in this, the fastest-growing area in America, was increasing at a terrifying clip. And everywhere Tess looked there were brand-new high-rise towers of tinted glass and steel. Tess Binder was surrounded by unimaginable wealth and awesome economic power. Driving to the brunch, she felt lost in a wilderness of looming dark towers.

The fashion show raised a good deal of money that afternoon, but for Tess it was a disaster. She *lusted* for the pantsuits and capes, and the 'little dresses with big impact', but prices for virtually nothing were starting at about $1,000, and one jacket she adored went for $15,000.

The women looked thinner because so many were wearing black. Fuller lips were definitely in: big swollen pouters, sometimes obtained by collagen injections or even fat cell transplants for more permanence. The fat cells were often siphoned from the fanny and funneled into the lips, which seemed ironically appropriate to the Gold Coast daddies who footed the bill. Most of the women just got the bee-stung effect by applying lipstick liner and matching lipstick, set by matte brushed powder, thus making themselves look poutier than John McEnroe. What with all the Manhattan black and blood-puddle red and swollen lips, the hot mommas resembled a coven of vampires.

At table number one were the Woodcrests. Morton Woodcrest wasn't just 'seven-one-four' rich – the dialing code for Orange County and title of a name-dropping local publication – he was 'F.F.H.' rich, 292nd in *Forbes*' 400. Tess thought that his wife, Zoe, was no longer just willowy, but so emaciated her spine jutted into her dress like a string of beads. Before Morton settled on his fifth wife, half the hot mommas at the club looked like Cambodian refugees because Morton liked them *thin*.

The brunch itself was so uninspired, everyone was bitching. The Arts Society had the gall to serve Belgian waffles, which anyone could get at Denny's all day. The fact that these waffles were served with strawberries and cream and cold curried chicken made matters *worse*. That combination had been déclassé for ten years. And the domestic champagne was simply undrinkable.

Everyone just knew that something as trite as Norwegian salmon poached in a tarragon *beurre blanc* would be next, and they were right! They could at least have served something simple and light, maybe some grilled trout with braised fennel. The Golden Orange hadn't seen such sneers and eye rolling since a consortium headed by easter Jews had moved in on the biggest land development in the area.

The whispered reminder that the proceeds from the fashion show and champagne brunch were for 'the arts' impressed no-one. When you're limited to a thousand calories a day, you'd better be offered more than waffles and lox. Most of the hot mommas managed only a few forkfuls of watercress and shiitake mushrooms.

There were, however, a lot of happy Mexican busboys and dishwashers who later loaded up on leftovers and guzzled champagne from opened bottles. Though most of them agreed with the hot mommas that the bubbly wasn't much. Couldn't touch Dos Equis, Corona, or any beer from Baja.

After Tess got home that afternoon, she poured herself a diet cola and sat barefoot on her patio, on the ghetto side of the island, facing Pacific Coast Highway. She promised herself she'd never go to another fashion show unless she could afford any silly goddamn piece of New York or Paris or Tokyo trash that struck her fancy. Tess Binder had never felt so *poor*.

Valium calmed her sufficiently to pick up the telephone.

The ten o'clock news had already dealt with the shoot-out in Laguna Beach by the time Buster Wiles arrived at Spoon's Landing. It was the first fatal shooting involving Newport Beach policemen in more than ten years.

Guppy Stover lifted her old gray head from her folded arms and greeted him with, 'Hey, I saw you on TV. Goddamn killer!' Then she yawned and shut her eyes.

Knowing how Buster counted calories, Spoon put a glass of light beer on the bar, but Buster said, 'We been shootin people all day and whadda I get? Light beer?' Buster was trying to look jaunty but his hands were shaking. 'Gimme a Wild Turkey,' he said. 'Neat.'

Winnie Farlowe spotted Buster from his table across the saloon where he'd been watching the Lakers on the big screen. Winnie got up and joined the big cop at the bar.

'Saw your little trauma drama on the news,' Winnie said. 'What the hell you doing down there in Laguna anyways?'

'Man, you got off the job *just* in time,' Buster said. 'Guy had an Uzi! I was looking up at *death*!'

Guppy Stover popped up again, smoothing her trademark evening gloves and adjusting her red velvet hair ribbon. 'What'd it look like?' she asked Buster. 'Death?'

'An Uzi,' Buster said to his drink. 'Looks like an Uzi.'

Unable to visualize an Uzi, Guppy closed her eyes again. Bored and drunk.

Buster Wiles bared his shockingly white teeth and squinted through one heavily lashed violet eye when he held Spoon's bucket glass up to the light. Satisfied that it was moderately clean, he settled on to the barstool and reached under his L.A. Raiders warm-up jacket to adjust the ride of his shoulder holster.

He was forty-four, but still had the iron-pumping build he'd cultivated when he won the surfing competition in Huntington Beach in 1966 before going to Nam. And he'd lost very little of his coppery mane to middle age. The present-day surfers said that Buster wasn't too hot on a board any more, but he still had pick-of-the-litter when he felt like making an appearance at any of the surfing events in Orange County. One of the reasons the department had taken Buster off motors, according to police scuttlebutt, was because in a uniform with helmet and boots, he had women of all ages *intentionally* cruising through red lights just to get stopped by the hunk with violet eyes. They called him 'Gideon' Wiles, he'd been in so many hotel rooms.

'So what happened down there, Buster?' asked Winnie.

Buster let out a vaporous sigh that seemed to enervate his mean-looking body. Then he said, 'Soledad Sam, ever run into him when you were on the job?'

Winnie shook his head and Buster said, 'Call him

Soledad 'cause he's got this tattoo of Soledad Prison on his shoulder. Anyways, he's this little speed tweaker, like our snitch. Spends his time in low-life meth labs breathin more ether fumes than all the patients at Hoag Hospital put together. Uses meth and other dirtbag drugs. But our snitch tells us Soledad Sam's been hired to transport a key of cocaine from this apartment house in Laguna Beach to a hotel up by John Wayne Airport. I mean, this little ratfucker's gonna be trusted with a *key*!'

'How much is a key these days?' Winnie asked.

'Thirteen gee per key. And this little germ never had more than a couple twenty-dollar rocks in his life before. So me 'n Novak, we don't really believe our snitch too much, but we stake out the apartment with a couple guys from Laguna PD, who didn't have to go to their tanning salon today or whatever they do down there. And jist as we're trying to figure out where our little dildo is at, he comes outta the apartment with something tucked inside his pants that's either the world's biggest hernia or a key of first-class blow.'

'Get to the Uzi,' Guppy Stover said belligerently, the first time Buster was aware that the old woman was listening.

Buster turned away from Guppy and continued in a lower voice. 'Anyways, we take down the chump and sure enough he's got the key! Says he got five ohs for takin on the transportation job and four more when he makes the delivery. He starts rollin over on everybody. Says he's a balls-up dude and if we talk to the DA and his parole office he'll even testify for us.'

'There's no business like snow business,' Winnie observed.

'So we strike a deal, sort of, when he says there's still maybe another key inside with these two outta-work musicians that share the place. We hook up Sal and go chargin back inside, based on his information. We bust *one* guy and find a few lines of blow on the table in the kitchen, but no keys.'

'*One* guy?'

'I'm gettin to that,' said Buster. 'Now it ain't a big apartment, so we figure he jumped out the window when he heard us comin up the steps. So me 'n Novak, we're searchin the bedroom when I see this mangy tomcat that stops lickin his balls long enough to mosey over to this big overstuffed chair, and the cat goes behind it to this slit in the upholstery and sticks his paw inside. And I says, 'Aha!''

'Wake me up when you get to the Uzi part,' Guppy mumbled to her drink.

'So I go over and shove the tomcat outta the way and I stick my arm inside the chair. And all hell breaks loose!'

Buster paused when three off-duty cops, including Novak the narc, came through the door and headed straight for the snooker table in the adjoining room.

Novak yelled, 'Draft beer, Spoon. And keep it comin!'

'Right on cue,' Winnie said, nodding in the direction of Novak the narc, who was sighting down the shaft of a snooker cue as though it were a rifle.

'Looks like he needs a drink,' Buster said. 'Anyways, the cat attacks! The goddamn thing goes right for my arm and starts gougin and hissin and spittin! I come straight up, and like, stumble back inside this closet. And I toss the little bastard up in the air where he hits the ceiling. But it ain't the ceiling. It's a trapdoor!'

'Uh oh,' said Winnie.

'Yeah! He knocks the little door cockeyed and there's the second guy we thought jumped out the window. And I'm starin at an Uzi on full auto, and I scream louder than the goddamn cat, and Novak over there, he runs in and starts crankin off rounds up into the crawl space, and that unemployed musician's gonna have a closed coffin after the undertaker gets a gander at the mess those hollow-points made of his face.'

'The guy get any off?'

'A burst,' Buster said. 'Before or after Novak capped him? I can't say for sure. Neither can Novak. What difference does it make?'

'An Uzi's a *gun* for chrissake!' said Guppy Stover whose attention span was exhausted. 'Why didn't you *say* so? Probably one of those assault guns George Bush isn't sure if he's for or against, right?'

Buster stopped talking when Novak the narc walked to the end of the bar, reached over and grabbed Spoon's private phone without asking permission. He looked grim.

He dialed a number and after a moment said, 'It's me, Ma. Yeah, I knew it'd be on television.' There was a pause and he said, 'Ma, I don't *know* if he had a family! Look, he was a doper! He woulda over-amped anyways. Overdosed, I mean.' Another pause and then in utter frustration, 'Of *course* I didn't enjoy it, Ma! I even got sick to my stomach that time Lorrie got her ears pierced! Remember?'

Turning to Buster, Winnie said, 'The cat? Why'd he attack you?'

'Oh yeah,' Buster said, and Winnie could clearly see the wonder in Buster's violet eyes. That's how they looked in Nam sometimes. Eyes full of wonder. 'Know why the cat jumped me? I was into *his* stash. The cat had a dead mouse stashed inside the chair and he was protectin it! A fuckin *mouse*! I almost got killed for stealin a dead mouse!'

'Have another drink,' Winnie said.

Bilge O'Toole entered the saloon, drunk, and spotted Buster. 'Saw you on TV!' he said. 'What happened down there?'

Buster rolled his eyes at Winnie and said to Bilge. 'There I was, thinkin I was forty clicks outta Da Nang. Charlie was in the wire. My piece jammed. I can't talk about it. Doctor's orders.'

'Vietnam flashback, huh?' Bilge clucked, lurching to the other side of the bar where eavesdropping showed some promise.

When they were alone again, Buster said to Winnie, 'I'm *real* sick a my job, Win. Slam dunkin these little two-oh and five-oh dopers. Endin up with kibbles 'n bits and a sack full a subpoenas to ruin my days off. I'm gettin real sick and *real* tired. Wish I could hurt my back like you did. I'd trade my strong back for your weak pension *any* day.'

Winnie's nose twitched. He sniffed the air like a pointer. Jasmine! He whirled around. She was sitting three stools to his left. She smiled.

'Hello,' Winnie said.

She was wearing a red and white sailor-striped tee, with a red chambray wrap skirt and white deck shoes.

Buster stared at his drink and didn't look up.

'Thought I'd have a nightcap,' she said. 'Went to the movies.'

'Any good?'

'Tedious. Brat-pack stuff.'

'This is my friend, Buster Wiles. Buster, meet Tess Binder.'

'I heard your name on the car radio,' she said to Buster. 'You were in a shoot-out today. How *are* you?'

'You'll have to try me and find out,' Buster said, his eyes slits of purple.

She didn't like that and neither did Winnie. She turned away and lit a cigarette with the gold lighter.

'Be cool, will ya!' Winnie whispered. 'She's a *lady*.'

'Sure. They all are.' Buster finished his drink, turned to Winnie and said, 'My life's takin a turn. I'm on the verge of . . . a *big* career change. Meantime, I ain't gonna let some faggot dust me with an Uzi! I'm gonna ask for an inside job, startin right away.'

'When we did police work together you wanted to do *real* police work,' Winnie said.

'Trouble with you, Win, the job was a way of life. That's why you're so lost now, flounderin around and beatin the livin shit outta your own liver. With me it was never more than a job. Best I could get with no skills other than ridin a board.'

'You're not really thinkin about leaving the department?'

'Thinkin hard, pardner. I got an offer to consider, a *real* offer. This thing today, it helped me make up my mind.'

'Yeah?'

'Can't talk about it yet.'

'Even to *me*?'

'Maybe I'm scared if I talk about it, it'll burn off like cloud cover in the morning. You know how superstitious I am.'

'Jist do yourself a favor, Buster. Think before you pull

the pin. It's cold out here in the civilian world. You'll never find the same kind a friends you have on the job.'

'Maybe I don't need em like you do. Things work out for me, I promise you'll be the first to know about it. You're one a my only friends, right? Meantime I'm askin the boss to give me a different job. I've *had* it with street work.'

'The heavyweight iron-pumping finalist of the 1979 Police Olympics?' Winnie said. 'Pushing a *pencil*?'

'I'm almost forty-five years old,' Buster said. 'When was the last time a middle-aged guy got shot by a pencil? Ya know what that guy sounded like breathin his last? Like the static on your stereo speakers. Like maybe he had a bad tweeter or woofer. Yeah, I don't mind pushin a pencil. Thirty-six grand a year ain't enough no more. Not for me. Man, I'm gettin *old*.'

Buster finished the Scotch and squeezed Winnie's shoulder, a bonding gesture of his that Winnie always hated. Buster had a grip like a five-pound pipe wrench.

The big cop crossed the saloon in half a dozen long strides without so much as a glance at Tess Binder. And that was definitely *not* like Buster Wiles, whose bedroom exploits, they said, kept the Orange County abortion clinics in business. He was a different man now than the guy Winnie had partnered with off and on for six years. Winnie felt very sad for his old pal.

'Your chum has a few problems, doesn't he?' Tess said, blowing a cloud of smoke that Winnie, a nonsmoker, would have resented from any but her vermilion lips.

'Burnout. Stress. Same old story,' Winnie said. 'Used to be a good detective. He's not all brawn, there's some brains up there.'

'Most unusual eyes,' Tess Binder said.

'Pansy purple, I used to say. Guy could haul out the old Catalina steamship with his bare hands and he's got eyes like Liz Taylor.'

'Lavender, I'd say,' Tess said. 'Maybe lilac. Hard to say in this light.'

Not *another* one lost to Buster Wiles! To test her he said, 'Guy's a hunk, huh?'

'If you care for the type,' Tess shrugged, lifting Winnie's spirits. 'Probably wears a pinkie ring when he gets dressed up.'

Winnie laughed at that, but reached below the bar to remove the opal pinkie with 'Win' in zircons that Tammy had given him for a birthday three weeks before she served him up a dose of bankruptcy.

'How about you?' Tess Binder asked. 'Were *you* a good detective?'

'How'd you know I was a detective?'

'The newspaper said you were a detective prior to your police retirement.'

'Yeah, well, I was . . . why not admit it? I was good as any. Some guys thought I was maybe the most dedicated. You put me on a case, I didn't know how to let up. Used to drive guys like Buster nuts 'cause I jist wouldn't quit. Especially if it was a good case.'

'What's a good case?'

'Somethin big.'

'Murder?'

'Yeah, like that. An unsolved murder is like . . . personal.'

'A personal insult?'

'Yeah, Buster said that to me one time. Like an insult to

65

me personally, not just to the corpse. We hardly ever had a whodunit homicide in this town. If we did, I'd solve it. If I had to kill to do it.'

'You loved being a cop, didn't you?'

Winnie was looking into her eyes now. Even three stools away, even in this light, he could see they were gray, and opaque, like the water off Newport Pier sometimes got. Usually around the Gold Coast when you looked into unusual irises, like hers or Buster's, you knew they were contact lenses. But Winnie was convinced that everything about her was real. He was getting that feeling again. His heart was contracting prematurely. He felt like a shellfish, jiggly and boneless. Tess Binder was so exciting she was scaring the living crap out of Winnie Farlowe.

He didn't know what else to say, so he said, 'Yeah, I *loved* being a cop.'

'Why're we sitting so far apart?' she asked.

Tess turned toward him on the stool and uncrossed her legs. A significant piece of body language, Winnie was sure of it.

He practically jumped over the two stools, the sudden movement making him wince.

'Your back?'

'Yeah, sometimes I forget and then I get reminded.'

'Can surgery correct it?'

'I'm scared a the knife. Besides, disks're iffy no matter what. I'm OK, long as I don't do heavy lifting. Oh well, could be worse, huh?'

'Not for you. It cost you your job.'

'You see right into a person.' Winnie turned ever so slightly toward Tess Binder while the drunks at the other

66

end of the saloon let out a cheer for Magic Johnson's fifth assist of the Lakers' game.

'You're not so hard to read,' Tess said. 'You're a straight-ahead guy. Seldom do I meet a straight-ahead guy.'

Winnie's heart started doing the trick again. He massaged his chest for a moment, then said, 'How about another round?'

'Got to go home.'

'Is it the noise in here? We could . . .'

'Got to go,' she smiled, turning gracefully and sliding off the stool, just as Carlos Tuna came staggering into the saloon, too drunk to have any chance of being served. Carlos, carrying Regis, caromed off the hemp-wrapped pillar in the center of the bar, causing it to shudder. Then he ricocheted off a chair, sending it crashing, and finally he was safely leaning on the bar. Regis was lucky he was armor plated.

'Coming back tomorrow?' Winnie called out hopefully as Tess moved through the gloom which had never looked more depressing to him.

'Probably,' she said, waggling her long fingers at him.

Carlos Tuna put his stud turtle on the bar and said to Spoon, 'Regis is depressed. Won't snap out of it. Ever since he met Bilge's Irma. Don't eat right or nothin.'

'Yeah, well I ain't got time for lovesick turtles,' the saloonkeeper droned, but he mercifully poured some beer into a saucer for Regis.

Carlos didn't bother to try for one, drunk as he was. Particularly after Spoon took one look at him and said, 'You're about as welcome as junk mail.' Then to Winnie,

'I got twenty on the Celts and right now Magic's shovin the ball up their ass!' Then Spoon hobbled back to the other end of the bar, where the TV mob was screaming in anguish because Bird just made a three-pointer and the Celtics had shaved the lead to two.

On the verge of his own crying jag, Carlos looked mournfully at Regis, who was trying to climb into the saucer of beer, splashing foam all over the bartop.

'I wish I never asked Bilge to bring Irma in here,' Carlos said to Winnie. 'I wish Regis never even *seen* Irma.'

Winnie was growing more and more depressed. Especially when, just before he left the bar, Guppy Stover, so blanched she looked like she'd been soaked in water all night, said to the beer-soaked reptile: 'Of all the gin joints in all the towns in all the world she had to crawl into *this* one!'

Winnie staggered out the door with an aching heart, thinking of star-crossed lovers: Bogart and Bergman, Irma and Regis. But mostly he thought of himself and Tess Binder, while the saloonkeeper took time out from Lakers' basketball to play 'As Time Goes By' for Regis on the battle-scarred bar-top with a pair of particularly filthy spoons.

6: *Night of the Lizard*

Winnie was going job hunting. So to speak. That is, he was so worried about paying his lawyer, among others, that he got up before ten a.m. And instead of putting on jeans and a T-shirt, he borrowed a suit from his downstairs neighbor, a failed mortgage broker now working out of an abandoned warehouse in Costa Mesa, selling worthless mining stock to wealthy coupon clippers.

The 44 Regular fit Winnie OK, but he wasn't used to baggy trousers and big shoulders, and when he stopped at Spoon's Landing for a pick-me-up, Spoon looked him over. 'That just-took-it-outta-the-washer-with-the-sleeves-rolled-up look of today ain't it, Winnie.'

'Think it's too much?' Winnie buttoned the jacket, then unbuttoned it. 'Maybe the green paisley tie don't go with the winter white?'

'Too yuppie-ish,' Spoon said. 'You're no yuppie.'

Guppy Stover, who'd begun drinking brain tumors at nine a.m., was already surly. 'Duppie,' she said. 'You're definitely *downwardly* urban. Goddamn duppie.'

Winnie said to Spoon, 'I heard they're lookin for a boat salesman over at that broker by Mariner's Mile. I think I could probably sell those big stinkpots, right?'

'Jist turn on them oh-so-sincere peepers and you could sell the Rushdie memoirs to one a the ayatollahs,' Spoon droned.

Which caused Guppy to say, 'That guy Rushdie oughtta move to Orange County. Our Eye-ranians couldn't leave the discos long enough to kill anybody.'

Winnie finished his drink and left, but hadn't been gone five minutes from Spoon's when the saloonkeeper took the phone call from Tess Binder.

He seemed to like Winnie and somehow that made it *more* depressing. Winnie walked along the row of motor yachts in the broker's boat slips, trying to be interested in what the guy was telling him about an Ocean fifty-three-foot sports fisher. And an Egg Harbor 46 that he'd just sold. And there were two Vikings in his inventory, one fifty-seven-footer having a custom wet bar that cost $20,000. He told Winnie about a 111-foot steel-hulled oceangoer built to Lloyds specs that he'd been offered for two million, and a seventy-four-foot Stephens Flybridge for a million and a half. But it was only when he'd spot a sloop or a ketch that Winnie would get a spark of interest. A Nordic 44 knocked him for a loop, and he fell in love with a Hinckley 52.

'I'd be better at selling sailboats,' he offered. 'I'm a sailor.'

'*Lot* more money in powerboats,' the broker said. 'Outsell sails five to one in this store. You sell one of the big babies, you made your year.'

'Yeah,' Winnie said without enthusiasm. 'Gotta be hard to move em though.'

'Be surprised. Good year, we got no problem moving them, even the hundred-footers. This year hasn't been too good. People don't know which way George Bush is gonna go. Don't know if we're in for inflation or recession or

70

more good times. Boat business'll be tender till Bush figures out who he is.'

Bush wasn't the only one with an identity crisis, Winnie Farlowe thought, studying the boat slips bulging with rapidly depreciating booze cruisers. Imagining himself trying to convince a Gold Coast millionaire that his life was incomplete without one of those greenback gobblers blocking the view from his waterfront home. As Winnie left, the broker told him he was one of the 'finalists' for the job, and would be called within a week, one way or the other.

By the time Winnie parked in front of Spoon's Landing, Guppy Stover had a whiskey glow and was telling some poor guy who merely said 'How ya doing?' about the son of a bitch who dumped her on Waikiki and wrecked her entire life.

'Got a phone call,' Spoon said to Winnie. His sweat-stained yellow shirt was unbuttoned all the way down the front on this hot day, exposing a wet pink hairy belly.

'Who, my lawyer?'

'Your squeeze,' Spoon said.

'What squeeze?'

The saloonkeeper removed his navy cap to scratch his bald head. Then he did something really ugly. He smiled. 'Come on, Winnie, tell old Spoon all about it!'

'*What* squeeze?'

'The one I seen you talkin to the other night. That two-legged tuna that looked like she was cruisin the Bermuda Triangle till she laid eyes on you. *That* one!'

'Tess Binder? You serious?'

'As a heart attack.'

'Called me here?'

'Asked me if you was gonna be in today. I said the day you don't come in we'd put your picture on a milk carton.'

'She coming in?'

'Wants you to meet her over at her club. Six o'clock. Think you can make it?'

'Can I *make* it?'

Winnie was so happy he bought a drink for Guppy, one for Spoon, and another for himself. Winnie was so happy he spent thirty bucks in the next two hours, and when Carlos Tuna shambled in, he looked at all the grins and said, 'Why's everybody so happy? They puttin *Roller Derby* in prime time?'

By the time six o'clock arrived, Winnie was half fried. He'd meant to limit the drinks, but he was nervous. Tess Binder made him that way, and when he was nervous he drank a bit more than he should. Just as he did when he was depressed. Or scared. Or lonely. Or on a night with a full moon, halfmoon or no moon. Especially when he got to missing police work.

Well, there was *some* truth to the accusation that he had a drinking problem, but he sensed a change was about to occur. Tess Binder was part of it. A woman like her showing such interest in him, well, if he could get some kind of employment, a job he was proud of, the way he was proud of being a policeman . . . OK, maybe not that kind of pride. He didn't expect to ever have *that* kind of professional pride again. That thing he felt during the fifteen years he was a cop, the thing about being a professional.

He thought of these things while driving to her club. He forgot them when he got in the parking lot and gave the VW convertible to the kid parking a Lamborghini. Then he saw a Testarossa that looked like the one his lawyer, Chip Simon, used to run down a pathetic kneeling paper clip, the way life had run down Winston Farlowe until he no longer knew who or what he was. Winnie staggered a bit when he got out of the VW and the valet parker had to grab his arm. Winnie mumbled something about weak ankles, but the kid's knowing look said, sure, just like the *rest* of the dipsomaniacs around this joint.

There was live music in the bar, a three-piece band with a female vocalist. And the place wasn't as dark as Spoon's Landing, which meant it wasn't as dark as Dracula's bunk, but it was dark enough to camouflage nips and tucks and bad sutures and lumpy implants and curdled silicone.

Winnie walked all the way around the rectangular midroom bar but couldn't find her in the teeming crowd. He started looking at the people the way a cop does, noticing that a lot of the women had skin so taut they were frog eyed, with that look of perpetual astonishment. The older guys had their share of cosmetic surgery too, the kind that softens and smoothes the eyes. But instead of looking like young men they end up looking like old women. Old guys with old women's eyes were a common sight even in Spoon's Landing. What *wasn't* common was the sight of a black face anywhere in The Golden Orange. The census always claimed there were a few, but nobody ever saw one. It was said that former baseball slugger Reggie Jackson lived around here but it was widely believed that by now he'd turned white.

Winnie elbowed a space for himself at the bar next to a guy who was doing well just to hang on. The guy was very tall, wore an auburn toupee, and was swaying like a palm tree in big wind. He looked pretty old up close, and you could weave a dock line from his gray wiry nose hair.

'Better adjust the horizontal hold, partner,' Winnie said when the guy lurched into him.

'I know you?'

Winnie thought it was the worst rug he'd even seen, especially on a rich guy. 'I'm new around here,' he said.

Winnie was delighted when the guy waved to one of the harried bartenders and yelled, 'Give my friend a . . .'

'Polish vodka. On the rocks.'

'Double?'

'Why not?'

When Winnie's drink arrived, the drunk in the funny red rug said, 'You won't like it here. Superficial. Everybody's superficial.'

'Well, superficiality's only skin deep,' Winnie said, standing on tiptoes, unable to spot her among the murky mob of drinkers.

'Look at the lizards slithering in,' the guy said disgustedly. 'Here to ferret out some lonely old broad before she gets Alzheimer's so bad her lawyer has to slam a lid on the money box. This is the night of the lizard. Drinks're cheap. Grab-a-granny night, we call it.' Then the tall drunk took a closer look at Winnie, swayed to starboard, and said, 'Wait a minute. *You* a lizard? Naw, you don't look like one.'

Winnie caught him in midstagger and said, 'You filed a fight plan?'

'*Another* drink for my friend!' the guy said to the bartender, who nodded and took an order for thirteen drinks from a perspiring waitress as the roar of the crowd increased in direct relation to the decibel level of the band playing in the other room.

'Anyway,' Winnie's sponsor continued, 'you're new, so you can hook your wagon to a star. Or your bumper hitch to a hearse. Some old broad with lips like wet clay and a house done in graveyard marble.'

'I'm sorta always hooking my wagon to a wagon, is my problem,' Winnie said.

Then the drunk pointed to a booth full of hot mommas on the upper level. They were sleek and slim and expensive, like Tess Binder. Women her age. Even across the room Winnie could see they were all looking for something.

'Stay away from *them*,' the guy said.

'Who they waiting for?'

'Not guys like you. FFH rich, not just seven-one-four rich.'

'Excuse me?'

'I tell you, stay away from *those* broads! None of them ever had an orgasm unless it happened on shop-till-you-drop day at South Coast Plaza. If local paramedics have to learn lifesaving liposuction it's because of *them*. Conversation? They could trivialize trivia.'

While Winnie Farlowe was watching *them*, Tess Binder strolled into the jammed barroom, walked directly toward *them*, kissed one of them on the cheek and sat down at their table.

'Do you know *that* one?' Winnie asked the tall drunk.

The guy swayed again, looked over the heads of the

75

crowd at Tess Binder and said, 'No, but they're inter-changeable. Choosing between any two of them's like choosing between Iran and Iraq.'

Two minutes later Winnie was standing at the booth full of hot mommas. Corky Peebles, in a torso-hugging cotton turtleneck, took a sniff but passed. She knew poverty when she smelled it.

'Win!' Tess said, beaming up at him. 'Sit. Have a drink.' Then she turned to the other hot mommas and said, 'Everyone, this is Win Farlowe.'

Winnie caught a few names, and sat down to hear the end of Rita Fisher's tale of *tragic* divorce, which everyone knew to mean she'd not been able to get Graham Fraser to abrogate the prenuptial agreement.

'. . . so there I was wandering around Crystal Court,' Rita explained. 'Alone. I mean, *really* alone in a crowd. My house on Lido? Gone. Even my birthday present? My five-sixty SL? Gone! Stolen by that barrel of guts! That heartless, three-hundred-pound monster. Him, he's still decimating herds of beef. Me, I'm living on tarragon sprigs!'

Tess said, 'You should've put mad money aside every chance you got. Next time, get a secret safety deposit box.'

Rita sighed. 'That doesn't work for me. Mad money's harder to keep boxed up than Elvis Presley.'

A few of the women clucked and murmured sympath-etically, but Winnie noticed that none of them stopped eyeing the new prospects who passed through the packed lounge in an endless flow.

'I told you, you should never've married that greedy swine!' said the ever-sensitive Corky Peebles. 'People like him, and Castro and Qaddafi, and Ted Kennedy, and . . .' She'd just run out of famous people she hated. 'They should all be put in a country where they only have a Sears store to shop in! They should have to live with mall withdrawal forever!'

It was clearly the worst fate that Corky Peebles could wish on another human being.

'After a while the need to shop sort of goes in remission,' Tess consoled. Then she turned to Winnie and said, 'Shall we go to dinner?'

As Winnie and Tess pushed through the crowd and got to the door, the drunk in the red rug was boozier yet. He was sharing the door table with a dog-eyed hot momma so thin you could pick her up like a beer mug, by her collar bones. He was saying to her: 'Grow old along with me! The best is *yet* to be! That's Robert Browning.'

The skinny momma, her silicone bursting out of a creamy pink silk blouse, had just eyeballed better pickings in the form of a rollicking up-and-coming mortgage banker. She jumped up and said, 'Mister Browning was correct *only* if you have a personal trainer, a good cosmetic surgeon and a great portfolio. Bye-bye, darling.'

The disgusted drunk spotted Winnie leaving with Tess Binder and cried out, 'Don't think *yours* is any different! They're so predictable! An organ grinder shows you more variety! Their natural inclination is toward spike heels with ankle straps and fishnet stockings! Don't be fooled, my friend! Hookers! *All* of them!'

'Who was that delightful man?' Tess asked, as she and Winnie walked through the lobby toward the parking lot.

'Guy I met at the bar. Wore those five-hundred-dollar ostrich shoes with warts on 'em? Went to the Andrei

Gromyko charm school. So pessimistic he should wear a shroud.'

'A real sweetheart. I could see that.'

He'd never stood beside her until now, and she was taller than he'd thought. In high heels, she was exactly at eye level with him.

'Where we going to dinner and do they take overdrawn Visa cards and when was the last time you rode in a VW ragtop that runs worse than New York City?'

'Don't worry about a thing, old son,' she said, handing the valet-parking kid her ticket. 'You're *my* guest.'

Old son. He *loved* it. They talked like that on *Masterpiece Theater*!

She drove a Mercedes, but not a new one. Winnie correctly guessed it was six years old, a four-door sedan without chrome wheels or pinstripes. Not a Golden Orange kind of car at all. A diesel, for chrissake!

She seemed to read his thoughts.

'One of my ex-husband's cars,' she said. 'The one he didn't want. The one that he gave me as a wedding gift, he took back. It was a Porsche nine-thirty Cabriolet. Red. My father did the same thing to me once. It's the way of men like that. The Lords giveth . . .'

7: *The Nymph*

The restaurant was on the oceanfront. It was one that Winnie had passed a thousand times. Once he'd even stopped for a drink and to watch the sunset on a day he was wearing a *Sail America* sweatshirt that didn't pass dress code: no collar. But the guy on the door, a mustachioed Parisian, who'd long since learned not to act like one, told Winnie not to leave. The Frenchman disappeared for a few minutes and returned with a *Members Only* windbreaker whose stand-up collar passed muster in The Golden Orange except at weddings. But the drinks were $3.75, so Winnie only had a couple.

Now he was back there at twilight with Tess Binder. The first thing he noticed was that the bar was jammed but nobody paid much attention to the magic hour light show. The sky looked eerily blood streaked, moments before the fireball floated down into the inky sea, always faster than Winnie expected.

'Forty-five seconds,' Winnie said after they found some standing room by the big window facing the ocean.

'What's that?'

'Took her forty-five to drop past the horizon tonight. I can see her from my kitchen if I stand on a chair and peek over the roof next door. Took her forty-five seconds tonight.'

'The sun's feminine?'

'Oh yeah, without a doubt,' Winnie said. 'Can't live without her, but she's dangerous.'

The Frenchman aimed his prominent Gallic nose at a pair of yuppies sitting at one of the tall cocktail tables and they jumped up and followed him. Winnie grabbed the two vacated stools and a leggy blonde in a tuxedo jacket, black tie, shorts and high-heeled pumps took their drinks order.

Outside the window, on the beach, an Asian lad flew his electric-blue and amber batwing kite. The kite looped and climbed, soared and dove. The boy made the kite dance along the sand and pirouette over the bodies of a pair of lovers lying on a beach blanket. Then the kite fluttered and hung in midair above the window of the restaurant, a brilliant jewel hovering in the twilight.

Perched on a high stool with her legs crossed, Tess didn't seem to notice as her full-split white skirt fell open. Winnie loved white stockings! The shawl-collar blouse was white linen, and Tess reflected red dusk back at Winnie. It was a bewitching moment: this vision in white glowing a creamy pink from reflected blood-red twilight.

When the drinks arrived, she touched his glass with hers. He figured she'd say 'Cheers,' but she fooled him.

'Chin chin,' she said.

He caught himself gulping, forced himself to put the glass down and tried conversation. 'Too bad you don't sail,' he said. 'I really dream of a racing boat but I got my eye on a more practical thirty-six footer. Way she's designed, one guy could sail her round the world. Self-steering vane on her stern controls the rudder. Built in the early sixties and modified with all kinds a stuff. She's a heavy boat. Won't go fast, but very stable. Doesn't oil-can when you go to weather.'

'What's that? Oil-can?'

'You know that hollow sound the boat makes in a chop? Baloom, baloom, baloom. Got lots a headroom down below. No engine. That blew up, but who cares?'

'Going to buy it?'

'Fifteen grand. The best sailboat bargain I'll ever see.'

'So buy it.'

'Gotta pay my lawyer four grand for walking me into court and introducing me to my worst nightmare. My lawyer, Chip, said he woulda *liked* to cut his fee to two.'

'So why didn't he?'

'Claims the senior law partners don't permit fee cutting, sympathy, compassion, pity, or mercy of any kind.'

She shrugged and said, 'You got off with probation. He was competent, wasn't he?'

'As Noriega's dermatologist or the department of motor vehicles. All *he* did is stay outta the judge's way so he could torture me for fifteen minutes. Oh yeah, Chip made a two-minute leniency plea with about a thousand adverbs in it. He's the adverb king of the Western world. Only guy in the universe who still says, "Jeepers!" As in "Jeepers, Win! I really *wish* I could shave the fee! Truly I do! Truly! Sincerely! *But . . .*"'

'So you won't be buying your bargain boat?'

'Only sailboat I'll have is in my bathtub. Come to think of it, I don't *have* a bathtub. Shower stall. Works half the time.'

'Why do I have a feeling you're trying to tell me how dreadfully poor you are.'

'And needy. Needier than public television. I figured we were eating at your club and it wouldn't cost me. Now

I'm nervous as the Borgias's food taster. I might as well come clean. I can't pay for a meal in a place like this. My credit card's more overextended than Mexico.'

Tess Binder looked into Winnie's soft blue eyes and saw not a trace of duplicity. 'You *are* ingenuous, Mister Farlowe.'

'Is that like ingenious? I used to be ingenious sometimes. Working on a homicide gave me ingenious moments.'

'And solid. A straight-ahead guy. You even have a forelock to tug.' She seemed amused, checking out the ill-fitting yuppie suit, the graying cowlick, but mostly the soft vulnerable eyes. 'Well, you can stop poor-mouthing even if it's true. I invited you to dinner so it's *my* treat.' She signaled to another waitress in tuxedo shorts, this one a redhead even taller than the blonde.

After that drink, part of him wondered what the hell she wanted with him, this woman who could read his mind. This woman whose eyes behind the tortoiseshell glasses were opaque, eyes he couldn't read at all. If eyes were windows, her panes were frosted.

Ten minutes later, the Frenchman showed them to their booth, which faced all the action down in the sunken barroom. The place was decorated like a don't-give-a-shit, make-believe brothel, complete with paintings of voluptuous nudes, all of which said: 'No fag designer ever laid a glove on *this* joint. We're earthy, but we ain't cheap.'

The food, as in most really successful Golden Orange restaurants, where the seven-one-four and the F.F.H. wealthy dine, was not faddish. By the end of the 1980s, cholesterol was making a comeback. If you felt like California cuisine you traveled to Beverly Hills or West

Hollywood, where a glimpse of movie stars went with the price of dinner. Cajun never did have a foothold in The Golden Orange. Even Southwestern seemed destined to go.

Hearty American fare was back with a vengeance, at least for men. And this was *very* much a man's world, this citadel of white Republicans. They'd dumped all that nouvelle nutrition the moment they learned that zinc doesn't guarantee an erection.

When the menus came, Tess told Winnie to shoot the works, so he ordered the mussels to start, then the abalone at thirty-nine bucks a pop. She ordered the local sea bass, supposedly caught by the dory fleet, that small bastion of oceangoing self-reliance working about five hundred yards from the restaurant, by the Newport pier.

There are fifteen to twenty fishermen in the dory fleet, a unique and eccentric band who, for a century, have launched their little flat-bottomed boats directly off the beach, smashing through the breakers into wind and spray and deep dark ocean. All alone usually, at two o'clock in the morning, they motor out sometimes twenty-five miles to set their mile-long lines, held down in a thousand feet of ocean by Coke bottles and bricks, each line set with over five hundred hooks from which a good day's catch of half a ton will be plucked by hands turned bone-white from exposure. All of this in an era when commercial fishermen use airplanes and sonar.

Of course, the brightly painted old wooden dory boats, littering the beach where they sell the day's catch, are there for atmosphere. Nowadays, the new boats of Japanese design have Yamaha engines, and Toyota trucks haul them out of the water at day's end. Still, the dory fleet retains a kind of Gypsy romance to tourists, and even to locals. They're part of the rind in The Golden Orange.

'Know something?' Winnie said, looking down to the bar level where beautiful young women were having drinks with middle-aged men they hardly knew or just met. 'This is a pickup joint.'

Tess said, 'Not the way *you* mean it. In the age of herpes and AIDS these women come here to get fed. These gentlemen are looking for dinner companions and the ladies just oblige. It seldom goes beyond that, or so I've been told. It's a tradition here.'

'So there really *is* hunger in America!' Winnie observed. 'And these Gold Coasters're doing their share to take care of it, at a hundred bucks a head. Maybe this is part of the thousand points of light George Bush was talking about at the Republican convention.'

Tess looked at a pair of young women, both with hair like tennis star André Agassi, and said, 'More like young animals being captured, fed and released by toothless predators. This is a nature show, Winnie. They do everything but tag ears around here.'

Winnie had two more Polish vodkas, and was starting to vibrate by the time dessert came.

'Got any cheesecake?' he asked the waitress. 'I'll have cheesecake if you got it.'

'And give him a scoop of white chocolate ice cream on the side,' Tess said. 'My old son hasn't had a meal lately.'

When the waitress was gone, Winnie said, 'Any son of yours would still be squeezing zits. You can't be a day over thirty-five.'

She looked very pleased at that, but said, 'You don't really expect me to tell you my age.'

'Me, I just turned forty. I'm feeling it. Only time I felt young was tonight at your club. Watching the grab-a-granny action.'

'Who told you about the grab-a-granny business?'

'The tall guy with the funny red toup on his head. The one that yelled at me when we left.'

'The one who called *me* a hooker.'

'Yeah, well, he was one a those drunks likes to shock little girls and people from Nebraska. I didn't pay no attention to what he was saying half the time.'

'If my father were alive I'd take you to his yacht club,' she said. 'Different crowd entirely.'

'I know a few people belong there,' Winnie said. 'Met 'em when I was still sailing a lot. Your dad was commodore, huh?'

'My grandfather. When I was a little girl Daddy made me sail Sabots and Snowbirds. Humphrey Bogart was racing his Albatross here in those days.'

'So you *are* a sailor!'

'Not if I can help it. Whenever I'd place below the top three in a race I'd get lectured for an hour. It's probably why I hate boats. Especially sailboats.'

'Bet you were an only child, with an old man riding that hard.'

'You win the bet.'

'Daddy's girl, huh?'

All the time she was talking about her father, Tess Binder looked away from Winnie, toward the night, toward the crashing surf beyond the long white sand beach. She didn't answer him at first, then she smiled sardonically and said, 'Daddy wasn't much for girls, as it turns out. Shall we go?'

'Sure,' he said, finishing the last bite of cheesecake.

'Let's go to *your* club.'

'*My* club?'

'Spoon's Landing.'

'Well . . . tonight's likely to be a little rough. The gang from the boatyards get paid.'

'Super! Let's go!'

'Hey, I *do* belong to a club,' he said. 'Sort of. Let's stop at my club for one and then to Spoon's.'

Ten minutes later, Tess, who looked as though she might be feeling the drinks, parked the Mercedes in the parking lot beside the American Legion Post on Fifteenth Street. The building happened to rest on some of the most valuable land on the Balboa peninsula, city-owned property on Lido Channel. Winnie had joined the Legion for three reasons: cheap drinks, pretty good steaks you get to cook, and a restful channel view. Those members who'd seen combat were mostly vets of the Second World War or Korea. There were only a few from Winnie's war, but everyone seemed friendly and real. He never could get used to older folks calling him 'comrade' all the time. Still, when you get an honest shot of good booze for a buck and a quarter, you had no bitch coming. And unlike Spoon's Landing, the worst argument he ever heard here was about whether or not you can talk during a salute.

The old babe who played the piano was in full swing when they arrived. All in all, the Legion was like any mid-America lodge. Tess seemed to enjoy the down-home hospitality, so they killed an hour listening to the piano, during which Winnie downed four vodkas because at that price you couldn't afford *not* to. Just before they left, the old lady played 'Where or When', and a widow of a Second World War naval aviator stood up and sang in a thin quavery soprano.

> *It seemed we stood and talked like this before*
> *We looked at each other in the same way*
> *then*
> *But I don't remember where or when.*

'*That's* how I feel about you!' Winnie said suddenly. 'Like the song!'

'What do you mean?'

'Since I first met you I've felt like I've seen you before. Maybe talked to you. Something.'

He shook his head slowly, groping for it. *Déjà vu.* A snatch of a melody. The smell of her perfume: jasmine. What?

'Haven't we met someplace before, babe?' she said. 'That what you mean?'

'No, I'm serious,' he said.

> *The clothes you're wearing are the clothes you wore*
> *We smiled at each other in the same way then*
> *But I can't remember where or when.*

'I'd remember you, old son,' she said. 'Shall we go?'

Winnie stopped when they reached the sidewalk outside.

'Anything wrong?' she asked.

'You ever drink at that jazz club in Laguna?'

'Winnie!' she said, shaking her head. 'I'm offended. Are you saying you could *forget* me?'

'No, I guess I couldn't,' he said.

The voice drifted outside, the tin soprano, so full of sadness.

> *And so it seems that we have met before*
> *And laughed before and loved before*
> *But who knows where or wheeeennnn.*

Tess chuckled and said, 'Maybe we were chums in some other life?'

'Maybe,' Winnie said. 'But I'd be happy to be your pal in *this* one.'

Spoon's Landing was, as Winnie feared, full of fishermen and boatyard gypsies and off-duty cops and other waterfront vagabonds. Four boozy cops in jeans and T-shirts were playing snooker and punching large holes in their paychecks. The L.A. Kings were playing hockey on big screen, and there were some petty but boisterous bets being made in the corner of the saloon. A dory fisherman in huaraches and cutoffs – a wiry guy with alligator hands – accidentally lurched into Tess before they got to the bar. He offered a leering apology, disappointed to see Winnie right behind her.

'I was afraid a this,' Winnie said. 'Looks like a panel for the Geraldo Rivera show. Sure you wanna have a drink?'

'Wouldn't miss it,' Tess said cheerily, and Winnie wasn't too bombed to see that she didn't seem all that sober either.

'Let's sit at the far side,' he said.

Spoon moved Guppy's empty glass twelve inches down

the bar to make room for the new arrivals and told her, 'Wake up and go home!'

The old woman opened her eyes, banged her hand on the bartop and said, 'Somebody stole my drink when I went to the ladies room! I demand another one!'

'Cut it out!' Spoon said.

'Cut *what* out?' Guppy's velvet hair ribbon was undone and dangling in front of her nose, unleashing an explosion of gray hair. '*I'm* the one got ripped off by one of your low-life customers! Look at 'em!' She waved her hand in the general direction of the dory crews. 'I've seen more gentility at a cockfight and better wardrobes. Their idea of style is tying the thongs on their deck shoes and they don't *need* socks 'cause their ankles're green.'

Then she located her glass and smacked it down on the bar, yelling, 'Publican! Bring me a screwdriver!'

'I'll put one through your heart!' said the saloonkeeper. 'This bar's inlaid with shell from Galápagos turtles! You can't *get* giant turtle shells no more!'

'Well, you shouldn't *have* a goddamn endangered bartop!' Guppy countered. 'You environmental pirate!'

'*I'll* buy Guppy a drink, for chissake!' said Winnie. Anything to quiet things down.

'She ain't gettin no drink!' Spoon said. 'She's been drinkin rum since noon. This always happens when she takes that noon balloon to Jamaica.'

Guppy smiled demurely at Tess, extended her gloved hand and said, 'Howja do, my dear. I'm Guppy Stover. What's Winnie doing with a lady like you?'

Tess Binder smiled and shook hands with Guppy, who then said, 'Don't get too close to those guys playing snooker. They're cops. And stay away from the bunch of thugs watching the hockey game. They think class is when most of the words on their tattoos're spelled right.' Then she pointed to Bilge O'Toole and said, 'Don't even *look* in his direction or you'll be wearing him like a fox stole. We're talking here about a guy that drinks from the faucet without a glass. He smiles at you, you'll feel like you just been flashed.'

The old woman, forgetting she was eighty-sixed, yelled to the saloonkeeper: 'Spoon, bring me a brain tumor! I feel like mixing.'

'I ain't serving drinks to a drunk!' Spoon said. 'If I wanted to get thrown in jail I'd attend a Grateful Dead concert. Go *home*!'

Bilge O'Toole, who probably had a higher blood-alcohol reading than Guppy, said, 'Stop whining about a drink! What is this, the days of whine and roses?'

Then Carlos Tuna moved in close, carrying his turtle, Regis, around his neck in a leather pouch designed for comfy riding. He stuck up for Guppy. Soon *everybody* was fuming and fussing about who should or should not be served an alcoholic beverage.

'What this is really about,' Winnie explained to Tess over all the yelling, 'is a debate over what Regis, who's Carlos's turtle, did to Irma, who's Bilge's turtle. They're looking for an excuse to fight. Jesus, where's the ghost-busters when we need 'em?'

'I'm enjoying myself immensely!' Tess said. And for once her gray eyes looked a bit less opaque.

Finally Carlos said to Bilge, 'Listen, I was you I'd go back down the bar with the rest a that barge garbage!'

'Careful, Bilge!' Guppy sneered. 'Don't mess with Carlos. He's one of those hard guys, blows his nose on the sidewalk.'

'He'll be *wipin'* it there along with his ass, he messes with me *or* my turtle!' Bilge countered, his face red and sweaty, his white hair standing in stalks.

'This'll be a one-punch fight,' Spoon said disgustedly to Winnie. 'Whichever one throws it, he'll have a coronary on the spot. They'll be hemorrhaging cholesterol if they so much as break skin.' Then he turned to both big-bellied turtle wranglers and said, 'Break it up, or you're *all* eighty-sixed!'

'I came here and paid good money for a laugh or two!' Guppy cried in utter despair. 'They had more laughs in *Wuthering Heights*!'

Tess had trouble hitting the ashtray when she snuffed out her cigarette. 'I think there's only one place to go,' she said boozily.

'Yeah?'

'My place. Wanna see my house?'

'I'll need a microsecond to think it over,' Winnie said.

Guppy Stover was being removed from Spoon's Landing by the proprietor himself when Winnie and Tess arrived at the Mercedes parked on the street in front.

The old woman's hair ribbon was long gone and her mass of hair had fallen forward, hiding all but her strawberry nose.

'Unhand me, you lout!' she cried, as Spoon gently propelled her down the sidewalk in the general direction of her apartment.

'You're not wanted here tonight,' Spoon said. 'Go home.'

'What am I, a pariah?' she cried. 'A leper? Why don't you *brand* me? Why not make me wear a scarlet letter? I bet Hester Prynne got kindlier pub service, you big tub a pelican puke!'

91

'That's what you get when boozers have an education,' Spoon explained to Tess just before she opened the door to the Mercedes. 'Always bringin up people I ain't met.'

Tess was quiet during the ten-minute ride from Spoon's to her home on Linda Isle. So was Winnie, but only because he was being lulled to sleep by the metallic chug of the diesel car.

His head bobbed when she said, 'What else did he say? That man?'

'What man?'

'The tall one at the club.'

'The guy wearing the rug? I don't know. Bought me a couple drinks and was filling me in on some a your members.'

'And what about my group? I mean, the women I was drinking with?'

'I don't know,' Winnie said, realizing that tonight of all nights he should've shut it off after the eighth or tenth vodka. 'Just more or less that they got the social consciousness of Marie Antoinette.'

'Well, he wasn't exaggerating all that much.'

'No?'

'About a few of them. Corky Peebles, for example.'

'I liked her haircut,' Winnie said, as Tess stopped at the guarded kiosk of Linda Isle. 'Reminded me a the Beatles when they started out. Very nostalgic.'

The uniformed guard waved and pressed the button to raise the wooden car barrier. Tess drove on to the island and made an immediate right. Into the ghetto.

A few homes on her side of the island were listed for $2.5 million, but there were a few you could pick up for as little as $1.2 million on leased land. Tess Binder's house was one of those. She detested it. She'd gotten by with the furniture that Ralph Cunningham gave her when he'd bolted. She could've bought different furniture on credit, but had refused to put a penny into a house she hated. She didn't even have the emotional energy to try to sell the horrible marble sculpture her husband had bought during their honeymoon in Florence. The 'art dealer' in Florence had told Ralph that the sculptor was a young Michelangelo. Tess said, sure, if Michelangelo had freebased for about ten years and had the taste of Imelda Marcos.

Winnie Farlowe was one of the few human beings she'd invited into the house since Ralph deserted her for his tennis partner and what would surely be a costly doubles match.

She was about to apologize and concede that the place was ghastly, when Winnie said, 'This is the most beautiful house I've ever seen! I love marble floors and a sweeping staircase and a crystal chandelier! Where does Scarlett O'Hara sleep?'

'So glad you like it, old son,' Tess said, leading him down into the sunken living room, tossing her purse on one of two sofas that Ralph had done in florid raw silk. She unsteadily turned on two lamps and pulled her shoes off, dropping them on the biggest glass and gilt coffee table Winnie had ever seen. 'I need a drink,' she said, walking to the mirrored wet bar. She *hated* smoked mirrors. *So* gauche!

Winnie moseyed around the room admiring an enormous oil painting from the Italian honeymoon. It was a Mediterranean version of Claude Monet lily pads that Tess had left on the wall only because it reminded her of

93

fresh water with limits. *Finite* water that did not come at you like an assailant, and rush away like a slave to the moon.

Winnie sat down on the sofa next to Tess only after she put a glass of Russian vodka on the table next to her double Scotch.

'Sorry I don't have Polish vodka.'

'I was thinking I had enough,' Winnie said, eyeing the drink.

'I *know* I've had enough,' Tess said, taking a good hard hit on the Scotch, closing her eyes as it slid down her throat. Winnie had never seen someone drink Scotch the way she did – erotically.

He caressed his glass while she lit a cigarette and tucked her legs underneath herself, revealing all of one thigh. Tess clapped her hands and a sensual saxophone riff surrounded them: Ellington's 'In a Sentimental Mood'.

'John Coltrane was the best ever on tenor,' Winnie said. 'Wish I coulda seen him in person.'

'I'm not a real jazz buff,' Tess said, 'but I like certain pieces. My husband owed his life to Japanese technology. Me, I'd rather have a radio you can see and turn on with a knob.'

'OK if I take my coat off?'

'I certainly *assumed* you'd take your coat off,' Tess Binder said, looking him right in the eye. She did it the same way she shook hands. Confidently.

The implication stopped him for a second. Those gray eyes behind the oversized glasses were impossible to read, especially since she kept going out of focus. He *knew* he shouldn't have another swallow of booze.

Then she did that trick again. She sipped the Scotch and

leaned her head back like a bird. He could almost *see* it slide down. He couldn't decide. Was it the booze in his belly or the Scotch slipping down that long graceful throat? Anyway, Winnie Farlowe was getting mightily aroused.

She sat catlike, exposing the muscular thigh. Those goddamn white stockings! Winnie was a sucker for willowy babes in white stockings. Made them all look like lascivious nurses in blue movies, the kind his team used to see at a movie house in Santa Ana when he was a high school kid playing football.

'Why're you afraid of me?' Tess asked abruptly.

'Shows, huh? Well, maybe after this Russian potata juice ferments I'll relax more.' He took a big hit on the vodka.

'Why do you drink so much, Win?'

'Oh, I don't *usually* drink so much. Not like this. Not like tonight.'

'No? Why tonight then?'

'You're buying.'

'You're lying.'

'I guess so. I'm jist nervous.'

'So why're you afraid of me?'

'Well, let's see . . .' His speech was getting slurred and he knew it. So he took *another* drink. Too late now!

'Lie down,' she said.

'What?'

'Here. On the sofa. Lie back and put your feet up.'

Tess dropped to her knees on the white carpet, lifted Winnie's legs on to the sofa and slipped off his cheap penny loafers. She plumped the sofa pillows behind his head, got up and swayed toward the fireplace. She lit a small gas fire for effect. The logs were fake. Then she came back and knelt beside him.

Winnie watched her take her jacket off and toss it carelessly on to the matching silk sofa on the other side of the glass table. She picked up his drink and held it to his lips, showing him an unreadable smile. She was acting just like a goddamn nurse! *Was* this one of those blue movies, or what?

'Comfy?' she asked.

'You kidding?'

He thought she was going to lean over and kiss him, but she didn't. She giggled softly. Wind chimes again.

'Still scared?'

'Sure.'

This time she chuckled out loud. 'Win Farlowe, you're perfect!'

'I know. You said. A straight-ahead guy. Can I ask you something?'

'OK,' Tess said. 'Anything.' She crept a little closer, resting her arm on the cushion beside his. He could feel the soft down on her forearm. In the firelight it was the color of polished brass.

'I mean, I wasn't conceived in a Cal Tech sperm bank. But I'm not stupid.'

'Of course not,' she said.

'I mean, I don't like poems that don't rhyme, but I'm no dummy.'

'You are definitely no dummy,' she agreed.

'So why me?'

'Why you, what?'

'Someone like you. Looks. Brains. Money. A real *babe*! I don't get it.'

'You're the world's only ex-cop who ever broke up a parade all by himself. You're different.'

'I'm different. Slumming, is that it?'

'You're going to force me to get specific? OK, starting with your looks, well, you look like . . . like daybreak at Catalina. When I was a girl and my dad took me over to the island for weekends, we'd sit out there on the water at dawn, fishing. Or rather, *he* was fishing and I was watching the sunrise. I thought, if there's one thing you can depend on it's that beautiful sunrise over the island. All this, after my mother and father had been screaming at each other all night and my fingers were bleeding from chewing my nails to the quick. Unlike you, I've always thought of the sun in masculine terms. Old mister sun rising up out of the sea at dawn. Anyway, I look at you and I think of that. That's how you strike me, old son. There's something *certain* and reassuring about you.'

'That's why you call me old son? You mean like in the big sun up there?' Winnie pointed toward the twenty-foot ceiling.

'Could be a subconscious choice of words,' she said. 'I don't pretend to understand myself any more than I've understood the men in my life: my father, my husbands, all three of them. But I think I understand a few things about *you*. You're a straight-ahead guy.'

'Got any kids?'

'No,' she said. 'Guess I couldn't bring myself to inflict the men I married on some helpless child. How about you?'

'My ex talked me into adopting her brats, I guess, so she could get a little more when her lawyer opened my veins. Never had any a my own. Sometimes I wish I had a son.

Me, I had a *great* old man.' Thinking of his father, he sighed, then said, 'So, how about all the guys around here? All the guys at your club? You don't like em?'

'They bore me or threaten me or repel me. Maybe they seem as ruthless as my father, I don't know. But you, you're *different*.'

'I don't scare you, huh? That figures. I don't scare anybody.'

'But I scare *you*?'

'I'm starting to get used to it,' Winnie said, and his hand inched toward her bare shoulder. His little finger lightly touched the flesh. She felt cool even with the fireplace heating up the room. 'It still don't exactly add up.'

'Stop acting like a cop,' Tess said, moving her shoulder so that three of his fingers were touching her. 'If you *must* have a motive, try this one: From the first moment I saw your photo in the newspaper, I was intrigued. You appear so vulnerable and yet look what you've done. I wanted to find out more.'

'Why?'

'I don't know. A time of life. Divorced for the third time. Facing middle age. Almost broke. Yeah, don't let this house fool you, it's mortgaged to the hilt. All alone, with my father dead less than a year. A father who left his property to someone *else*. Well, I saw your photo, when you were walking out of jail with your lawyer, and I thought: That man, I've *got* to meet him.'

'What? Pity?'

'*Self*-pity, maybe. You'd *acted*! You *did* something, though I'm sure you regret it now. Still, through frustration or rage or whatever, you did something and it made people notice you. Me, I'm afraid to *do* anything to

98

change my life. With you I somehow feel that anything's possible. There, is that enough of a motive for you, Officer? And please don't say I'm trying to make a father figure out of an ex-cop. Believe me, old son, you are *nothing* whatsoever like *my* father, Conrad P. Binder.'

'How come you use your maiden name?'

'My last husband took everything else so I thought he should get back his name. Never liked it anyway. Anything *else* you'd like to know? About motives or clues or evidence or whatever else a cop looks for every time he meets a woman who likes him?'

She was smiling when she said it, but she turned away and dabbed at one eye and removed her glasses.

'Hey!' Winnie said propping himself up on one elbow. 'Hey.'

She turned back to him, and once again her eyes were opaque and unfathomable and absolutely dry. 'Hey, what?' she said.

'Hey, lady,' Winnie said softly. 'Hey, lady, I didn't mean to make you sad.'

She leaned over and kissed him. Then she took his hand and held it to her face. Then she turned and kissed the palm of that hand, and then every fingertip. 'You wouldn't mind walking me upstairs, would you?' she whispered.

'I'm as helpless as a kitten up a tree,' Winnie Farlowe said.

He followed Tess Binder through the living room to that sweeping staircase. She led him by the hand, but stopped for a second when he had to grab the rosewood banister.

'I'm OK,' he lied.

Tess led him through a set of double doors and switched

on a lamp. The master bedroom was the biggest Winnie had ever seen outside a movie. It was done pretty much like the living room with statuary and paintings in gilt frames. The carpet was white but seemed heavier and whiter than the one downstairs. Tess pulled back the ivory silk bedspread. He'd never slept on peach-colored sheets. He'd never *seen* peach-colored sheets.

Tess said, 'Hop in there and warm the linen. I'll be right back.'

She was gone for nearly five minutes. Winnie got undressed, wondering if it was OK to leave his clothes on the black leather chaise, a high-tech job that looked like a stealth bomber in flight. It was the only object in the entire house that Tess had picked out herself, and it clashed outrageously with the costly kitsch her husband had collected.

Winnie decided what the hell, stripped, tossing his things on to the black leather chaise, and jumped into bed. He was glad she hadn't seen his ragged boxer shorts.

He was under the covers when she reentered the room, wearing a primrose peignoir. Tess switched off the light, but instead of coming to bed, she walked to the window and threw open the drapes. Winnie could see the headlights behind her from Pacific Coast Highway, and heard voices from the restaurant parking lot across the narrow, yacht-chocked channel. Tess stood with her back to the room for a full minute. He wished she'd hurry; the booze was hitting him hard and his eyes were getting heavy.

When she finally turned toward him, she stood motionless in the moonlight, next to a marble sculpture that Ralph had loved but left. The nymph extended a hand toward Winnie Farlowe. He found himself growing more alert. Agitated. Something! What was it? He couldn't guess what the nymph might be offering with her open-handed gesture. The hand was empty. *Déjà vu?*

> *We looked at each other in the same way then*
> *But I don't remember where or when.*

Tess Binder opened the tie on the peignoir and let it fall to her hips. Then she tugged again and let it fall to the floor. Winnie could see that she was small-breasted like the nymph, but a tad more voluptuous in the hips. The nymph was a size four.

He looked from Tess to the nymph and back again. They were the loveliest things he'd ever seen in his life: the nymph and Tess Binder. Both of them so cool and still and bewildering in the moonlight. He was sober enough to hope he'd remember it all in the morning. He forgot about the song, and that glimpse of something half remembered.

'Well, old son,' Tess said finally.

But it sounded like the voice came from the cold marble nymph.

8: *Straight-ahead Guy*

When Winnie's eyes popped open he fully expected to find the twin buzzards perched on his bed, maws gaping and bloody. Instead, he found peach-colored sheets and a faint smell of jasmine and for a moment he couldn't remember where the hell he was.

Then he saw Tess sitting on that black futuristic chaise, staring through the open French doors, a cigarette glow reflecting off her glasses. She was wearing only the peignoir even though the offshore wind was cool and damp. Seeing her cleared his mind and he wanted to make love to her all over again. And he *did* remember most of that. He plumped his pillow and she turned toward him.

'Hello,' she said.

'Hello, lady.'

'It's three o'clock, go back to sleep.'

'I know it's three o'clock,' he said. 'I always wake up at three o'clock.'

'Why?'

'The blood sugar,' Winnie said. 'The booze makes it do a swan dive. Then you wake up and meet your hobgoblins. Mine're a couple of real characters. They stay with me about two-three hours on average. You got any?'

'Men,' she said. 'Cruel heartless men I've known.'

'Lemme visit the head and then you can tell me about 'em if you want,' Winnie said.

He got out of bed. Suddenly self-conscious of his nakedness, he sucked in his gut and hurried into the bathroom. He wasn't sure, but she might've chuckled.

When he returned and jumped into bed, he said, 'Gold faucets in the sinks and tub! They real gold?'

'They're as real as the Gold Coast itself,' she said. 'They complement the stained-glass window, don't you think? My husband could've designed it, it's so like him. This statue was one of his investments in *art*.'

Tess always figured that Ralph was the only man in the entire history of The Golden Orange to have a life-sized marble nymph in his bedroom. Completely left to his *own* devices he'd probably have painted in the nipples and pubic hair like a Saudi sheik on Sunset Boulevard.

The ice in her voice made him pause, but he said, 'Yeah, well, I like the window. All those sailboats and dolphins.'

'Newport Beach *belle époque*,' she said. 'Nineteen seventy-nine. That's when my husband's company built this one. He could've afforded any house he wanted on this island, but he had that *arriviste*'s insecurity. Wanted to be able to liquidate and run if the market failed, but it's hard to run with a house. On the other hand, some of the people around here are *fearlessly* nouveau. One conspicuous consumer completely remodeled his house five times in a four-year period. One of our YPOs.'

'What's that?'

'Young Presidents' Organization. Have to do twenty million a year and have at least fifty employees, or something like that. They kick you out when you turn fifty. He's nouveau Jewish, that one. When I was growing up there wasn't a Jew at any of my father's clubs, which're

103

probably still restricted – *de facto* if not *de jure*. Even my club was probably only fifteen per cent Jewish until about ten years ago.'

'You got a problem with Jews?'

She shot a look at him and said, 'Of course not.' Then she turned back toward the darkness.

'Me, I only got a problem with money,' Winnie said. 'Problem is I got none, and no prospects for any. But I like talking about it. Unless it bothers you.'

'Not at all.'

'What's it cost to join your local golf club?'

'The initiation fee's about a hundred and thirty thousand. Waiting list of a year, at least.'

'I used to play a little,' Winnie said. 'Read where it costs over a million to join in Tokyo and you gotta wait years. Guess the rich and shameless don't have it so bad around these parts. Not compared to Tokyo.'

'I never *needed* to be rich, Win,' she said. 'Comfortable, yes. I'm used to certain comforts, I don't deny that.'

'Wanna come to bed?'

'In a minute. After I finish this cigarette.'

'I saw this guy in your club tonight,' he said. 'Real wrinkled old guy. The kind where you wanna swag his neck? Wearing either a solid gold Rolex or the hubcap off his wife's Mercedes. And I thought, *this* is the guy I handled a burglary for one time. Residential job out on the peninsula. They stole his wife's full-length lynx which cost a hundred grand. And they also got his gold-plated license-plate holder. That cost twenty grand, with its own burglar alarm on it. I had to make a supplemental report for them after he got through thinking it all over. About the insurance and all? So I went to your club, this was, oh, seven, eight years ago. I took the report on his yacht. One a those eighty-footers where you could fill the slips below the waterline with concrete and he'd never notice 'cause it never goes out. And I thought, there's something very very wrong with my life.'

He paused to clear the vodka mucus from his throat, and she said, 'What was wrong?'

'I got a conscience,' he said. 'I got this baggage *he* didn't have. I mean, I knew the report was bullshit so he could rape the insurance company and IRS. And his wife was there and had to excuse herself to go pick up the poodle at the doggie day-care center. I bet there's lots like her making annual visits to a plastic surgeon where the croaker's floor is slushy with sucked-out pheasant and fried squid in pumpkin sauce, and the goddamn sludge from kiwi and angel-hair pasta can wear out a dozen Roto Rooters. And I thought, Where's the justice here? Me? I had a few chances at bad bucks during the years I policed this town, but there I was, bankrupt as Eastern Airlines.'

'Are you saying your conscience held you back, is that it?'

'That's it.'

'Any regrets that you have this policeman's over-developed superego?'

'Sometimes. Know some a the things I *hate* about cop shows on TV? They always say, "Put out an APB." Me, I never put out an APB in my life which is just this thing when nobody can find the suspect and already gave up. Another thing that gets me on the cop shows is when they go, "Use extreme caution." Like, after a guy shoots a bunch a people with an AK-forty-seven. If they gotta *tell* you to use caution you gotta be brain-dead, right? But

105

more than all that, I really hate where they say, "The defendant was sentenced to life three times and he showed no emotion." They even say that in the newspapers all the time.'

'Why do you hate it?'

''Cause he can't show any emotion. He's a sociopath, most likely. His feelings are deader than ten-cent phone calls. All this brings me back to the guy on his yacht, phoneying up that supplemental burglary report. And me, I'm sitting there helping him screw the insurance man and the taxpayers. And I know it and he knows it, but he don't give a shit if I know it. He's a sociopath, no doubt. And he's glad of it.'

'Ever get *tempted* to do something illegal for money? When you were a cop?'

Tess Binder snuffed out the cigarette and got up from the chaise, but didn't come to bed. She walked toward the window, toward the cold marble nymph. She stood by the wall and Winnie could feel those smoke-gray eyes watching him from dark shadows.

'Once, maybe,' he said. 'There was this doctor. He had this rich wife, even richer than he was.'

It was a case he'd worked on just before his injury. He was teamed with Buster Wiles at that time, before Buster became the cynical burnout Winnie had introduced to Tess at Spoon's Landing. It began as a simple follow-up to an anonymous phone call.

'I've got to meet a homicide detective,' the anonymous caller had said. 'There's going to be a contract murder. Meet me at two o'clock. End of Balboa Pier. I'll be wearing a black T-shirt.'

106

Winnie and Buster had absolutely nothing going that day, having finished their routine paper work. It was a bright summer day, and they could always get a hamburger at the faux-forties diner out on the end of the pier. So even if the anonymous tipster turned out to be just a nut case, they decided to make an appearance. They found him standing by six fishermen, who were doing OK from the looks of the battered buckets full of dead fish.

Buster approached the guy and said, 'You the one that called?'

He was as tall as Buster, but lean and stringy. Ruddy and fair, he was one of those beach lovers who were candidates for skin cancer but refused to wear hats. His lips were raw, and he had a couple of precancerous flakes on his nose and cheeks and old dermatology burns along his forehead and eyebrows. Winnie had gotten sick of warning guys about Haole-rot, back in his lifeguard days.

The tipster had seen too many cop movies, because he pretended not to have heard Buster. He looked past both cops, then walked toward the west side of the pier away from the blazing sun. When he was gazing toward Catalina, with a detective on either side of him, he said, 'Let's make a deal.'

'You're tuned to the wrong channel,' Winnie informed him. 'We don't make deals.'

'My name's Harvey Devlin,' he said. 'I've been indicted for a misunderstanding. Involves junk bonds. I'm a broker.'

'If it's a mistake, what kind a deal you lookin for?' Buster asked.

'My lawyer thinks I'm sure to be convicted for some sort of fraud. All I want is someone to put in a word for me

107

with the judge when I'm sentenced. I think I've already decided to plead guilty and not have a trial.'

'Yeah, well, we don't know much about junk bonds,' Winnie said. 'And anyway . . .'

'You know about murder,' the bond broker said, turning to look at them.

Buster moved closer. 'So whaddaya wanna tell us about murder?'

'What's the crime when somebody offers you money to kill someone? Conspiracy?'

'Maybe,' Winnie said. 'Probably soliciting murder. Easier to prove.'

'OK,' the broker said, and he looked both ways and then down the pier toward the beach. He *had* seen too many movies! 'There's a doctor that lives on Lido Isle. Out by the end in one of the bigger houses. Cosmetic surgeon with three offices. Done some business with me in the past, and one time we scored pretty big with high yield bonds. So, I did some bragging one time. Said I could arrange anything he ever wanted, from broads to murder. He took me seriously. Wants me to arrange a hit on his wife.'

Buster asked: 'Why's he want her dead?'

'Who knows? Money has to be part of it. Always is. Around here anyway.'

'So if, and I'm saying if, our boss and the DA's office was interested, would you agree to wear a wire and go to your doctor pal and let us record his statements while he offers to hire a hit on his old lady?'

'I'll do it!' the bond broker said. 'But it's not going to be easy. When he first mentioned it to me he made me pull up my shirt and even ran his hand inside my belt and

108

down my legs. He frisked me pretty good. I've seen part of his portfolio, which is worth about fifteen mil. He's not stupid.'

'It can be done without a wire.' Buster said. 'But it's not as easy. We'd have to rely on your testimony.'

'I'm willing to testify, and I think he'll hand me the payoff money on the spot. Soon as I give him the IUD.'

'What IUD?' asked Winnie.

'Hers. That's what he wants as proof. I'm supposed to hire a guy to fly to Aspen where she summers. And do the job and remove her IUD and bring it back as proof. He doesn't want a Polaroid of her dead body, or her wedding ring, or any other goddamn thing. Not even a newspaper report that she's dead is enough to make him happy! He wants her IUD. Says he'll pay me on the spot.'

'How'll he know it's hers?' Winnie asked.

'He put it in. Maybe he marked it or knows the brand. The guy's a little weird. Anyway, he wants her IUD as proof she's dead.'

'Just a sentimental old fool, ain't he?' said Buster.

While they took down all of the pertinent information that afternoon on Balboa Pier, and the sun was powering its way westward, a sea gull wheeled and shrieked and dove toward a bait box on the west side of the pier. An Asian fisherman yelled at the gull and chased it just as the bird was getting airborne with his booty. The frustrated gull dropped the fish along with a load of guano. It plopped on Winnie's right shoulder.

'I hope this ain't an omen,' Buster said.

The deal was to go down in four days. The bond broker's imaginary hit man was to fly to Aspen that weekend with expense money supplied by the broker, along with instructions as to the wife's habits and living arrangements. She was to be strangled when she answered the telephone in her bedroom at nine p.m. on Saturday, when he usually placed a call just to make sure she wasn't out at a disco. The broker's hit man was to enter with a key supplied by the doctor, and leave the door unlocked when he departed, as though she'd forgotten to lock it.

The broker middleman was instructed as to removal of an IUD, and agreed to have his man do his best to rape her, either before or after the murder, whichever was easier for him to accomplish. This to supply a better motive for murder. And then the killer was to fly back to John Wayne Airport.

When the bond broker said that he didn't know if his man could commit rape either on the dead or soon to be, the doctor said, 'Just offer him an extra thousand. He'll get an erection.'

The police in Colorado, and the doctor's wife, were alerted. Everything was arranged for the Saturday night payoff on Lido Isle. The intended victim had had her IUD removed, and as an ironic gesture, had put it in a Tiffany jewel box for presenting to her husband. The box was express-mailed to the Newport Beach Police Department.

The only thing that went wrong was that the doctor changed the deal to Friday and nobody was ready. The bond broker finally located Winnie at his home number, after trying unsuccessfully to reach him for six hours on Winnie's day off, telling him that the doctor's wife had to be killed that night or all bets were off. This caused Winnie to phone Buster at home, speed to the station, pick up the Tiffany box, and meet with the bond broker at a bar on Lido peninsula. They were twelve minutes late getting the bond dealer and the Tiffany box to the one a.m. rendezvous at the four-million-dollar waterfront home on Lido Isle. And they had no backup team.

The bond broker was inside for less than fifteen minutes. When he came out so quickly, Winnie and Buster figured the doctor hadn't taken the bait. They followed the broker, who drove to the Lido Isle bridge, as instructed. There, the broker parked his Jaguar XJ-S and waited for the detective car to pull in behind him.

The cops were astonished when the broker dumped several stacks of currency into Buster's lap. Then he said, 'I did my part. I'm trusting you to blow in the DA's ear for me.'

Winnie remembered that Buster couldn't take his eyes off the bucks, and Winnie finally had to say, 'Let's go pop the doc.'

When they barged into the house, guns drawn, the first thing the doctor said was, 'I beg you, gentlemen! Let's be reasonable!'

He was dressed in a maroon silk robe and wore monogrammed velvet slippers, blue ones with a gold crest on each toe. He had his hands up facing drawn guns, but he didn't look terrified, just disappointed.

Winnie said, 'Let's go in the bedroom and get dressed, Doctor. I have to advise you that you have the right to remain silent . . .'

Five minutes later, both cops had holstered their guns and were letting the doctor get ready. They walked him to drawers and closets to retrieve clothing: underwear, a golf shirt, matching slacks and sweater, tasseled loafers. He looked like he was going out for eighteen holes instead of to the slam.

When he was completely dressed, he went to the dresser and smoothed back his pearl-gray hair with a silver-inlaid brush in each hand. Then he turned and said, 'Gentlemen, can we negotiate?'

'We got nothing to trade,' Winnie said.

'And neither do you, Doc,' Buster said.

'Please, gentlemen, may I?' He turned and went to a wall safe inside a huge walk-in closet filled with business suits and shoes. He began turning the dials. Winnie started to say something, but Buster was interested.

When the surgeon gave the tumbler the final turn and the lock clicked open, Winnie drew his two-inch stainless steel revolver and put the muzzle of the gun on the bone behind the doctor's left ear.

'I don't think there's a piece in there, partner,' Buster said to Winnie.

'I assure you there's not,' the doctor said reasonably, as though he was used to people tapping on his skull with a Smith & Wesson.

Winnie shined his light in the safe and watched in amazement as the doctor removed stacks of money. One-hundred-dollar bills. Twenty-one stacks. He had an armload when he finished cleaning out the safe. He calmly turned and walked to the king-sized bed and dropped the money on it.

Then he said, 'I want you to know that I'm not attempting to bribe you. One felony crime is quite enough.'

'What are you attempting to do?' Winnie asked.

'I'm protecting myself from burglary,' the doctor said. 'You're taking me to jail and someone might break into my house and ransack my safe. I was hoping you might . . .

safeguard this money. You could hold it wherever you like.'

'Maybe you better put it back in the safe,' Winnie said. 'And set your burglar alarm.'

'There must be a hundred thou here,' Buster said. He walked toward the bed like a priest to an altar. Reverently, was how Winnie remembered it.

'There must be two hundred and ten thousand,' the doctor said. 'But I can make four times that much in the next six or eight months if I don't lose my license.'

'You asking us to go outside and ice the junkman?' Winnie asked.

'Pardon me?'

'Your pal, the junk bond broker. You obviously know he's working with us. You want us to cap him and dump him in the bay?'

'I wouldn't mind,' the doctor said, smiling ironically. 'He's set me up.'

'You've set yourself up,' Winnie said.

'What's the nature of my crime?'

'Soliciting murder,' Buster said.

'Ridiculous. I imagine that that's a very technical and complicated charge. I mean, my word against his, isn't it? And I certainly haven't admitted anything to you, have I? I admit I paid him twenty-five thousand. I owed it for a bond deal he did for me. That gentleman has a very shady reputation in the market. As for me, I've never even gotten a traffic ticket. He's trying to blackmail me.'

Winnie looked up sharply when Buster, still staring at the pile of money, said, 'That's a lot a Ben Franklins.'

Winnie said, 'Yeah, well, we're wasting time, so let's take the doc and . . .'

'Tell me, Doctor,' Buster said, 'how you gonna continue your plastic surgery practice after we bust you? I mean, you gonna still be able to cut and stitch after the state jerks your license off the wall?'

'It takes a severe episode of ethical misconduct or moral turpitude for a physician to lose his license in this state,' the doctor said. 'I don't think merely an arrest or even an indictment would justify it.'

'How about a conviction?' Winnie said.

The doctor shrugged and said, 'Easier said than done. Soliciting murder? I don't know why he'd say such a thing. But I would imagine that your reports could be a little vague and weak. I know your informer lacks credibility given his reputation. And your personal assessment of his credibility, well, I imagine that if you believed my story you'd write your reports a certain way, and inform the district attorney that the case is probably untenable. If those things come to pass, I probably wouldn't even be brought to trial. And I'd certainly never be convicted of anything. What do you think?'

It was Buster, not Winnie, who drew the handcuffs and said, 'Time to hook you up,' cuffing the doctor's hands behind his back. 'Siddown on the bed next to the Ben Franklins.'

Then he turned to Winnie and said, 'I wanna talk to you, pardner.'

He walked Winnie to the doorway leading to the staircase, where they could watch the handcuffed surgeon and still talk. Buster stared at Winnie for a second without speaking. Then he said, 'He didn't offer us a bribe.'

'The implication is there.'

'The implication is that we can have it all. All two

hundred and ten thou. This guy wants to keep his life-style going. This guy . . .'

'Is a bag a pus!' Winnie said. 'But since he didn't really offer us anything directly, let's just let him tuck his Franklins back in the safe and take him on down and book him for soliciting his wife's murder. 'Cause he's getting me so mad I might jist kick him down the fuckin staircase and I think maybe that's polished granite down there at the bottom in the entry hall and it looks real hard.'

'But he's right, Win! We might not be able to make a case against him no matter how hard we try. He's right about our bond broker. That guy's a bigger hemorrhoid than this croaker here.'

'Let's get the money back in the safe and book this maggot,' Winnie said. 'I gotta check out Spoon's new waitress. I'm sure you got something to do too, don't you, Buster?'

Buster stared at his partner for several seconds. Sweat was beading on Buster's forehead, and Winnie felt his own flesh getting cold and clammy. Then Buster showed his 'this-is-just-a-shuck' gleaming white grin. And his violet eyes stopped throwing sparks, and he said, 'Sure. I guess we'd never be able to make a case for attempted bribery even if we did pretend to go along with him. That's what I was thinking we could do, *pretend* to go along.'

When they got back inside, Buster was all business. He said, 'OK, Doc, on your feet. You're gonna witness us putting your money back and I'm gonna let you set the lock and the alarm. Don't wanna get accused of not protectin your goods. It's a shame but I think you're gonna get your knife taken away. Goddamn Gold Coast tragedy, ain't it, Doc?'

For the first time the surgeon looked worried. A tear even formed in his left eye, which made Winnie Farlowe very happy.

When Winnie finished his story, Tess, who had stood motionless in the shadows the entire time, stepped out into the moonlight.

'What happened to the doctor?' she asked.

'Did about ten months,' Winnie said.

'And the license?'

'Probably in some other state where they need a guy who's real hot at sucking out all those pizzas topped with buffalo steak and macadamia nuts.'

'So you think your friend Buster was on the verge of accepting the money if *you'd* gone along?'

'I don't wanna think so,' Winnie said. 'Buster was a good friend. Still is. And a good cop when he wants to be. I don't like to think he could do business with that sociopathic doctor.'

'So it appears you'll live your life as a poor man, Winnie Farlowe,' she said.

'Guess so,' Winnie said. 'Must be written in my genes somewhere. Kismet. Winnie Farlowe's a . . .'

'Straight-ahead guy,' she said, sliding the spaghetti strap chemise off her shoulders and letting it fall to the floor.

He could see her glasses flash in the moonlight. She took two steps and leaped into bed playfully. She rolled on top of Winnie and took his face in her hands.

'So am I through after tonight?' he asked. 'You dumping me or what?'

'What the hell makes you think that?'

'I can't afford to take you out even for hamburgers except maybe on Thursday night when they drop the price at this joint I know.'

'So if you're *that* broke with no job and no prospects, what do you plan to do about it?'

Winnie looked up to her, then enveloped her bare torso in his arms, tracing the valley between those health club back muscles. He kissed her shoulder for a moment, thought it over and said, 'I dunno. I just *don't* know.'

'You may just have to depend on the kindness of strangers,' Tess Binder said.

9: *Oasis*

At ten o'clock the next morning, having had a swim and eggs Benedict with Tess Binder at her club, Winnie was back in his apartment trying to put together a suitable wardrobe for a desert weekend. Tess had said she'd pick him up at noon and that he 'shouldn't ask questions'.

She wasn't dumping him. She wanted more of what he offered, whatever the hell *that* was. She said he was funny. She said he made her feel more like a woman. She wasn't tired of him. Not yet!

Winnie was tuning the radio on an L.A. jazz station when there was a knock at the door. He opened it to find Buster Wiles and a huge young cop named Hadley, a rookie he knew only slightly. They were wearing tan shorts and white sneakers with their tan uniform shirts and Sam Browne belts: the outfit of the police department's beach patrol.

'I *don't* believe it,' Winnie said to Buster. 'You?'

Buster drew out a little towel he'd tucked inside his Sam Browne, mopped his neck and grinned. 'Easter week, baby. They need some big beef out here to bust all these Newport Beach felonies.'

Winnie knew that 'felonies' meant writing beer tickets, citations for drinking in public around the Fun Zone and the piers. During Easter week the town's population of seventy thousand could double, with twenty to thirty college and high school kids crammed into every available rental. Not to mention tens of thousands of day-trippers.

'Peninsula looks like Calcutta already,' Hadley said. 'Million beer cans on the beach.' The young cop had the cylindrical legs of a juvenile elephant, and a back you could shoot snooker on.

'Like a war zone,' Buster said. 'They're tryin to reinvent the South Bronx with white people.'

'I didn't think you'd *really* leave narcotics,' Winnie said.

'I told ya I'm through putting myself in situations where some cretin can spit slugs at me with an Uzi on full auto. Beach patrol, baby. Six miles a tits 'n ass. I mighta had a shot at being a trash cop – pardon me, an *environmental services coordinator* – but I figure litterbugs in progress're harder to catch than bank robbers. So I managed to slide into the beach patrol. You should see the new four-wheeler the other team uses for sand safaris. When Hadley's drivin, he digs those foot-deep trenches around anything bigger'n a thirty-four B cup. Needs a coolie with a shovel fillin in behind him.'

Winnie said, 'Now I know who to call about all the dog crap, and people that park in front a my carport.'

'That's what we're here for, baby!' young Hadley said, imitating Buster Wiles. 'People around here don't give a shit about burglars and muggers, but they want red zone parking to carry capital punishment!'

Buster looked at the old Adidas tennis bag Winnie had thrown on the daybed in his living room. There were two pair of faded socks and more ragged underwear packed in it, along with a freshly laundered aloha shirt and jeans.

119

'Blowin town before the rent's due, or what?' Buster asked.

'Going to Palm Springs for the weekend,' Winnie said. 'Well, not exactly Palm Springs. La Quinta. Ever been there? Out where they built that monster golf course? Where they play the Skins game on TV?'

'Heard of it,' Buster said. 'Desert ain't for me. Dries out my sinuses and makes me sneeze for a week.'

'I'll take along some nose drops,' Winnie said.

Winnie worried for the furniture when young Hadley sat down at the kitchen table, lifting one of those massive legs on to a chipped and rickety kitchen chair. The kid said, 'You can't escape spring break out there in Palm Springs. They got just as many vacationers as we do.'

'Yeah, well, I'll be with a friend,' Winnie said. 'We'll be staying outta their way.'

Buster didn't say anything but he looked curious, so Winnie said, 'I got a sponsor for this trip. Somebody's taking me.'

Slyly, from Buster: 'That new waitress at Spoon's musta had a good week, huh?'

'Naw, she's outta the tip zone with her bad attitude,' Winnie said. 'She can't afford an on-time guy like me.'

Buster turned to the kid and said, 'Come on, Junior, Winnie's bein mysterious and we got a wienie wagger down by Seventh Street we oughtta try to catch sometime this year or next.' He said to Winnie, 'Guy wears a winged Mercury hat like an FTD florist. Rings people's doorbells, but instead a presentin them with a parcel a pansies, he shows them the blue thimble.'

'This couldn't be the career change you had in mind the

120

other night?' Winnie asked, as the two beach cops walked to the door. 'Working the beach patrol?'

'Not quite,' Buster said. 'But it'll do for a while. By the way, poverty-stricken as you are, it's only fair to warn that ya can't sleep in your car between the hours a nine p.m. and nine a.m., 'less you wanna risk the wrath a the beach patrol.'

'Oh, *thank* you, Officer!' Winnie said. 'I'll just sleep on the beach during the day and drive around all night.'

'And you can't fish in the bay after six p.m., jist in case you're hungry enough to eat the mutants that live off the refuse from all the illegally dumped Porta Potties.'

'I see you already learned every one a the felonies,' Winnie said. 'And no dogs on the beach, right?'

'I can overlook that one,' Buster said, before closing the door. 'We got lots a Cambodians and other gooks fishin off the piers nowadays. They'll catch 'em and *eat* 'em for us.'

As they were descending the treacherous wooden staircase, Winnie heard Buster say to his young partner, 'Don't introduce me to any more broads with no eyebrows and no personality. I been datin one like that for thirteen years. In fact, she caused *both* my divorces.'

She was prompt. She pulled up in the alley behind Winnie's apartment at noon and tooted the horn. He practically jumped down the termite-eaten staircase. A weekend in the desert with Tess Binder!

The drive to Palm Springs usually took two hours when the getaway from the coast was early in the day. It was very hot during spring break, and there was the usual crush in down-town Palm Springs, with thousands of teens and young adults cruising Palm Canyon Drive. Drinking beer and smoking dope. Tearing the clothes off girls dumb enough to cruise in convertibles. Getting busted by the roving police patrols.

Tess knew enough to avoid it at this time of year. She passed the Palm Springs cutoff and stayed on Highway 10 all the way to Washington Drive and then turned south toward the Santa Rosa Mountains. All she'd say to Winnie's repeated questions about their destination was that she guaranteed he'd like it.

He figured she'd rented a condo at PGA West, especially when the signs pointed toward that huge golf course development.

'Hope you don't wanna play golf this weekend,' Winnie said.

'Why?'

'I saw that monster course on TV. They got bunkers bigger'n Kuwait.'

'We're not playing golf, old son. We're going to swim and lie in the sun.'

'Yeah? That's OK with me.'

'And make love.'

'That's *definitely* OK with me.'

'And ride horses.'

'Horses? Wait a minute!'

'I'll teach you. I used to ride at the polo field out here. That's *another* thing my dad wanted in addition to a little sailor: a little rider. And what'd he end up with? A woman who wouldn't be caught dead in jodhpurs. When I think of boots I think of hours of dressage, with Daddy standing

122

over the trainer saying, 'Tessie isn't tired. Tessie *loves* it. Don't you, Tessie?'

'Didn't have much of a relationship with your father, did you?'

Tess took her eyes off the road for a minute. She looked at Winnie with some surprise and said, 'I adored my father. He was a *god* to me.'

Tess turned abruptly on to a dirt road in La Quinta, meandering toward the Santa Rosas. Around them were ranches and groves full of orange trees and date palms. 'All this'll soon be gone,' she said. 'What with all the land developers and earth movers.'

Finally he said, 'Hey, lady, where the hell you taking me?'

'Here,' she said and turned the Mercedes on to another narrow road, this one paved with asphalt. She continued along the road for five hundred yards, turned right and stopped.

It was a man-made oasis: three acres of date palms and orange groves and eucalyptus, and a huge tile fountain in the center of a motor court. Beyond the motor court a hacienda: Spanish colonial revival, a two-story with red Roman tile roof and blindingly white stucco walls rounded off at the corners.

'It was built in the heyday of California architecture,' Tess explained. 'Nineteen twenty-eight.'

The house had small single windows covered with iron grilles, and a green awning, held by wrought-iron pikes, sheltering the front door. Winnie smelled real jasmine like Tess's perfume, and saw a pergola with trellises covered with bougainvillea. There were stables to the right, just past the motor court, in keeping with the architecture of the house but obviously built in recent years. Winnie could see a white horse poking its face through the window of its stall.

'Who owns this place? Zorro?'

'It was my father's weekend home,' Tess said. 'Which he called *El Refugio*. His refuge.'

'Who owns it now?'

'My father's friend, Warner Stillwell.'

'He buy it?'

'My father left it to him.'

'To a friend? Why didn't you get it?'

'I got some money,' she said. 'Enough to survive on, Daddy thought. Come on, let's look at the stables. I want you to meet my pals.'

As Winnie and Tess crossed the motor court, the shaggy barrels of dried fronds beneath the green of three gigantic Mexican fan palms rustled in the wind. Winnie and Tess had to turn away from a gust that suddenly burst through the canyon, capriciously exploding into whirling dust devils in the open desert beyond. When the wind became still, lavender petals from the bougainvillea littered the grass beneath the pergola.

'Desert breezes,' she said. 'Unpredictable. And these mountains? I never feel *safe* here. Flash floods, burning heat, sudden gusts of parched wind. The desert gives me a sense of . . . foreboding.'

The stable was cool and shaded. A horse whinnied, then another. They walked past several empty stalls before Winnie saw the white Arabian horse. She poked her dish-face at him and batted her brown eyes. He patted her nose gingerly. When she tried to nibble his fingers,

Winnie jerked his hands and Tess laughed.

'She won't bite,' Tess said. 'Sally's a love. She doesn't see many people any more. Just needs to be ridden.'

They passed two more stalls and a loud snort startled him. Tess walked to the stall door and said, 'Hello, handsome.'

He was a huge horse, seventeen hands high. Silver with a black mane and a white star on his forehead.

Tess reached for his head and whispered to him, 'How's my big boy? How're they treating you?'

'You wouldn't have any silly thoughts going round in that busy brain a yours, would you, Tess?' Winnie said. 'About *me* riding that brute?'

'You'll be riding Sally. I'm riding Dollar.' Then she turned to the silver horse and said, 'You still love me, don't you, handsome?'

'Last horse I rode was on the merry-go-round at the Balboa Fun Zone. I was drunk and fell off. Didn't know horses got this big 'less they were pulling beer wagons on TV. He's some stallion.'

'Gelding,' she said. 'Used to be a stallion, but he was unmanageable. Once he kicked the door off his stall and ran all the way down to the fire station. Took my father five hours to get him home. And still Daddy refused to geld him.'

'What changed his mind?'

'Dollar kicked Warner and broke his femur. Then he bit me on the hand. Had to have sutures.'

'That did it?'

Tess took Winnie's arm and began walking back to the motor court. 'No, that didn't do it. My father was a great romantic. He'd *never* have gelded that animal. I did it when Daddy was on a winter cruise with Warner. I tamed Dollar. Daddy was furious of course, but then, I never could please him.'

When they got to the cactus garden in front of the house, an old Mexican in a cowboy hat turned the corner, pushing a load of manure in a wheelbarrow.

'Miss Tess!' he said.

'Jaime, this is Mister Farlowe,' she said.

Winnie smiled, put out his hand and said, 'Winnie's my name.'

The old man wiped his hand on his jeans, pumped Winnie's hand and said, 'Hello, sir. Happy to meet you.'

Tess continued walking Winnie toward the house, saying, 'Jaime, we're going to have lunch and a swim, and late this afternoon I'd like you to put the tack on Sally and Dollar.'

'Yes, Miss Tess,' the old man said. 'Will you need me on the ride?'

'No, we won't need a *vaquero* behind Mister Farlowe,' Tess grinned. 'He'll show Sally who's boss.'

'Oh, my!' Winnie said, following Tess into the house. 'Does Sally need a *boss*? Oh, my!'

Three steps led down into the large living room, which looked even larger because of the adzed open-beamed ceiling. The boards between the beams were stenciled with decorative Moorish patterns. There was a huge fireplace, and Navajo rugs covered the large red Mexican tiles on the floor. The house was full of South-western art, Indian artifacts and potted palm and cactus.

There was a partner's desk by a window with leather executive chairs on each side of it. Beside the fireplace were two well-worn comfortable leather easy chairs, side by side: matching chairs with ottomans.

They walked back to the foyer, where the ceiling was low enough for Winnie to see the hand-adzing on the beams.

'I'm speechless,' he said.

'Daddy had taste,' Tess said. 'The architect who built this was famous for many houses in Beverly Hills and Pasadena. He built this one for my grandfather actually, but Daddy redecorated it, oh, about thirty-five years ago. Very little's been changed since then.'

'I'd *never* leave here,' Winnie said. 'if it was mine.'

'Oh yes you would,' she said. 'You haven't experienced a desert summer. Come on, I'll show you the rest.'

Tess's shoes clicked on the red tiles that covered the entire ground floor of the rambling great house, which was mostly in shadows now that the afternoon sun was passing the Santa Rosas. There was a long heavy wooden table in the center of the dining room, with padded leather side chairs. There was a small table off in the corner of the dining room with barrel chairs and cushions covered by a woven Indian design. This corner could be lit by the wrought-iron floor lamp and used as an intimate nook for dining away from the main table.

Tess noticed Winnie looking at the little table for two, and she said, '*That* little table wasn't here when I was a girl. When my mother was alive.'

The kitchen was surprisingly small, given the scale of the house. But Tess explained that the architects of California's Golden Age didn't worry about kitchens, in that the lady of the house wouldn't be doing much work in there anyway. Meal preparation was for servants.

'We're all alone in the house,' Tess said. 'Lauro and Alicia won't be back till Sunday. They've taken care of this place since nineteen forty-nine. They're even older than Jaime. The whole place is old. Sometimes it makes *me* feel old.'

'It makes me feel like I'm in an old black-and-white movie!' Winnie said. 'I'm crazy about it! So where's the guy that owns the place?'

'Warner's not in good health. He goes to the hospital from time to time. I phoned and got his permission to use the ranch for a few days. He's good about that. Any time I want the place, I just have to phone. He has a cottage in Laguna Beach where he goes, and leaves this place to me.'

'How often do you come?'

'Last time was two years ago,' she said. 'Or was it three? I had a sudden urge to ride with my father. But Daddy said he was getting too old to ride. That trip wasn't a pleasant one.'

'Think they might have a beer in the fridge?' Winnie looked at his watch, making sure it was late enough to drink. Late enough had come to mean after 11.30 a.m., which was close enough to lunchtime, the hour that Golden Orange high-rollers guzzled booze at power lunches. Or so Winnie supposed.

'Now for the most dangerous part of this holiday,' Tess said, opening the double doors of the refrigerator. 'And I don't mean horseback riding. I mean eating *my* cooking. Grab a beer. No, grab two, and get yourself out to the pool for twenty minutes while I create.'

The 2,500-square-foot patio was guarded on three sides by the walls of the house, with lemon and grapefruit trees partially enlosing the fourth side. A swimming pool was in the center, a classic oval design, bordered with multicolored ceramic tiles. The pool was spotlessly clean and had an ancient diving board set into the deck with polished brass fittings. Winnie was sure of one thing. Someone had *loved* this house and still did.

He couldn't decide between a chaise or a hammock. Finally he decided on the hammock by an overhanging balcony with a dark wooden balustrade. The terrace on that balcony appeared to belong to an upstairs bedroom and was overgrown with jasmine. The smell was more intoxicating than booze.

The last time Winnie had tried a hammock was in Nam, and he'd been a *lot* thinner then. He tested the lines that secured the thing to a pair of Indian laurels seventy feet tall, their tangle of limbs entwined as one. It was a custom hammock made of white braided cotton with a blue-striped head pillow. Winnie got into it gingerly, and put one bottle of beer on his chest and the other beside him on the red tile. Potted pink and white hibiscus was flourishing at the base of the Indian laurel trees. The beer was Mexican, appropriate to a house like this.

Winnie Farlow decided that no matter what happened, no matter how soon all this with Tess Binder might end, this romantic day in this romantic place was going to be the happiest day of his life. He'd finished the second beer and was dozing, the sway of the hammock putting him to sleep, when he heard Tess open the French doors in the dining room.

'Come on in!' she yelled. 'Let's see how brave you are!'

When he got inside he found that she'd set two places, one on each end of the dining room table. There was patterned silverware and linen napkins and a chafing dish in the center.

'I cheated,' she said. 'When I phoned, I told Alicia to prepare something I could finish up when we got here. So if this is any good, Alicia gets at least half the credit.'

It was. Tess served him chorizo and eggs, and a dish of guacamole on the side with corn tortillas and home-made salsa that he knew a *gringa* couldn't have made.

'*Love* it!' Winnie murmured three times during the lunch. He glanced at the intimate dining area in the corner, perfect for two, and wondered why they'd eaten at the big table. Tess hardly touched a bite.

'I'll do the dishes,' Winnie said when he'd finished.

'Of *course* you'll do the dishes, you lazy lout,' she said, 'while I put our things away in the guest bedroom, the one directly overlooking the pool. After your chores you can go up there and get out of your clothes and I'll meet you on the diving board.'

'Shoulda brought my Speedos,' he said. 'The swimsuit I brought is the kind that comes off if you dive.'

'Swimsuit? You kidding?' She finished her glass of Chardonnay and headed toward the staircase that had risers decorated with more patterned Mexican tiles.

By the time Winnie got the dishes into the dishwasher and found his way upstairs to the guest room, he heard a splash. He looked out the French doors and saw Tess Binder, naked, swimming strong laps from one end to the other.

Much as he wanted to run out there, he couldn't. He'd been a detective too long. Too much was troubling him. He couldn't put it together, and she wasn't telling him everything. He was getting a little at a time – very little. Like many former police detectives, Winnie Farlowe hated mysteries.

The guest bedroom was spacious and comfortable, under-closeted by modern standards, but the room was large enough for an eight-foot armoire on either side of the twin beds. Twins. Winnie didn't much care for *that*. He was sure that this was a seldom-used bedroom.

When he was dressed in his swim trunks and Top-Siders, Winnie wandered down the hall and, on impulse, entered three other rooms. One was a servant's room beside an inside staircase that probably went down to a service porch behind the kitchen. The other two were being used primarily to store things long abandoned: tennis racquets, golf clubs, riding trophies for dressage and show jumping. Winnie examined a few of them and they all bore the name of Tess Binder. As a kid she may have hated riding, but she could do it. He found boxes of books and photo albums, probably stored here after the death of Conrad Binder, and oak filing cabinets, six of them.

Continuing down the shadowy hallway past a ceramic tile of the Madonna set into the wall, he found a room with the door closed. He opened it a few inches, then nudged the door wide. It was another bedroom, larger than the guest room, and this one *had* been lived in. For a long time. This was Winnie's kind of room. There was a fireplace in the windowless wall bordered with patterned tile. It was a *real* fireplace, not a Gold Coast fireplace, blackened and smelling of eucalyptus and oak and ashes. Like the rest of the house, this room was done in South-western decor, but it seemed even more masculine than the others. The chairs beside the fireplace sagged with the contoured imprint of a man. Or *two* men, since there were two chairs side by side. The entire house suggested partnership.

131

On the carved walnut mantelpiece were photos in an array of frames, of Tess mostly. But there were lots of pictures of a broad-shouldered handsome man: fishing, playing golf, jumping a black horse, chasing a lob in tennis whites. The man had dark curly hair and a friendly smile. He was various ages in the photos.

Winnie walked to the four-poster and examined the photograph on the lamp table by the window. It was the same man, but he was nearly sixty in this one. He wore an ascot and a white long-sleeved cotton shirt with epaulets. He wore breeches and boots. He had aged very well indeed. He had his arm around Tess, who was about thirty years old. He looked at her like a loving father would.

Winnie entered the bathroom and opened the medicine cabinet. Empty. He opened the drawers under the tiled countertops and it was the same. No-one had lived in this bedroom for some time.

Before he left the room he opened the armoire and found suits and blazers, cleaned and pressed and hung neatly. This had obviously been Conrad Binder's room. Winnie was beginning to admire that handsome, stylish, athletic man in the photographs. But the man didn't look anything like Tess. Winnie expected to find a painting or photo of Tess's mother, but there was none. No pictures of a woman except for Tess herself.

There was one last bedroom at the end of the hall. The door was closed, but what the hell, he'd gone this far. Winnie turned the heavy brass knob and pushed the door open. Another bedroom, also masculine, but this one without a fireplace. This one had the drapes thrown wide which offered a dramatic mountain view with the desert in the foreground. He could hear Tess still splashing in the pool, for the French doors were open on to that jasmine-covered balcony overlooking the patio.

More photos. Photos everywhere. On the mantel, covering the bureau, on the dressers, blanketing the walls. And above the king-sized bed there was an oil painting, a portrait of a middle-aged man in a dark blue three-piece business suit. He sat on the edge of an enormous desk in the standard mogul pose. Behind him in the portrait was a wall of windows through which whitecaps crested on the ocean. The painting suggested a tall office building in The Golden Orange, overlooking the Pacific.

There were some shots of Tess, but most were of this man at various times in his life. In the earliest ones he looked to be about thirty-five, a more sedentary man than the dark, curly-haired athlete in the other bedroom. In most he posed quietly, often with a book in his hands or one resting beside him on the pool deck, or, in one photo, in his lap as he sat sunning himself on the deck of a cruise ship. This man was also handsome, but fairer. His hair had turned silver in the later photographs. Tess Binder looked a lot like *this* man, except that in the close-ups, you could see that his eyes were pale blue. In one, presumably the latest, the man was perhaps seventy years old.

Winnie went to the door, listened, but heard nothing except Tess swimming relentlessly. He entered the bathroom and found that it was like the one in the adjoining bedroom. There was a tub, a shower stall, a tile counter with drawers and a medicine cabinet. Winnie opened the cabinet. It contained toiletries and medication of various sorts, mostly over-the-counter stuff. He examined a prescription and saw that it was a blood pressure drug issued by a Doctor G. Lutz in Palm Desert for Mr Warner D. Stillwell.

Before he left the bedroom Winnie found a photo he'd almost overlooked. It was on a small reading table on the window side of the king-sized bed. There was a reading glass and two financial journals on the table. Winnie picked up the photograph and examined it in the light.

They were young then, probably in their late thirties. Warner Stillwell and Conrad Binder – the man whose photos and portraits filled *this* room – were clowning on the diving board just below this master bedroom. They wore swimsuits, and Conrad Binder had on tennis shoes. He was pretending to be losing his balance while Warner Stillwell pretended to be pushing him into the pool. They were both fit and tan, having a very good time.

Winnie put the photo down, left Warner Stillwell's bedroom and closed the door. He was feeling depressed and anxious and suddenly sad. *Now* this didn't seem like a place for a fantasy weekend. *Now* this seemed like a real house where two men had grown old together. And now there was only one.

When Winnie got downstairs he found Tess standing naked on the diving board, panting from the mini-marathon she'd just swum. She was looking down on him with those impenetrable gray eyes, so unlike the transparent blue eyes of her father. Licking water drops off her lips, she stood there as if to say, Well?

She was so smooth and tan, so firm and strong from the waist down that Winnie unconsciously hid behind the bath towel he was carrying.

134

'Win, what're you doing in swim trunks?' she demanded with a little grin.

'Helps me hold my gut in,' he said. 'I got the drawstrings so tight, my eyeballs ache.'

'Take those things off and let it all hang out!' Tess commanded. Then she laughed, took two steps, leaped straight up on the spring board, and did a one and a half, cutting the water with hardly a ripple.

'Kee-rist!' Winnie said, shuffling to the hammock and plopping himself into it. Suddenly his lower back was hurting.

Tess erupted from the pool in one lithe movement, pulled herself up to the pool deck and crossed the grass toward him, sweeping her butterscotch hair back behind her flat tiny ears.

'What *are* you doing, Win Farlowe?'

'You make me feel old, lady! Older than iron. Older than coal, even. I can't compete with you in *anything*!'

'Oh dear!' she cried with mock alarm. 'My old son's turned forty and it's *depressed* him!'

Then she stood over him, dripping pool water on to him and the hammock.

'You ain't gonna dump me outta this are you?' he said. 'I might break a hip, old guy like me.'

'What if I told you a secret I wouldn't tell *anyone* else, even if they sentenced me to life imprisonment at my club?'

'So tell me.'

'I'm *older* than you. I'm forty-one.' Then she paused and said, 'No, goddamnit, that's a lie! I'm forty-three!'

'Forty-three! So get a wrinkle for chrissake!' Winnie looked her over from point-blank range. 'Turn around.'

Tess pirouetted for him, and he said, 'Not a *dimple*! Nothing! Ageless! You're smooth as that marble statue. The one in your bedroom. Come to life jist to intimidate me.'

Tess looked very serious then, even solemn. She said, 'I don't think you'll ever stop being a cop. Analyzing everybody and everything.' Then the solemnity vanished, and she gave him an impish smile and said, 'I know how to make you stop being your gloomy old self. I'll give you something *else* to worry about. Danger!'

Tess grabbed him by the swim trunks and pulled. He yelled, 'Whoa!' and almost tumbled out of the hammock, and his back *did* hurt. When he got righted, his swim trunks were around his knees.

'Hey, wait a minute!' he hollered, but she stripped them off.

Then Tess Binder squealed and leaped into the hammock and they both swayed back and forth precariously while Winnie held on.

'Hey, at *least* lemme outta here first!' he cried, while she giggled loud enough for Jaime to hear her from the stables. She apparently didn't mind.

When the hammock stopped swaying, she scooted to a kneeling position over him, balanced the hammock and said, 'Ready?'

'This *can't* be done,' Winnie said. 'Why don't we go over there on the grass? Or on the lounge chairs so we don't fracture our skulls on the tile deck?'

'No *danger* over there,' Tess said. 'You'll remember it this way. I don't want you to ever forget a moment of our time together. You'll never forget me, will you, Win?'

She ran her hands down his body, balancing the

hammock with her knees. She crept forward, astride him. She smiled, and as her eyes went on down his body, her hands became busy.

'This can't be done,' Winnie croaked.

'I haven't steered you wrong yet, have I?' Tess replied.

10: *Shells*

The fun and frolic and the six beers at poolside had exhausted him and he'd gone up to their room thinking Tess would follow. When he awoke he looked at the other twin bed and saw he'd been napping alone. It was nearly six o'clock.

Winnie got out of bed, went in the bathroom and shaved. He dressed in jeans and a long-sleeved cotton shirt he'd brought along for the desert evenings. He wore deck shoes and heavy socks to protect his ankles from the stirrups. Then he went down to face Sally and show her that she was boss and it was OK with him.

He found Tess in the stables with Jaime, discussing an oat mix he'd been giving to Dollar.

'Hi, sleepyhead,' Tess said, as the old man led the horses outside.

'Tell me you weren't gonna let me sleep through this,' Winnie said. 'Tell me there was no way to avoid it.'

'No way,' she said. 'I wouldn't let you miss this ride if your life depended on it.'

Winnie looked at Sally, saddled and already moist with sweat. She was tied to the hitching post and looked impatient. Tess put her foot in Jaime's cupped hands and jumped up on to a little English saddle on Dollar's silver back. She was wearing breeches and boots, a blue cotton blouse with a matching scarf around her hair, and a neckerchief.

'Thought you hated riding boots,' Winnie said.

'I keep them here for emergencies like this.'

'This really ain't an emergency,' Winnie said, walking reluctantly toward the Arabian. 'I mean, I could probably live my life with no regrets if we called this whole thing off.'

Sally was saddled western, a relief to Winnie. He reached up, grabbed the horn, but couldn't get his foot in the stirrup. The horse moved a step, and Winnie would have fallen on his ass except that the surprisingly strong Mexican cowboy caught him and held on to Sally. Jaime boosted him with his bent shoulder under Winnie's buttocks. Once in the saddle, Winnie's back started aching even before the horse stirred.

Tess turned the silver horse in two circles, held the reins expertly in both hands and clucked to him.

'There, there, big boy,' she crooned. 'There, there, handsome.' Then she turned to the cowboy and said, 'Go on home, Jaime. See you in the morning.'

'I should stay, Miss Tess,' Jaime said. 'Mister Warren likes me to give them a good brushing after a ride. I don't mind staying.'

'I still know how to unsaddle and brush a horse. You go home, Jaime,' she said firmly.

'Yes, Miss Tess,' the old man said. 'I see you in the morning.'

'Sleep in,' Tess said. 'You don't have to come to work till ten o'clock.'

'Yes. Thank you, Miss Tess,' the old man said.

Winnie got to thinking how it is with *them*, with rich

people. The old Mexican cowboy didn't work for her. She didn't own the property, but she gave orders and he obeyed them. Rich people.

Tess walked Dollar behind Sally and said to Winnie, 'Just squeeze her with your thighs when you want her to go. She's western-trained, so just lay the reins against her neck when you want her to turn. And out of respect for flattened disks we are *not* going to trot, canter or gallop. We're just going for a walk.'

'Oh, thank you!' Winnie said. 'You're my hero for sure!'

After they got going he almost enjoyed it. He *would* have enjoyed it except every time Sally stumbled, or stepped over a ditch, or climbed a rise, his back hurt. But the scenery was magnificent. The Santa Rosas were sometimes chocolate, sometimes pink, depending on the setting sunlight. The golden light looked silver when it streamed through the canyons, and the sky at dusk was streaked with color: pastels, lavenders, even scarlet. It might be even more beautiful than the ocean sky, he thought.

When they got deep into the mountain shadows, the smell of sage mixed with the aroma of leather and horse sweat. Now he *did* enjoy himself, sore back or not. It was dramatic.

The mountain loomed over them. Tess was right. The stark volcanic landscape, swept by desert wind and pitiless sun, gave a sense of foreboding. Winnie had the feeling of being watched by the forces of nature in this place where nature could strike with ferocity.

'Where do you want to have dinner?' Tess asked, dropping back to ride beside him.

'How would I know? I'm a stranger in these here parts, ma'am.'

'I mean, in or out?'

'Let's see, how about out?'

'Fancy restaurant or desert homey?'

'Homey,' he said. 'One a those down-home places where the desert rats hang out. You know, where the owner's some good-old-boy that when he tries to fix his place up, he puts in little cutesy stuff like dwarf statues and windmills. Kinda place you don't know whether you're supposed to eat or play miniature golf. I always been lucky in those kind a places. Never got a dishonest meal from people like that.'

'I know *just* the place,' Tess laughed, and suddenly Dollar tried to break into a run, but for Winnie's sake, Tess reined him in immediately.

'Easy, Sally!' Winnie said. 'Easy, girl! You and me, we don't have to try and compete with those athletes! Easy, girl!'

They rode along for another five minutes and Winnie was starting to hurt enough that he began worrying about the ride back. He wondered if he would look too much like an invalid if he got off and walked partway.

Tess pointed up to the sheer side of the cliff, to a pale discoloration on the rosy rock.

'That's a waterline,' she said. 'An ancient lake once filled this basin. That's forty-two feet above sea level, that line.'

'Yeah?' Winnie reached back and grabbed on to the saddle to relieve some pressure. The unbroken line was clearly visible along the rock face.

Tess noticed Winnie's discomfort and said, 'This might

141

be a good place to rest before we start back.' She halted Dollar and jumped off in a way that would have had Winnie on his knees writhing in pain.

'Whoa, Sally! Whoa, girl!' he said to the skittish Arabian, and Tess grabbed Sally's bridle while Winnie climbed down with utmost care.

'You've survived so far,' she said.

'Yeah, the last guy this lucky with an animal was that guy Androcles. He didn't get eaten either.'

'That's the latest level of Lake Cahuilla,' she said, gesturing up to the waterline. 'During the last couple thousand years the lake was born and died several times, depending on what the Colorado River was up to.'

Winnie looked up and could actually see shells protruding from the rock. 'I never knew about this!' he said. 'A freshwater lake?'

'An inland sea in prehistoric times. The last lake went from horizon to horizon.'

'Look!' Winnie said, kneeling down in the sand. 'Shells! Hundreds a them!'

'Thousands,' she said. 'From freshwater clams and other creatures. Several million years ago something happened. A fantastic upheaval. Mountains bursting up from the water.'

'Up from the sea,' Winnie said, genuinely fascinated. 'Maybe that's how we all came about. Up from the sea!' He examined the shell fragments in his hand and said, 'Looks like oyster, some of 'em.'

'Originally it *was* seawater,' she said. 'There're beds of oyster shells a thousand feet up the mountainsides in this valley, but it's been fresh water for thousands of years. Those're freshwater shells you've got.' Tess then got down on one knee and started sifting sand, picking out larger unbroken shell specimens.

'Like tiny seashells,' he said. 'But smaller than the ones from the ocean.'

'They're pearly and cute,' Tess said. She put several into Winnie's shirt pocket.

'Thousands and thousands a years!' Winnie said, sitting back on his heels, looking up at the mountain. 'Makes being broke and hungry in Orange County kinda unimportant, don't it?'

Tess moved toward him and, still kneeling on one knee, her boot buried in white sand, took his face in her hands and said, 'My poor, poor boy. Are you hungry as well as poor? Don't worry, Auntie Tess'll see to it that you're never hungry again.' Then she took off her glasses and kissed him. It was the longest, most tender kiss yet. When she broke away, he reached for her.

'Hammocks're one thing,' she said, jumping to her feet, 'but not on a sand dune. Besides, the desert scares me.'

Then she took his hand and pulled him to his feet.

'Damn, you're strong,' Winnie said. 'I wouldn't wanna arm wrestle. And I bet *nothing* really scares you.'

'You'd lose that bet, old son,' she said. 'You surely would.'

If she hadn't tied both horses to a stunted tamarisk tree, they might have bolted. A gunshot ricocheted off the face of the rock ten feet from Tess. The pop echoed through the canyon.

'Down!' Winnie screamed, and his shout frightened the horses. Dollar reared, breaking the limb of the dying tamarisk. The splitting wood sounded like the crack of a rifle. Then the horse panicked.

'Whoa, Dollar! Whoa!' Tess yelled. And *another* ricochet preceded an echoing pop from a gun fired hundreds of yards downwind.

'FORGET THE HORSE! GET DOWN, GOD-DAMNIT!' Winnie screamed.

Tess lost her glasses, scrambling behind the rocks, but Winnie picked them up before diving after her on his belly.

Dollar galloped in the general direction of the house. Sally was uncertain. First she started after Dollar, then she turned and looked toward the cowering humans. She whinnied in confusion, then galloped toward home, her reins trailing in the sand.

'What is it, Win? What is it?' Tess cried.

'Some maniac! Some asshole! Some stupid son of a bitch!'

Tess started to peek over the top of the rock, but Winnie jerked her back down. His heart was pounding so hard his own voice sounded ten feet away and he could almost hear his heartbeat thudding off the canyon walls. It sounded like the drumming of a sailboat in rough sea: Baloom! Baloom! Baloom!

Winnie crawled out on the trail, ready to leap back behind the rocks if the shooter fired again. He squatted, then he duck walked. Then he advance ten feet and stood up.

'Gone!' he said to Tess. 'The asshole's gone! I *think*.'

'Where were the shots coming from?'

'I don't know, but let's get the hell outta here! We'll be lucky to make it back before dark. Is that when the rattlesnakes come out? After dark?'

Winnie was limping by the time they got close to the ranch.

He'd stumbled a dozen times, walking behind Tess on the horse trail while the twilight shadows faded into desert night. Even when the Milky Way spilled across the vast open void, like the heavens he often saw miles out at sea, he couldn't really pause to admire that desert sky. He was *hurting*, and fearing all the sounds from crawling flying hopping slithering desert creatures who hunt and prowl only when the blazing sun vanishes.

Winnie was trying *not* to fear a two-legged desert prowler, having by now all but convinced himself that the shots had been fired by a careless hunter or some cretin who liked to scare the shit out of dudes on the riding trails.

When he saw the white walls of the hacienda a hundred yards ahead, he said, 'I think we're gonna live.'

Before going to the house, Tess walked straight to the stables, where she found both horses in their proper stalls nibbling alfalfa, their bits still in their mouths. She switched on the stable lights and unsaddled the animals, who hadn't suffered any injuries and seemed to be content.

When the horses were secure she put her arm around Winnie's waist as they crossed the motor court toward the house.

'How's your back?'

'It'll be OK tomorrow,' he said. 'But I don't think I'm up to going out tonight.'

'Neither am I,' she said. 'You have a drink and a bath and rest. I'll fix dinner.'

The moment they got inside the house Winnie picked up a phone in the living room.

'What're you doing?'

'Calling the cops, of course. Who patrols this area? Sheriffs?'

'Should we do that?'

'Whaddaya mean, should we *do* that? Some asshole took a couple shots at us!'

'You said it was probably some kid.'

'Exactly why we gotta report it. Some nutcase kid out here shooting at people on horses? Who patrols this area?'

'Riverside County sheriffs,' she said. 'Indio office.'

Winnie was lying on the leather sofa in front of the fireplace when the uniformed deputies arrived. He pulled himself painfully to his feet while Tess admitted a buxom young woman and a middle-aged Latino who walked like his feet were hurting even more than Winnie's back.

'I'm Win Farlowe. Retired, Newport Beach PD.' Winnie shook hands and motioned them to the side-by-side chairs. The female deputy was carrying the reports and did the writing.

'This your place, sir?' the Latino asked.

'Not hardly,' Winnie said. 'I'm jist a guest.'

'It's my . . . it *was* my father's home,' Tess said. 'Now it's owned by Warner Stillwell. He's away for a few days and we're guests. My name's Tess Binder.'

While the young woman wrote, the male deputy said, 'So somebody took a shot at you?'

'Two,' Winnie said. 'Off on the trail about, oh, two miles back in the canyon.

'More like a mile,' Tess said. 'It's just *seemed* that far to a tenderfoot.'

'You sure it was a shot?'

'Two shots. Yeah, they ricocheted. If they hadn't a ricocheted I wouldn't a been sure. Gunfire sounds funny out there in all that space.'

'Rifle or handgun?'

'Don't know,' Winnie said. 'Popped like a handgun. I'd guess handgun, but I can't say.'

'From what direction were they fired?' the young woman asked.

'North-west, I'd say,' Tess volunteered. 'There's a big stand of tamarisk trees by the cliffs, about, oh, a hundred yards from the trail. In the past I've seen guys in off-road vehicles shooting at cans. My father used to call you about them. In fact, your people once sent a helicopter but didn't catch them.'

The Latino said, 'So it coulda been just somebody shooting at beer cans?'

'Coulda been,' said Winnie. 'But the first round was pretty close to her.'

'Did you see where it hit?'

'No, but I heard it. I heard it hit and zing. I don't think I could point out the exact spot. All those rocks and cliffs look alike.'

'Well, we'll sure get this down on paper,' the Latino said. 'If you hear any more shooting out there don't hesitate to call us.'

'Would you like some coffee?' Tess asked. 'Or iced tea? I've made some tea.'

He said, 'Iced tea would be great.' Then to Winnie, 'Bet you're glad to be off the job, huh? Living in Newport Beach? Man, you got the life!'

Tess prepared another light Mexican meal for him: chicken tacos, frijoles, some tossed salad, and Alicia's homemade salsa. She served it to Winnie in the living room, where he sat in front of the big fireplace in one of the leather chairs.

147

His body exactly fit the contour of the one closest to the hearth.

When he mentioned that to Tess she said, 'Daddy's chair. Warner has always been slender. Daddy was more your size.'

After his fourth beer Winnie got up the nerve to pry. '*Two* well-worn chairs?' he said. 'They sat here for hours. For years. Each in his own chair.'

'They did everything together,' she said. 'For thirty-five years. Until Daddy died seven months ago.'

'What happened to your mom?'

'Died of stomach cancer when I was twelve. Daddy raised me, and Warner helped. He used to work for Daddy.'

'Yeah? What'd he do?'

'Anything Daddy wanted done. Warner was a failed tennis pro with no other skills of any kind. At first he was our houseman, back in the early days. Back when Mother was sick. Daddy actually hired him to clean and cook and help look after me. My father was in mortgage banking and did lots of business back east and even in foreign countries.'

She got up and put the dishes on a tray.

'Can I help with the dishes?'

'You stay there and rest that back. I want my boy in the pink tomorrow.'

'We're not going riding again!'

'Maybe in the hammock,' she said, not looking back, as she clicked across the rusty red Mexican tiles. 'If you're up to it.'

When Tess came back it was with a vodka for him and what looked like Scotch for herself. She sat down in

Warner Stillwell's leather chair and sipped from a glass. It was a four-ouncer, with very little ice.

The vodka emboldened him. He said, 'Kinda . . . unusual for an employee to end up inheriting the estate, isn't it?'

She smiled ironically.

'You're too good a detective for that,' she said. 'Why don't you just come out and ask?'

'They were lovers, huh?'

'Take a look at their rooms,' she said. 'Daddy's pictures are plastered all over Warner's room and vice versa. It started before Mother died. They must've been like an old married couple at the end.'

Winnie glanced down at the arms of the leather chairs. They were shiny, a patina like polished walnut. Thirty years of use. An aging married couple, as comfortable together as a pair of old boots. 'You, uh, said your dad was kinda tough on you. How did Warner treat you?'

'Don't misunderstand. Daddy was demanding. On me. On Mother. On everyone who worked for him at his bank. Mostly on himself. On everyone except Warner. Warner had the dominant role in their relationship at the end, but Warner was never that way with me. He tried to be more of a father to me than Daddy did. He tried too hard. He was always just Warner to me. I never could forget that at one time he was our *houseman*.'

'Did that make such a difference?'

She glanced at Winnie sharply and said, 'To me it did. It might be hard for you to understand. When I graduated from Stanford and came back home, Warner was completely in charge of the Newport property *and* this one. Oh, he *tried* to spoil me, always giving me money and gifts, but I never forgot that he was giving me Daddy's money. *My* money, if our family was like every other one I knew about. Warner was giving my my own money. My future inheritance. I came to hate it.'

'So what happened?'

'To whom?'

'To all of you. How'd it come about that *your* inheritance went to *him*?'

'When Daddy turned sixty-two he sold the bank and liquidated all his stock. I was on my second miserable marriage by then. Daddy hated my second husband worse than the first, but not as much as he came to hate Ralph Cunningham, my last one. Anyway, Daddy and Warner decided to live here permanently. Oh, they traveled a hell of a lot. They loved cruise ships. Must've made ten crossings on the *QE2*, not to mention two voyages around the world. They spent a whole lot of money, those two, while they grew old together.'

'Can't take it with you,' Winnie said. 'Not a bad idea.'

'When you have a daughter you can *leave* some,' Tess said. Then she looked at her glass and said, 'God! I feel like Guppy from Spoon's Landing. Who took my drink?' She got up and clicked across the tiles to the kitchen. When she returned she wasn't fooling around. She'd brought a bowl of ice cubes and both bottles: Scotch and Russian vodka. She filled his glass first.

When Tess sat back down she said, 'I was *shocked* to find out how little they had in the bank after Daddy died. Those old men had gone through everything, apparently. I was left two hundred and fifty thousand dollars, which had been kept in trust, and Warner got this place. And that was all there was. I used part of the money to continue

150

living on Linda Isle after Ralph abandoned me. Ralph gave me the furniture that's in the house.' She paused a moment and said, 'Men are such generous and compassionate creatures.'

'Some are,' Winnie said.

'Well, there you are,' she said. 'I'm an abandoned orphan with a net worth of whatever I can get out of the Linda Isle house. I assume I can get back my down payment of one-fifty, less commissions. You see, I'm buying it from Ralph. At a price *he* could live with.'

'A hundred and fifty,' Winnie said. 'You're not so rich. I know cops worth more than that.'

She laughed out loud, then said, 'Does this mean you're going to abandon me too? Will I be left on the beach by yet another man?'

'I'll *never* dump you, lady,' Winnie said, reaching for her hand across the arm of the leather chair. 'I'll hang around long as you want me.'

Tess Binder looked at Winnie, at his hand, back into his eyes. Then she removed her glasses, and put them on the table. She knelt down on the Navajo carpet, knelt at his feet and put her cheek on his thigh. Her face was turned toward the fireplace and her shoulders started to heave as though she were crying.

'I always find a way to make you sad,' he said. 'Without meaning to.'

She sniffled and said, 'You make me very *happy*, old son.'

'You're tired,' Winnie said. 'Me too. Let's go to bed.'

He finished the drink and Tess helped him up. She put her arm around his waist as they climbed the staircase to the guest room.

'We can sleep together in Warner's bed,' Tess said. 'After all, he shared it with my father and I'm my father's child.'

'No,' Winnie said. 'I don't think I'd like that. Much as I wanna feel you next to me. No, somehow that wouldn't be right. Let's go to our room.'

'Right as usual,' she said, kissing his cheek.

Tess allowed Winnie to undress her and tuck her into one of the twin beds. She looked very sleepy when he kissed her once on the forehead, then on both cheeks, and said, 'I think you should go right to sleep. You had quite a day.'

'See you in the morning, old son,' she said gratefully. Then she added, 'Oh, by the way, I found an old book downstairs. All about the Coachella Valley and the inland sea in prehistoric times. I put it in the bathroom on the counter.'

'Would the light bother you if I read?'

'I'm gone off already,' she said, closing her eyes.

'Tess,' Winnie said, just before he undressed. 'One more thing. What did your dad die of?'

She didn't turn over. With her back to him and only a little of her sunstreaked, butterscotch hair showing from under the blanket, she said, 'Suicide. My father shot himself with a pistol.'

11: *The Hotline*

She was up long before Winnie. He'd drunk so little the night before (by his standards), he'd received no three o'clock visitors. Could it be that Tess Binder kept the buzzards away? In fact, he'd slept for ten hours without waking. The book about the Coachella Valley was open on the table beside the bed where he'd fallen asleep after reading the chapter dealing with freshwater shells, like the ones Tess had put in his pocket.

He put on his swimsuit, a black knit shirt, and deck shoes. When he came down to breakfast he was carrying the book and the little shells. Tess had just come in from the stables and greeted him with a kiss.

'Want breakfast or lunch?'

'I *never* sleep this late,' he lied. 'I can't believe it.'

'Breakfast, I think. How about an omelet? I make killer omelets.'

Winnie sat in the kitchen at an oak table that must have been a hundred years old. The table had been cut, gouged, scraped and rubbed shiny from thousands of meals prepared on it. Winnie read, and drank his coffee, occasionally pointing out something in the book while Tess made breakfast.

'Listen to this,' he said. 'It says here that ancient fish traps and oyster shell beds and marine fossils *way* above sea level are all around these parts. And you know that high tide line on the cliffs? That's from the last freshwater lake about five hundred or a thousand years ago.'

'You're quite a little tourist, aren't you?'

'Definitely. My old cop friends know all about that. I used to go on fishing trips with the guys to Baja and they'd be drinking and I'd be off checking out the local scenery, looking for artifacts and stuff. Buster Wiles always called me Winnie the Explorer.'

'You didn't drink with the guys?'

'Not much then. Not like I do since I left the job. You know, I offered to sign a waiver with the city to release them against any medical claim if they'd just let me stay on. But the city attorney didn't think a waiver'd hold up if my herniated disks *really* blew out later. So I had to retire.'

'And the pension isn't enough?'

'I could squeak by, living the way I do. Driving a ragtop VW that runs like the Beirut post office. But I owe a few more years a child support to my adopted daughters. My wife's second ex-husband told me those little monsters caused his triple bypass. Nearly died a blood complications. They had to change his oil about six times, seventy-eight pints a blood. I donated two, myself. Tammy couldn't 'cause her nail polish wasn't dry.'

'A lot of men might fight it, the spousal support.'

'I made the deal with my eyes open. I signed the marriage certificate. I signed the adoption papers. A deal's a deal.' He paused and said, 'I'm sadder than a country song, huh? Guess you feel like giving me a telethon.'

'No, just one killer omelet.'

While Winnie ate his omelet and drank more coffee, Tess sat and glanced through the book. 'I've never been much interested in the history of this valley,' she said.

Winnie washed down a mouthful of omelet spiced with jalapeno chilis, and said, 'Earliest evidence of Indians goes back about twenty-five hundred years. The really old camps were probably wiped out by earlier lakes. The prehistoric lake was over a hundred miles long.'

'Did you learn any more about the little shells?' Tess asked, picking one up and holding it below her earlobe.

'Cute,' Winnie said. 'They'd make cute earrings on your tiny ears. Might look nice as a necklace too, couple hundred strung together.'

'They *are* freshwater clam shells, aren't they?'

'Some a them. Some a the others . . .' He took the book and turned the page. 'The thin pearly shells are clam. The one you got in your hand, that's called a univalve. From mollusks. They were pretty new to the scientists about a hundred years ago.'

Winnie took five white shells from his pocket, each no larger than a button. 'Like baby sea snails,' he said.

'Save them,' Tess said. 'Souvenirs of our desert holiday.'

'I don't need shells to help me remember *this*,' Winnie said, but Tess smiled and put the shells back in the pocket of his black knit shirt.

'You should've been some sort of scientist.'

'Oh yeah,' he said. 'Can't you jist see me all blissed out over a new study on slime molds? But I shoulda gone to college. My dad always told me he'd support me all the way through if I wanted to go. And I was a Nam vet, so I did have options for an education. But no, I had to become a cop. Took some junior college classes over the years, police science mostly.'

'You're an orphan,' she said. 'Like me.'

'My mom's still alive. Lives with my sister and brother-in-law up in Tustin. I'm jist a half-orphan. Talking about not going to college reminds me, you know the song I hate worse than any in the world? "My Way". You know: "Regrets I had a *few* . . ." Well, I had a few thousand in my life. I got a few new ones every single day.'

Tess got up from the chair and cleared the table, popping a chili into her mouth like it was a grape. When she took his coffee cup, he thought she was going to refill it, but she put it on the tile counter by the sink. Then she took off her glasses and pulled her loose cotton blouse over her head. She stepped out of her sandals and was wearing only her khaki shorts.

'*What* the hell?'

Tess walked over to him and sat astride his lap. She kissed and licked him with a tongue hot from jalapeño.

'Here?' he said, between kisses.

'Here, on *this* table.'

'Real old table.'

'It might not hold us. There's the danger.'

'I got myself a daredevil here,' Winnie Farlowe said. 'Hope I got enough nerve for you, lady.'

When he stood up with Tess Binder clinging to his neck and her legs wrapped around his hips, he didn't feel any pain. His back started hurting an hour later when he climbed into the hammock.

Winnie asked Tess if they could stay home again that night, and she said she wouldn't have it any other way.

They made the ride back the following day before the late afternoon traffic was heaviest, not talking very much during the drive. Winnie spent the two hours wondering if someone like Tess Binder had satisfied her curiosity, or whatever it was, and wouldn't need to go slumming at Spoon's Landing. Wondering if, when he kissed her good-bye, it would be his last closeup of the opaque gray eyes behind tortoiseshell glasses.

When she drove across Pacific Coast Highway on to Balboa peninsula, Winnie was dozing.

'Home again, big boy,' she said and his head bobbed.

'Yeah, so I am.'

'Santa Ana winds're blowing,' she said. 'It's hot!'

'Not like the desert,' he said.

He was wrong. High pressure in Nevada, Utah and Arizona, and low pressure offshore allowed air to flow from land to sea. Compression on the mountain slopes was funneled through the canyons and made the air strike Los Angeles and Orange counties like an open-hearth furnace. During the first week of April, heat records were broken and it stayed hot for days. It was 99 degrees Fahrenheit when Tess turned into the alley behind Winnie's apartment and parked. He got his bag from the trunk and walked around to the driver's side.

'Santa Anas,' he said. 'Feels like God's blow dryer's hitting me in the mouth.'

In a way, she looked as unapproachable as she had the first time he saw her at Spoon's Landing. He thought he should thank her and shake hands. But then he fancied he could smell jasmine, could still taste her tongue burning with jalapeño. He remembered that hammock beneath him and could almost hear her squealing with excitement. He stood gazing at her with a forlorn expression.

'What is this?' she said, finally. 'An HFH goodbye?'

'What?'

157

'Ho-fucking-hum. Is that all I'm going to get out of you, old son?'

Tess Binder opened the door of the Mercedes, stepped out on to the alley and grabbed a handful of Winnie's hair, pulling his head down. The goodbye kiss broke the record of the one he'd gotten at the hacienda.

When she finally pulled back she said, 'I'll call you. I've got some thinking to do. OK?'

'I'll be around,' Winnie said. 'You won't have no trouble finding me. If you're looking.'

'I'll be looking, old son,' Tess Binder said, jumping back in the car.

When Winnie arrived at Spoon's Landing at four o'clock that afternoon, he was greeted by a newspaper headline, from the joke newspapers they do for tourists. Spoon had taped it over the mirror behind the bar. The headline said: NEW SKIPPER HIRED TO PILOT THE EXXON *VALDEZ*.

Below the headline there was a photo of the ill-fated oil tanker's drunken skipper, Joseph Hazlewood, and another of Winnie Farlowe leaving jail after the Christmas debacle.

The column led with: 'Crew will never know the difference.'

'This came a little late for April Fool's Day,' Spoon explained. 'Where the hell you been? I almost called the beach patrol. Had 'em check sand bumps for feet.'

'I was with a lady,' Winnie said.

'Yeah,' Spoon said doubtfully. 'Computer dating service really works, huh? So what'll you have? Your see-through drink? Polish vodka?'

Winnie missed Tess Binder already, and he realized that he might get blind drunk if he wasn't careful. Spoon's droning voice was depressing.

'A beer,' Winnie said, finally. 'Better make it a beer.'

The first didn't make him feel any better. Neither did the second. Then he ordered a Polish vodka.

Cops arrived at 4.15, five of them: Novak the narc, two new ones Winnie didn't know, Hadley, the big cop who worked beach patrol with Buster, and Buster Wiles himself.

Buster introduced Winnie to the two new cops, and Winnie was bagged enough to buy everyone a round of beers even though he was down to his last twenty bucks. Buster and Winnie shared a table away from the other cops, who began shooting a raucous game of snooker.

One of the young cops yelled to the dour saloonkeeper, 'Come on, Spoon, get in the game! I hear you're a snooker-shootin party animal!'

'Sure. Spoon's a party animal like Howard Hughes was a party animal,' Buster said disgustedly. 'Like Rudolph Hess was a party animal.' Then he turned to Winnie and said, 'Young coppers these days? Idea a fun is drivin a pickup over chuck holes. Or belly-bumpin people off barstools. I don't know where they get 'em. Gimme a fuckin headache, is what they do.'

'Still on the beach patrol?'

'Long as I can keep the job.' Buster nodded.

'Still contemplating a career change?'

'Sooner'n you think,' Buster said.

'Still can't talk about it?'

'Soon.'

'I admit, you got me curious,' Winnie said.

'That's jist like you. You're the most curious guy I ever worked with. Gotta know how *everything* works. I said you'd be the first to know, and if it don't work out, I'll be here till I retire. Or till I run into another psycho with an Uzi that shoots straighter.'

The young cops playing snooker were getting noisier. Hadley had guzzled four ounces of bourbon with the glass in his teeth and his hands behind his back. When he finished he wiped his chin and marched triumphantly around the snooker table, slapping palms with the others.

'You fuckin kids decide to break out a cornet or slide trombone, I'll cite you for no parade permit!' Buster Wiles barked. Then to Winnie: 'Wanna go divin tomorrow? I heard they took some real big abalone by Dana Point. Been thinkin about takin a drive down. I can borrow an extra tank and wet suit.'

'I haven't dived since . . . come to think of it, since you and me went to Catalina on Woody's Bertram twenty-eight. He still got the same boat?'

'Yeah, but he don't go out much no more.'

'Guess you can still borrow it?'

'Anytime,' Buster said. 'We could go out for a couple days fishin if you want.'

'Thanks, Buster, but diving doesn't interest me much any more. Getting too old. Cold water makes my back ache sometimes.'

'You think *you're* gettin old? Man, I'm forty-five almost! I even catch myself watchin the Phil Donahue show sometimes. Sittin there lookin at all those guests that jist missed the electric chair but got Phil convinced the naughtiest thing they ever did was paint happy faces on the hobbyhorse in nursery school. Far as I'm concerned, purgatory'd be an eternity of watchin the Phil Donahue show. Hell'd be watchin him interview movie stars.'

'Lemme get my schedule together,' Winnie said. 'We'll do some fishing soon. I been out looking for a job, you know.'

'You ever thought about being a PI? You could give whatzisname a call. Kilroy? You know, the PI up in Santa Ana? He runs a pretty respectable business.'

'Me, a PI?'

'Ain't exactly police work, but sometimes you might get a decent case,' Buster said.

'I was thinking about selling boats.'

'You can sail 'em, but I can't see you sellin 'em,' Buster said. 'You're too straight. Too much of a straight-ahead guy.'

'That's what *she* calls me!'

'Who?'

'Tess Binder. The woman I introduced you to the other night.'

'Oh, yeah, the *lady*. That her name? Binder?'

'Yeah, she called me a straight-ahead guy too.'

'When they flatter you, watch out.' Buster got up and went to the bar while one of the young cops dropped some coins in the jukebox, looked at the selections and, seeing nothing he even recognized, punched three numbers at random. The first spooked Winnie. It was Frank Sinatra.

It seems we stood and talked like this before
We looked at each other in the same way
then
But I can't remember where or when.

161

Winnie was astonished. He yelled to Spoon, 'Hey! How long's that song been on the jukebox?'

'Since about the last time Carlos Tuna bought somebody a drink,' the saloonkeeper answered. 'Back when Wayne Newton still sang like a girl.'

'I never noticed before,' Winnie mumbled.

Buster came back with a double vodka for Winnie, and said, 'Guy sittin by Guppy at the bar? Tried to get me in a game a liar's poker. He's got a dollar bill with a knife crease in it. I says, "Sure, pal, how 'bout we have a little side bet too? I'll bet two-oh that your dollar bill's got about six of a kind on it, probably aces." Suddenly, he don't wanna play no more.'

Winnie said, 'I seen him around. Works a bar like a minesweeper. Stealing tips.'

Then Buster said, 'What's the name a that bitch . . . sorry, that *lady* you were with? Binder?'

'Yeah, Tess Binder.'

'They fished a guy outta the surf over by Little Corona last year. Name was Binder. Let's see, Charles? No. Chester?'

Winnie said, 'Conrad? Conrad P. Binder?'

'Yeah, that's it,' Buster said. 'Conrad Binder. Suicide. Shot himself down there on the sand one night. Fishermen spotted him the next morning. Crabs had a luau.'

'When was it?'

'Oh, August. Maybe September.'

'I was drinking pretty heavy then,' Winnie said. 'Feeling real sorry for myself right after they retired me. Guess I missed it in the papers.'

'Local guy. Stockbroker or something.'

'Mortgage banker.'

'Was that it? Anyways, he smoked himself down there on the sand and the tide moved him around. The Harbor Patrol got called first, but you know how *they* are. Offshore's supposed to be county, but up to the surf line is ours. I bet they got a gaff and pushed the body so there'd be no doubt who handles it. Can't figure why anybody'd wanna be on the Harbor Patrol. PR job. Triple A on-the-water, far as I'm concerned.'

'Where'd he shoot himself?'

'Little Corona.'

'I mean, head? Temple? Mouth?'

'Temple, I think. I didn't see the body. The other dicks were talkin about it. You know, one day a guy's a prominent retired banker, next day the crabs're eatin his face. Ends up in a room with rubber wallpaper, wearin a toe tag.'

'Why'd he kill himself? Any note?'

Buster shrugged and said, 'I don't really know much about the case. Ask Sammy Vogel. He handled it. I think the guy was sick. Cancer or somethin. Maybe heart.'

'They find the gun?'

Buster thought for a moment and said, 'I think they did. Pretty sure. Why?'

'Why? 'Cause if they didn't, how can they be sure it was suicide? Jesus, Buster, you been working dope so long you're zombied out.'

'They *musta* found the piece. There was no talk about a homicide. Guy went down on the beach one night, probably sang a medley a the Beach Boys' greatest hits, and busts a cap in his own skull.'

'You're a real romantic, Buster,' Winnie said, signaling to Spoon for refills.

'How come so much interest in this guy, Binder? You ain't been makin it with that lady in white, have ya?'

Winnie was suddenly stopped cold. There it was again! That maddening sensation of *déjà vu*! The song was playing in his mind! Playing at the wrong speed.

We smiled at each other in the same way then
But I can't remember where or when.

'Talk about *me* bein zombied out!' Buster said, finally.

'What?'

'You're zonin. How 'bout comin back to planet earth?'

'It's that goddamn song!' Winnie said, snapping out of it.

'What song?'

'The one jist finished on the jukebox.'

'I didn't notice.'

'I *know* I've seen that woman somewhere before. Maybe *talked* to her. Maybe . . .'

'What woman?'

'Tess Binder. I've been . . . *seeing* her in my mind. But . . . like, I've seen her *before*. Like, like . . . in a *dream*.'

Spoon was putting the drinks on the table. The saloonkeeper had an unfiltered cigarette dangling from his lip, and his Mister Roberts naval officer's cap was perched on the back of his head. His aloha shirt was unbuttoned and his hairy belly was dripping sweat, on this, the afternoon of one of the most fiery Santa Anas in Southern California history.

'Hey, Spoon, Winnie's gettin spooky!' Buster said. 'Rememberin people from another life. Better dial the Shirley MacLaine hotline.'

'Don't remind me a Shirley MacLaine,' the saloon-keeper droned. 'The night a couple years ago when her I-lived-other-lives story was on television, the customers wanted to watch it. There she is, old Shirley, dancin around with some young dude she was boffin. He kept saying he created himself. He was God. She says, "I'm God!" He says, "No, *I'm* God!" "No," she says, "*I'm* God!" I'm goddamn *bored*! I turned on a ballgame and that's what led to the fight where somebody tossed a bottle and busted out my big screen. Cost me nearly a thousand bucks for repair. Don't mention Shirley MacLaine in *this* joint!'

When Spoon finished droning and shuffled back behind the bar, Buster said, 'Anyways, if you're all that interested in the Binder deal check with Vogel. There mighta been somethin questionable about it, but not to my knowledge. What's wrong? Your little friend Tess suspect foul play?'

'No, it's jist that, well . . . he offs himself with a handgun. And somebody took a shot at us with a handgun.'

'Somebody . . . wait a minute! Where? When?'

While Winnie briefly described his desert holiday with Tess Binder, leaving out hammocks and kitchen tables, Tess was having a tall glass of iced tea on the beach at her club. The temperature on the sand had reached 100 degrees. Corky Peebles's power bob had lost its sizzle. Everything seemed to droop after twenty-four hours of relentless Santa Anas. Nature had unplugged the power in *all* the power bobs.

Corky was limp and lifeless on the sand, defanged and declawed. An FFH millionaire showed up, but not a single feverishly hot momma could so much as budge. On a day like this you could actually *see* what was rumored: Each hot momma averaged three eye jobs and one and a half facelifts. The unlifted hands looked parchment dry, the flesh seeming to curl like old wallpaper. After her ice melted, Tess went home.

When Winnie was finished with his story, Buster said, 'You been off the job too long. I think you're looking for new employment. I mean, just 'cause your girlfriend's old man ices himself don't mean there's some connection with a gunshot in the desert. Which may not have been a gunshot? Which may have been an accident in the first place? Maybe you shouldn't look into a PI job, Win. You got too much imagination already.'

'Yeah, maybe,' Winnie said. 'Jesus, it's hot! Maybe the Santa Ana winds're making me goofy.'

'Must be it,' Buster agreed. But then the big cop sipped at his drink, put it down and said, 'On the other hand, where *was* this guy when the shot was fired? The one you say Binder gave the ranch to? His boyfriend?'

'Warner Stillwell? Supposedly went to the hospital for a few days. She don't know what's wrong with him.'

'Maybe *my* brain's gettin scorched from these Santa Anas but . . .'

'Yeah?'

'But, with old man Binder and his daughter outta the way . . . Naw, that don't work out. You said Stillwell *already* has the property.'

'Wait a minute!' Winnie said. 'What if there's *more* property? Assets. Stock. Gold. I don't know, whatever rich people stash for a rainy day. What if there's a lotta

166

assets Tess don't know about? Maybe assets he can't get till she dies. Make sense?'

'Ya got me,' Buster shrugged. 'I'm jist a dope cop. *Former* dope cop. By the way, I decided to put a move on the boss to get the environmental services job. Hazardous waste dumpin, chemical spills, midnight flushers in the bay. Trash cop. I was born for that job. Officer Trash. Anyways, I don't know about probates and wills and like that. Maybe you oughtta talk to Sammy Vogel if you really think there's somethin to all this. And if there is, maybe you better get another girlfriend . . . No, wait a minute. *Don't* get another girlfriend! If her dead old man's ex-boyfriend *is* tryin to snuff her, it must mean she's got somethin he wants. She might be rich and don't know it. How about arrangin another introduction for *me*, Winnie!'

'You took enough a them off me over the years,' Winnie said, finishing his vodka. 'This one's a keeper. *If* she ever calls me again.'

'Yeah, well, she wasn't my type anyways. I can't stand broads wearin white. Means there's a black heart under there.'

'She was wearing *red* the night you met her.'

'Yeah, but she's the white linen type if ever I saw one,' Buster said. 'Am I right?'

'You *do* know women, Buster,' Winnie agreed.

Buster Wiles looked up and said, 'Uh oh,' but couldn't get away in time. Tripoli Jones had just come in and spotted them at the corner table.

He wasn't Libyan, he'd gotten his nickname from the Marine Corps hymn. Tripoli Jones was a living embodiment of 'Once a Marine always a Marine'. He made Ollie North look like a draft dodger, everybody said. Two drinks and the fifty-eight-year-old telephone lineman was back at the Chosin Reservoir fighting his way up icy Korean slopes, firing a BAR with one hand. When he was ten years younger, Tripoli Jones was more dangerous than New Year's traffic. They said he'd busted more skulls than Harley-Davidson, but he'd had a triple bypass that had slowed him down some. And he *despised* Vietnam vets.

Without being invited, Tripoli Jones sat next to Winnie and said, 'Whatcha doin, boys? Reliving Nam? Remembering all the good Thai stick you smoked?'

'Time to go,' Buster said.

'That movie *Platoon* was about *your* war, all right,' Tripoli Jones sneered. 'The enemy is *us*. What bullshit! The enemy is the left-wing assholes that make that garbage. Always easy to tell the good GIs from the bad ones in those pinko movies. The good ones all smoke pot, the bad ones're the rednecks drinking beer.'

After his film analysis, Triploli Jones signaled to Spoon for a beer.

'We don't *really* have to go back to the thirty-eighth parallel tonight,' Winnie said. 'Do we, Tripoli?'

'What'd us Korea vets get when *we* came home?' Tripoli Jones said, sneering to the ceiling this time. '*They* get psychiatrists and a slab a granite in Washington and Jane Fonda. What'd *we* get? Who gave a shit about the fifty-four thousand dead? But *we* don't sit around and whine about flashbacks and Agent Orange and posttraumatic stress disorder! Shit! We killed gooks and came home and worked for the telephone company, is what *we* did!'

'Yes, Tripoli,' Buster sighed. 'And *we* jist smoked dope and made babies in Cambodia and Vietnam and Thailand.'

'And two in Burbank,' Winnie said. Don't forget those.'

'The *whiner's* war, is what,' Tripoli Jones said. Having gotten it off his chest, the loyal legionnaire yelled to Spoon, 'Bring my comrades a drink!'

Then he got up and staggered over to the snooker table to see if there were any other veterans around.

'Can't stand a roamin drunk,' Buster said. 'If they stay put, you can avoid 'em.'

'His wife's in here looking for him five nights a week,' Winnie said. 'Guy needs a beeper collar.'

Spoon brought them the drinks from Tripoli Jones just as the phone rang. Spoon shuffled back to the bar, picked it up and said, 'Yeah, he's here.' Then to Winnie he yelled, 'For you. *Mister* Farlowe.'

Winnie had run out to his car and was starting the engine before he even realized he'd forgotten to say good-bye to Buster Wiles. Tess Binder had asked him to come to her house right away. She said she was frightened for her life.

The gate guard at Linda Isle looked at his clipboard and said, 'Go right in.' He didn't even give Winnie's battered VW ragtop a second look. Probably figured Winnie was a boat cleaner or maybe one of the car polishers who regularly visited the island.

Tess's house was one with an electric gate buzzer. Winnie figured such precautions were overkill. In all his years with NBPD he couldn't remember a significant burglary on Linda Isle except for a few inside jobs by employees or local kids. It just wasn't worth it for opportunist thieves to overcome kiosk security, or to raid by boat.

The gate buzzed and clicked open. Tess stood at the door waiting for him in an off-the-shoulder white jersey and a sarong skirt. She didn't look as scared as she'd sounded on the phone. She threw a suntanned, well-muscled arm around his neck and kissed him. A long one. A probing one. When she finally stepped back he said, '*That* don't feel like a scared kiss.'

'It's a scared kiss and a grateful kiss. Come on in.'

Tess led him to the living room, to the sofa he well remembered. She offered him a double vodka without asking. She'd stocked up on Polish vodka. She had a diet drink.

After he'd taken a few sips she said, 'I hadn't planned on seeing you so soon. I wanted to give it a rest. I wanted to sort it out and see how I really feel about you, but something happened. I had to call.'

'So tell me.'

'When I got home, I did my mail and watered a few plants. I'd planned to skip dinner and was upstairs when the phone rang. I answered, but the caller hung up. I was about to get undressed and take a shower. It's so bloody hot I went to the French doors. You know, the ones beside the bed?'

'I'm not likely to forget.'

That brought a little smile, then she continued: 'I opened the doors and the Santa Ana wind just seemed to rush in. Took my breath away. Something made me look across the channel. I saw a man. He was in the parking lot by the restaurant, standing by an old blue car. Looking up at my window. Oh, he pretended to be just admiring the boats docked in the channel. I stepped back from the window but kept an eye on him. He walked around for a while, then he came back.'

'Is that when you called me?'

'No, I waited. I had a cigarette. He was still out there, but sitting in the old blue car. Then he got out and walked over to the water and pretended to look at a big sailboat. He walked along the railing and I could see him the whole time except when he'd disappear behind one of the big powerboats. I don't have binoculars, but I think I know who it was.'

'Who?'

'I *think* it was Hugh Starkey. They call him Hack. A guy who used to work for my dad and Warner. Hack took care of Daddy's boat for several years and often went out to *El Refugio* to do their cars or other odd jobs. The man finally got back in the old blue car and drove away. I think it was a Plymouth.'

'Is he gay?'

She nodded. 'He's about, oh, now he'd be about fifty years old, a big strong guy. Always had his hair permed, and dyed it black as he got older. I think it was Hack Starkey and he was trying to figure how to get in this house!'

'So whaddaya suppose he had on his mind?'

'I don't know, Win! Look, I have a confession. I've been thinking about that gunshot out on the trail.'

'Yeah, so've I.'

'Well, Starkey knows his way around the ranch. He's ridden those trails with Warner. In fact, during the last couple of years Hack and Warner seemed a little *too* friendly.'

'Tess, I'd like to talk about your dad's death.'

'Oh God!' She got up and went to the wet bar. She poured herself a double Scotch. When she came back her hands were shaking.

'Tell me about his suicide. How it happened. Who informed you. Details. I know it's tough.'

Tess sighed and took a good long hit on the Scotch before saying, 'I didn't even know Daddy was ill. He couldn't have been *terribly* sick yet, but . . . well, according to Detective Vogel at the police department, my father simply walked down to Little Corona Beach, one night last summer. One warm, starry night, last summer. And he put a gun to the side of his head. And he did it. They found nothing by way of a note. His wallet and money were still in his pocket.' She paused to sob for a second, gained control and said, 'Why does a man go off to a lonely beach to do something like that, Win?'

'I don't know,' he said, taking her hand. 'They do it in unpredictable ways. Did the police find the gun?'

'Yes. It was Daddy's gun. A thirty-eight-caliber revolver he'd kept at the ranch. His body eventually slid down the beach when the tide came in. By the time he was spotted by a fisherman, Daddy had been in that cold water all night. They found . . . what do you call it . . . dark marks on both sides of his body?'

'Lividity?'

'Yes. They said it indicated he was lying for several hours on one side and then the tide turned him over on the sand and he lay for several more hours. He was nearly afloat in the water when a fisherman finally spotted him the next morning.'

'And the gun was still on the beach?'

172

'Yes, partly buried by the tide. He'd had it registered with the Indio sheriffs.'

'What happened to it?'

'I gave it to Warner when it was returned to me with Daddy's things: his wallet, wristwatch, his Stanford graduation ring, his clothes and shoes. I kept all the other things, but I gave the gun to Warner. I wanted to throw it away, but where do you throw a gun? I thought about tossing it in the ocean. I thought about burying it in the ground. Finally I just gave it to Warner.'

'Tess, was there *any*, I mean, *any* suggestion of foul play?'

'How foul can it get?'

'I mean, that it was anything other than suicide?'

'No!' she said quickly. 'None whatsoever. There were powder marks on his temple. What do you call it?'

'Stippling. From the gunpowder tattooed under the skin.'

'The coroner and the detective from Newport Beach, everyone was satisfied. Especially after they talked to Daddy's doctor and found out about his . . . illness.'

'You said he was sick, but he *wasn't* sick. What was it?'

And then she *did* cry. Tess buried her face in the back cushion of the sofa and began to weep. Winnie sat helplessly and touched her shoulder once or twice. He guessed.

'AIDS?' he said.

'HIV,' she said, still sobbing. 'It wasn't AIDS yet. But he was carrying the virus. His doctor and the pathologist concurred.'

'How about Warner? Is *that* why you say he goes to the doctor periodically?'

Then she wiped her eyes with the heel of her hand, put her glasses back on and said bitterly, 'I don't know. He *must* have it. The virus at least. He *must* have given it to my father. Where *he* got it I can't say.'

'He's an old man, isn't he?'

'Seventy-two. Old men get it too. But he's a fit, athletic man who looks ten years younger. I *know* he gave the disease to my father!'

'How can you be sure?'

'Win, goddamnit! My father wasn't an IV user, or a junkie, and he didn't get a transfusion, and you don't get it from toilet seats! How *else* could he've gotten it? Are you implying my father picked up hustlers from bars? Hustlers like Hack Starkey? Are you suggesting *that*?'

Winnie put down his drink and took her in his arms. 'I'm not suggesting anything. I just wanna help you.'

'I know,' she said, holding on tight.

'I wanna check out a few things. Maybe I can help, maybe not.'

'You can help by staying with me tonight. Please don't leave me alone tonight!'

Still holding her, he said, 'I won't leave you.'

When she looked up she tried to smile. 'You can even use my toothbrush. I've never let anyone share my toothbrush. Not *anyone*!'

12: *Betsy*

Both Tess and Winnie (who had a very brief buzzard visit at 3.30 a.m.) slept late the next morning, and while they slept, Buster Wiles was drawing ever closer to his career change. The Santa Ana wind condition had drawn 300,000 to Southland beaches. Even on this weekday the peninsula was gridlocked, and the beach patrol had started writing beer tickets at ten o'clock in the morning.

Balboa peninsula, a crooked finger of land bordered by the ocean on one side and lower Newport Bay on the other, is less than five hundred yards wide at its widest point, and about four and a half miles long. Balboa Boulevard, which divides the peninsula, is lined with apartment houses that charge big bucks to short-term tourists, as well as to students in for a fling.

During this onslaught by the Santa Anas, the peninsula was a circus. At the Newport Pavilion the big catamaran was loaded to capacity for the hour-and-a-half run to Santa Catalina Island. Kids mobbed the merry-go-round and Ferris wheel at the Balboa Fun Zone and lined up at Skee Ball machines in the arcade. The Balboa and Newport piers looked in danger of collapse, overrun by fishermen and others desperate for an offshore breeze that just wasn't there.

The ribbon of pavement that borders the vast white beach of Newport was jammed with bicyclists and roller skaters. And the sand was a patchwork of 'saltwater taffy', those living breathing morsels of sweetness in French-cut bikinis.

Three 'jogglers' from the local colleges, a young woman and two young men, sprinted along Ocean Front, amazing the acres of sun lovers. The young woman, dressed in a polka-dotted tank top and Capri-length striped tights, juggled four red balls. The young men juggled five balls each. Both of them wore three-piece outfits consisting of solid cotton T-back tops and matching briefs over striped knee-length Lycra trunks. All three jogglers wore Reeboks and mismatched socks, since mismatched socks were up-to-the-minute. At least, for the moment.

The section of water on the ocean side of the harbor jetty, known as the Wedge, was jammed with kids daring the *reeeelyawesome* waves that sometimes roar to twelve feet and break bones against jetty rocks, a legendary site for body surfers and boogie-boarders, featured in the surfing classic, *Endless Summer*.

Buster found himself partnered with Hadley again, and the young cop's mouth started revving before they'd finished their first cup of morning coffee. Buster had gotten to the stage in life where he couldn't stand extended conversations with any person under the age of thirty-five, much less having to spend eight hours a day with a twenty-two-year-old. Much less one like Hadley who thought he could score with surfer bimbos and beach bimbettes by telling fecal jokes.

'Knockers 'n fannies far as the horizon!' Hadley cried, as the cops walked along the surf line. 'A sea of tender flesh with nary a ripple on the surface! Hey! Scope-out on *that* one!'

176

He'd spotted a tall one in an apricot bikini. They were lying in rows, all this Golden Orange saltwater taffy, in taffy-colored French-cuts and thong bikinis: lemon, licorice, tangerine, strawberry. They were soft and pliable and tasty, these lithesome saltwater taffy morsels.

'Yeah, she's got the shape-of-a-shape,' Buster said, sweat beading on his forehead and lip. 'Maybe when she grows up, huh?'

'She'd be *perfect* if she had a liquor license,' Hadley giggled. 'And if she'd give *me* a license to lick her!'

Hadley didn't laugh, he *brayed*. The bimbette with the shape-of-a-shape looked up at Hadley, curled her lip and whispered something to a friend, a more full-figured bimbette who lay face down, her top undone for no tan line. But they both took a peek at Buster and smiled sympathetically.

Hadley said, 'She reminds me of one I met at Smedley's party. They call her Fangs. Thinks your dick's an artichoke leaf. Likes to drag the meat off.'

While Hadley brayed again, Buster adjusted the ride of his holstered gun and wiped his face with the white hand towel he'd tucked inside his Sam Browne. Buster's uniform shirt was already soggy. He said, 'I know you seen *Beverly Hills Cop* eighteen times, and I know Eddie Murphy brays like a jackass too, but he's got forty million so nobody *tells* him!'

Buster suggested they go get a soda pop. When they reached the sidewalk on Ocean Front – which borders the beach all along the peninsula – a gorgeous red-haired skater in a hot-pink thong bikini throttled back to eyeball Buster. She cut him a *big* smile, and posed on one wheel when Buster turned on those thick-lashed lilac lamps of his.

'Do you have the time, Officer?' she asked.

'For *what*?' Hadley piped up, causing Buster to shake his head wearily.

Buster looked at his watch and said, 'It's *only* ten-thirty, but believe me, it feels like five o'clock in the afternoon.'

The redhead was only about twenty years old and Buster had long since given up *that* kind of trouble.

Hadley was wild about the fine coat of freckles covering the skater's legs and shoulders and back, and said, 'If I was your boyfriend I'd love to play connect the dots!'

'Yeah, I know,' she said sardonically. 'With your tongue, right? I hear that *all* the time.' Then, to Buster: 'What is this, simian rivalry?'

It was the first time Buster smiled all day, but she was *still* too young. 'We gotta go before I get heatstroke,' he said. 'I'm even too weak to drink from a straw.'

'I'm staying down on Seventeenth Street,' she said quickly. 'Maybe you could come by tonight and tell me if it's a safe neighborhood?'

Then Buster broke her heart by saying, 'Sugar, I got handcuffs older'n you,' while he mopped the back of his neck with the towel and headed toward the hamburger stand.

'Hey! I kinda *like* handcuffs!' the skater said, with a forlorn gaze at Buster's buns inside those cute police department shorts.

When they were seated at a stool having a root beer, Hadley said, 'She was all-time, that redhead! The look she gave you, you could wear out two dildos with. If you half tried, Buster, you could draw bigger crowds than Bruce Springsteen or the fuckin Chinese pandas. These surfboard Suzies want you more than Day-Glo earrings. How 'bout you *take* some and give me your leftovers? Man, life's a beach, don't ya know?'

Buster ran his hands through his hair, surprised that even his *scalp* was soaked. He sighed and said, 'Now comes the terrible truth, Sonny. Old Buster has a taut cord attached from his cock to a troubled psyche, OK? See, the cock has to have some slack so it can grow. Mine ain't *got* none these days.'

'Why?'

'I got problems up here.' Buster tapped his head.

'What problems? My mom says you used to be king a the beach around here.'

'Fact is, I need to get in another line a work. If this was Nam I'd shoot myself in the foot to get a ride home.' Then he realized what Hadley had said. 'Your *mom*!'

'You tired a police work?'

'Give yourself another fifteen years,' Buster said. 'It won't seem so impossible.'

'Different strokes,' Hadley said. 'Depends on what gets you off, I guess, I'd *pay* to do this job. All those wood burners on the beach? Yeah, I'd *pay* to do this job!'

'Depends on what gets you off,' Buster said. 'Me, I can't stand the thought a lookin at another computerized police report with all those little boxes on 'em. I've filled in more little boxes in my time than a gynecologist. I'm ready for a career change.'

'What could you do? All you know is police work, right?'

'Somethin akin to my trainin. Maybe a job in a lab. Maybe shockin mice till they go bonkers. That's like police work. Only in police work, *I'm* one a the fuckin mice! Now let's go write some beer tickets, kid.'

On their way to ticket the early-morning boozers in the parking lot by the Newport Pier they ran into Cockatoo Clyde. As usual, the little fat man was surrounded by parrots and cockatiels, canaries and love birds. They perched on his shoulders, or on his head, or sat obediently on temporary perches that encircled him on the sidewalk. Clyde did shows for tourists and bimbettes.

Buster found the vivid and beautiful creatures strangely depressing. He had a terrible feeling something was going to happen on this scorching day. Something that *wouldn't* be beautiful. In fact, he got a sinking feeling in his stomach when Hadley paused and disgusted a bimbette by saying to her: 'Know how to turn a canary into a hummingbird? Cut off its feet!'

'You're real smooth and sophisticated,' Buster said to his partner. 'Like dago red in a fruit jar.'

They continued walking along Ocean Front. When they got to Fifteenth Street, they saw a pair of young Asians looking into the window of a BMW 325i. The local cops say that when two or more Vietnamese go within fifty feet of a German car, there's *de facto* probable cause to stop and frisk. They say that Vietnamese thugs down from Westminster's Little Saigon can strip a radio out of a Mercedes faster than you can tune it to a Dodgers game.

The two Asians spotted the cops and started moving fast, toward Balboa Boulevard.

Buster was *much* too hot and tired, but Hadley said, 'He's carrying something!' Then he yelled: 'Hold it!'

And the chase was on! The taller Asian held the BMW radio like a football.

Buster put out a call for assistance over his hand set before lumbering after the fleeing Asians. Hadley, who had good speed for his size, powered along in a hang-it-out sprint. The young cop was almost sideswiped by a red pickup on Balboa Boulevard, and a kid with a baseball hat on backwards stuck his head out the window and yelled, 'You'd write me a jay-walking ticket for that, you shithead!'

The shorter and slower Asian headed east toward Main Street, a shady tree-lined thoroughfare near the old post office. The other Asian doubled back toward the beach. Hadley figured they had their wheels parked back there, maybe in the vicinity of the BMW, but since the tall one was carrying the radio, Hadley stayed with him, hoping Buster could keep up with the slower shorter one.

Meanwhile, Buster was trucking along breathlessly, cursing Asian boat people and rookie partners and the Santa Ana winds and his life in general as he ran across the boulevard by the Balboa Cinema. A car had to careen toward the oncoming traffic lanes, forcing Buster to leap on top of a parked car to keep from getting creamed. Another car screeched and fishtailed and dove to a stop just in time.

Horns were blowing and people were screaming, but no harm was done except to Buster's nervous system as a geyser of adrenaline blew through him. Then Buster, too, wondered if they might've stashed their car somewhere near the place where they'd first been spotted. He chugged back toward the beach.

The taller Asian ran back to the sidewalk along Ocean Front, dodging in and out among strollers, skaters, runners, loiterers, and cyclists in Spandex. With the radio still under his arm he juked and jibed, and looked back at Hadley once too often.

He crashed into the three jogglers. Red balls went flying. Bodies covered in polka dots and stripes did back flips and cartwheels and whoop-de-doos. The jogglers smashed into two kids on beach bikes who collided with two skaters going the other way. People shouted and screamed, arms flailing, legs akimbo. Metal and flesh skidded along the pavement. Big wheels and little ones spun upside down in the air. Hadley plunged through all of it without losing a step.

And he made it to the corner. Where he stepped on *one* little red ball, a joggler's ball, belonging to the girl who could sprint all-out while keeping four of them in the air.

The young cop's legs went horizontal! He did a head-first, belly-flopping, boogie-boarding slide along fifteen feet of sidewalk, upending a tourist from Tacoma who had already decided that folks were a little different in California.

Hadley yelped, rolled over and gaped in horror at his knees and shins. The stolen car radio lay broken in the street ten feet away. The cassette player was jammed and a tape had popped out. Hadley limped over, retrieved the stolen property and sat down on the curb.

Buster had been prowling through the alleys behind the row of rental units along the beach, looking for a likely car that might belong to the two suspects, when he spotted the tall Asian two hundred yards farther west along the beachfront!

The thief was now bare-chested, using his shirt to mop sweat and blood from the abrasions on his chest, arms and forehead. He looked like he'd been dipped in olive oil, his lean sweaty body and shiny black hair gleaming in the pitiless sunlight. Buster yelled: 'Stop, you little slopehead, or I'll blow you back to the boonies you came from!'

The Asian was losing it, running in slow motion. He wasn't breathing, he was rattling. He turned a corner away from the beachfront, back toward Balboa Boulevard again. Where he had his luckiest break of the week. He had *just* enough time to dance off the sidewalk.

When Buster rounded the corner – having decided to sprint all-out for another fifty yards and then, fuck it – he *wasn't* so lucky.

An exploding palette! Color! A kaleidoscope of emerald green and blood scarlet and lemon yellow and cobalt blue! Buster heard exotic cries he hadn't even heard in the jungles of Vietnam! Shrieks and whistles and screams! Colors dove and swooped and wheeled and hovered before his eyes!

Buster Wiles found himself sitting splaylegged on the sidewalk. Cockatoo Clyde sat opposite him, looking every bit as dazed as Buster, but a lot more terror-stricken. Clyde was swarmed on by birds scurrying to safety. His cockatoos and parrots and canaries and cockatiels and lovebirds and parakeets screamed in rage and fear, even biting at their master in confusion.

Buster was covered with a mosaic of feathers and bird shit. Terror-loosened bird bowels had simply let go! Buster was awash in green and white, and strangely enough, a kind of magenta slime. He could *taste* bird shit: It was even dripping down his nose.

'I got a headache,' the dazed cop said in a soft demented voice to the equally dazed bird man. 'If you promise not to bitch to my boss about me scarin your birds, I promise I won't tear your face off and *eat* it.'

The bird man gaped at the ferocious, bloodied, psychotic-looking cop, and said, 'Can I just *say* something, Officer?'

Buster's voice was so soft he could hardly hear himself speak. He said, 'Yes, if it's not critical of me. Because life is fuckin me over real bad and I feel like I might have a stroke any minute now, and I'm jist about as dangerous as an English soccer fan. So if I was you, I wouldn't say nothin *critical*.'

Cockatoo Clyde gulped and said, 'I was just going to tell you, Officer, that the man you're chasing staggered into the alley over there and fell down.'

It took Buster Wiles about two minutes to get to his feet and limp toward the alley. Halfway down, the Asian was leaning against the wall of a garage. He wasn't going to run, but he wasn't going to go the easy way. He just stood there, waiting for Buster.

Buster Wiles's temples throbbed with pure fury. His eyeballs were seared, swollen with rage. He advanced toward the Asian, who stood stoically but with some defiance in his delicate face. He wasn't really as young as Buster had first thought. His face said: 'Where I come from I got used to men with guns beating the living shit out of me. One more time won't matter.'

Suddenly, a ten-year-old Pontiac chattered through the alley, almost pinning Buster to a telephone pole before he leaped to safety! He found himself on his ass again. The Pontiac was driven by the *other* Asian, who squealed to a stop near his pal, just as a Newport Beach patrol unit slammed to a stop at the opposite end of the alley.

The driver started to reverse the Pontiac without having rescued his partner, but Buster was on his feet and had drawn his revolver, very willing to crank off every round. The car stalled and the driver leaped out and tried to run back out of the alley with the rejuvenated partner hot behind him.

Buster smacked the little one with his side-handle baton when the guy tried to scamper past. The little one did a forward somersault, but got up running, blood streaming down the back of his head. The tall one made it past Buster.

Another Newport Beach patrol unit pulled up on the other end of the alley, and Buster, along with a female cop named Babs Morris, found themselves rolling on the sidewalk with the shorter thief, a biting, spitting, gouging little boat person who didn't want to go to jail that day. Buster was already exhausted and Babs Morris didn't have all that much upperbody strength. The little Asian managed to slug her twice on the side of the face and kick Buster in the groin.

A crowd of college kids, already drunk by noon, came pouring out on to the street from where they'd been watching a game of volleyball on the beach, and immediately took sides with the game little Asian. Buster got the guy in a chokehold, while Babs Morris looked for the handcuffs that he'd kicked out of her hand. Buster tried his best to pinch off the Asian's carotid arteries with what was left of his strength.

The college kids yelled things like:

'You don't have to kill the guy!'

'Let him up, for chrissake, he can't breathe!'

'Does it take *two* cops to arrest *one* little guy?'

'Just put the handcuffs on him and stop *hurting* him!'

By then, there were five patrol units screeching toward

the alley with lights gumballing. Two cars slid to a stop and the cops jumped out and piled on. One of them knelt on the Asian's back, and at last he submitted to handcuffs and was dragged to a police car.

Buster rolled over and looked at the crowd still yammering and twittering. To him those college kids looked like they were standing on the other side of an aquarium. Or *he* was.

He staggered to his feet and limped toward the mob of kids. He picked out one who was making chirping noises like the Bedouin women in desert movies. The kid quieted down when Buster was six feet away, when he saw a pair of eyes emitting a death beam.

The kid said, 'Hey! Hey, wait a minute!' when Buster slowly drew out his handcuffs. 'You can't arrest me! I haven't *done* anything!'

Those violet eyes floated in a sea of lava. Those eyes were coming at the kid like little purple asteroids from a galaxy far away.

Buster was lunatic-furious. He said, 'I ain't gonna arrest you! I'm gonna *deputize* you!' Then Buster snatched the kid's arm. And while the crowd started hollering about police brutality and civil rights and such, Buster bent that arm straight up, and whispered, 'Do you swear to uphold the law and defend the Constitution? Yes? Fine! I hereby deputize you!' Then he slapped the handcuffs in the kid's hands and said, 'Now let's see *you* catch the one that got away without hurtin him! Make sure any bruises and broken bones belong to *you*, not him, YOU LITTLE MAGGOT SUCKIN FRATERNITY VERMIN!'

A sergeant who had just arrived, ran up, took Buster in tow and pointed him toward a patrol car. Then he went to the college kid, retrieved Buster's handcuffs and said, 'He was hit in the head by the suspect. Concussion. You understand.'

While Buster sat in the sergeant's car for safekeeping, the crowd of college kids went back to volleyball and drinking beer. And the patrol units at the scene cleaned up the carnage of the day.

Hadley rode back to the scene of the car burglary and pointed out the BMW to a patrol officer, who ran a radio check on the license plate. It came back as an LAPD stolen, with a hold-for-crime-scene-investigation, *and* the unusual request to notify West L.A. detectives when the stolen car was recovered. And just after a tow truck arrived to hook up the stolen car, there was another radio message that Hadley and Buster should go to the station.

While they were being driven to Newport Beach PD by Officer Babs Morris, who had a black eye, Hadley said, 'That BMW wasn't even jimmied! Probably the jerkoff that owns it left it unlocked! Might as well write "steal me!" on it, you leave a BMW unlocked up there in L.A.'

Buster didn't seem to be hearing Hadley. His bell was still ringing and he couldn't focus all that well. Finally he said, 'Somethin's wrong. This is supposed to be a safe place to do police work. Yet in the same week, I get shot at for stealin a dead mouse and almost killed by a fuckin cockatoo.'

Babs Morris turned and looked at Buster Wiles very strangely. With her one good eye.

When they got to the station Sammy Vogel was waiting for them.

'You mean, this *ain't* about me jackin up that smart-mouth college kid?' Buster said. 'I was figurin he probably called in to beef me.'

The bald little detective scratched his shiny pink jaw and said, 'That BMW you guys impounded? It was hot.'

'Yeah, we know,' Hadley said, 'with a request to notify LAPD.'

'That's because it was stolen during a residential burg where a woman and her daughter got murdered,' Vogel said. 'The car belonged to the victim.'

That stoked young Hadley. 'A double murder? They know who did it?'

'No,' Vogel said, 'but they know about a serial murderer with the same MO. They call him the Audio Killer.'

'I got a headache,' Buster said. 'Whaddaya want us to do?'

'Just wait here at the station for LAPD, is all. Don't go anywhere. They probably wanna see if your suspect could have anything to do with their case.'

'No way,' Buster said. 'Our gooks were jist two opportunists. Happened to see a BMW that wasn't locked and went for the radio.'

'I got the radio back,' Hadley said to Vogel, 'but the guy I was chasing got away.'

'Yeah, well, I don't suppose LAPD cares about a recovered radio. They're looking for a serial killer. Any chance for prints on it?'

'Sure,' Hadley said. 'I picked it up real careful. The guy's prints're all over it.'

'I mean the *killer's* prints!' Vogel said. 'Not *your* guy. The guy that killed the people and stole the car. *His* prints. He's fruity over cassette players, this Audio Killer.

188

He mighta played one of his tapes on that car radio.'

Suddenly Hadley reached into a half-ripped pocket of his shorts and took out the audiocassette, holding it by the edges. He said to Vogel, 'I almost forgot about this. It popped out.'

Vogel took the cassette from the battered young cop. It was plain, without a commercial label. It had *Betsy* scrawled across it.

Vogel crossed the squad room to a cassette machine on top of a filing cabinet. He put the cassette in the machine, holding the edge between his thumb and forefinger. He punched the button on the machine.

There were two other detectives in the squad room. Everyone stopped when, after a few seconds of tape hissing, they heard a woman weeping hysterically. Then she cried out: 'Pleeeeease! Pleeeeease!'

Then she tried to scream, but it was muffled by something. Then someone made gargling noises.

Then they heard the tape hissing again, followed by someone panting into the mike. Then there was a gasp and something that sounded like wheezing. Then the tape hissed again. Then it all stopped.

Buster looked at Hadley but nobody spoke. The action on the tape resumed with the sound of a small child crying. Then a man's voice said, 'Mustn't cry, Betsy. There's no need to cry.'

The child's voice said, 'Where's my mommy? I want my mommy.'

The male voice said, 'Sure, Betsy. You'll be with your mommy soon. *Real* soon.'

Then the child was screaming in terror. Then she was screaming in agony. They could easily detect the difference.

The screaming went on for perhaps thirty seconds before it was muffled, and a man's panting excited voice said, 'Betsy. Betsy!'

Then the sound stopped and the tape hissed again.

Buster and Hadley waited in the lunch room for the LAPD detectives. Buster had a diet drink while Hadley just sat quietly. But the hair on Buster's forearms was still electric, and he shivered up his back as he thought about the tape. He had watched Hadley's young face go gray during the playing of the cassette. There had been a white line around the cop's mouth, his lips were pressed so tightly together, and Buster thought he'd seen tears in the kid's eyes.

The LAPD detectives arrived at 5.15 p.m., apologizing for the delay. They seemed satisfied that the Asian thieves had nothing to do with their double murder, but they were extremely excited to get the cassette. A dusting for latent prints had produced nothing except smudges from Hadley's own fingers. But the voice of the serial murderer was on that tape, their first and only lead to the Audio Killer.

'I'm gonna have our boss write you guys an attaboy,' one of the detectives said.

Ordinarily, Hadley would've been thrilled by a commendation, but he'd been subdued since hearing the Betsy tape. After the LAPD cops were gone, and Buster and Hadley had had their abrasions tended to and were in the locker room changing to civvies, Hadley finally said, 'Know how old the little girl was? Betsy?'

'No.'

'Three years old. I asked them and they said she was three years old.'

190

'Yeah, well,' Buster said. 'Well.' He couldn't think of anything else to say.

'Guys from Santa Ana PD always say that here in our town a beer ticket's a felony, right? And they always ask, whadda we get? One-point-seven homicides in a bad year? Well, I'd rather be here and deal with a million frauds and ripoffs than deal with *one* a those kinda homicides. Or something like the Randy Kraft case.'

Hadley was referring to Orange County's most notorious murder trial ever. Randy Kraft, a forty-four-year-old computer consultant, was linked to the drugging, strangling and mutilation of forty-five young men, sixteen of them in Orange County, between 1972 and 1983. Like the Audio Killer, Kraft also relived his moments, and kept a diary with cryptic allusions to various victims. If all of Kraft's killings ever became known, he might be the USA's premier killer, even topping Ted Bundy, no mean feat in the land of recreational murder.

The audiocassette with *Betsy* scrawled across it was not uncommon, the LAPD detectives had pointed out to Hadley. Modern American serial killers were even using videocameras to memorialize their deeds.

'Know how I feel today, Buster?' Hadley said, when he finally put on his Nikes, ready to go home. 'I feel like *I'd* be the one looking for a career change if I had to deal with stuff like that. Like Betsy.'

Buster had a roaring headache, and other parts of his body hurt just as much. He'd asked for and been granted the next two days off. He dragged himself painfully to his feet, and just before Hadley left the locker room, Buster said to him, 'This job *sucks*.'

Hadley turned in the doorway, looking very young and

191

sad. He said, 'You didn't *always* feel that way. Did ya?'

Overflowing with venom, Buster Wiles said: 'Only difference between this job and my ex-wife is, this job always *will* suck!'

13: *The Bell Buoy*

The temperature in downtown L.A. was 106, which beat the record for the date by fifteen degrees! The surge in energy use from all the air conditioners in L.A. and Orange County had knocked out traffic signals. School-children were being kept off the playgrounds, and lights were turned off in classrooms.

Winnie had convinced Tess Binder to get out of the house and spend a large part of that scorching afternoon cruising in Newport Harbor. Tess borrowed a twenty-foot open-bow runabout, powered by an inboard-outboard engine, from her next-door neighbor. She packed a picnic basket full of light snacks, cold beer and California Chardonnay, and she sunbathed while Winnie piloted the boat.

Newport Beach is composed of eight islands, one natural and the rest man-made. Tess knew every island and every channel as well as Winnie did, but wasn't interested in the sights. She reclined across the bench seat in the open bow and rolled down her purple high-waist bikini. To Winnie she was as firm and sleek as an ocelot, and yet she'd never left him to go to a gym or even talked about it. Winnie wore baggy cotton shorts and a faded red tank with a screen print of a catamaran flying a hull on the front. He'd gotten enough confidence by now to stop sucking in his gut.

Winnie took the runabout under Newport Boulevard into the narrow channels by Balboa Coves, passing a gondola going the other way, a motor-powered gondola with the pilot in a Venetian striped jersey and a straw gondolier's hat. The steaming tourists in the gondola drooped like dead dandelions.

'Remember Corky Peebles from my club?' Tess lowered her oversized sunglasses to peek at Winnie, who leaned back, steering with his bare feet.

'Which one was she? The other blonde?'

'No, the one with the bobbed black hair and the gorgeous body.'

'Oh yeah. The one that looked at me like I was a strange spot on a hotel pillowcase. I remember her.'

'If she were with us, she could do a running commentary of who lives in which house, as long as it's someone with a net worth of more than ten million.'

'Why just ten? Why not FFH numbers?'

'There's only a handful of those in the harbor, but there's a lot of the others.'

'Seven-one-four rich, right?'

'You learn fast.'

'Told ya I wasn't too dumb, lady,' Winnie said, holding a cold beer to his face and letting the water drops fall on to his chest.

'And as far as *Forbes*' Four Hundred, well, if someone slips three places, or jumps two on that list, Corky knows about it. And knows if he plays, or if his wife plays, and with whom. She's always ready to strike when there's an opportunity.'

'Tell me, Tess,' Winnie said, noticing for the first time that her hands were older than the rest of her. 'What would it take for someone like . . . like Corky to be content?'

'The Sultan of Brunei couldn't make Corky content.'

'Well, yeah, but let's take someone like . . .'

'Me, you mean.'

'OK, you.'

'How much is your pension worth?'

'Come on, I'm serious.'

'OK, seriously, I don't need much. If I'd gotten my father's ranch I would've waited till it appreciated and sold it and bought a condo and scraped by. Now, well, I'll have to do what you're going to do. I'll have to get a job. And I've never had one.'

'In your life?'

'In my life. Men've always taken care of me. First Daddy, then my three husbands. Men who treated me like a Rolls-Royce hood ornament.'

Later, when Winnie passed Harbor Island on the main channel side, Tess said, 'There. That's the best location on the water as far as I'm concerned. I used to think my inheritance would be large enough to buy a house on Harbor Island, a house that didn't need too much remodeling. One with a nice lawn.'

'How much would that cost now?'

'With a turning basin view? Oh, six or seven, I suppose. For a decent one.'

'Million?'

'Of course. The guy who bought the John Wayne house has a hundred and twenty-seven foot mega-yacht worth *ten* million.'

'You were expecting *that* kind of bucks when your father died, and you got nothing, right? So tell me, how

195

the hell could those two old guys spend so much?'

'You'd have to ask Warner Stillwell. I've asked him and he just shrugs it off. Refers to all the cruises and the villas they leased in the south of France and Portofino. That sort of thing.'

Winnie steered quietly for a long time. It was very hard for him to conceptualize real wealth. And to realize that by Golden Orange standards Conrad P. Binder wasn't even all that rich. The old family home in Bayshores was a scraper, according to Tess, torn down within a week after the new buyer cleared escrow. Winnie finally had to concede that he simply had no idea what it meant: rich.

Then Winnie began thinking about the hot mommas. What would they do on a day like this? Maybe they'd go up to South Coast Plaza or Fashion Island to browse in air-conditioned shops. How much would they spend?

Suddenly it occurred to him. 'Know what?'

'What?'

'I lived around here all my life and I never even bought so much as a pair of socks up there in Fascist Island. Imagine that!'

'That *is* amazing,' she said.

He nibbled on a sandwich and drank beer. Tess occasionally ate a carrot or a celery stick and sipped Chardonnay. Winnie noticed that the wine had a store sticker price of $25.95 so she couldn't be *that* broke. He had less money than that to tide him over until the next pension check arrived.

Winnie kept the boat in lower Newport Bay, though he preferred the natural beauty of the upper bay, where there was still undeveloped land and lots of wildlife. Winnie's grandfather had helped float the barge Theda Bara rode on there, during the filming of *Cleopatra*. But Winnie figured the back bay would be a few degrees hotter so he decided to avoid it.

There were over sixty thousand boats in Orange County, but few were cruising the harbor in these melt-down Santa Ana conditions. By the Lido peninsula they cruised past a Feadship, a 102-foot motor yacht.

'I've been on that boat,' she said. 'It's a Van Lent design from Holland. Steel built. The plumbing's gold plated. Even the screws're gold plated!'

'A lotta that around here,' Winnie said. 'Gold plating.'

On such a hot windless day, without billowing spinna-kers and flashing catamarans and wind surfers, Winnie wasn't as distracted as he would've been with sailboats to admire. He began thinking about murder.

Neither of them had yet brought up today the subject of Conrad Binder, or the gunshot in the desert, or the man loitering across the channel from Linda Isle.

She was the first. She said, 'Have you thought about it, Win? Hack Starkey watching my house? That gun-shot?'

'I can't put it together,' he said. 'It jist doesn't shake itself down to anything logical. Why would Warner Stillwell or anyone associated with him – like this guy Starkey – why would he want to see you dead? He's already got everything.'

'Everything isn't that much to begin with, since they apparently managed to spend all Daddy's money during the years between his retirement and his death.'

'How much do you figure that was?'

'I have no idea. Several million. Maybe more. I just don't know.'

'How much is the ranch actually worth?'

She paused and said, 'A house and a few acres? A bit more than a million. Land's not as valuable out there as it would be near Palm Desert or Rancho Mirage.'

'So by *your* standards, even if he didn't already have the land, that wouldn't be enough to kill over?'

'That's very little money.' She smiled. 'By *my* standards.'

'But he's got the ranch. So what would he gain? See, it just doesn't work out.' Winnie paused for a moment and said, 'You got a copy of the will?'

'Of course,' she said.

'Can I have a look when we get back?'

'You can have anything I've got,' Tess Binder said.

Tess said she wanted to go outside the jetty, which Winnie had planned on avoiding in that he'd have to cruise past Little Corona, the beach where Conrad Binder had ended his life. He stayed on the peninsula side of the main channel when he passed, staying as far as possible from Little Corona Del Mar Beach. He watched her with sidelong glances, but she never turned her head in that direction.

When they got out of the breakwater, past the jetty, past the five-mile-per-hour speed limit, he throttled forward. The nose lifted and the boat planed. He sped down past Corona Del Mar, past Pelican Point, and Arch Rock, so covered with bird guano it looked snowcapped. The inky water changed to aquamarine along that stretch of coastline, and the beaches near Cameo Shores were dotted with people lying at the base of the sandstone cliffs, hoping for relief from the heat.

The chop got a bit severe halfway to Laguna and they were getting bounced around, so Tess suggested they turn back. But before reaching the jetty once again, Winnie steered around the green bell buoy marking the harbor entrance. Five ocher-colored California sea lions lay on top of each other on the buoy: three females and two big bulls. The bell was clanging with each wave, wake and swell, the tapper only inches from the heads of the sea lions, who didn't seem to mind.

'Back when I was a kid, one big guy, Quasimodo I called him, used to lay there all the time,' Winnie said. 'All day long with that bell clanging in his ears. Had to've gone deaf after a while. Big ugly old guy. Wonder what happened to old Quasimodo?'

The sea lions ignored the boat, as they did all boats that didn't get close enough to deliberately frighten them. And they wisely ignored the trash that people tried to feed them.

'My dad and me used to rent a little boat at the pavilion and fish out here. Those were the best days of my life. Those days fishing. Jist my dad and me.'

Winnie noticed that one of the sea lions had a fishing line wrapped around her neck, slicing deep into her flesh. He pointed to the animal.

'What's wrong?'

'She's got a line wrapped around her. She'll get infected, maybe die, if she doesn't get help. Assholes! They drown them in their gill nets! They hook them! They strangle them with their lines! *Assholes!*'

Suddenly Winnie turned the boat toward the jetty and gave it throttle.

'What're you doing?'

'We gotta report this right away,' Winnie said. 'She needs help.'

Tess started to say something, but decided not to, Finally she smiled a little and said, 'Aye, aye, skipper. Straight ahead. It's the only course you'd *ever* steer.'

By the time they got back to Linda Isle and Winnie had called the National Marine Fisheries Services, and buttoned up the neighbor's runabout, Tess said it was cocktail time. She poured drinks for herself and Winnie while he took a shower. When he came down there was a double vodka for him on the glass table in the patio, along with a sheaf of documents.

'I'll just have a bath,' Tess said, 'while you look through all that stuff.'

The traffic was heavy on Pacific Coast Highway, an endless line of cars leaving the beach at day's end, heading inland, back to the more stifling heat. Winnie's glass sweated a puddle almost immediately, and he splashed a few drops on to the documents when he put the glass down. He wiped the page on his shirt and began to read the last will and testament of Conrad Philip Binder, Jr.

The first two pages were legalese, and then came the interesting part. The estate of Conrad Binder had been left to his trust, with Warner Daniel Stillwell as executor. The most significant paragraph was offset:

I hereby leave my ranch, commonly known as *El Refugio*, in the county of Riverside near La Quinta, to my friend and companion Warner Stillwell for his use as resident of said property during the remainder of his life. Upon his death the property shall be distributed to my daughter, Tess. If Tess does not survive Warner Stillwell, the property shall be distributed outright to him.

Winnie had started on his second tub of vodka when Tess came down in a terry robe with a towel wrapped around her wet hair.

'Boring reading, isn't it?' she said.

'Not all that boring.'

'Why do you say that?' She sat down with her drink and looked disgustedly at her ghetto view: Pacific Coast Highway and the riverboat restaurant, probably jammed to the gunwales with tourists.

'You never told me you were going to get the ranch eventually.'

'I thought I did.'

'You didn't.'

'Well, I get it after Warner's gone. Believe me, I could be an old lady by then. He's got Ronald Reagan genes.'

'Are you aware Warner Stillwell gets the property if you die?'

'Of course I'm aware of it. But he already *has* the property.'

'Yeah, but he can't dispose of it. He can't sell it. He can't eat it. He can't blow it up. He can only use it. As a residence.'

'So what? That's all he *wants* it for. That's his home. Aside from a quite humble bungalow in Laguna Beach, that's all he's got.'

'Maybe he's sick a living out there in his desert paradise. Maybe he's lonely for . . . Oh, for boys, let's say.'

'There's lots and lots of boys in Palm Springs.'

'Maybe he likes the Laguna boys better, I don't know. The point is, he might be tired a living out in the desert and he's only got a handful a years left and he wants to live them in Laguna. Or where did you say they rented those villas?'

'The south of France, near Nice. And Portofino, in Italy.'

'Yeah, so the only way he could *sell* that property is if he outlives you.'

Tess got up and started pacing nervously. She put her drink down and sat again. 'Winnie, you can't turn this into a murder conspiracy! *El Refugio*'s not worth that much.'

'Three acres? A house like that? Maybe you're wrong. Maybe it's worth more than you think?'

'People don't murder other people for that kind of money!'

Winnie looked at Tess for irony, but saw none. He couldn't even address that statement. Rich people!

Winnie said, 'Tess, I've known people who'd kill you for . . .'

'But not people like Warner Stillwell.'

'People like *you*, you mean. And your dad, and all the other folks you grew up with.'

'I know it sounds terrible to you but that *is* what I mean. That's just *not* a lot of money!'

'Who's this lawyer Martin Scroggins?'

'Daddy's lawyer. And now Warner's. And mine if I need him. His firm's been in business since my grand-

202

father's day. A very respectable Los Angeles firm, with an office here in Newport.'

'I'd like you to talk to Mister Scroggins.'

'About what?'

'This will.'

'Do you want me to ask him if the selling price of a small ranch is enough for me to fear for my life?'

'I wanna help you, Tess.'

'I'm sorry,' she said, and patted his hand. 'I don't mean to be flip, it's just that I'm trying to pretend I'm not scared. That man watching my house . . . I don't know. It's got me unnerved!'

'I can't stay here guarding this place forever.'

'Why not?'

That one stopped him. He thought he'd see that mischievous grin of hers, but all he saw was a pair of gray eyes behind tortoiseshell glasses. Unfathomable gray eyes. Like pebbles on the beach, washed clean by surging tides.

'I *would* like you to talk to Scroggins.'

'OK, I will. Tell me what to ask.'

'I want you to be absolutely sure there're no stocks, bank accounts or other real property that your dad owned.'

'But a laywer would have to tell me about that. He *would've* told me about that.'

'Can you go see him?'

'Let's both go tomorrow.'

'A phone call'll do. Lawyers turn on the meter the second you make an appointment.'

'They do the same thing with phone calls, believe me.'

Winnie bent forward then, testing his back gingerly. 'Let's go inside,' he said. 'I gotta stretch out flat for a while. My back's got more kinks than a lawyer's conscience.'

While Winnie lay supine on the floor of Tess's living room watching the six-thirty world news on TV, Buster Wiles made a run to Spoon's Landing looking for Winnie Farlowe. Buster found the zoo howling as usual, and the zookeeper perched on a stool behind the long bar. Spoon's voice droned endlessly about the twenty bucks he'd bet that the Edmonton Oilers couldn't shut out the Great Gretzky even once during the Stanley Cup play-offs.

The rest of the bar conversation centered on the 4.6 earthquake that had struck Newport Beach at 1.07 p.m. that afternoon. Not a big quake, but the two jolts felt powerful; the epicenter was right on the Newport-Inglewood fault. The outrigger hanging from Spoon's ceiling had to be rewired to the termite-infested ceiling timbers, and Spoon had lost a dozen glasses and a picture frame that held one of the last-known photos of Al Jolson, the family's favorite singer when Spoon was growing up. Spoon always said that he hoped Jolson's ex-wife, Ruby Keeler – who often came to The Golden Orange during the summer – wouldn't write an exposé of Al Jolson just because there was a natural title in it: Mammy Dearest.

Of course, Buster hadn't felt the earthquake, in that he was too busy out on the street being attacked by canaries and lovebirds. He wondered now if maybe the earthquake had made him less surefooted while he was chasing the

Asian thief. Maybe he'd actually gotten dumped by Mother Nature, not by Cockatoo Clyde.

Buster explained his battered condition by telling the denizens of Spoon's Landing all about his day's misery, but leaving out the part about Betsy, refusing even to *think* about that cassette. The big cop was so despondent he ordered one of Spoon's 'pizzas', prepared and frozen every Thursday by the saloonkeeper himself when he got his delivery of cheese and pepperoni from a guy in Costa Mesa, and a load of anchovies from one of the crew who manned the fishing boats that do the full and half-day runs out of Newport Harbor.

Bilge O'Toole, who'd closed his live-bait shop early that day, heard Buster place the order. And when Spoon was out of earshot, he said to the cop, 'When was the last time you ate one a Spoon's pizzas, Buster?'

'I don't remember,' Buster said. 'I musta been drunk if I did it.'

'They're tougher'n fiberglass, but they don't smell as good,' Bilge informed him.

Tripoli Jones, sitting on the other side of Buster, concurred. 'The anchovies must come from Alaska. Nothin that didn't die in an oil spill could taste like that. Put a dozen of 'em in a juicer, you could pour it in your crankcase.'

'I don't care *what* it tastes like,' Buster mumbled. 'I ain't that hungry anyways after the day I put in.'

'So save it for the beach,' Bilge suggested. 'Use it for a boogie board. Where were you when the earthquake hit?'

Tripoli Jones said, 'I was up on a pole by city hall gettin ready to check a line when the pole started to cha-cha. I did a lumberjack slide. My hands got so shaky I coulda threaded a sewin machine if it was movin. I had to come straight here for a drink!'

Spoon logged that as the most novel drinking excuse of the year so far: *An earthquake made me do it.*

'I started praying,' Carlos Tuna said. 'Regis got tossed off the kitchen table and pinballed out on to the porch. I started saying Hail Marys. I thought it was the *big* one!'

Spoon moved his slimy cigar stub from one side of his mouth to the other, and said: 'A day to go down in Newport Beach history. A town where every thirty feet there's a bar or a bank, with more masseuses than the Ottoman empire. Fifteen square miles a greed and white-collar crime. And people *finally* pray because of a little four-point-sixer!'

'Well, in Lubbock, Texas, two hundred forty-seven people saw the Virgin Mary this month!' Carlos said. 'Weird stuff's going on. I think the end is near.'

'If the end is near, I wanna *live* a little before I go,' Buster said to his beer glass. 'Gimme a double shot a Wild Turkey, Spoon.'

'Careful, Buster,' Bilge warned. 'You'll be gettin those three a.m. visitors like your pal Winnie. Like the ones Carlos gets, and Guppy. Me, I only get 'em on Tuesdays, Thursdays and sometimes on Monday. They don't come on weekends.'

'Nobody gets in my place at three a.m.,' Buster said, ''less they can do it with a gut full a hollow-points.'

'The ones Bilge's talkin about ain't scared a guns,' Carlos informed Buster. 'He's talkin about *life*! The old lady you still love? The one you still hate? The kids that never call you even on Christmas? The boss that spends his Sunday multiplying loaves and fishes but comes to

206

work on Monday like *The Nightmare on Elm Street*?'

'That's what my three o'clock dreadlies look like, come to think of it,' Tripoli Jones said. 'But they're wimps and pussies compared to the *real* monster you face at three o'clock in the morning. Your *youth*. The youth that was me. The me I lost!'

Buster Wiles was having a major epiphany. He said, 'I'm almost forty-five already. Forty-five! I can't believe it. Where's *my* youth?'

'You got some good years left, Buster,' Carlos said. 'But not as many as you think. It's gonna all start to go soon. Them big muscles a yours? They're gonna fall like ethics in Washington. Better take charge a your life now, if you can.'

'You get our age,' Guppy said, 'your life'll be more outta control than Central Park.'

'And then your blood pressure starts to take off,' said Tripoli Jones. 'And it's harder to bring down than Fidel Castro.'

'One day you look at yourself,' said Carlos. 'You say to yourself, people know me for miles around. But that's *all* I got!'

'Shit, they don't know you for *blocks* around, even,' Bilge O'Toole said, getting predictably surly, turning on his nemesis, Carlos Tuna.

Becoming more surly yet – and *that* was as predictable as beach litter – was Tripoli Jones, who said, 'The fuckin guy two stools away don't know you and you been drinkin here for fifteen years!'

Buster Wiles left the fiberglass pizza on the bar, finished his drink, and decided to get out now that the geezers might be drunk enough to start a fight.

For the rest of the evening he was determined to enjoy what was left of his youth. He was going to take better care of himself and pump iron two hours every other day and cut the booze down to almost nothing. In effect, Buster Wiles was making that career decision to take on a job that would change his life.

14: *Zeros*

By the weekend, the heat wave was breaking, at least in The Golden Orange. Los Angeles was still uncomfortable and the desert was a furnace, but the coastal communities had begun to settle down to more normal temperatures. Winnie had made only two brief trips to his apartment during that entire weekend. Sometimes it would seem as though Tess had forgotten about the man who'd been watching her house, but when Winnie would suggest that he go home so she could tend to ordinary business, she'd look frightened and beg him to stay.

'I need to be baby-sat,' she said, and yet when he'd look for fear in her eyes he'd see only gray pebbles.

When she'd wrap those strong arms around his neck and work him over with her muscular tongue, Winnie didn't look for anything.

On Monday morning they got up early to keep a hastily arranged appointment with Martin Scroggins, attorney-at-law. By mutual agreement they had a breakfast meeting at the yacht club, the one formerly commodored by Conrad P. Binder, Senior, where Scroggins himself had been a member for more than forty-five years.

'Seems strange to come in the front door,' Tess said to Winnie as they walked through the corridor. 'I used to always arrive by boat when I was a kid. They put up with a lot of nonsense from me and my chums in those days.'

The club was done in blue and white fifties nautical, like most of the older yacht clubs, with racing trophies and a sailboat model on display, and the corridors lined with pictures, dating back several generations, of commodores in blazers and brass buttons and yachtsman caps.

Tess paused before a portrait of a handsome sunburnt commodore with a long straight nose and round glasses and a stern expression.

'My grandfather,' she said. 'I think Daddy was disappointed when *he* never became a commodore too. That's probably why he seldom came here during the last ten years of his life.' Then she added, 'Of course, he couldn't see that he never had a chance of being commodore after he . . . after Mother died and he took on Warner as his companion.'

'Did he have a blind spot about Warner?'

'In most ways,' Tess said. 'Like many men of his generation with a . . . confused sexual identity, Daddy thought other people wouldn't guess. He could be very naïve, my father.'

The patio offered a panoramic view of the turning basin, where there was decent wind but little boat activity on a Monday morning. They sat at a table under a blue umbrella, and Tess switched to sunglasses with white frames. She wore a white linen dress with a double row of black vertical buttons and black scalloped trim across the shoulders. To Winnie she seemed overdressed compared to the other more casually attired breakfasters at the yacht club.

Winnie saw an older man emerge from inside and look toward the tables, blinking in the bright sunlight. He said, 'That must be Scroggins. He's all gray, just like I imagined.'

It was true. Martin Scroggins wore a gray suit, a gray silk tie with the tiniest of patterns, and his thinning hair, absent the rinse popular with men his age at Tess's club, was the color of a tarnished butter knife.

'Good eye, Officer,' Tess said. 'That's Martin, all right.'

'He's so invisible he stands out,' said Winnie.

Scroggins saw Tess, waved and quickly came to their table, giving her a peck on the cheek. He was so tall he had to duck under the blue umbrella to shake hands with Winnie.

When they were seated Martin Scroggins immediately signaled to a waitress for coffee and menus. He was not a man to lollygag.

'Have you been well, Tess?' he asked.

'Well enough.'

'Yes, I was sorry to hear about your divorce.'

'Be sorry for the last two,' Tess said. 'Not this one. Ralph Cunningham was a real bastard.'

Scroggins gave Tess a patient understanding nod. He looked to be a man with an understanding of *all* the Binder problems, Winnie thought.

'I had hopes he'd be the one for you, Tessie,' Scroggins said. 'I know your father hoped so too.'

'Daddy hated Ralph's guts.'

That embarrassed the elderly lawyer. He cleared his throat and took a sip of water.

Tess said, 'Winnie's a retired Newport Beach police-man, Martin. I wonder if you two ever saw each other in a courtroom?'

'Can't say that I ever tried a criminal case around here,' Scroggins said, smiling at Winnie. 'Oh, occasionally when a client would have a problem with one of his kids, I might attempt to get a drunk driving reduced to a reckless. Something like that.'

'Don't think we ever met,' Winnie said.

When the menus came Martin Scroggins ordered a very hearty breakfast. Tess asked for a slice of toast, no butter.

Winnie said to Tess, 'I'm gonna have an omelet. Even though I know it won't beat *your* omelets.' He saw that Martin Scroggins didn't miss the implication of Tess having made breakfast for him.

When the waitress was gone Scroggins said, 'How can I help you, Tessie?'

'It's about Daddy's will, Martin. I have a few questions about the trust giving *El Refugio* to Warner for the remainder of his life.'

Martin Scroggins glanced at Winnie again, very uncomfortably.

'Winnie's aware of everything,' Tess said. 'It's all right, Martin.'

'Yes, well, a trust by its nature is a device whereby some taxes can be saved and the property can be controlled. The decedent's wishes will be honored, and, believe me, your father was adamant about his wishes.'

'No, you don't understand,' Tess said. 'I guess what I'm trying to find out is, how is it that there was so *little* in the estate?'

'What do you mean?'

'Well, I only got two hundred and fifty thousand.'

'Yes, but your father believed Ralph Cunningham would do right by you during the term of your marriage. He didn't think you'd *need* much money. After all, Cunningham's worth quite a lot.'

'Are you saying Daddy didn't anticipate that my third marriage mightn't outlast our champagne bubbles?'

'Exactly. He thought you were . . . well, as he put it, *mellowing*.'

'He wouldn't put it that way. *Maturing*, you mean.'

Scroggins didn't say anything.

Tess said, 'All right, so he thought that a quarter of a million should keep a well-married lady in necessities through Warner's lifetime?'

'I think so,' Martin Scroggins said. 'In any case, your father and I both knew Warner well enough to agree that if something *did* happen, some emergency or need, Warner would do whatever he could for your well-being. Your father even told me that if you ever found yourself divorced again or in dire financial straits, Warner'd welcome you to live *with* him. Warner loves you like his own, Tessie.'

'Dear God!' Tess Binder said, taking her cigarettes from her purse. 'Living at the ranch? Me? Dear God!'

Scroggins was very uneasy. He signaled to a waitress for more coffee. While the young woman poured, he said to Tess, 'Your father's thinking was sound, in my opinion. It's quite common for a trustor to leave his estate to his wife as a life tenant to use for her lifetime, and then to his child in fee after his wife passes away.'

'And Warner was his wife,' she said matter-of-factly.

Martin Scroggins cleared his throat and said, 'Surely, you can't be having money troubles?' He glanced at Winnie again, but Winnie looked away and drank his coffee in silence.

'Surely, I *am*,' Tess said. 'Ralph was a swine. His prenuptial agreement is unbreakable. He gave me nothing but household things.'

'Well, perhaps until you're on your feet, you might consider talking to Warner. Really, he could *use* you out there now. He's lonely with your father gone. It's only him and the servants.'

'Have you been to *El Refugio* lately?'

'No, not since your dad died.'

For the first time, Winnie spoke. He said, 'Do you know Hack Starkey?'

Martin Scroggins looked wary. He said, 'Yes, I know him. I should say I know *of* him. I can't remember ever actually meeting him.' The old man looked back at Tess and said, 'He did odd jobs for your father and Warner, I believe.'

'Mostly for Warner,' Tess said. 'He was Warner's man Friday.'

Scroggins dropped his eyes while sipping his coffee, and said, 'I wouldn't know about what services he may have performed. There was certainly no provision for anyone else in the trust. Just you and Warner. And even if Warner, as life tenant, and you as remainderman, were to agree to change or terminate the trust, in my opinion, it can't be done. The trustor, your father, specifically addressed that possibility. He knew what he wanted.'

Martin Scroggins brightened when breakfast came. He had a hearty appetite for an older man, and after waiting just long enough to be polite, he wolfed his breakfast while Tess made small talk with Winnie.

Winnie ate quickly, only saying to Tess, 'This can't touch your omelet. Your *killer* omelet.'

Tess winked at Winnie when Scroggins was occupied with dipping a slab of ham into egg yolk. Then she said,

'Things're always better when they're made on an old-fashioned kitchen table.'

After the lawyer obsessively mopped up the last drop of yolk, he said, 'Tessie, so far, I don't know if I've been very helpful to you.'

Tess said, 'You see, Martin, I can understand how Daddy would think I was being provided for by my husband, and that a pittance would suffice.'

'A quarter of a million,' Martin reminded her.

'Is a pittance these days and you know it.' She added, 'Around here.'

'Once again, I could suggest the ranch,' Martin Scroggins said. 'Why it's . . .'

'A living hell in the summer!' she said. 'And limbo the rest of the time.'

Martin Scroggins was clearly disappointed. 'Your father and Warner wouldn't agree with that. Neither would I.'

Tess reached over and patted his hand. His fingers were extremely long, and pencil veins crisscrossed the hands, petering out at the jutting wristbones. 'I didn't mean to sound like a brat,' she said. 'It's just that I've been abandoned. I don't *have* anything, Martin, except for the equity in my house.'

When Scroggins glanced at Winnie again, Winnie said apologetically, 'This is the only shirt I got without a fuzzy collar or a hole in it. Usually, I dress like a shipwreck. I couldn't feed a pet gerbil.'

Tess smiled at Winnie and said to the lawyer, 'For once, I haven't latched on to a man who can help me. Not in that way. He helps me in every other way.'

Martin Scroggins got very serious. 'I'm trying to understand what I can do, Tess.'

'Martin, is there anything . . . anything else that could be converted into cash? I mean, aside from *El Refugio*, which I realize can't be sold during Warner's lifetime.'

'What are you saying? Do you think I'd withhold information from you?'

'No no no,' Tess said quickly. 'But, I don't know how . . . I just can't *believe* they could have devastated Daddy's money in only six or eight years! It's incredible that there wouldn't be anything left except the cash I got and enough for Warner to live on.'

'Tessie, they *didn't* devastate his fortune!' the lawyer said. 'Sure, they traveled a lot and lived very well, but your father was entitled to that. He earned that money. And Warner certainly wasn't left with some vast secret bank account after your dad died. I believe there's enough to cover bills and enough to run the ranch for several years.' Then he showed his first bit of exasperation. He said, 'Tess, that ranch isn't Warner's. It's *yours*. Or it will be when Warner's gone. Your father didn't abandon you!'

'But Martin, where did all the *cash* go?' Now Tess was showing exasperation. 'That's what I want to know.'

'The ranch!' he said. '*El Refugio*, of course.'

'What're you talking about? A three-acre spot of green in the middle of the desert?'

Suddenly Martin Scroggins stopped toying with his crust of toast. He stared at her for a moment to see if she was being serious. 'You don't mean *three* acres.'

Tess looked befuddled. 'Of course that's what I mean.'

'Tessie,' said Martin Scroggins, 'your father bought land from his neighbor in nineteen seventy-one. The

216

neighbor was a speculator who'd gotten in enormous trouble and needed liquidity.' Then he stopped and said, '*Surely* you know all about this!'

Tess Binder leaned forward in her chair and said, 'Martin, this is the *first* I've ever been told about an additional land purchase.'

Scroggins was unraveling. He looked from one to the other and back again. 'But . . . but I don't understand!' he said. 'I assumed . . . no, I was told! I distinctly remember that I was *told* by Warner Stillwell during a telephone conversation that you were aware your dad's liquid assets were used to buy the land. It was such an incredible bargain. A steal, really. He said that he and you and your father had discussed it!'

'How . . . much . . . land . . . did my father buy with those monies?' Tess demanded.

They even *talked* different, Winnie thought: *those monies*.

The old lawyer's voice was suddenly weak. He said, 'Why, half a section. Three hundred and twenty acres. But Tessie . . . how could you *not* know?'

'*You* never told me!'

Winnie discovered that he was leaning forward himself, staring at the unblinking sky-blue eyes of Martin Scroggins, looking for a hint of duplicity, but seeing none.

'Tessie, I've been in practice for forty-seven years,' the lawyer said. 'I would *never* withhold any part of a transaction from a party who . . .'

'Why didn't you send a copy of the deed with my copy of the will when Daddy died?' Tess pressed ever forward while the old lawyer retreated.

'It was *there*, Tess! After the estate closed and I recorded the probate decree, I sent the decree to Warner. And a copy to *you*! My God, Tess, could my secretary have . . .'

Then he stopped and Winnie knew he was thinking: my secretary! That bitch! What? How?

'I got the copy of the trust and the will,' Tess said. 'There was *no* copy of a decree in there describing the assets.'

'I can't explain this!' the lawyer said, and when he raised the cup to his lips, his long bony hand was trembling. 'I assure you that Warner told me you knew all about the decision to buy the land. After all, it'll revert to you someday. Why would Warner tell me that? I don't understand! I've got to phone him!'

'I take it that Daddy himself never told you I was aware of the purchase of hundreds of acres?'

Scroggins paused and Winnie saw Tess watching the lawyer *very* closely. Finally the lawyer said, 'He *may* have. I can almost remember discussing it with Conrad on the phone. But I can *distinctly* remember discussing it with Warner.'

'But you can't say for sure that Daddy told you?'

'No, I can't, but I have a feeling he *must* have.'

She seemed to relax a bit. She leaned back in her chair and lit a cigarette. Martin Scroggins continued to stare and shake his head in disbelief.

'So,' he said, 'until this meeting you thought you were only going to inherit the house and a few acres of grove?'

'That's right,' Tess Binder said. 'That's exactly right.'

'I *must* contact Warner Stillwell immediately!' Martin Scroggins said.

Tess leaned forward so suddenly she bumped the table and the coffee spilled. 'No, you mustn't!' she said. 'This is something that . . . well, it's a family matter and I have to sort it out.'

'But I was your father's attorney! And I feel as though I'm *your* attorney even though I've never represented you directly. My God, Tess, you were unaware of the dimensions of your future inheritance, and I feel responsible! I've got to find out how it happened. How you *wouldn't* have received your copy of the recorded deed. I mailed it to you, let me see, a very short time after your father died.'

Tess asked, 'In the same envelope as the will and the trust?'

He thought for a moment and said, 'No, a bit later. I think. But you see, I assumed, I mean, I'd been *told* you knew all about the land purchase!'

'I'm not *blaming* you, Martin,' Tess said. 'I'm not blaming anyone. I just want to sort this out myself and I don't want you to get involved. Not yet. After I make an inquiry, then you can help me.'

'Yes, of course, I'll help,' he said. 'But Warner *told* me you knew about the land!'

'Yes, well, maybe both he and Daddy assumed the other one told me. Perhaps it was all a big mistake. Perhaps your letter with the copy of the deed was lost by the postman. We have so many new carriers these days.'

Winnie pitied the old man. He'd lost his aplomb completely. The lawyer looked at Winnie and said, 'How *could* it be a mistake?'

Tess turned to Winnie and said, 'Well, Win, I think we should let Martin get to his office, shouldn't we?'

Martin Scroggins was shaking his head and muttering when Tess leaned over and kissed his cheek. He stood up reflexively and Winnie put out his hand. The lawyer's palm was damp.

'Could I just ask one question?' Winnie asked.

'Yes, of course,' Martin Scroggins said.

'How much is the place worth now?'

'Well, I wouldn't know,' the lawyer said. 'You'll have to ask a broker out in La Quinta.'

'Any idea at all?'

'No,' said Martin Scroggins, 'except that Conrad believed that with PGA West having put in such a big development out there, the entire area was going to boom. He'd heard rumors of a big new airport and believed that with half a section he could find an eager developer, easily. That's land for a few hundred condos and an eighteen-hole golf course, which is what Conrad had in mind.'

'So, he didn't give you a *round* number?'

'No, but it's one of the last choice areas reasonably close to Palm Springs. I believe he'd tested the water with a developer from Rancho Mirage and turned down fifty-five thousand.'

Winnie said, 'For all that land?'

'Fifty-five thousand an *acre*,' said the lawyer.

Winnie said, 'Fifty-five . . .' It stopped him cold. 'That's too many zeros for me! The Japs didn't send that many zeros to Pearl Harbor!'

'By the time it becomes Tessie's it'll be worth twenty to thirty million,' said the lawyer. 'There can only be one *other* explanation for all this . . .' He hesitated, glancing at Winnie again.

'We've gone *this* far, Martin,' she said, 'so speak your mind.'

'It might be that your father thought you *still* weren't

ready. I mean . . . well, three marriages? A life that's been . . .'

'Unproductive?'

'Yes, you know how he . . . doted on you.'

'Not from my point of view. I paid a price, being his only child.'

'Well, it might be that he and Warner decided you shouldn't know about the extent of your father's estate. That it'd be better for you to think your inheritance would be a more modest one.'

'That doesn't explain Warner's failure to notify me *after* Daddy's death, does it? And the fact that the copy of the land deed never arrived in my hands.'

'I simply *cannot* explain that part of it,' the lawyer said.

Neither spoke until they were halfway to Linda Isle in Tess's car. Then Winnie said, 'I think we jist found a motive for what's been going on.'

'Yeah,' she said. 'Warner didn't plan to live out his days in Daddy's refuge. Warner must have *other* ideas, connected somehow with Hack Starkey.'

'I'll tell you one thing, lady,' Winnie said. 'I'd work partners with you anytime. I've seen veteran detectives do a lot worse in an interrogation. That old man's scared you'll slap a malpractice lawsuit on him.'

'I just hope he keeps his mouth shut,' she said. 'I want *you* to tell me what to do about Mister Warner Stillwell.'

'I don't think that lawyer's gonna blab anything to anybody,' said Winnie. 'He's glad you're not mad at him. Far as you're concerned he'll be quiet as a snowfall.'

When they were near Tess's club, Winnie looked at his watch and said, 'Think it's late enough for a drink?'

221

Tess kept her eyes on the road and said, 'Whatever you say, old son.'

'Might help me to relax and think clearer. A beer maybe.'

'Or two?'

Winnie said, 'You don't think I'm an alcoholic, do you?'

'Don't get paranoid. There's a big difference between a heavy drinker and an alcoholic.'

'Sure, it's when booze starts swinging a wrecking ball at your life.'

'Right,' Tess said, glancing at him. Not with disapproval, he was sure of it.

The valet-parking kid who took Tess's Mercedes nodded at Winnie in recognition. He was starting to feel part of it all: The Golden Orange!

While they were still at the yacht club, during a silence when Martin Scroggins had been devouring his breakfast, Winnie had been eavesdropping on a foursome at the next table, discussing a *Los Angeles Times* story about the scientific world going coconuts over the claims of the Yank and the Brit who had either achieved cold fusion, or confusion, with less energy than it took to run their experiment. But if others in The Golden Orange were excited about science attempting to approximate the Promethean gift of fire, at *Tess*'s club events of greater significance to hot mommas were being breathlessly bandied about. A certain pair of houses had sold! Corky Peebles was practically hyperventilating when she spotted Winnie and Tess on the patio at a white table under an umbrella. Corky blazed a silicone trail across the deck, wearing a halter top, with breasts out to here, and shorts with a glittery blue anchor on each buttock. Every head in the place turned on its axis when she jiggled by.

'Did you hear!' she cried. 'The house across from Margie's is in escrow for nearly seven mil! That tops the price for John Wayne's place!'

'No, I hadn't heard,' Tess said.

'But that's *nothing*!' Corky breathed. 'The *other* one? The *big* one, sold to some . . .' When she thought about the ramifications of the buyer – FFH rich – she said, '. . . some Oriental gentleman for, are you ready? Fifteen million!'

'Truly unbelievable,' Tess said, trying to look unimpressed, but Winnie could see that she was. And why not, *he* was!

Tess said to Winnie, 'It's a nineteen-thousand-square-foot house with underground parking for nine cars.'

'And a twelve-thousand-bottle wine cellar,' Corky added.

'And a three-thousand-foot master bedroom,' said Tess.

'And it's got what they call poured-in-place concrete construction,' Corky said to Winnie, eyes alight. 'With steel I-beam construction. It can take a hit of *eleven* on the Richter scale!'

'If the next *is* an eleven, *that* guy's gonna be king a the coast,' Winnie said, and Corky's eyes went even wider.

'That's right!' she said. 'You're absolutely right!'

She wiggled her fingers then, and jetted back to the hot mommas on the other side of the patio, leaving a vapor of wrinkle cream in her wake.

'She's now finding out if the gentleman's married,' Tess said to Winnie, 'and whether he likes round-eyed women, and if there's anything new out of Cal Tech regarding earthquake predictions. If the big one comes and he's the

223

only rich man left she'll get him if she has to ride it out on a rubber dinghy.'

'I'm starting to like her,' Winnie said, *trying* not to gulp his beer. 'She's got more moves than Bekins Van Lines.'

Tess said, 'Don't get too comfortable around here with the likes of Corky. I don't get the ranch until Warner dies. Could be ten years. Maybe fifteen.'

Winnie said, 'Whaddaya mean by getting comfortable?'

'I'm not planning on letting you get away from me,' she said. 'But you'll have to wait a long time till I can afford a waterfront villa.'

Winnie gaped. She was barely smiling. She was gazing at him with gray pebble irises behind rose-tinted lenses. Wearing her white dress. The goddamn white dress!

'What's the matter, love?' she asked.

Winnie realized that his mouth was hanging open. He snapped his jaws shut and said, 'I guess I looked like a stroke victim, huh? One a those guys with his mouth frozen open like he's gonna laugh but it never comes? I guess I looked like that, huh?'

'Something wrong?'

He didn't mention the white dress. It made him feel dizzy to think about it. He wanted it to go away. That maddening sensation of *déjà vu*, something just beyond a curtain of white linen. Then it was *all* gone.

'Maybe it's what you said. Something made me drift. Becalmed. No wind for my sails. A sailor in irons.'

'Why?'

'Hearing you even *suggest* you're gonna hang in there with a guy like me? I mean, you might *think* you know what you're doing, but . . .'

Then Tess Binder leaned forward in her chair and

224

touched his hand the way she'd touched Martin Scroggins's hand. She said, 'Win, when I make up my mind about something, I always know *exactly* what I'm doing.'

She leaned even closer and kissed him. When she pulled back he glanced over at the hot mommas, at Corky Peebles, who saw the kiss and turned to her tablemates to whisper.

Winnie said, 'Corky's looking at me, thinking, a house jist sold for fifteen mil and Tess's playing kissy face with a guy that wears sneakers a Shangai longshoreman wouldn't be caught dead in.'

When Winnie excused himself to go to the restroom, Corky Peebles scurried back to Tess's table.

'You just *got* to tell me!' Corky demanded. 'Why *him?*'

Tess blew a cloud of smoke in Corky's direction and smiled mysteriously, saying nothing.

'*Why*, Tess?' Corky cried, her power bob bouncing in frustration. 'I mean, sure, he's sorta Our Gang cute, but he couldn't get mugged in Harlem!'

'Maybe he's a superb lover,' Tess said, broadening the smile that was driving Corky mad.

'Puh-leeese!' Corky cried. 'How could anybody in the whole wide world even *attempt* to reach orgasm with a guy that wears a Timex watch?'

When Winnie returned Corky waved bye-bye and wriggled away.

Tess said to Winnie, 'Want to talk about more *ordinary* things? Like murder?'

'Sure,' he said. 'You and me, that makes me start to sweat, and think about an old song I don't understand. Murder, *that* I can understand.'

Tess lit a cigarette and said, 'OK, here's how I see it:

Warner waited a discreet period of time, eight months after Daddy died. Now he wants to sell the ranch and go back to Portofino or wherever. But he can't. He can only live in it. Unless I die.'

'Wait a minute, Tess,' Winnie said. 'Start at the beginning. Your dad bought that land without you knowing. Must a cost him a few million, four or five maybe. So your father *didn't* blow his money. He invested most of it but jist didn't tell you.'

She puffed on a cigarette, looking toward the main channel beside the club. Except that her view was blocked by a large yacht fisher, custom built in Australia and said to have cost its owner three million dollars. And there were other *more* expensive yachts blocking the view from where they sat on the club patio.

Winnie followed her eyes and thought, That *is* the view here. Landlocked yachts. The ultimate in conspicuous consumption. The water itself is set decoration!

Finally she said, 'Yes, of course. From the beginning, here's how I explain it: Warner told Daddy that *he'd* discussed the land purchase with me. Daddy assumed that I knew all about it.'

'Something *that* important? Doesn't wash,' Winnie said. 'He'd talk it over with you himself, your father.'

'Remember, I told you that Warner was the dominant one in their relationship? Besides, Daddy had something more pressing on his mind.'

'What could be more pressing?'

'Maybe he was preoccupied with the HIV virus. He could've known about it for years.'

Winnie thought a while and said, 'That could obsess a guy for sure, but dumping all that cash in a huge land

226

purchase? Naw, he'd tell you if he wanted you to know.'

'OK then, goddamnit! Martin Scroggins was right! Daddy and Warner decided that I *shouldn't* know. That I was too . . . immature, and always had been. And when my marriage to Ralph Cunningham failed, as Daddy knew it would, *then* he'd tell me all about it. Then he'd tell me I wouldn't be a pauper after he was gone. That I'd be well provided for.'

'Yeah, I'd call that well provided for,' Winnie agreed.

'He probably developed symptoms last year. And he started thinking about it: AIDS. The dreadful agony. The . . . the *humiliation* of it. He couldn't see any way out except to take his gun and go back to where he'd been happiest, back here where he'd been a husband and a father . . .'

Tess stopped then and sniffled. Winnie waited a moment and said, 'OK, *that* scenario I can almost buy. A guy like your old man, living all those years in a closet . . .'

'He *thought* he was closeted. Of course, everyone knew.'

'Yeah, well, he had to get outta this world right away. I can see that part. And he figured after he was dead Warner'd let you know about the land. About how you'd be rich in a few years after Warner was gone.'

'Don't count on a *few* years, old son,' Tess said. 'Warner is an amazing physical specimen for a man of seventy-two.'

'Yeah, but you said he's probably got the virus, if not AIDS itself. Otherwise, how would your dad . . .'

Tess's chin trembled, so Winnie stopped right there. He signaled to the waitress. When she came over he looked at his watch and said, 'I'll have a vodka on the rocks. Polish if you got it. It's late enough.'

Tess at last addressed the painful subject. 'OK, let's assume that Daddy got the virus but Warner doesn't have it. Or, let's say they *both* have it but Warner's optimistic. Maybe he believes in that Tijuana AIDS clinic that claims to have a handle on it. Or he thinks a cure's on the way. He always was more of an optimist than Daddy. Let's assume he isn't about to kill himself. On the contrary, he's going to enjoy life. He wants to try to spend those millions in the years he has left. Now, go with *that* one.'

'Where you're trying to take me, I got trouble going,' Winnie said. 'See, all this would rest on a personality switch. Warner Stillwell's spent half a lifetime with your dad. Let's say, he only *pretended* to love your father because a the life-style he was provided with. Still, the man's over seventy. He's got it made the rest a the way, long as he stays on the ranch and continues what he's been doing, and . . .'

'Hack Starkey!' she interrupted. 'Maybe he's been heavily involved with Starkey. Maybe Starkey doesn't want to live on the ranch. Maybe he wants to do the things with Warner that Daddy did with Warner.'

'Return to Sorrento?'

'Something like that.'

'And Starkey persuades him that *you* gotta go, so the ranch can be Warner's to sell. But Starkey's not a professional killer and he butchers the shot he takes at you out on the trail. And he's a pretty sloppy guy on a surveillance too, when he's checking out your house.'

'Exactly.'

'I don't like it,' Winnie said. 'How do you explain the will and the trust arriving at your house, but *not* the land deed?'

'There was something I deliberately withheld from Martin Scroggins. Something that would've made him interrogate Warner Stillwell immediately, no matter what.'

'Yeah?'

'At the time those documents were sent, I was *staying* at the ranch. Arranging for the funeral at the desert cemetery after the coroner was through with Daddy's body. Making notifications. Doing a thousand little things. Helping to see Warner through his grief, at least I *thought* he was grieving.'

'Who had access to your mailbox on Linda Isle?'

'Anybody on the list I've given to the gate guards.'

'Who would that be?'

'A housekeeper comes in once a week, a girl from Guatemala who's worked around this island for years. Then there's the water delivery man. Corky Peebles and three other girlfriends're on the list as well. I put Ralph Cunningham on the list in case we had more business about the divorce. And Warner Stillwell, he's on the list. Hack Starkey could've come and claimed to be Warner Stillwell.'

'How would he get inside your house?'

'The maid and the service people get the key from the guard and return it when they've finished with their work. Warner and Daddy, they had their *own* key, in case they ever cared to drop in unexpectedly, but they never did. They were old-fashioned gentlemen who'd never come unannounced.'

'Would the gate guards keep the logs from last year? And would the logs have license numbers of your visitors?'

'I assure you our gate guards are not policemen.'

'OK, so Hack Starkey coulda got in and stolen that piece a mail. Still, I don't like the notion that Warner suddenly turned homicidal over big bucks because your dad *conveniently* killed himself. That's the part I don't like. I don't like convenience when it comes to a murder for profit. Which is *not* a crime of impulse.'

'At least you have a motive. A motive for murder.'

'What I'm thinking now is, I'd like to get rid of all the convenient events here. We been talking about a motive for *your* murder. How about all this being a continuing plot? For a double murder? Your father first, then you.'

Tess spilled her beer across the table. But she scooted back quickly enough to keep it from staining that white linen dress.

15: *Higher Power*

Buster Wiles wasn't sure if the hollow banging that woke him was from his erratic heartbeat or the cheap plumbing. He felt like he'd fought an orangutan in an elevator. He knew he'd be hurting in the morning, but not like this! From the neck down he was covered with ugly abrasions and bruises: purple, black and lime green. He couldn't remember ever bruising green before.

Worse than all of that was the hangover. Everything he couldn't see felt swollen and inflamed. His nerves twitched and danced. His hands seemed palsied, and every arhythmical heartbeat sloshed painfully to his head. Buster needed a surgical collar to support a skull this big.

Buster tried to take a cold shower but the jets hurt. He tried to dry with a soft towel but the towel hurt. Buster limped outside his apartment and stood naked on the back porch to dry in the sun, blinded by the light. He ran the risk of some kid on the way to school seeing him and maybe telling a teacher who might call the cops, but he figured the way things were going in California these days they'd probably need videotape of the crime as well as a signed confession that he waved his whanger before anybody would bother. That made him think of last night's news. The notorious McMartin Preschool Molestation Case was entering its third *year* in Los Angeles Superior Court, and had already cost the California tax-payers fifteen million dollars. If due process in California had come to three-year trials, why should *he* worry about the misdemeanour of exposing his shattered body on the back porch of a crummy apartment in Newport Beach, USA?

Buster was hurting too much to make coffee. So he just sat facing the morning sun and thought about Life, *his* life in The Golden Orange. About living in this little city with its police force of 145 officers, where the average cop can't afford to live if he wants a decent house. And how very soon there'd be only 144. He thought of many seemingly unconnected things. For instance, he thought of how he helped to protect one of the biggest Rolls-Royce dealerships in the world, he, the driver of a Ford Escort. He thought of how a Mercedes was considered a Chevy Nova around these parts, and if you don't at least drive a Lotus Turbo keep it to yourself, they say.

Buster Wiles knew that these disturbing thoughts were flooding his swollen brain because he needed to rationalize what he knew he was going to do. What he *had* to do if the remainder of his life was to have comfort and meaning and dignity. If he was to enjoy what was left of youth. If there was any of that left to a man of forty-five.

The time had come for Buster Wiles to address the Cop's Syllogism, which has led thousands of burned-out, overwhelmingly cynical members of the law enforcement business into alcoholism or drug addiction, police corruption or suicide.

The Cops' Syllogism is very simple and exceedingly dangerous: 'People are garbage. I am a person. Therefore . . .' Once it's consciously or unconsciously acknowledged and accepted, whatever follows is something *bad*.

And so at last, after months of grappling with a tottering superego, the conscience of Buster Wiles had at last collapsed, and lay like a bloated corpse in the surf. There was no turning back now. As soon as he was recovered from the ravages of this morning he would proceed with his 'career change'. He was going to take the assignment, absolutely.

'How are *you* today,' she said, hobbling down the alley.

Buster lowered his face from the sun's rays, but didn't move and he made no effort to cover his nakedness. He just sat there in a folding chair, almost dry enough to go in and get dressed, and looked blandly at the old crone pushing a shopping basket through the alley.

He'd never known where she lived. She wasn't exactly a bag lady, more of a pack rat, always wearing layers of dresses. Always pushing a shopping cart loaded with junk. The nameless old woman lived somewhere between Twenty-eighth and Thirty-third streets, near Winnie Farlowe, or so Buster supposed. Yet he wouldn't have been surprised if she owned ten thousand shares of Xerox. Around here, anything was possible.

Her stockings were rolled around ankles as white as the shells that lay on Buster's porch near a pair of black swim fins so old and rotten he didn't care if an alley thief stole them.

She looked over at Buster again and said, 'Fine, I hope.'

Buster said, 'Huh?'

'I just asked, how are you today?' said the nameless old woman. 'And you didn't answer.'

'I don't like trick questions,' said the utterly naked man, suddenly stricken with nausea.

233

The smell of food woke Winnie up. He knew at once she was making him a killer omelet. He jumped out of bed, for once not reluctant to slide from between those peach-colored sheets. He showered, shaved, put on a clean Reyn Spooner flowered shirt, jeans, and Top-Siders. Forget the socks; he didn't have to impress her any more. The omelet was ready by the time he got downstairs.

'We have become wonderful one-times-one,' she said. 'I don't even have to call you.'

'The killer omelet did the job.' He sat down expectantly. 'Don't you *ever* eat?'

'I haven't been going to my aerobics class. I don't dare eat.'

'I got regrets heavier than you,' he said. 'Not even a piece a toast?'

'I'll watch you eat and I'll drink coffee.'

The omelet wasn't perfect in that the jalapeños weren't fresh like the ones at the ranch. But Winnie told her it was heavenly, and when he'd finished he said, 'When am I going home again?'

'I'll let you know in a year or two.'

'Am I a prisoner here?'

'Yes.'

'Know one a the things I admire about you?' he said. 'I like how you talked to your cleaning lady yesterday afternoon. You aren't one a those women they're ever gonna call "Uh".'

'What do you mean?'

'Well, I been around these parts long enough to see how

Nouveau Newport talks to servants. Like, "Oh, call me Jill! *Don't* call me Mrs Roderick!" But the Salvadoran maid ain't about to *ever* call her Jill, so she ends up callin her "Uh". Gets real difficult sometimes when the maid's gotta yell for the lady a the house. She goes: "Uh! Uh! Telephone! Uh! You there, Uh?" You been dealing with servants all your life. You got no problem.'

'I know you well enough to guess that *you're* the one getting around to a problem.'

'What worries me is, what they're gonna call *me*. The help, I mean. If I keep hanging around with you? See, I look like Winnie. I talk like Winnie. I *am* . . .'

'A love. You're a love. Now stop worrying about our future together. Those things have a way of working out.'

'Or not,' he said.

'So what's our next move insofar as my problem is concerned? My little problem with murder?'

'OK,' Winnie said. 'First thing I wanna do is look through your dad's stuff. Specially his wallet. Maybe there's a name. A phone number.'

'Whose?'

'I don't know. That's why I gotta look. Or maybe a credit card receipt from when he bought gas on the way from the ranch to Little Corona Beach. And if not, I wonder how much gas was in his car when they found it.'

'It was parked by Ocean Boulevard, just above the beach. The keys were still in it. I guess a man doesn't worry about car theft if he's going to shoot himself. Warner had it driven back home to the ranch.'

'A killer might not worry about theft either, if he's in a hurry to unwrap and dump a body he's just taken outta the trunk.'

'Would it have taken two men to do it?'

'Almost certainly.'

'Hack Starkey and Warner? That's what you think?'

He shrugged and said, 'Can I see his stuff?'

She retrieved it from the hall closet: the cardboard box still bore the coroner's tape. Winnie took the box into the dining room so he could spread things out on the table.

'Do you mind if I go shopping while you look through his things? I haven't had the guts to open that box yet.'

'Sure, I understand,' he said.

After she'd gone Winnie looked at his watch and saw that it was absolutely not late enough to have a drink. So he had a beer. It was only a light beer, he told himself.

He sipped the beer while unfolding the clothing from the box: a short-sleeved shirt with a button-down collar. A pair of tan poplin trousers, cordovan loafers, blue cotton socks, boxer shorts. Everything was badly wrinkled and the shoes were caked with salt brine. Beach sand littered the bottom of the box.

The wallet was brown calfskin and its contents had been bagged separately. Winnie removed the credit cards, the driver's license, a photo of Tess wearing a mortarboard when she'd graduated from Stanford, a photo of Warner Stillwell as a young man, and ninety-six dollars in cash. He didn't find a gasoline receipt or anything remarkable in the wallet. He was disappointed that there was no address book.

He was folding up the clothes when he glanced in the box and saw it: half a shell. He retrieved it from the box and held it in his palm, a shell no larger than a pearly button. Winnie's heart started pounding almost as it had the evening he'd first seen a shell like this. Back when someone had fired gunshots, probably with evil intent.

Then Winnie found a *whole* shell caught in the cuff of Conrad Binder's trousers, where the cuff was stitched to the leg. He now held in his hand one-and-a-half freshwater shells from an ancient lake near a place called *El Refugio*.

He almost ran to his car to look for Tess, but he realized she could have gone anywhere to shop. He sat down to plan his next move. He picked up the telephone and called the Newport Beach Police Department to make an appointment with Detective Sammy Vogel. But before he left Tess Binder's house he poured three fingers of vodka. Just to calm his nerves.

The excitement mounted the moment he walked into the station. Winnie Farlowe was involved in police work again! Sort of. Then a teenager – one of the police cadets who work at the front desk – said, 'Can I help you, sir?' And he knew he was just another outsider.

Sammy Vogel took him to the lunchroom, where, at this time of day, they could have some privacy.

'How you keeping in the outside world, Win?' the detective asked, after he bought them both a cup of coffee.

'Can't complain,' Winnie said, sitting at what used to be his favorite table. He'd drunk a lot of coffee at this table.

'Glad to see you didn't get your dick trimmed for that Christmas caper?'

'Yeah, probation,' Winnie said. 'I can handle it.'

'So, what can I do for you?'

'It's about Conrad P. Binder? The guy that you fished out last summer?'

'Oh yeah,' Vogel said. 'What about him?'

'I'm sorta friendly with his daughter, and, uh, she has some ideas.'

'Yeah? About what?'

'Are you sure, *absolutely* sure he iced himself?'

'You mean could he've been capped by somebody else?'

'Yeah.'

'No way. I was there when they posted the body. There was stippling in his scalp.'

'Yeah, but somebody *else* coulda put the gun there and pulled the trigger,' Winnie said.

'The gun was found beside him, on the sand.'

'Prints?'

'You kidding? Sand. Surf. Elements.'

'I'm jist trying to find out if it was . . . *possible*. See, she was told there was lividity on both sides, so she got to thinking maybe the body was shot somewhere else and then transported to Little Corona and dumped on the beach. Did the car have a lotta gas in it?'

The balding little detective then began a session in snideness. Sammy Vogel had always been a state-of-the-art smirker. He talked with his hands and fingers as though he was signing to the deaf. 'Tell her she watches too much TV. Lividity was caused by the body being turned over on the beach by the tide. It flipped him like hamburger, front to back. After several hours on each side he gradually drifted down toward the water.'

'He was actually floating?'

'Not quite. And the car had half a tank, because he'd filled it the day before, out near La Quinta. His housemate verified it.'

'Usually you need a hard surface for lividity.'

238

'I told you he was lying on the beach. Wet sand is hard.'

It was plain to see what reaction he was going to get, but in that he'd gone this far, Winnie reached into the pocket of his jeans and took out the button-sized shells.

'They're freshwater shells. From the Coachella Valley. By La Quinta, to be specific.'

'I didn't know there was an ocean out there,' the detective said, smirking.

'There used to be an inland sea. I could probably take these to an expert and prove they didn't come out of the Pacific Ocean.'

'So?'

Winnie removed a whole shell from his shirt pocket. It was identical to the others. He put them on the table, three in a row.

The smirking detective said, 'This a new variation of the old shell game?'

Winnie pointed to the one from his shirt pocket, and said, '*This* one came from the cuff of the pants Conrad Binder wore the night he died.'

'What're you talking about?'

'Did you find any other shells like this? Maybe in his shoes or . . .'

'There were no shells,' Sammy Vogel said. 'Damn it, Win, whaddaya trying to stir up here? That was a suicide! I got his stuff from the coroner myself. There were no shells that I ever saw. Whaddaya trying to do here?'

'Well, what if he was shot by somebody out there on his property? What if they dragged him through the desert sand and dumped him in the trunk of a car for a couple hours? Lividity might form on one side after a long drive to Newport. Then they carried him down to the beach and dropped him on the *other* side. And there you find him with freshwater shells in his cuff.'

Vogel hesitated a moment, then said, 'I think you been hitting the bottle just as hard as people say you are. I think your IQ's dropped to eighty. Eighty *proof*.'

'You don't have to get hostile, Sammy.'

'Hostile? Me? You come in here and imply that one of *my* cases – a *suicide* – is suddenly a whodunit murder? Because of a little seashell? Why should I get hostile?'

'Not a seashell. A freshwater shell. In his cuff, and half a one in the box his clothes were in. Maybe fell outta his shoe.'

'Who says this was in his cuff?'

'I found it there. His daughter had the box all this time, unopened. I went through it this morning and I found the shells.'

'Well, I guess you'll have to join the Baker Street Irregulars, Winnie,' said Sammy Vogel. 'But you are *not* going to turn this suicide into a whodunit. In the first place, even if there *was* a desert shell in the cuff of his pants, so what? The guy coulda picked up that shell anytime. Christ, he *lived* there! Why couldn't he have a shell or two stuck in his clothes? The guy shot himself and the tide did the rest. Period. Ask the coroner if he killed himself. By the way, the guy was sick. He had a reason for pulling that trigger.'

'Yeah, I know about the HIV.'

'OK, Win.' The detective stood up. 'It's been great seeing you again, but . . .'

'You know anything about a guy named Hack Starkey? Real name's Hugh Starkey. Used to work for Binder.

Used to spend a lotta time out there working around the ranch. Lives in Laguna, I think. I wanna talk to him.'

'You talk to anybody you want,' said Sammy Vogel, 'but I'm not gonna run his name through CII if that's what you're thinking. And I'm not gonna get involved in this because if you start bugging innocent people you're gonna get your ass in a lawsuit. And maybe you got nothing to lose, but I do. So long, Win. If I was you, I'd consider getting in touch with my Higher Power.'

'What's that?'

'Go to an AA meeting. You'll hear some speakers who were dysfunctional drunks at one time. I've been dry three years now. Before that, my thought process was getting the way yours is now. The brain starts blowing its horn and careening around like a Cairo cabbie. Think about going to an AA meeting. I go every Tuesday and Friday night. You wanna go with me sometime, gimme a call. I'll take you and bring you home afterwards. Otherwise, *don't* call me, Winnie.'

Winnie spent an hour fast-walking to Balboa Island and back for exercise. He tried unsuccessfully to watch a movie on TV, then washed and vacuumed his car in Tess's garage, a job he hated above all others. After that, he showered and put on a cotton knit shirt and chinos. He even wore socks and a belt. He was going to *work*.

'The last time I saw you looking this excited, we were suspended in midair on a hammock,' Tess said, when she came in the house with a bag from Louis Vuitton.

'Sit, lady, I've got some news,' he said.

Tess went into the kitchen and got a diet drink from the refrigerator and a Mexican beer for Winnie. She wore a brand-new white and mint-green chemise dress, and he thought she looked radiant.

Triumphantly, he pulled the shell from his shirt pocket and showed it to her.

'Yes?'

'This came from the cuff of the pants your dad wore the night he died! And this . . .' he showed her the shell fragment, 'came from the bottom of the box that contained the clothes! It could've also been in his cuff or maybe his shoe!'

Tess didn't say anything. She stared at the shells as though she'd never seen one before. She took a sip of her diet drink and said, 'Is it possible, Win? Is it *possible*?'

'I think so,' he said. 'Your father was killed at *El Refugio* and his body was driven down here!'

'But is it *proof*?'

'In a court of law? Of course not.'

'What're you going to do?'

'I've got a few ideas.'

'You're not going to the police?'

'I already have.'

That startled her. 'You *have*?'

'Yeah, but Sammy Vogel kissed it off. He was always a little bit lazy. Sleepy Sammy, we called him. He thinks a guy that lived out there in the desert might limp through life with shells in his shoes. Says it was suicide. Period.'

Tess thought for a moment and said, 'I suppose he's right. He could've been out hiking and caught a shell in his cuff.'

'We know different, you and me,' said Winnie. 'And now I know those shots were no accident. It was a botched attempt on your life.'

'Hack Starkey?'

'*Gotta* be,' Winnie said.

'So what's next?'

'A little police work.'

'I thought you said the police aren't interested.'

'Hey, lady, you're looking at an ace detective! I get to do police work again. And I get to help the girl I . . .'

'Don't stop now.'

'The girl I been hired to protect.'

'Oh, I'm *hiring* you, am I?'

'Sure, now that I know you're gonna get that ranch someday, I'm gonna bill you soon as you're rich.'

'I'll pay whatever you ask,' she said, and then she put her glasses on top of her head, and moved on to Winnie's lap and kissed him. Then she asked, 'So what now?'

'I gotta locate Starkey. Vogel won't help me, but somebody will. Maybe I'll call Buster.'

'I wouldn't,' Tess said.

'Why not?'

'I didn't like him.'

'Well, yeah, he was in his smart-mouth mood the night you met him, but he's OK. A good cop when he lets himself be.'

'He didn't seem trustworthy. From what you've told me about him, he *isn't*. He might want something in return for any favor he did.'

'He'd be doing it for me.'

'He'd probably send *me* a bill or something. Can't you get somebody else?'

'OK,' Winnie said. 'Maybe I shouldn't even mess with the guys I used to work with. There's a PI in Santa Ana, Pat Kilroy. Used to be a cop here. Got retired on an injury same as me. He owes me one from the old days.'

'That might be better,' she agreed. 'Keep the police completely out of this.'

She kissed Winnie again, one of her muscle-tongue specials, and said, 'Police work can wait a few minutes, can't it?'

'How many?'

'Oh, I think I'll need about thirty,' she said, tugging on his belt.

Tess seemed willing to let him out of her sight at last. But when Winnie was ready to leave, she made him promise he'd come back to sleep with her no matter how late it was.

When he got home to check his mail, the apartment had never looked gloomier. Tess Binder had taken up so much time lately the spiders now controlled his kitchen. He sat down with a stack of mail, bills mostly, and wrote some checks. Then he called Kilroy and was lucky to catch him at his desk.

'Pat, it's Winnie Farlowe,' he said. 'I need a job done.'

'Win!' Kilroy was a four pack-a-day man with a voice like a rivet gun. 'Long time. Glad to see you came outta that ferry hijacking OK.'

'Yeah, I been meaning to call you, Pat. Thought we could have lunch sometime. But now I got this lady friend needs to locate a guy named Hugh Starkey. Hack, they call him. She says he's white, about forty-eight to fifty, six-feet-two, two-ten, gray hair dyed black, brown eyes. No real job. Lives in Laguna maybe. Maybe hangs around gay bars.'

'You had one of the guys run him through CII?'

'No, this is one I don't wanna use the cops for. I'd like you to handle it for me.'

'I can call you in ten minutes if he's got a rap sheet. How far you want me to go if there's no record?'

'I could check voter's registration myself. Maybe you could check with DMV. He's gotta have a driver's license. And if we end up with nothing, I'd appreciate it if you'd run him through the major credit institutions. He's gotta have a financial rap sheet. That kinda guy owes money to everyone.'

After hanging up, Winnie looked around and couldn't stand it. He had to do a *little* housekeeping in case the landlady dropped in for something. He was down on his knees dueling with spiders when the phone rang. It was Kilroy.

'That was fast,' Winnie said.

'Hugh Willis Starkey,' Kilroy said. 'Has a misdemeanor record. Gotta be him. Last busted by the highway patrol for DUI. Let's see . . . two years ago. Gave an address in Laguna Beach.'

Winnie wrote down the address of the apartment house and said, 'Could be a transient place.'

'Might be,' Kilroy said, 'but there's no point me going any further till you check out this address.'

'Absolutely,' said Winnie. 'Only thing bothers me, this is too easy. I figured the guy was gonna be more of a challenge. Wish I could get his mug shot right away.'

'Gimme a couple hours,' said Kilroy. 'I'll have one of my people deliver it. Where you gonna be, Spoon's Landing?'

It made Winnie squirm, his reputation. But he said, 'Yeah, jist have it dropped off at Spoon's Landing.' Then he said, 'By the way, Pat, would a guy with a misdemeanor record have any trouble getting a PI license?'

'What kind of misdemeanor?'

'Oh, DUI, let's say.'

Kilroy was savvy. 'You mean like BUI? Boating under the influence?'

'Yeah,' Winnie admitted. 'I'm talking about *me*. I been thinking about your line a work. I was a pretty good detective at one time.'

'Sure you were,' said Kilroy. 'I think you could probably swing it, the license, I mean.'

'I was wondering, maybe you might need another guy sometime? Doesn't have to be full time.'

Kilroy hesitated and said, 'I can always use part-time guys that know what they're doing, but . . . well, I got a strict rule. I won't hire someone if I even suspect he's got a problem with booze.'

It was Winnie's turn to pause. Then he said, 'Don't let the boat parade thing fool you. I don't drink that much. Certainly not more than I can handle.'

Kilroy said, 'Yeah, well, maybe we can talk about it.'

'OK. Thanks for the help,' Winnie said.

When he hung up he grabbed the bottle of beer he'd just opened and started to pour it down the sink. Then he thought it over. One lousy problem with booze in his entire life! That goddamn boat parade! Well, shit! He knew what he could handle and what he couldn't. He wasn't going to let people intimidate him. He tipped the bottle up and drank it. Then he went to Spoon's Landing to await the delivery of Hack Starkey's mug shot.

Winnie was surprised to find Buster Wiles sitting at the

bar. And shocked to see the bruises, contusions, abrasions and swelling over Buster's face and arms and hands.

Winnie took the stool next to the big cop, and said, 'Who designed that face? Salvador Dali?'

'I tried to leave you a note from my roof. But my fuckin brain's so squishy I couldn't spell Farlowe and decided to climb down. If my life don't change for the better, I swear I'm gonna *bite* it. I can't live like this.'

'What the hell happened?'

Buster turned painfully and said, 'Oh, yesterday I spent a riotous, fun-filled day at the beach, is all. Till I ran into a pair a dinks that evened up the score a little bit for all that napalm we used to lay on 'em.'

'You look like an eggplant. In fact, your eye looks like *cooked* eggplant.'

'This is what happens when you get teamed up with twenty-two-year-old baby cops who tell you their mom thought you were king a the beach, and maybe to prove somethin you get carried away and start chasin someone along the oceanfront when what you should do at your age is strictly *drive-by* police work. Hand tickets out the window of a patrol unit or shoot the motherfuckers from inside the car with an assault rifle. But under no circumstances should you be tryin to run after thievin slopes with some fuckin kid cop who actually says stuff like, "Life's a beach!"'

Buster turned back to his drink and hunched his mulish shoulders and signaled to Spoon for another round. Winnie decided to drop the subject of Buster's wounds, except to say, 'I take it you *won't* be going to work today?'

'I oughtta take the *week* off,' Buster said. 'My head feels like a bag of plastique. A comb might blow it up.'

'If you got nothing to do and feel up to it, I could use some help.'

'Doin what?'

'I gotta find a guy.'

'What guy?'

'Guy named Starkey. I'm expecting his mug shot here pretty soon. Kilroy's getting it for me.'

'I'm surprised you didn't ask one a the guys at the office if you wanted a mug shot.'

'Gonna keep the PD outta this. I think this guy's trying to kill Tess Binder.'

Buster hurt himself turning to face Winnie. 'What's that broad doin to you?'

'It's a long story. If you're willing to help me I'll fill you in on it while we drive down to Laguna.'

'For what?'

'I wanna talk to the guy.'

'You wanna ask him why he wants to shoot your little pal?'

'What made you say shoot? I don't know how he'd pull it off.'

Buster said, 'Most a the world these days, that's the way they do it. California's got more guns than the Warsaw Pact.'

'You gonna help me?'

'Can't. I almost got killed by a flock a canaries yesterday. My luck's run out.'

'Actually, Tess'd be very unhappy if she even knew I was talking to you about it. You didn't make a great impression on her that night.'

'Sure, she's got you running around lookin for imaginary snipers. Pretty soon she'll be wearin your nuts for earrings. They're all the same, broads like her. Two-steppers. Remember those snakes in Nam? They bite you and you're dead in two steps.'

'I think she's all right,' Winnie said.

Buster nodded doubtfully and said, 'Well, I can't help you. I only do police work when the city pays me for it. And then I only do it if there's a sergeant watchin me.'

'What I need is, I need a backup for when I talk to this guy. I want somebody with a gun behind me. Jist in *case*.'

'It ain't gonna be me,' said Buster. 'Don't you still have your piece?'

'Yeah, but a medical retirement doesn't entitle me to run around carrying a concealed weapon.'

'Sorry, Win. Why don't you try one a the other guys you partnered with?'

'Since my boat parade caper the guys seem to avoid me. I'm bad news. They think I might get involved in another . . .'

'*Débâcle*'s the word you're searchin for.'

'Yeah, they think I'm an alcoholic.'

'Well, you're not. You jist drink a little too much. Maybe Kilroy'd back you up. Maybe his guy, that one that brings the mug shot. Why not ask him?'

Winnie let it drop and ordered another drink and one for Buster. They were both watching a golf tournament on ESPN, when a guy walked in and said to Spoon, 'I have something for Win Farlowe.'

'That's me,' Winnie said.

He looked older than Spoon. Buster's left leg out-weighed him and had more hair on it. He might've been consumptive. He handed Winnie the envelope and said, 'With Pat Kilroy's compliments, Mister Farlowe.'

249

When he left, Winnie said, 'How'd you like to rely on *him* for a backup?'

Buster said, 'Don't get me in trouble, man! I'll go along to watch you *talk* to this guy, but that's it!'

'That's all I want,' Winnie said. He'd rarely seen Buster so adamant. Buster's hand wasn't steady when he picked up the drink. 'I'm on the verge a new things,' Buster said. 'I don't want you screwin me up jist because you gone loopy over some little squeeze from Linda Isle.'

'I won't get you involved,' Winnie said. 'We'll go in *my* car.'

As they were leaving, Tripoli Jones reeled into the barroom, too drunk to be walking, let alone driving the car that he'd parked with two wheels on the sidewalk.

Spoon took one look at him and said, 'Forget it. No way. Go home.'

The former marine muttered and cursed and staggered into the men's room, where he took a header. When he came out he insisted that somebody had installed speed bumps in there.

16: *The Hound*

The cops referred to The Golden Orange as 'le Côte de Fraud.' That, because there were so many major and minor fraud cases emanating from the Gold Coast. Still, The Golden Orange someday may become the financial heart of the American Southwest, they say. The cops referred to it as Goyim Heights, whose West Bank, they said, is Security Pacific.

Fraud and financial scams in The Golden Orange were on the mind of Winnie Farlowe during the drive down Pacific Coast Highway to Laguna Beach early that evening. It was warm enough to keep the top down, but the VW was noisy, and when he got out of Corona Del Mar the engine whined, unable to pass a slow-moving Cadillac Fleetwood.

'We ain't in no hurry,' Buster said. 'I'd like to survive the drive so somebody can shoot me. It's more dramatic, right?'

'I'm getting curious about your career change,' said Winnie. 'Something's going on. You seem a lot different somehow.'

'I said I'll let you know if it comes about, OK?'

'Remember the boiler room?' Winnie said. 'The guy you and me busted? Worked out of an apartment?'

'Which one? I busted lotsa guys sellin those so-called

251

precious metal stocks. A frying pan contains more precious metal.'

'I was thinking of the guy that was selling all that gold to out-of-state buyers at two hundred an ounce. Only it was still in the ground and their money was supposed to get it out within fifteen months.'

'Yeah, what was his name?'

'You got pretty friendly with him. You should remember.'

'He was a decent guy for a thief,' Buster said.

'And the way he put it, it didn't seem so bad,' said Winnie. 'If the investment cost more to get the gold out, well, the company would pay the difference, he said. Amazing how people went for it.' Then Winnie looked at Buster. 'I remember you said they could afford it, those investors. Average investment was only, what? Five grand? A few lost twenty, but nobody got hurt too much, you said.'

'Guy drove a Lamborghini,' Buster recalled. 'And his girlfriend had an Aston Martin Lagonda.'

'Yeah, that's right,' said Winnie. 'He did OK with oil and gas investments too. Except I got more gas in my belly right now than he ever owned. What I'm wondering, is your career change along the lines a something like that? You always said a guy with half a brain coulda pulled it off.'

'I ain't gonna discuss it, Winnie,' Buster said. 'It jist might be something along those lines, and if it is, so what?'

'You wouldn't do something that'd get you in big trouble, I hope. I wouldn't like to see that, Buster. Those boiler-room scams can get a guy chucked into a single room with three roommates. For about five years.'

'He beat us in court if you remember,' Buster said. 'He's probably got a job in one a those giant buildings with black windows up in Irvine, makin a million in salary and three million in stock options. Remember that boiler room *you* busted on Christmas Eve that time? That guy . . . whatzisname? I heard he owns a six-million-dollar yacht he keeps in Sardinia. Had the Prince of Monaco aboard for lunch. So how bad did you hurt him with that case?'

'Well, I'd hate to see you do something that . . .'

'Don't be worryin about me,' Buster said. '*You're* the guy goin around tryin to put yourself into the middle a somethin that smells worse than red tide in still water. Me, I'll prob'ly live out my old age as a scuba scrubber. Stuck to boat hulls underwater with a toilet plunger in one hand, scrubbing off slime with the other. That's something like police work, come to think of it.'

The open highway between Corona Del Mar and Laguna Beach is about all that's left of undeveloped coastline along that stretch of Orange County. Surfers still park their cars along the ocean side, and climb down the cliffs to unspoiled beaches, to ride in swirls of turquoise and midnight blue.

'How'd it be to live in a place like that?' Buster asked, pointing toward a huge home perched on a cliff overlooking Reef Point. It had a lighthouse wing with a green copper roof, and a redwood observation platform all the way around. The sky beyond looked inflamed and feverish.

'I'd prefer the one on *Brideshead Revisited*,' said Winnie. 'Less rooms to clean. You know, I really appreciate this, Buster. You coming along with me.'

'I had important things to do,' Buster said. 'Like takin

253

the knots outta my telephone cord, but I'm a real balls-up guy. So tell me, whaddaya gonna say if we find this guy Starkey?'

'I'm gonna interrogate him,' Winnie said.

'Case you ain't noticed, Win, you don't have a badge no more. What's your authority to make people sit still for an interrogation?'

'He's a gay-bar drifter from what I know. He'll look at two guys like us and see *cop*. We lean a little bit, he'll roll over, belly up. That's what I'm betting on.'

'Yeah, well, I ran into lots a sissies from gay bars that Heinrich Himmler couldn't make snitch off a pal.'

'I'm betting he will. Or at least he'll tell his boss we're on to him.'

'What'll *that* accomplish?'

'I told ya I wanna scare the crap outta Warner Stillwell. He'll realize it was a bad idea and it ain't gonna work. And he'll have to be content to live out his life on the ranch.'

'That's it, then?' Buster said, incredulously. '*That's* the fallback position here?'

'Yeah, but I hope I can persuade Starkey to dime the old man. I'd like to make a case the DA'd *have* to prosecute. Like that attempted murder on Tess. Or maybe even the murder of Conrad Binder.'

'You get that much outta this guy and you can hire on with the KGB.'

'At least we'll throw a scare into old man Stillwell if nothing else.'

'And your lady friend'll be safe from future attempts?'

'Something like that.'

'And she jist waits around till the old guy croaks and gets her inheritance? And *then* what? You think she's gonna remember you? You think she's gonna remember you next *month*?'

'I don't worry about that part,' Winnie said. 'Far as I'm concerned, she's a good friend who needs help. I'd help *you* if you were in trouble. Like you're helping me right now.'

'Don't go all sentimental on me,' Buster said. 'I start cryin and the salt'll hurt all the raw meat that used to be my left eye.'

Buster was silent during the drive past Irvine Cove and Emerald Bay – gated communities with homes on both sides of the highway. From there south, Laguna Beach wore a string of coves like a necklace: Santa Ana Cove, Fisherman's Cove, Diver's Cove, and the main cove where the crowds gathered on the sand to watch basketball or volleyball, or to scope-out the hardbodies, most of whom were male.

Buster looked at the bohemian Laguna street scene, and said, 'I'd hate to work the beach patrol around here. You don't know which bums might be artists. You can't tell a future Picasso from a bag a garbage.'

Winnie left his car at the Hotel Laguna with a valet-parking attendant rather than fight for a parking space on the street. It was a landmark hotel, frequented by Barrymore in the thirties and Bogie in the forties: a flat-roofed block of stucco with a quixotic belltower.

'Want a drink before we go to work?' Buster asked.

'Just one,' Winnie said, but immediately provided Buster with a minor shock by changing his mind: 'No, better *not*.'

They quickly found the ramshackle apartment house on Mermaid Street. It could be described as 'Laguna casual', which meant even more so than the Balboa peninsula.

Buster said, 'This is the kind a place where dressy-as-it-gets means wearin a tank top that ain't inside out.'

The man who answered the door didn't remotely resemble the face on the police mugshot, and didn't seem to recognize that he could be talking to cops.

'Hack Starkey?' he said. 'He the guy used to live here before me? Young guy with a wooden leg? If it ain't him, better talk to the landlady in number one.'

When Winnie knocked, the landlady yelled, 'Door's open!'

She sat at an easel painting a beach scene with pastel watercolors, which she probably hoped to peddle at the summer Sawdust Festival, a 'people's' art show where folks like her tried to catch the overflow from the Laguna Beach Pageant of the Masters, in which real people and painted ones become entwined in life-size tableaus of famous works of art, so that the viewer isn't sure which figure breathes. People with binoculars pack the Laguna Bowl every night during the festival, trying to guess which ones in a massive reproduction – like 'The Last Supper', for instance – could be a flesh-and-blood citizen of Laguna who'd practiced all year turning to stone.

The landlady flip-flopped into the living room in worn-out rubber thongs, a glass of whiskey in one hand and a palette in the other. Her nose had more busted veins than the Klondike.

'I ain't got an empty apartment,' she said.

'I'm looking for a former tenant,' Winnie said. 'Hack Starkey? Middle-aged guy with dyed black hair?'

She gave them a closer look, saw cop written all over them and said, 'Yeah?'

256

Winnie knew the look, and that if he said he wanted the guy for attempted murder, she'd say, 'Moved. No forwarding address.'

So he said what usually gets cooperation: 'We wanna talk to him about a report that he molested a kid.'

'Yeah? How old?'

'About six,' Winnie said. 'A little boy.'

'That dirty cocksucker!' she said. 'He moved, oh, eight months ago. But I hear he hangs around town in the gay bars. That son of a bitch! I hope he tries to run and you shoot him down!' Then she looked at Buster's battered face and said, 'Want me to lay hands on those wounds? I can usually drive out evil spirits in a couple minutes. You'll feel better.'

To Winnie's astonishment Buster said, 'I *do* got some evil stuff in there.' Then he sat down on the greasy sofa and said, 'Let 'er rip.'

The woman shuffled over to the refrigerator and got an egg. Then she drew a glass of water from the faucet. She put her red pudgy fingers gently on Buster's head and passed the egg in circles over his face. Then she broke the egg into the water and studied it.

'What's the verdict?' Winnie asked.

She said, 'Yeah, there *are* some unholy things in there, son, but I don't think I can help you. I can tell you this: You better *deal* with it.'

They thanked her and left, deciding she was a fairly ordinary resident of Laguna Beach.

The first gay bar they tried was The Tango Tavern. It wasn't as dark as a movie by Ingmar Bergman, but it was even gloomier. Six guys scattered around the bar looked as though sixteen-inch guns wouldn't faze them.

Buster said, 'These dudes're down for the count. A barrel of amyl nitrate ain't gonna start their rockets. They need a *big* booster. Your guy into drugs by any chance?'

'Not that I know of,' Winnie said.

Winnie went straight to the dour and listless bartender and flashed the mug shot. The bartender looked at the photo and said, 'Not in *this* joint.'

It gave Winnie a boost to see that the bartender didn't ask to see police ID. He *still* had the look!

Buster said to a patron who resembled Alice Cooper, 'I'm lookin for an old boyfriend. Had his toes amputated to fit in size three's with four-inch spikes? Seen him around?'

The guy just *stared*. Buster thanked him, saying he'd seen more signs of life in an oyster bed.

The next stop was The Flaming Sunset, already rocking out at 8.45 p.m. The fire department poster said the saloon was OK for 145 persons. Buster said he saw that many guys holding other guys in their laps. He and Winnie squeezed into a corner close enough to the bar to spot anyone with the world's phoniest-looking dye job.

A table six inches away was packed with androgynous drinkers, one of whom said something moderately amusing. Causing the one closest to Buster to cut loose with a shrill squeal.

Buster turned to the youth and said, 'Butch it up, for chrissake! Mother's on the way!'

The ceiling held enough baby spots and electrical tracks to mood-light the San Diego Freeway.

'This lighting could make even Spoon's Landing look like champagne and violins,' Winnie observed.

'That's the truth, Ruth,' Buster agreed. 'Wonder if the

cops gotta handle many drive-by slappings around here.'

There was live rock music playing on the other side of the barroom, but getting through the teeming multitude would be impossible.

'I ain't seen a cocktail waitress,' said Buster.

'Any female person'll be a waitress, I imagine.'

A female person finally squeezed her way through the crowd and looked at them with a please-order-something-simple expression.

'Beer,' Winnie said. 'Any kind.'

'Me too,' Buster said.

Buster was taller than Winnie, but he wasn't looking around much, so Winnie was on tiptoes half the time. He saw lots and lots of dye jobs, all colors, and most of them bad, but not Hack Starkey. After finishing their beer they managed to bump their way closer to the bar itself.

Winnie could finally see that it was a piano trio supplying the music on an elevated stage, and they were pretty good. Winnie hoped they wouldn't play 'Where or When'.

'Better stay sober,' he said to Buster, 'or you might end up with a truck driver picking your pocket and he won't be looking for money.'

Buster was bored with their mission. 'You say the guy's about fifty? This is a younger crowd. Let's try another joint, one a those where they lace your drinks with minoxidil for the hair and Retin-A for wrinkles.'

The third place they tried was called Malcolm's Lounge. It was more of a proper restaurant, on the ocean side of Coast Highway. A jazz combo was playing something from Thelonious Monk. It took Winnie a minute to realize it was 'Mysterioso'.

'Far from the yammering crowd,' Buster said. 'I think

the guy next to me at the bar was fallin in love with me. Can you catch AIDS from slobber and drool?'

Winnie said to the bartender, a bleached, over-the-hill surfer, 'I'll teach you a drink I learned from a bartender named Coley, who claims he invented it. Toss two double shots of Absolut Citron into a shaker. Pour in a splash of Cointreau and squeeze in some juice from a fresh orange. Strain it into a chilled cocktail glass, garnish with a lemon twist and pour one for me and one for yourself. You'll make big tips on this one.'

'This is called working up an informant,' Winnie whispered to Buster while the bartender carried out his instructions. When the bartender put the two cocktails on the table, Winnie picked his up, sniffed it, sipped and said, 'Perfect. This drink'll sell *very* big with ladies.'

The bartender sipped and nodded. 'What do you call it?'

Winnie thought for a moment and said, 'I call it . . . let's see, I call it The Golden Orange Cocktail.'

'The Golden Orange?' the bartender said. 'Not bad.'

When the bartender was down at the other end of the bar, Buster said, 'Any drink that goes over with ladies'll pay the rent in this place. They could serve 'em with an endive hotdog to all the Nellies.'

When the bartender came back to see if they wanted a refill, Winnie beckoned him closer and said, *sotto voce*, 'Now I gotta ask *you* a favor. I gotta find a guy named Hack Starkey. Middle-aged with a bad dye job.'

'Got a *lot* of bad henna rinses around here,' the bartender said.

Winnie took out the mug shot and said, 'I work for a private investigator. Been given the job a finding this guy

260

that scams old pensioners outta their savings with phony investment schemes. We jist wanna serve a subpoena on him, make him go to civil court and pay some of it back. No big thing.'

The bartender picked up the mug shot and Winnie knew he'd scored a hit. But the bartender hesitated. Winnie said, 'The Golden Orange'll make you twenty bucks a night in extra tips.' Then he put a twenty on the bar and pushed it forward, saying, 'Here's the first one.'

The bartender looked at the twenty and said, 'I think this is the guy that lives near The Windjammer Tavern, down by Sugarloaf Point. Used to come in here, but not in a long time. I think he's sick.'

When they left the bar, Buster said, 'Your ship come in? *Twenty*-dollar tips?'

'Tess loaned me a few bucks.'

'A perfect little helpmate,' Buster said. 'Pretty soon you'll tell me she's buying a saloon.'

Near The Windjammer Tavern could only have meant the small frame house on the ocean side of the highway, which, from the looks of it, was destined to be scraped. In the side yard was a filthy old kidney-shaped swimming pool bordered by a rusty chain-link fence. It was a very dark night and there was no yardlight. They opened the gate and picked their way through litter.

'If this guy's a hit man he ain't gettin rich off his commissions,' Buster noted. 'That pool looks like a vat a cioppino.'

Winnie knocked and a skeletal figure in a tattered terry bathrobe opened the front door. Winnie almost gasped when he saw what the man from the mug shot had become.

'Mr Starkey,' Winnie said, 'we'd like to talk to you.'

Hack Starkey stepped back into a small foyer, and supported himself against a table that held a single vase of paper flowers. He turned and limped into a badly lit, cluttered living room where an orange-striped cat sniffed at a paper plate containing the residue of something coagulated. Something the man must have eaten within the last week or so.

He had to use both hands and then his elbows to settle himself into his recliner rocker, his forehead beading with the effort. His hair was no longer black. Two inches of gray showed, and the top layer was the same color as the tabby cat. Wisps of gray facial hair hung like Spanish moss from his bony jaw. His flesh was saffron yellow, but his fingers were saddle-leather brown. He lit a cigarette with the stub of another that he'd plucked from one of three overflowing ashtrays.

The tarnished lamplight was behind him and when he raised his face toward Winnie, his eyes disappeared in their sockets.

'You *are* policemen, aren't you?' he wheezed, but when Winnie nodded and fumbled as though for his police ID, Hack Starkey dropped his palm as if to say it wasn't necessary.

'We, uh, jist need to ask a few questions about your boss, Warner Stillwell,' Winnie said, sitting on the edge of the sofa.

Hack Starkey looked toward the TV in the corner of the room, and fumbled with a remote control. It fell on the floor and Winnie could see that picking it up would take major effort. Buster picked up the device and shut off the television.

The house didn't need vacuuming, it needed a street sweeper. Buster used a magazine to dust two fur balls from a kitchen chair and dragged it into the tiny living room. He shot a glance at Winnie that said, *This* is your hit man?

Winnie said, 'I jist wanna talk about your boss a little bit? A confidential police matter.'

Wheezing, Hack Starkey said, 'He *never* was my boss. Mister Binder was my boss. Mister Stillwell let me go right after Mister Binder killed himself.'

'How long did you work for Conrad Binder?'

'Off and on, about thirteen years. I did jobs for him when he had the house at Bayshores. Paint the house. Clean the barnacles off the dock. Detail his cars. Then gradually he had me spend time at the ranch. I painted that whole ranch house, all by myself. One time I stayed there for three months.'

Hack Starkey was suddenly wracked with a rattling cough. He grabbed a handful of tissues from a box and gagged up some phlegm. Buster shuddered, and shot another glance at Winnie. The look said: Let's boogie on *out* of here!

When Hack Starkey stopped coughing, he leaned his head back and wheezed some more. He inhaled from an aerosol device next to him. There were various prescription vials and bottles on the table, and an empty glass. Winnie picked up the glass and walked into the squalid kitchen. He filled the glass with tap water and brought it back to the sick man.

Hack Starkey nodded gratefully and drank. His Adam's apple bobbed like a Ping-Pong ball in an air tube.

'You should be in a hospital,' Winnie said.

The man, his coughing spasm under control, said

wheezily, 'I have been. I will be again. I'm suffering from drug side effects as much as anything.'

Winnie picked up the vials and saw the name of a Dr Wentworth in Laguna Beach. Then he spotted one that contained medication prescribed by a Dr Lutz in Palm Desert. The prescription was ten months old and had been refilled twice.

'When was the last time you saw Doctor Lutz?' Winnie asked.

'Just before Mister Binder died.' Then Hack Starkey said, 'He was Mister Binder's doctor. I've had that one refilled twice. I got a local doctor now. He's giving me AZT and pentamidine. I think it helps but I'm not sure. I got my hopes pinned on HIV-Immunogen. That's Doctor Salk's new treatment. He found a cure for polio. Maybe he can . . .' Hack Starkey paused. The horror in the faces of his inquisitors told him what they thought about his hopes. They were looking at a death mask.

'There's a minor police problem connected with Warner Stillwell that we have to clear up,' Winnie said. 'Tess Binder told me you were Mister Stillwell's man Friday.'

Hack Starkey attempted a sardonic smile and said, 'I worked only for her dad. He signed every check I ever got. Mister Stillwell never liked me very much. He's a jealous man, Mister Stillwell.'

'Were you surprised when Conrad Binder shot himself?'

Hack Starkey puffed on a cigarette and said, 'He was a great person. He loved life.'

'Do you know why he did it?'

The dying man looked at Winnie Farlowe in disbelief. Then he pointed to his sunken bony chest and said, 'Ain't too hard to figure, is it? His T-4 count had been real low

264

for nearly two years. Doctor Lutz was monitoring it, but his side effects from the medication were bad. Severe anemia. He was just starting to feel real sick when he took that gun and ended it.'

'Were you at the ranch after his death? When Tess Binder arrived to take care of funeral arrangements?'

'Mister Stillwell sent me to pick her up at Palm Springs Airport. He didn't leave his room for three days after Con . . . after Mister Binder died. Can I ask you a question, Officer?'

'OK.'

'Was something stolen? Is that it? Is something missing from the ranch and Mister Stillwell's pointing the finger at me, is *that* it?'

'Would that surprise you?'

Hack Starkey tried to laugh, but he rattled. 'Mister Stillwell never did like me. I was young compared to him. Mister Binder was good to me and Mister Stillwell didn't like that neither.'

'OK, was there anyone *else* working for those two old men? Besides the Mexican servants? Anyone else who may've run an errand to Newport Beach within a week or so after Conrad Binder's death?'

'There was no-one else. Mister Stillwell fired me a few days after the funeral. There was nobody else.'

'Was Mister Stillwell jealous of Tess Binder?'

'He loved Tess Binder. I think he was closer to her than her father was, but I don't think she loved him. Used to call him "mother" behind his back. You know, like, "Hack, where's my father and *mother*?" I think she hates gay people. She was a spoiled child. Married a string of losers. She didn't even see her father during the last year of his life, but she always wanted his money.'

'How do you know that?'

'She'd call him and I'd hear him yelling over the phone. And he'd say something like, "Absolutely not!" But pretty soon he'd write a check and tell me to run down to the post office and send it to her by express mail. They *both* spoiled her: Mister Binder and Mister Stillwell.'

Winnie was suddenly very much aware that Buster was studying *him*, not Hack Starkey. Winnie said apologetically, 'A couple more questions, Mister Starkey. To your knowledge, is Mister Stillwell sick too? With AIDS?'

'He used to go to Doctor Lutz for a minor blood pressure problem, but AIDS? I think Mister Stillwell hasn't had sex in twenty years and resents anybody *else* having it. He used to be an athlete. He's very strong and healthy. There's no way he could have AIDS. I'd bet my life on it. If I had a life worth betting.'

'But Tess Binder said she thinks he goes to the hospital from time to time.'

With a shrug of the eyebrows, 'Not to my knowledge. He goes to that fancy spa down below the border from time to time. The guy's over seventy but looks middle-aged. Mister Binder once told me Mister Stillwell's parents both lived past ninety. Him, sick? I doubt it.'

Winnie stood up and Buster followed. Winnie said, 'One last question. Did you give the disease to Conrad Binder?'

Hack Starkey looked up, and in the yellow lamplight Winnie could see that his eyes were yellow too. He said, 'Do you think you could leave me in peace now?'

Winnie and Buster turned to go, but when they were still in the foyer the doomed man rattled and said, 'I

266

imagine his daughter blames me for it. And if it makes her feel better to have someone to hate, I don't mind. He used to come here to Laguna Beach at least once every two or three months by himself, and stay at a motel. He was a good-looking man who still had emotional needs, even at his age. I don't know who *he* got it from, but what I think is, *he* gave it to *me*.'

On the drive back to Newport Beach, Winnie said, 'Obviously she was mistaken about seeing Hack Starkey watching her house. It must've been somebody who resembles the way Starkey *used* to look.'

'Maybe she's jist another hysterical broad,' Buster said. 'Hack Starkey's a corpse. Drop me at a car wash. I need to be steam-cleaned.'

'But she's not the hysterical type. Doesn't panic easy. I think Warner Stillwell has himself a Hack Starkey kind of guy. I trust what she tells me.'

'Last broad I trusted was my mother. My stepfather used to get drunk and kick the shit outta her when my little brother and me weren't handy. Only thing he never abused in that house was his basset hound. One day I got this idea to take a piss on the floor right in front of his favorite chair and blame it on his dog. So he'd beat the dog instead a my mother. And it worked. Next time he got drunk I pissed on the rug again and he beat the dog again. Then one night when he was out gettin *real* drunk I took a crap on the rug. When he came home he beat that hound to death.'

'How did that make you stop trusting your mother?'

'When she saw the dead dog she broke down and told him the dog was innocent. Before he could catch me I

267

jumped out the window and ran away. I ended up livin with my uncle down in Huntington Beach and never went in my mother's house again. And I stopped trustin people, especially women.'

Neither spoke again until they turned on to the Balboa peninsula. Then Buster said, 'My little buddy I was talkin to in The Tango Tavern? He asked me if I knew what they call a gay legend. Give up? A *myth*-ter! I thought I'd laugh my tits off.'

17: *A Bright Shining Gumdrop*

By the time they got back to Spoon's Landing, Winnie's back was aching and stiff from the ride, the dampness and the stress. Somebody out there was a threat to Tess Binder, he was *almost* sure of it. He wondered if he should warn her to avoid the channel side of her house at night. It seemed crazy, but the shots out on the trail were crazy too. If Warner Stillwell had hired an assassin, the guy was a wild card.

When he parked in front of Spoon's, Buster said, 'Havin a nightcap?'

'Better not,' Winnie said. 'Tess's expecting me.'

'I got an idea might help ya.'

'OK. Order me a drink. I gotta call and give her a report.'

They found the usual crowd plus a lot more who were venturing out for the first time now that the spring revelers were back in school. There were two empty stools at the far end of the bar separated by the presence of Guppy Stover, with her elbow on the bar and her head in her hand.

While Winnie went to the pay phone, Buster bellied up and said, 'Gimme a Wild Turkey, Spoon. And Polish vodka for Winnie.' Then to Guppy he said, 'Mind movin down? Me 'n Winnie wanna talk.'

That did it. 'Winnie?' she sneered. 'What's to talk about

with Winnie? Even Bilge O'Toole can't get a rise outta Winnie, and Bilge argues with turtles. Every opinion Winnie ever had is noncontroversial. Like, "I'm against war. I'm for better schools. I hate lawyers." Why would you wanna sit and talk to a *bore* like Winnie Farlowe?'

Before Buster had an answer, Spoon put the drinks on the bar, accidentally clinking Guppy's.

'Hey, watch it!' she said. 'You oughtta get a curb-feeler on those shot glasses, the way you bang into things! And it wouldn't kill you to buy a lady a drink!'

Winnie stepped up to the bar then, and Guppy said, 'Here he is now, salt of the earth Winnie. Well, this joint's a bleeding canker sore and canker sores don't need salt of the earth.'

'I'd love to buy you a drink, Guppy,' Winnie said sweetly. 'Would you be terribly inconvenienced if I asked you to move down?'

Guppy was defanged. When Spoon poured her the free drink, she smiled coquettishly at Winnie and said, 'Thank you, darling. It's a pleasure to find a real gentleman in this little corner of hell.'

When they were at last seated together, Buster said to Winnie, 'So what'd your little friend say when you told her you struck out with Hack Starkey?'

'Not much,' Winnie said. 'She couldn't get over how I found him so quick. Thought I'd need a week to find a drifter like him.'

'Anybody pop a cap at her tonight? Or does she have her imagination under control?'

'She told me that when she went down to the pharmacy tonight she saw a car that *mighta* been the same one the guy drove. The guy she thought was Starkey.'

'Get a license number?'

'Guy got away.'

'They always do,' Buster said. 'UFO's, Bigfoot, Elvis. The way I see it, you gotta bring this to a head before she drives you outta yours.'

'You said you had an idea.'

Buster downed the whiskey and smacked his lips. 'Like you said before, it's time to quit dickin around and go right to the source. Confront this Warner Stillwell *now*. Tell him what you know and what you expect.'

'He might laugh in my face. What can I prove? Less than nothing.'

'Yeah, but you can tell him you laid it all out to a lawyer and to some a your old buddies at Newport Beach PD. And you got a to-whom-it-may-concern note pinned to your girlfriend's underwear that says if I die suddenly, Warner did it. He'll likely call off his pal, if that gun-slingin cowboy even exists.'

'I'm jist not sure it's time to talk to him.'

'It's time. Tell him two can play the game, and if he don't resign himself to livin out the years he's got left, right there on the ranch, you might have to give him a little tit for tat. Like a rat-a-tat-tat from a fuckin assault rifle! There's a lotta things you can tell him to discourage this game you think he's playin. The bottom line is you gotta quit bein a volunteer victim for Tess Binder.'

'Maybe you're right.'

'She can get on with her life and wait for the fortune she's gonna get some day. Who knows, maybe before that she'll get lucky and catch somebody that's on the rebound from one a those other little hose monsters at her club. Maybe he'll fall in love and have a double ring ceremony on his yacht. *Without* a prenuptial agreement. And she can hire you to go along on the honeymoon as cabin boy, right?'

Winnie gaped at Buster for a moment. Then he said, 'You're about as romantic as lunch in the morgue.'

'I jist know people. People like her? They're the easiest.'

'I'm worried about you. You don't even smile no more. You jist smirk. You probably smirk when you've having sex.'

'For sex you gotta get too close to people. I'm tryin to figure out how to do it from a distance.'

'One thing did come outta tonight,' Winnie said. 'I got *another* motive for Conrad Binder's murder. When Binder got sick, Warner Stillwell knew for sure his housemate was screwing around with another guy. It musta made him crazy.'

'This is gettin too convoluted,' Buster said. 'Look, is this case about love or money?'

'Maybe both,' Winnie said. 'Life's seldom either or.'

'You're too complicated,' Buster said. 'You always were. I'm jist a simple guy. To me a murder boils down to sex, revenge or money. And anybody that kills for sex or revenge has *bad* head trouble. Now I gotta go home and put this beat-up old body to bed.'

The barroom bitching started rather early that night. Tripoli Jones tasted Spoon's Special Lobster Salad and yelled, 'Your lobster oughtta have dates on 'em like milk cartons: open before April first. This lobster's *rancid*!'

Spoon hollered back, 'You want a money-back guarantee, go buy a car battery!'

The ex-marine then yelled to the multitudes, 'Anything

happens to me from eatin this, I want a hose down my nose, and Ollie North's lawyer!'

Winnie tiptoed up the carpeted stairway, planning to slip into bed without waking Tess, but she was lying awake. He wondered how many sets of those sheets she owned. They always seemed fresh and they were always the color of the flesh of a slightly overripe peach.

She didn't speak until he slid into bed beside her. Then she turned on her side and said, 'I don't know what to do, Win. Tell me what to do.'

He was sober enough to know that his speech was slurred. 'I'm not sure, Tess. I got a couple ideas we can talk about tomorrow.'

'We *have* to do something. I can't live like this! Looking for a killer wherever I go! I hoped it was Hack Starkey, and that when you found him you'd make him stop somehow. I still can't believe you found him so easily.'

'It wasn't that easy,' Winnie said, not without some professional pride.

'I don't want to end up like Daddy!' She threw her arms around him and pressed her naked body against his. 'Please don't let me end up like Daddy, Win!'

'You won't,' he said, stroking her hair, smelling jasmine. 'I won't let anything happen to you.'

As they kissed, she rolled Winnie on top of her. He was lying diagonally across the bed, and was getting aroused, but when he glanced up at the marble nymph with her hand outstretched, he saw that she was offering him something. *What?*

273

'What's the matter, love?' Tess said. 'Too tired tonight?'

'It's just . . . it's . . .'

He almost had it! There! It was there! The amorphous spangled image of a woman in a white dress! Reaching out!

'Too sleepy tonight, old son?' she asked, easing him off her body. 'It's OK if you're too sleepy.'

Then it was *gone*. Winnie Farlowe felt a touch of panic. He thought about going to the library the next morning to read up on the *déjà vu* experience.

Winnie said, 'I *musta* met you in another life! Either that or I'm going nuts. Which is very possible.'

'*That* again? Still think we met somewhere before, huh?'

'I need to plug into one of those New Age brain wave machines,' Winnie said. 'I need their synchro-energizer to unscramble my brain waves. It's like we met in a *dream*, you and me!'

Tess sighed and said, 'Go to sleep, love.'

Before he closed his eyes, Winnie leaned over to Tess and said, 'There's another thing bothering me besides this dream I can't remember. You said Warner Stillwell goes to a hospital from time to time. That led you to believe he had AIDS, right?'

'Yes.'

'Starkey told me there's nothing wrong with him. He doesn't have the HIV virus.'

'He *would* say that,' Tess said. 'He'd like you to think badly of my father. Even if Hack Starkey isn't physically able to do me harm, that doesn't mean he isn't good buddies with Warner Stillwell. They were thick, those two!'

'He denies that too. He claims that he and your dad

were . . . buddies. That he worked for your dad, not for Warner Stillwell.'

'Of course, Daddy paid him! It was Daddy's money, wasn't it? But Hack Starkey was Warner's man, I tell you. He's *still* Warner's man. Who's paying his medical bills now? Did you ask him?'

'No.'

'Why not? I thought you're the ace detective.'

'Tess . . .'

'Well, you seem to believe this . . . this deviate instead of believing me!'

Winnie sat up with his back against the padded headboard. He tried to take her hand, but she turned her back to him.

'I believe you, Tess! Why wouldn't I?'

'Find out who's paying the medical bills. I'll bet it's Warner Stillwell. For past services rendered! And I'll bet Warner has AIDS. I resent and detest what you're hinting at! That my dad got AIDS from that . . . that creature, Hack Starkey!'

'Go to sleep, Tess,' Winnie said. 'I don't mean to hint at anything. I can't. I don't know *what* the hell to think.'

He awoke at The Drinker's Hour, but without the buzzards Fear and Remorse. Since meeting Tess Binder, his waking life had been filled with excitement and confusion and even *hope*, all of which helped to banish the demons. But none of that could thwart biology – the drop in blood sugar. So he lay awake for nearly three hours staring at the darkness, trying not to hear the song that was tormenting him. Instead, he heard the jazz melody from Thelonius Monk's 'Mysterioso'. It made him think of his evening in Laguna Beach. Of Hack Starkey's death mask. Of the old woman trying to drive out the evil in Buster Wiles.

Winnie was feeling clammy and anxious. He had a slight sensation of dread. He countered it by deliberately thinking of his childhood. Of shooting baskets in the driveway with his dad. His dad had always seemed so big and powerful. His father had seemed eternal.

Once again, Tess got up long before he did. Once again, the omelet was ready when he got down to the kitchen.

She was wearing a white jersey with green vertical stripes on the front, white shorts, white deck shoes. She smiled and left the frying pan long enough to kiss him. 'Sorry for last night,' she said.

'Nothing to it,' Winnie said. 'I'll be twice as nice today to make up for it.'

'It takes two to tangle, and I was a bitch,' she said, putting the omelet on his plate.

As before, she sat and drank coffee and watched him eat. Once, she reached over and brushed his hair back from his forehead. When his cup was half empty, she refilled it. She wanted to make him another omelet, but he declined. When he wanted to help with the dishes, she pushed him toward the patio with his coffee cup.

Winnie sat watching the traffic snaking its way along Pacific Coast Highway. He saw an outrigger racing team of six college girls powering past in the narrow channel. All of them were tan and fit, muscular specimens with strong paddling strokes and great shoulders. California girls.

When Tess came out and sat beside him, she said, 'I don't *really* know if Warner Stillwell has AIDS. Once he told me he had to check into the hospital from time to time, so I just assumed it.'

'It may be,' Winnie said. 'Doctor Lutz in Palm Desert might tell you if you call and say you're concerned.'

'To tell you the truth, Win, maybe I don't *want* to know for sure. I guess in my heart I always suspected that what Starkey told you last night might be what happened. That he and Daddy were the ones who got . . . *involved* for a few . . . *perverse* moments. I guess in my heart I thought it could've happened that way. I guess I preferred to believe that Daddy was an innocent victim of Warner Stillwell's philandering.'

'I understand,' Winnie said. 'It's OK, Tess. It's OK.'

She put her hands up under her glasses as though it would block out memories. When she removed them she looked at him dry-eyed, and said, 'I can take anything as long as it's the truth.'

'That's the toughest thing of all,' Winnie said. 'The truth here is awful slippery. It's like a . . . like the words to a song.'

Tess said, 'You're staring at me in that odd way again.'

'Was I? Sorry.'

'What should we do about Warner Stillwell?'

'What would you say if we just met him head on?'

'How?'

'Like arrange a meeting. Maybe here or out at his ranch. Just confront him with what we know.'

'That somebody took some shots at me? That somebody spied on me?'

'Yeah, and that if something should happen to you all of a sudden, he'd be a very sorry old guy one way or the other.'

'Sounds like bad melodrama.'

'It's better'n sitting around waiting for a guy to take another shot. He might aim better next time.'

'There must be some other way.'

'I'm out of ideas.'

'The Ensenada race is coming up,' she said.

'Yeah, April twenty-eighth. I crewed for a friend a mine three years in a row. We came in second in our class one year.'

'My father had a lifelong friend named Dextor Moody who always throws a party at his yacht club on Catalina Island the week before the race. Some of the sailors use it as an excuse to tune up their boats. They do a shakedown cruise to Catalina, and then back the next day. Daddy and Warner almost never missed that racing party. Dexter was about the only friend from the old days who accepted Warner, and I'll bet he'll take Warner over to the island on his yacht.'

'I don't see how that's gonna help us.'

'Warner will *not* come alone, no matter what his health's like. He'll have a companion drive him from the ranch, and accompany him on the boat.'

'How about one of his servants?'

'They're too old and not the type for a yachting party. There's a very good chance that Warner might bring *him*! The man who's stalking me. Is that a reasonable assumption?'

Winnie looked at the gray pebbles and said, 'Search me, lady. Nothing reasonable's happened to me since I met you.'

'Do you regret it?' she asked softly. 'Meeting me?'

'You know the answer to that.'

'This might be . . . dangerous.'

'I doubt it. He's not gonna take a shot at you at a yacht party.'

She grinned seductively and said, 'Are *you* feeling dangerous this morning?'

'Why, you got a hammock around here?'

She got up and patted his hand. 'Old son, daytime performances are just the ticket for middle-aged folks. Have you ever tried it from the cockpit of a sailboat?'

He sometimes thought the most enchanting thing about her was her imagination. Tess ran upstairs and quickly changed into a trendy mariner's outfit: a double-breasted, waist-length jacket with crested gold buttons and baggy sleeves, and white linen pants, with the white deck shoes. She told him she had to phone a yacht broker. When she reappeared, she posed provocatively and said, 'How's about a date, sailor?'

When they got in the car she informed him they were going sailing, but while driving down Coast Highway to the boat dealer, she suddenly asked Winnie if he needed a drink.

'I never *need* a drink,' Winnie said.

'Of course you don't,' Tess Binder said, turning the Mercedes into the driveway of the club. 'But it's almost noon. It's certainly not too early.'

He said to Tess, 'Maybe if we're gonna sail I shouldn't have any booze. I feel responsible for somebody else's boat.'

'The people I borrow boats from wouldn't care if you sunk them,' she said. 'In fact, they'd probably appreciate it. They could collect the insurance and buy a bigger one with more prestige. Let's have just *one* drink.'

279

He was starting to think that being with her was like traveling with his own bartender. He had to admit that a brew sounded good.

They took a table under an umbrella and he ordered a Mexican beer. He was a bit irritated when Tess ordered iced tea, no sugar.

'How come I'm the guy that has a real drink?' he said.

'I'll order something else if you want.'

'I don't *need* somebody drinking with me, Tess!' he said. '*You* suggested we have a drink in the first place!'

'Oh, please, let's not quarrel again,' she said, slipping her hand into his. 'We're going to have a *lovely* day.' When the waitress came with the beer, Tess said, 'Changed my mind. I'd like a beer too.'

Before he had time to object to *that* move, Corky Peebles blazed on to the patio from the private beach fifty yards away. She wore a see-through coverup over a gold bikini, with gold sandals. On the third toe of her left foot she wore a tiny gold band.

'As inevitable as dawn,' Tess said to Winnie. 'She comes up like thunder 'cross the bay. Where she's living with a girlfriend until she can find another husband.' When Corky came closer, Tess smiled and said, 'My, you've got an eary start on your tan this season!'

Corky stopped at the table, nodded at Winnie and said to Tess, 'I know it's déclassé nowadays, but I'm an old-fashioned girl. Besides, I look pretty good with a tan, yes?'

When she turned to Winnie, slit-eyed, he said, 'Absolutely!' And noticed a little scar on each of Corky's hips near the bikini line. Then he realized that Tess had similar marks, tiny, but they were there.

Corky said, 'Have you heard what Doris got from Bob for their honeymoon trip? The luggage, I mean?'

'Tell us,' said Winnie, glad that Tess had insisted on the beer. It tasted great.

'Crocodile luggage with gold fittings. Only gold *plated*, of course, but still.'

'How much did it cost?' Tess asked.

'A hundred and twenty-five thousand.'

'What a crock!' Winnie said, but Corky didn't react. Then he said, 'Crock?' Still nothing.

'She can't hold on to Manley,' Corky said. 'Men don't like her after they get to know her. Manley'll be available soon, you'll see.'

'He does seem sweet,' Tess said.

'One of those self-made street guys, though,' Corky offered. 'Thinks it was skill that made his waterfront house quadruple right after he bought it in seventy-five. When really it was dumb luck and a volatile market. They just can't admit things like that, those self-made types. How do you pass an evening with guys like that? What do you talk about? Like, one time I went with them to Beverly Hills when people still ate nouvelle. He looks at his plate and goes, "I don't know whether to hang it or drink it." Then he asks for ketchup! How do you pass an evening when you *marry* guys like that?'

'Reminds me of a self-made rich guy that comes down to Spoon's Landing,' Winnie said. 'Mouth like a mule skinner. Always had a load a snuff in his cheek, so big it looks like he forgot to take it outta the can. He says most a the wives only get to act out by voting for a Democrat once every four years.'

They nodded politely, but neither women seemed

interested, so Winnie signaled to the waitress for another beer.

'And have you heard about Blanche's husband?' Corky asked. 'The new bank he founded went belly up and he's being sued by thirteen foreign investors. Had to file Chapter eleven and he's forced to countersue them. But get this! He's syndicating his lawsuit! Fifty thousand shares of common stock at five dollars a share! He prepared a formal stock offering, and from any settlement judgment you get back your investment and a percentage of remaining proceeds.'

'He always had imagination,' Tess said.

'Shares in a lawsuit,' Winnie said. 'That's pretty amazing all right.'

While the women chatted, Winnie looked at his watch and ordered a vodka. He was definitely feeling a buzz by the time Corky left their table to join another hot momma on the beach. Winnie watched as together they approached a very fat, older man who was having a tall drink at the beach hut. One woman sat on either side of him and he pecked them both on the cheek.

As Tess signed the bill, Winnie pointed to the fat man and said, 'Who's that guy? Is he FFH rich?'

Tess squinted, then removed her sunglasses and put on the clear ones. 'Oh, that's Miles Jarvis,' she said. 'He's seven-one-four rich.'

'They work in pairs,' Winnie said. 'Corky makes the approach, the friend closes the deal.'

'They're not *hookers*, Win!' Tess said defensively. 'They have marriage in mind.'

'I'd say those ladies're entrepreneurs. Corky hopes to make a marriage *deal*. And her little pal's the *closer*! I think

I know what that tall drunk in the red toup was trying to say about the hot mommas around here. Like junk bonds: irresistible, but not worth it in the long run.'

He thought they were going to borrow a sailboat there at the club, but Tess surprised him by driving him to one of the yacht brokers on the main channel. She said it was an 'upmarket company', one of those yacht brokers where all the salesmen wore jackets and ties and the inventory in the boat slips was worth millions.

The broker was a tall good-looking guy about Winnie's age, with a terrific tan and teeth as white as Buster's. He was definitely commodore material for the old club, Winnie thought, as soon as he got old enough. He wore a blazer and slacks and a rep tie with deck shoes. He even wore socks.

'Boyd Schuyler, meet Win Farlowe,' Tess said after he'd kissed her on the cheek.

'Hear you're a pretty good sailor,' the broker said, and Winnie wondered if the guy knew he was the guy that stole Christmas from the boat paraders.

'How about showing Win some of your stock?' Tess asked.

They walked down the ramp, where there were huge power yachts in the first row of slips, and Boyd Schuyler said, 'A sailor probably isn't interested in these.'

Winnie gazed past them at a thirty-six-foot sloop in the second row. Boyd Schuyler followed his eyes and said, 'You in the market for a Swan, Mister Farlowe?'

Winnie didn't even bother to ask the price. He said simply, 'I got to sail a Swan thirty-eight one time. Did a favor for a guy and he took me out.'

283

'Bit too much of the heavy furniture feel for me,' Boyd Schuyler said. 'When Tess phoned she said you're the performance-boat type.'

'I'll take whatever you're willing to let us borrow.'

As they continued along the dock, the yacht broker said to Winnie, 'I guess you've sailed all the standard stuff?'

'Used to own a twenty-nine-foot sloop.'

'Do you know the Baltic?'

'Never sailed one,' Winnie said. 'I know it though.'

'It's like the Swan in that there's the feeling of security and the traditional warmth down below. *You* might like that, Tess.'

Winnie thought he saw Boyd Schuyler give a subtle nod to Tess when they got to the penultimate boat slip. The yacht broker said, 'I wonder if you'd like to take a look at this forty-footer? She's an ultralight. Only displaces ten thousand five hundred pounds.'

'That's a mini-sled!' Winnie said.

'Let's take a look, shall we?' said the broker.

He took Tess's hand and helped her up on to the deck of the sloop, with Winnie right behind her.

The broker said, 'We sailed a fifty like this and beat a Swan forty-six to Cabo San Lucas by nearly twenty hours. She surfs *sooner* than a heavy boat.'

Winnie was confused. Why was he showing them a terrific new boat like this? What had Tess told him?

'She's got a very long waterline and a planing hull, and for this dealer demo we put a furling one-fifty on her. Lots of little things. Deck hardware's through-bolted with stainless steel fasteners and backing plates.'

'She's a proper bag,' Winnie said. 'I'll bet she *flies*.'

'But she'll hold up under washing machine conditions.

284

The deck's cored with plywood inserts where there's high stress. The hull and deck're bonded and through-bolted with aluminum toe rails. Go on down the companionway and have a look at the main cabin. The cabinets and bulkhead are bonded directly to the hull. No floating bulkheads.'

Tess said, 'I want to see if this boat's got any lady features.'

When they got down in the cabin, Boyd Schuyler said to Tess, 'You've got two roomy quarter berths or doubles, and a large locker. You can stand upright in the head and the galley has a three-burner stove and oven and a stainless steel double sink. You've got double iceboxes and even a trash bin. She's not a cruiser, but there's comfort.'

'OK,' she said, 'I can make an omelet down here. I approve.'

'All seating is arranged so you have a three-sixty view out the cabin windows,' said the broker.

When Boyd Schuyler saw Winnie admiring the navigator's station, running his fingers along the Bruynzeel mahogany chart table, the broker said, 'Plenty of electronics, as you can see. Wind speed, autopilot, depth, VHF and Loran. The station is convenient to the cockpit and the whole electrical system is controlled at a breaker panel.'

'What kind of engine?'

'A twenty-seven-horsepower three-cylinder diesel.'

'Tell me, Boyd,' said Tess. 'How much does this boat cost?'

'Well, Tess, we like to quote prices without sails and electronics. That would be at a hundred and fifty thousand.'

'This boat *has* sails and electronics, Boyd,' she said. 'How much?'

He laughed and said, 'For you, Tess, we'll do the best we can. I'd have to sit down and do some computing. Probably another twenty thousand, more or less.'

'OK,' she said. 'Let's take her for a sea trial.'

'She's ready,' Boyd Schuyler said. 'If *you* are, Mister Farlowe.'

Winnie was astonished. 'You're not coming?'

The yacht broker shook his head and said, 'Tess said I'm not needed and that's good enough for me.'

Before Winnie's heart stopped banging, the boat was cruising along the channel, under power. He was so nervous about sailing a new boat like this that he wouldn't hoist the main and shut off the engine until they got past the Balboa ferry.

'How could you do this?' he finally asked Tess, who sat beside him in the cockpit.

'What?'

'Pretend you're interested in buying this boat?'

'Why wouldn't I? Haven't you ever test-driven a Porsche or some fancy car you knew you couldn't afford?'

'Actually, no,' Winnie said. 'I never had the guts.'

'Boyd's used to it,' she said. 'Do you think everyone who walks in there hands him a check and sails away in the sunset?'

'No, but this! She's a hotdog racing boat!'

'All the more reason you should be the first to sail her, old son,' Tess said, kissing his earlobe as he steered past the pavilion.

When he finally hoisted the jib, the ultralight sloop

leaped forward. Twice, a windsurfer flashed across the bow, and Winnie was thrilled by the boat's responsiveness when he maneuvered out of the way.

Winnie pointed to the sheets and said to Tess, 'Wanna pull the strings?'

'What's that?'

'Work the sheets.'

'Aye, aye, skipper,' she said. 'I'm the right wench for a winch.'

Winnie laughed. Everything made him laugh. He was sure there was good wind out on the ocean. This was his day! He decided to pretend that she was his, this agile sloop.

Reading his mind as always, Tess said, 'What would you call her?' Then she looked over the stern, patted the transom and said, 'Right here. What name would you paint on her rump?'

'I've always liked pretty names,' he said. '*Jasmine*, maybe.'

'Horrible!' she cried. 'A boat that can sail almost as fast as the wind needs a name with sex appeal. How about *La Venganza*?'

'What's that mean?'

'*The Revenge*. That's a great name for a fast boat.'

'She's also a sweet boat. Why not a sweet name? Like *Tessie*?'

'Ree-volting!' she said. 'This is *La Venganza*. She's sexy. She's dangerous!'

'A boat called *Revenge*? Well, it's not bad, I guess. For a fantasy boat.'

When they cleared the jetty, he brought the boat up on course to weather.

When he tacked for the first time, he yelled, 'Ready about!'

'Ready, skipper!' Tess shouted back.

'Hard a-leeeee!' Winnie laughed, noting that there was hardly a luff before Tess trimmed the jib.

The tack was buttery and fast. The sails roared, then filled, and they were jetting forward again, away from the buoy and the sea lions, a blue plume of spray in their faces.

'OK!' Winnie shouted. 'Let's pop the chute!'

Tess took the helm, and Winnie found the spinnaker down below. The spinnaker was blood-red with a slashing yellow stripe. In a few minutes they were in a race with the wind.

'She's built to run!' Winnie said, tasting salt in his teeth.

The big sloop sped southeast in the sunlight, glinting like a knife, down past Corona Del Mar, where the water dramatically changed to midnight blue and the sea creatures visible in the water all wore black wet suits with Day-Glo stripes and bobbed like seals.

He anticipated a sudden wind change and decided to play. 'Now, let's *drop* the chute!'

'Aye, skipper,' Tess responded, moving very quickly. She could sail a boat, all right.

And then, magic! A school of dolphin flashed across the bow, doubled back and swam under the sloop when he jibed. The dolphins stayed right with him on a close reach as the boat heeled so steeply that Winnie yelled to Tess, 'The rail's in the water!'

They were playing with him! The dolphins were enjoying their day as much as he was. He took her on a broad reach again, and Tess ran to the bow and lay flat, looking over the stem as the dolphins flashed beneath her in a game of sailboat tag.

Then the lead dolphin veered off, headed toward the shore, and the others followed. Winnie saw that the wind was blowing fifteen knots and they were sailing nine or ten! A hotdog boat!

Then, a last bit of enchantment. A silvery translucent bi-plane took off from the sea just off starboard. A flying fish. Then another. Then three more. A good omen!

The day disappeared on Winnie Farlowe. The first time he looked at his watch, he was shocked. It was after six when he came about and sailed very close to the shifting wind, back toward the harbor.

This time, despite the speed of the vessel slicing toward them, the sea lions were not troubled. Without an engine roar, they merely watched as Winnie sailed so close to the buoy that Tess could've almost touched the whiskers of a jealous bull, who covered the bodies of two small females. The tapper on the buoy sounded musical! Winnie laughed out loud.

By the time they approached the breakwater, Tess was in his arms almost dozing. The sky was ablaze and the sun was getting ready for the magic hour show.

'We did everything but spot a whale,' Winnie said.

'Next time, old son,' she murmured. 'We'll do even better next time.'

But Winnie Farlowe sensed that there could never be another day like this one.

'You know, Dennis Connor's entering the Ensenada race,' Winnie said. 'He'll sail the *Stars and Stripes* catamaran with a soft-sail rig instead of the airfoil wing he used in San Diego.'

Tess said, 'When I was married the first time, my husband forced me to crew with him on that race. Galley slaves had it better.'

'He'll be going after the record,' Winnie said. 'Ten hours, thirty-one minutes and two seconds. I was in the race when that record was set. Nineteen eighty-three. Newport to Ensenada, Mexico, in ten hours, thirty-one minutes. Of course, our boat needed another five hours, but still, that's a hundred and twenty-five miles! Think of it!'

'And what'd you do when you got there?' Tess asked. 'All my husband and his friends did was go to that ugly party they throw in a building they'd condemn if it was on the US side of the border. Everybody falling down drunk and throwing up. A convention of Hell's Angels shows more class.'

'Jist a bunch of sailors letting their hair down,' Winnie said. 'Imagine what it'd be like to race *this* boat in the Ensenada race!'

'I simply can't imagine,' said Tess Binder, observing the boyish glow in the eyes of Winnie Farlowe.

Tess suddenly stood up on the cockpit seat and stripped off her sweater and pants.

Winnie looked around the jetty for fishermen and said, 'Jesus, Tess!'

He didn't see anyone, but she obviously didn't care if he did. She unfastened her bra and stripped off her panties. When she sat on his lap he looked around and saw a lone fisherman trudging along the jetty at day's end with two buckets, a gunny sack and a fishing pole. The fisherman

wore a painter's cap with a Coors logo on the front, and
had a belly that got in doorways five minutes before he
did. The guy was looking downbeat and discouraged, as
though he'd been skunked. Until he happened to glance
over at the sailboat gliding by in light twilight air.

Tess rose up and gave him a victory sign, and the
fisherman yelled, 'Whoooooo-eeeee!' at the naked blonde in
the cockpit of the sloop.

Then Winnie lost control of *everything* and the boat was
all over the channel. Once he giggled and cried, 'Prepare
to jibe!' and 'Jibe ho!', followed by screams of laughter
from Tess Binder. With the naked woman climbing all
over him, Winnie finally had to furl his headsail and drop
the main.

By the time Tess finished with Winnie, and got herself
dressed, the sun had almost set. A breeze was blowing in
from Catalina where the island seemed to rise from red
dusk. Winnie was sprawled back in the cockpit and
caressing the tiller when they slid by the old pavilion, the
Victorian dowager of the Balboa peninsula. The pavilion's
observation tower and cupola glimmered in twilight
beneath a crystal sky.

Winnie felt almost sad enough to cry. He'd never had
such a perfect day, not as a grown man. There were
perfect days only when his father was alive. When he and
his father went out on boats. When they were boys
together, he and his father, on perfect days like this.

'My dad used to say her crown looks like a candy kiss,'
Winnie said, and he was surprised when his voice
quivered.

'Who?'

'The old pavilion,' he said. 'And after dark when the

291

lights go on, the crow's nest on top looks like a bright shining gumdrop.'

'A bright shining gumdrop.' Tess chuckled. 'That's my boy! A bright shining gumdrop.'

When they arrived at the yacht broker's, they found the office dark and empty. Winnie steered the sloop into the slip, tied her up, stowed the spinnaker, removed the battens, and covered the main.

'Is he gonna be mad that we're so late?'

'Of course not!' Tess said. 'Just toss the key through the letter slot. I'll call him tomorrow and tell him we're thinking about it. Maybe we'll need another sea test before we make up our minds.'

'You're amazing,' he said.

'You'll never forget this day, will you, old son?'

'Not as long as I live.'

Tess chuckled again. Like wind chimes. Then she said, 'It tickles me every time I think of it.'

'What?'

'A bright shining gumdrop. You're my precious precious boy. A bright shining gumdrop!'

18: *Two Harbors*

For once, she didn't let him sleep late. 'Wake up, old son! Come on, sleepyhead!'

Winnie had been having a dream about the nymph, something that caused him to toss and sweat. The nymph had tried to speak to him at last. She'd hovered over him and he could see her gray marble eyes. Winnie jumped up, but his head didn't. It was somewhere on the other side of the bed, and somebody was beating on it with a mallet, like a slab of squid.

'Got a busy day. Breakfast's ready. No omelet. Bacon and fried eggs, over easy with hash browns. Come on!' She clapped her hands three times and left him alone to deal with the hangover. The echo was like rifle fire.

They'd stayed home last night. The last Winnie remembered, he was lying on the living room floor watching the old war movie where John Wayne takes Iwo Jima, actually filmed on the very spot where he now spent his nights and days: Linda Isle, then called Shark Island, a name that Nouveau Newport didn't appreciate after the sandspit was developed for residential property. Especially since a few of the home buyers had been referred to as sharks in their time, as in land, loan, etc.

He'd had a *lot* to drink last night. He was becoming increasingly worried about that, but it wasn't entirely his fault. Tess kept refilling his glass! He taught her how to make The Golden Orange cocktail, and every time John Wayne shot a Jap she'd be in the kitchen mixing another batch. He remembered telling her he was outdrinking her three to one, maybe four to one. She'd laughed and said she was holding her own.

His hands were shaking and he was bilious. He belched, and a sour ball erupted from a deep well of toxic waste. He'd been poisoned by too much of a good thing, too much of The Golden Orange. He tried to get up. This time, his head stayed with its body.

When he finally lurched into the kitchen, pale and shaky, but showered and shaved, Tess took his breakfast plate out of the oven.

'Sorry to roust you out of bed so early, old son, but I've got news!'

He said, 'Tess, I don't wanna drink anything today. I'm so sick I actually look like the picture on my driver's license.'

'Oh, never mind that,' she said. 'You'll feel better at lunchtime. I had a slight hangover too, but it's gone. Listen, I've got *real* news!'

'Do you have some aspirin?'

She fetched the aspirin from a cupboard and poured his coffee.

'Listen! Dexter Moody's yacht party at the isthmus begins tonight with a picnic tomorrow! I rang him and he said he'd like us to come!'

She never said *phoned* him or *called* him. *Rang* him. *Masterpiece Theater*. Cute, but not when his head was a squid getting pounded into steaks.

'I don't quite understand.'

'We're going to Catalina, silly! We'll take the catamaran

to Avalon and taxi to the isthmus for the party. After which we'll sleep at the B and B over there. And, are you ready for *this*?'

'With you I gotta be ready for anything,' Winnie said, picking at the fried eggs with his fork.

'Warner Stillwell's going to arrive tomorrow!'

That got his attention. 'Who with?'

'He'll be coming with some people from China Cove. They have a big custom powerboat called *Circe*. We'll be there when they arrive.'

'So tomorrow I meet him?'

'We'll have a long talk, Warner and you and me.'

'Let's see how it goes first,' Winnie warned. 'See who's with him. Maybe I'll talk to him *alone*.'

'You're the skipper,' she said.

His hands were trembling so much he spilled coffee on his eggs. He was *not* going to have a drink until this thing with Stillwell was over. In fact, he decided he'd go on the wagon for a month just to prove he could do it. He didn't like the way he looked and felt this morning. It *scared* him.

'Hurry, slowpoke,' Tess said. '*The Catalina Flyer* leaves in forty minutes. We've got to pack a few things.'

'I want you to promise we're not gonna drink *anything* till this is all over,' Winnie said. 'My brain feels like I leased it out.'

'Whatever you say, Cap'n. We'll drink plain orange juice.'

'I feel like I been drinking *Agent* Orange juice,' Winnie said, hoping his hands would stop shaking before noon. 'By the way, who was *Circe*? A goddess or what?'

'She was a bad bad girl,' said Tess Binder.

The sailmaker was yelling at two employees when Buster Wiles climbed the stairs to the cavernous sail loft. The sails were laid out on the huge varnished floor with drawings under the Kevlar material. Six men sat at sewing machines in pits below floor level.

Woody saw Buster and growled something else at the two employees, who seemed very glad for the interruption.

'Problems, Woody?' Buster said to the sailmaker.

Woody was so weather ravaged and bald it wasn't easy to guess his age, but Buster thought he was about seventy.

'Can't find decent help these days,' the sailmaker grumbled, wiping his sweaty face with the tail of his green T-shirt.

Buster said, 'I could hear you clear from the street. Had a sergeant once could air out a guy like you do.'

'What good is it? They come and go like grunion, these beach bums.' The ponderous sailmaker had a Frankenstein gait from a fused right knee, and practically clanked down the stairs to the glassed-in cubicle that served as his office. Designs and brochures and sail samples were everywhere. He opened the desk drawer and handed Buster a set of keys attached to a flotation cork.

'OK if I don't bring her back till tomorrow?' Buster asked. 'Thinkin about maybe goin down to Dana Point. I know a guy down there lets me tie up all night. Sells outboards. Name a Guthrie. Know him?'

The sailmaker shook his head and walked with Buster out to the street, where the cop had double-parked by one of Woody's vans. 'Keep it a week if you want,' the sailmaker said. 'Don't know why I don't sell that boat. I can't use it. Leave here for half a day and these idiots'd probably burn the place down. Can't get decent help no more.'

The cry of The Golden Orange, from the hot mommas to an old guy in a sail shop. Can't get decent help.

'The police department can't run very long without me so I'll be back tomorrow,' Buster said.

The old sailmaker looked in the back of Buster's car. The entire seat and the floor were taken up by scuba gear. 'You oughtta get a hatchback or a van. Gonna ruin your upholstery with that stuff.'

'I'm lucky I can afford gas on my salary,' Buster said. 'Those two douche bags I divorced grab half a what the city pays me. They got hearts like an Iranian judge.'

'You might take some lobster and abalone around Catalina this time a year,' the sailmaker offered. 'Not too many tourists, now that spring vacation's over.'

Winking, Buster said, 'I'd rather stay around Dana Point. There's this waitress down there. She can dive without tanks. Lungs out to here.'

'Have fun, kiddo,' the sailmaker said. 'Gotta go back inside or those morons'll cut up my goods to patch their crummy jeans.'

The boat slip that the sailmaker had leased from the city of Newport Beach was only a few minutes from his shop. Woody's twenty-eight-foot Bertram was seedy from lack of use. Two gulls and a pelican were living on the fly bridge. Buster hauled his gear to the dock beside the boat and hopped aboard. At first he was afraid the batteries were dead, but then he remembered that Woody had installed an anti-theft battery bypass. He reached into the engine compartment and turned the bypass switch on. After he ran the blowers, the engines fired at once.

It wasn't a particularly warm morning, but Buster felt exceptionally clammy. He took off his windbreaker and began to transfer his gear from the dock to the boat: a black wet suit, mask, fins, a weight belt, two tanks, a black hood, a light, a knife . . .

America's largest catamaran, *The Catalina Flyer*, left its berth by the Balboa Pavilion at nine o'clock sharp. The huge cat held five hundred persons, and could make the twenty-five nautical-mile crossing in seventy-five minutes, weather permitting.

Winnie had been aboard the catamaran only one other time, and for this trip he sat on the top deck forward, facing the wind. Hoping for revival.

'I need an oxygen tank, is what I need,' Winnie said to Tess, who looked gorgeous in a lime-green cableknit sweater, with her butterscotch hair blowing free. For the first time he noticed the tiny line of scar in front of her ear, when the wind blew the hair back.

'You'll be in the pink after we get there, old son,' she said.

Tess eventually went below for coffee, but Winnie stayed put. He passed the time by breathing deeply – trying to purge every vein and artery with a fix of sea air. He avoided contact with other passengers. They were youngish couples with small children, and older people whose children were grown, people not ruled by school schedules.

Santa Catalina Island was bought from the pioneering Banning family by the Wrigleys of Chicago in 1914. The island is now mainly controlled by a conservancy, a nonprofit charitable foundation, which was deeded forty thousand acres by the Wrigleys and is responsible for keeping its eighty-six per cent of the island in a natural state forever.

The island is twenty-two miles long and eight miles wide at its widest point. Formerly a verdant paradise without large herbivores, the island has been ravaged by animals introduced for man's pleasure. The Spanish brought the goats, the Yankees introduced feral pigs and deer for hunting, and Hollywood brought the buffalo for the filming of Zane Grey's *Vanishing American*, the famous author himself being a resident at Avalon. The buffalo ended up on the cutting-room floor, but stayed on Catalina Island, where they roam the hills and, when the herds are cropped, end up in buffalo burgers and buffalo tacos.

Now, what with thousands of wild pigs eating the acorns, wild bison and deer eating the grasses, and wild goats eating everything, there is a constant effort on the part of the conservancy to keep the animals under control and the shallow soil intact. Still, Catalina is a beautiful place, and Winnie was always glad to return.

The ocean swells were three to four feet during the crossing, but Winnie knew they sometimes reached sixteen feet from trough to peak, this being a treacherous stretch of ocean. After an hour had passed, when the big cat slowed with Avalon Harbor dead ahead, Winnie was starting to feel better. He always loved the sight of the Avalon Pavilion off starboard. Tall as a twelve-story building, with art deco murals, the once fashionable casino is now used as a big-band ballroom, art gallery and cinema.

In the summer months the harbor of Avalon is under siege by an armada of yachts, and moorings have sold for more than $175,000, Catalina Island being one of the few destinations available to mainland yachtsmen. The narrow beach in Avalon is jammed in the summer, and the streets are mobbed.

Avalon is a very small town on a dot in the ocean, and doesn't offer much variety in the way of entertainment. Winnie knew that if he lived here he'd *really* become an alcoholic. The thought of it made him look at his hands. They'd finally stopped shaking. He was starting to regret he hadn't eaten his breakfast, but it was too early for lunch.

The sailboats and power yachts occupied most of the moorings, and shore boats taxied their passengers ashore for two bucks a head. The cruise ships and *The Catalina Flyer* were allowed to dock at the quay.

After Winnie and Tess disembarked and were strolling along Crescent Avenue, the main promenade, Tess said, 'No point rushing to the isthmus. We've got lots of time to kill.'

Winnie looked at his watch and Tess eyed him knowingly.

'I'm *not* looking to see if it's late enough for a drink,' he said.

'I didn't say you were.'

'I'm just seeing if it's too early for lunch.'

'We can eat any time you like,' she said.

They chose a restaurant favored by many of the two thousand locals, off the main promenade. Tess ordered a salad, no dressing, and Winnie asked for a cheeseburger and fries. While they were waiting for their food, Tess said, 'Greasy stuff takes care of the alcohol in your system. It's the best thing when you've been drinking. I don't think a beer'd hurt you.'

'I'm *not* drinking today!' Winnie said.

She reached over, and touched his cheek and said, 'You don't mind if I do?'

'Why should I mind?'

He was surprised when she didn't order a beer. She didn't even order a glass of white wine. She ordered a *double Scotch* at eleven o'clock in the morning! And she asked for a bucket glass.

'I'm on holiday,' she said apologetically. 'I'm going to have *fun*.'

When the drink came, Tess got animated. She picked it up and clicked it against Winnie's water tumbler.

'Chin chin,' she said. 'I'll do the drinking for both of us.'

She sipped, threw her head back like a bird, and said, 'Mmmmmmm.' He watched her throat muscles work on the Scotch. He could almost see it gliding down that graceful throat. He *loved* bucket glasses. They seemed more nautical – a heavy solid honest bucket glass.

He caught a glimpse of pink. Her tongue flicked along her chrome-red lipstick. She sucked the liquid like a she-wolf. Winnie waved to the waitress. He ordered a double vodka on the rocks. Tess said nothing.

'Unfortunately,' he explained, 'this is the only thing for a hangover. One a these and I'll feel OK.'

'You look OK now,' Tess said seductively. 'You look good enough to eat. One more of these and I might decide

301

to *do* it. Maybe we could try it on a glass-bottom boat? Give the divers and the fish a show.'

The cheeseburger arrived and it was OK. So were the fries. The drink was a *very* honest one. Tess said he still looked a little shaky and should probably have another.

Winnie ordered another double vodka. He had three before they left the restaurant at twelve-thirty. He and Tess were in a great mood. She kept repeating that he looked 'extraordinarily sexy'.

They walked down Crescent Avenue to the pavilion and watched some scuba divers sitting on the seawall, shucking clams.

'Let's come about, skipper,' Tess said.

'OK, where we going?'

'I know a lovely little tavern in the town.'

'There *is* no lovely little tavern. Too many tourists in them.'

'This one's different.'

'Don't you think we oughtta do something besides drink?'

Tess looked around, and saw that the tourists were all watching the divers. She ran her hand down inside his belt tickling his lower belly with her long vermilion nails. Her gray eyes narrowed, vulpine and sly. 'I *will* do something besides drink if I can get you in a dark corner of that lovely dark tavern!'

'Let's go find your tavern,' said Winnie.

As he'd predicted, there was nothing lovely about it. It was just a bar where islanders did their drinking. It was dark, but there were *no* corners. The room was round.

'Oh, well,' Tess said. 'It used to look different when I was younger.'

They ordered doubles. There were only three other customers. Winnie had to use the men's room, and when he got back there were two *more* drinks in front of them.

'Where'd these come from?' he asked.

'I finished mine while you were gone,' she said boozily. 'I wanted another so I ordered another for you.'

'You finished yours just like that?'

'Like *that*,' she said. 'I'm on holiday!'

'I had good intentions,' Winnie said weakly.

Tess reached up and pulled Winnie down by the hair. She thrust that muscular tongue straight into his left ear, and said, 'I want *bad* intentions, big boy. This is holiday time!'

Winnie raised the bucket and said, 'I'm catching up!'

'That's my boy!' Tess said, and Winnie drank guilt-free, proving yet again that the superego is alcohol soluble.

They ordered yet *another* round, and Tess, whose voice seemed to be getting thick, said, 'I gotta make a call, sailor. Gotta check on our B and B.'

'Thought you already booked the room.'

'Yeah, but I've got to make sure it's ready. I hate getting turned away from inns, like Mary and Joseph.'

While she was gone, Winnie noticed that his jaw was going numb. Greasy food or not, he'd had *enough*. He put the drink down, but then he saw that there was half a shot left in the glass. He drained it and put the glass down again.

Lousy joint didn't serve anything but crummy American vodka. He noticed that the fish in the aquarium on the wall seemed to be swimming. Then he looked closer and saw that it was a plastic fish in a three-dimensional wall hanging! He blinked hard and the fish stayed put.

'Guess what?' Tess said when she returned.

'What?'

'Our room's ready.'

'So let's go.'

'We've got some time to kill. One more for the road?' Tess raised her hand and called for two more doubles.

By the time they were back out on the street, Winnie was walking unsteadily. Tess led him to the taxi stand and the young driver helped Winnie up into the van.

'That vodka,' Winnie said. 'They oughtta can it and sell it to the cops. Tasted like Mace.'

Buster filled the Bertram at the waterfront gas station next to the Balboa ferry. The kid pumping gas said, 'Going after abalone?'

'Anything I can get,' said Buster Wiles. 'Sometimes you gotta take what life offers.'

'Guess so,' the kid said, topping off the tank. 'Hope you have good luck!'

'Gotta *make* your luck sometimes,' Buster said.

The day was heating up, and the sun crashed down on Buster Wiles up on the fly bridge. When he neared the end of the jetty, he thought the wind would cool him off, but it didn't. He took off his sweatshirt and felt chilled with only a T-shirt underneath, but in a moment he was OK. In fact, his underarms were damp with sweat. He'd been sweating all morning.

When he cleared the jetty, he gave her some throttle. He did *not* turn south-east toward Dana Point. The lazy sea lions on the bell buoy were indifferent to Buster Wiles, who steered a compass bearing of 240. Toward the isthmus of Santa Catalina Island.

The west end of Catalina was by far Winnie's favorite part of the island, and he was grateful for a respite from booze as the taxi wound along the road from Avalon over the mountains to the isthmus. During the hour-and-a-half drive, Winnie gazed at Mount Blackjack, the second highest elevation at two thousand feet, on an island without flat land. His father had taken him camping there when he was ten years old, and Winnie felt nostalgia welling up in his throat. It took a moment to subside. It was shocking to think that he was older now than his father had been when he took his son to the top of Mount Blackjack on a nature hike with his Cub Scout troop.

When they approached Little Harbor on the offshore side of the island, Winnie was a bit more sober and said to Tess, 'God, I forgot how beautiful it is! The white rock and black rock and the clear water!'

The driver had to slow when a mother buffalo and a calf, their hides caked with the chalky red dust of the island, crossed the road in front of the taxi, disdainfully trampling some prickly pear as though the yellow blossom cactus weren't there. Finally the road snaked its way down into Two Harbors, Santa Catalina's narrowest point, where Isthmus Cove on the north and Catalina Harbor on the south are separated by a narrow strip of land only half a mile wide.

Here the cloud shadow on the hillsides gave the rugged

landscape a look of moss and velvet before the summer burn. Cat Head juts out of Catalina Harbor on the south like a mini-Gibraltar, and the little harbor below Cat Head was dead calm with perhaps thirty boats moored and anchored: yachtsmen, fishermen and divers arriving early for the weekend.

A three-masted Chinese junk, the *Ning-Po*, lies in shallow water there in Cat Harbor, a boat with a colorful history. First used by smugglers in China, later captured by Chinese Gordon himself – who later passed into legend at Khartoum – the junk became a prison ship and finally ended up as a restaurant, a movie prop, and now a sunken oddity.

Sailing into Two Harbors through Isthmus Cove was the way Winnie loved best. So many times he'd come from the mainland for a weekend to fish the kelp beds with his dad. He'd always gotten that same feeling, his throat swelling up when he saw the chalk cliffs off to port, and Bird Rock off to starboard – home of gulls, pelicans and cormorants – a rock that guarded the harbor like an iceberg. And in fact many a careless skipper had been sunk by this 'iceberg' when his bottom struck the protective reef to the south, so shallow it juts out of the water at low tide.

Winnie and his father used to moor in Isthmus Cove and fish for halibut, yellowtail, albacore, mako shark, and his dad's favorite, white sea bass. Winnie often thought that if his father were alive he wouldn't have let himself deteriorate after he'd been forced out of police work. His dad would have saved him from himself. And then it occurred to him that he was still a lost little lad, longing for a father's protection. Did that *ever* end?

From the charcoal-gray, rock-strewn beach at Isthmus Cove the land rises up gently across the isthmus, with steep rugged hills ascending on both sides. Shaggy, wind-shaped eucalyptus and artfully placed palm trees provide a picturesque backdrop for the village at Isthmus Cove. Hollywood palm trees were uprooted when Sunset Boulevard was widened during the movie town's Golden Age, and the trees were shipped to Two Harbors to give the village the look it needed for filming *Rain*, *Hurricane* and *Mutiny on the Bounty*. Many of the wood-frame buildings with tarpaper roofs, including the general store, were constructed as a backlot in the thirties, and now serve as homes for the 130 souls living at Two Harbors.

Older yachtsmen still tell tales of the days when 'Christian's Hut', built for the Clark Gable–Charles Laughton epic, became a favorite saloon for the legendary binges of Errol Flynn, Victor McLaglen, David Niven, Ward Bond, and of course, John Wayne, until it burned down and was never rebuilt.

The dive-boat skippers claim there's fifty-foot visibility in the water by the kelp beds and reef off Isthmus Cove, making it a diver's paradise. Winnie remembered two trips he'd made here with Buster Wiles on the Bertram belonging to Woody the sailmaker to dive for abalone and lobster by the reef. On one of those trips they were outside the cove near Ship Rock, another small outcropping snowcapped with guano, when Buster had suddenly surfaced with a lobster in each hand.

Buster's violet eyes were dilated with fear! He'd been surprised by a large mako, which had come from nowhere and knocked the mask off his face. Still, Buster had clung to his lobsters, and later they cooked them on the beach by the pier and shared them with two young women from the Avalon Safari Tours, both of whom fell in love with Buster while he told them about the mako shark. He'd had good times there at Two Harbors, Winnie and his friend Buster Wiles.

Instead of going straight to the lodge on the hilltop, Tess asked the driver to let them off by a general store down in the village. The taxi fare was ninety dollars, and Tess gave the kid a hundred and waved goodbye.

'Need something from the store?' Winnie asked.

'Need a drink,' she said. 'That Catalina red dust, I've got it in my teeth.'

There was one restaurant in Two Harbors, with a bar inside and another bar outside on a wooden deck. They chose the outside bar and sat on the stools rather than at a table.

'It's glorious,' Tess said. 'We're going to have a warm glorious weekend!'

'Hot,' Winnie said. 'Hot for Catalina at this time of year.' Then to the bartender, 'Double vodka. Polish if you got it.'

After the second one Winnie started to regain the buzz he'd lost during the taxi drive. After the next the buzz became a roar. After the fourth he knew he was getting drunk.

'Think we better go find our room?' he said. 'It's almost four o'clock. What time's the party start?'

'Dexter said to be there at six. Sunset in paradise, that sort of thing.'

'Which club is it?' Winnie asked. 'There's several little yacht clubs around here.'

'I don't know the name of it. The one near Cherry Cove. Walking distance, according to Dexter.'

'I know that one,' Winnie said. 'A *long* walk. Maybe we oughtta eat something now. I'm getting loaded.'

'No, you're not,' Tess said.

'I'm drinking two for every one a yours!' said Winnie. 'Or three.'

'I'll let you know when you're drunk, old son,' she said. 'I was married to three drinking men. I know the symptoms. You're *far* from drunk. Anyway, we'll get a ride to the party from our B and B landlady.'

At 4.45 they left the bar and walked to the hilltop lodge, past the old Civil War barracks where the Union troops were supposed to protect the California gold from pirates during voyages from San Francisco to New York and Boston. The B and B lodge, once the home of the island's first family, was a charming old building overlooking both harbors from a hilltop promontory. Their room was comfortable and cozy. Tess told Winnie to shower first while she lay in bed watching the five o'clock news.

When it was her turn to shower, Winnie went down to the public room, whose fireplace had a century-old smell of eucalyptus and oak. He strolled outside and climbed the hill to enjoy the view of Cat Harbor. To ponder where life would take him now that he'd met Tess Binder.

While standing there on the hilltop, full of nostalgia from early memories of this place, he couldn't stop thinking of loss: his father, his career, his youth. He was full of alcohol and self-pity. He walked a little way up the road toward the Cat Harbor side where the path was littered with buffalo chips: Catalina frisbees. He saw a doe standing between a scrub oak and a dramatic, wind-sculpted cypress. The doe turned and pranced atop a rise and was gone. It was so ephemeral, that glimpse of something delicate and lovely. Winnie was almost drunk enough to run after the doe for one more glimpse, but he knew he'd never catch her. She was gone forever.

He thought if he didn't get a drink he was going to start crying and might not stop. At that moment, for the first time, Winnie Farlowe considered that possibly, just *possibly*, he might be a sick man. He *might* be what Sammy Vogel had mentioned: a dysfunctional alcoholic. He promised himself then that with or without Tess Binder's help he was going to quit drinking. For six months. Maybe forever. Starting tomorrow.

Then he looked down toward the lodge. She was standing outside with her back to him, looking toward Isthmus Cove, her hair blowing back from her neck, her white dress clinging, backlit. She had a gardenia in her hair and she wore black-and-white spectator pumps, the kind they wore in some of those black-and-white movies they used to film in places like this. He imagined how she looked from the front with that dress hugging her thighs, that white side-slit dress, her bare legs tanned and shimmering.

The things that happened for the first time
Seem to be happening again . . .

In his drunken state the song seemed to be going at the wrong speed again. It was too slow. The lyrics and the melody were grotesque.

310

And so it seems that we have met before
And laughed before . . .

He put his hands over his ears. He felt like screaming. He *was* going crazy! He *might* have screamed except that Tess turned and saw him and waved. The song faded. Winnie returned her wave weakly and began descending the hill. He needed a drink.

When he reached her, she put her arm around his waist and said, 'Well, old son, shall we go to a party?'

'You look absolutely beautiful,' he said.

'Thank you, skipper.' She leaned her head against his shoulder.

'I'm already pretty drunk,' Winnie said. 'And I know I'll get drunker tonight.'

'I'll watch over you. Go ahead and enjoy yourself.'

They stood there for a moment looking down at Two Harbors, at the sun on its downward reach, leaving a trail of fire behind. 'I guess before I get too drunk I just wanna say that . . . that I think I got a problem I got to control. I think I'm gonna stop drinking tomorrow and . . . and . . .'

'Yeah?'

'I wanted you to know that drunk or sober I woulda enjoyed this time you and me've had together just as much. And . . . well . . .'

He studied her, that white linen dress, those black-and-white pumps and bare legs, the gardenia in her hair, its scent mixing with jasmine. A single strand of pearls and no other jewelry, the only vivid color coming from her lipstick red as blood. And he said: 'No matter what happens, I wanna say you're more beautiful than that sky out there. And I love you more than my memories of this

311

place. You're here and now and *real*. And that's all I wanted to say before I get too drunk to say it.'

For the first time Winnie Farlowe actually saw tears on the cheeks of Tess Binder. All the other times she'd bury her face and sob. Now she wasn't sobbing. She was tearfully looking into his eyes. He removed her glasses and touched her cheeks. Then he licked the salt from his fingers.

When their landlady dropped them off, they walked down the hill to the yacht club, hand in hand. Tess didn't speak at all, not until they were looking at the outcropping of rock called Lion's Head, the guardian of Cherry Grove.

The yacht club was already full of people and every mooring was taken. The shore boat from Isthmus Cove was taking groups of people through the emerald water to the little pier by the club.

Tess looked very sad when she finally spoke to him. She said, 'If I were to say that with you I feel something I've never felt before, would you believe me?'

'Yes! I feel the same!'

'I want you to believe me,' she said. 'I want you to believe I'd spend my life with you. If such a thing were possible.'

'Tess,' he said. 'Tess!'

Tess Binder's eyes! He was always trying to peek within. Whenever he'd get close to succeeding, she'd suddenly draw those gray curtains or switch off the lamps.

Even now she pulled away, and suddenly she became her playful old self. 'We don't have time for that!' she said.

'It's time to go down there and party, old son! A full moon makes me howl!'

'It was full *last* night,' Winnie informed her. 'The moon, sun and earth, they won't quite line up. Not tonight.'

19: *Dark Water*

The yacht club was very ascetic by mainland standards, even by Avalon standards. But for the isthmus it was posh. Which meant that the plumbing worked and the floor was in one piece and there were cabañas and dressing rooms, and a few bungalows that were actually heated in winter. Yachtsmen, even if they were FFH rich, prided themselves on rustic informality. The location was, like all the isthmus, probably more beautiful than any coastline on the Southern California mainland. The water was turquoise and emerald, and clear. And the bottom was sandy white, the nearest thing to tropical water that California has to offer.

And since this was an isthmus yacht club where people came directly from their boats, the dress code was campground casual, even at a yacht club luau. Tess was overdressed, but Winnie, in a Reyn Spooner aloha shirt, white cotton trousers and deck shoes, looked about right for the soirée.

The food had been prepared on the mainland and delivered to the restaurant at Two Harbors for last-minute touches. There were three bartenders and six young women serving food at this, the largest annual yacht party on the west end of Catalina Island, hosted by Dexter Moody.

An eight-piece orchestra from Newport Beach that

314

usually played weekends on Balboa peninsula had been brought in to play tunes from the big-band era. There were at least three hundred people swarming over the yacht club and spilling out on to the grassy lawn and the beach itself. The music could be heard clearly all the way to Two Harbors.

In the club lanai, Winnie was astonished to see a suckling pig on one buffet table, another table heaped with five kinds of shellfish, and a third with eight or ten desert choices. About thirty people were already dancing in the main room while others heaped food on to plastic plates and took the feast outside on the grass.

A smiling silver-haired man with a lei around his neck stood beneath a mounted pair of harpoons, and greeted guests who lined up to meet him.

Tess, pulling Winnie by the hand, went to the front of the queue and kissed the man on the cheek.

'Dexter, meet Win Farlowe,' she said.

Dexter Moody smiled warmly at Winnie, made polite small talk to the annoyed woman they'd just shunted aside, and still managed to ask Tess how she'd been and why she hadn't called him lately.

Winnie kept his eye on the nearest drinks table, and while Tess spoke with Dexter Moody, he went for it, delighted to see that they had Russian *and* Polish vodka out here, past land's end, in a tiny speck in the Pacific Ocean. Rich people!

By the time Tess joined Winnie he was on his second double. He ordered a Scotch for her and said, 'Some party.'

'Want me to introduce you around? I know a couple dozen of these people.'

'I'm only interested in *one* person,' Winnie said, and she squeezed his hand for that. 'Think we oughtta grab a slab off Porky before he's all gone?'

'If I know Dexter, he's got a whole flock of suckling pigs out back. Or herds, whatever.'

'Maybe we *oughtta* eat something.'

'Let's not spoil our edge by eating,' Tess said. 'Let's dance it off instead.'

Winnie finished his drink and ordered a fresh one, which he left on one of the lanai tables. They danced for fifteen minutes, slow dancing, swing, even the twist from the old days. Tess was as graceful as he knew she'd be. She was good at everything. He only hoped the orchestra wouldn't spoil the party by playing 'Where or When'.

After they both worked up a light sweat, they went outside on the patio to cool off. Winnie's drink had been picked up by a waitress, so Tess told him to grab a table while she went for another. She came back with *four* drinks, two for each of them.

'So we don't have to keep making trips to the bar,' she explained.

When Winnie hefted the glass, he noticed there was only one ice cube in it. 'Vodka they got, but no ice?'

Tess giggled, but Winnie said, 'Must be six ounces a booze in these drinks. We gotta be careful or we'll be spending the night out back with the suckling pigs.'

'I'll show you suckling, big boy,' Tess said. Then she touched her glass to his and said, 'Chin chin.'

Tess sat with her legs crossed, one pump dangling from her toes. She had tiny toes. He couldn't figure that out. Why long fingers and tiny toes? Then his eyes moved up her legs. Shiny, tan, bare legs. Shimmering shins! He almost laughed out loud.

They didn't dance again, but Tess would occasionally spot someone she knew and run across the dance floor to chat. She always took her drink with her and always came back with a fresh one for him.

He couldn't understand it. The way she moved, so erect, her shoulders thrown back with that boarding school posture of hers. Always seeming dead sober even when she *said* she was drunk, and giggled, and acted silly.

Winnie had gotten to the games stage. He looked at a ten-foot sailfish on the wall over the bar. He squinted and closed one eye to try to make it hold still. Soon the sailfish looked like it had grown fur. Then it slowly started swimming.

He turned to a woman sitting at the next table and said, 'Somebody better spear that fish before he gets away.'

Tess came back briefly to tell him she ran into a friend she hadn't seen since her Stanford days, and she asked if he was all right. When he nodded, she placed another drink in front of him, another triple or whatever they were, in a bucket glass. Then she was off again.

By nine o'clock he couldn't read his watch. He had no feeling in his chin, lips or fingers. It was too late to eat. Too late to do anything. He had to stop to think what side of the isthmus he was on. For a second he thought he was looking at Cat Harbor. That made him giggle. The sailfish was bouncing around like they were smack in the middle of a squall.

'A very clever sailfish,' Winnie said to the woman at the next table who'd been gone for half an hour. He started to get up and was astonished when he reeled and fell back in the chair. The bartender had screwed up. This was American vodka.

A face hovered over him. Funny sideburns and whiskers. It was either a wild lynx or a Prussian general. It said, 'Easy, mate. Maybe you ought to head for your boat?'

Winnie rubbed some feeling into his lips, sniffed the lousy American vodka and said, 'I love the smell of napalm in the morning.'

When Tess finally joined him again, she had a fresh drink for each of them. She put them down on the table and said, 'You feeling all right?'

'How do I look?' Winnie asked.

Then he noticed there was a man with her, an imposing man Dexter Moody's age. The man said, 'Maybe he'd better not have any more.'

'Maybe not,' Tess said. 'Do you think you should stop drinking now, Win?'

That made him mad. He grabbed the drink and gulped it, but spilled half on his shirt. 'Who's he? A cop? I know when I had enough!'

Tess turned toward the man and said, 'I can handle him.'

The man shrugged and walked away, and when he did, Tess sat and whispered urgently: 'You've got to pull yourself together! Something's happened we hadn't counted on!'

'Let's go home.'

'Pay attention!' she said. 'This is important! Are you listening?'

'Yeah,' he said, seeing one and a half Tess Binders.

'Warner Stillwell's here! The *Circe* came a day early. They've just called from Isthmus Cove. The shore boat's bringing them here any minute.'

'Tomorrow,' Winnie said. 'We can talk to him tomorrow.'

'No, goddamnit!' Tess said. 'Not tomorrow! Tonight! It *has* to be tonight! Get on your feet, Win. Let's go outside and get some air.'

Five minutes later, Winnie and Tess were sitting on the deck looking toward the light on Ship Rock, the light to warn mariners.

Winnie kept focusing on the warning light, and tried to understand what Tess was saying.

'There's four of them,' she said. 'The owner of the *Circe*, his wife, another woman and Warner. He didn't bring his assassin.'

'Where is it, Tess?' Winnie asked, hopelessly confused. 'The *Circe*?'

'I told you! At Isthmus Cove. It's a big boat, so they've anchored out by the reef. The shore boat should be arriving any minute. Win, what should we do?'

With a hiccup: 'I think maybe we should talk to him tomorrow.'

'I wish you hadn't drunk so much!' she said. 'I *told* you not to drink so much, didn't I?'

'You told me?' Now he was seeing *two* instead of one and a half Tess Binders. 'You told me?'

'Remember, Win,' she said. 'I warned you *not* to drink so much. I told you several times. You *do* remember, don't you?'

He was getting nauseous. Tess seemed to be badgering him and he couldn't understand why. He knew he was a bit bagged, but that was no reason to badger him. He kept staring at her. He wanted to feel the outline of her face to see which one was hers. He wanted to do something everyone in the world thought he couldn't do. He wanted to do something extraordinarily difficult. He wanted to stand up.

Then it was too late. The shore boat arrived at the dinghy dock with a load of twenty-five noisy people. They were chattering and laughing as they crossed the pier. Tess didn't take her eyes off their silhouettes, backlit by the moon reflecting off the still water.

'It's him!' she whispered. 'The second man walking on the right!'

Before Winnie could say anything, she was on her feet, hurrying toward the advancing revelers. She was fifty feet away when she greeted a party of four. Winnie sat and peered toward the darkness, but heard only muffled words and laughter. The group of four approached him.

'Everybody, this is my friend, Win Farlowe! Win, this is everybody!' Tess shouted.

People spoke to him. Men shook his hand. One of them, a handsome older man in a yellow aloha shirt, seemed especially friendly. He looked familiar, but out of focus, like everyone else. Then they all disappeared inside with Tess.

Winnie continued to sit, staring at the light on Ship Rock that warned yachtsmen away. If he could make the light hold still, if he could make it be *one* light, he thought he might risk trying to walk.

When Tess came back she was alone. She said, 'I'm shocked that Warner drove down from the ranch all by himself! He's been staying with Giles Bledsoe who owns the *Circe.*'

'What's it mean, Tess?' Winnie asked. 'What?'

'It means you'll have to deal with Warner alone. You're not too drunk, are you? Win, I *asked* you not to drink so much. Don't you remember?'

'I don't know, Tess,' he said. 'I guess you did. I don't know what happened. I jist wish everything would hold still!'

'Goddamnit, pull yourself together!'

Even in his condition it startled him. 'I'm OK,' he said.

'I'm going to arrange it so you and Warner are together, understand? I'm going to help you to be alone with him, so you can *deal* with him.'

'I'll deal with him,' said Winnie Farlowe, but the light was still dancing on Ship Rock.

She left him alone again, and he had strange and bizarre thoughts: Why am I sitting in a kayak? What if I turtle, and can't get right side up?

Winnie was only marginally more lucid ten minutes later when a festive group of twenty people burst out on to the patio, led by Tess Binder, who said, 'Win, you should've tasted the suckling pig. Dexter had it cooked in banana leaves!'

'Let's go everybody!' one of the yachtsmen yelled. 'Bring your A-coupons! The tour's about to begin!'

'We're going to visit the *Circe*,' Tess whispered to Winnie, helping him to his feet. 'Come on!'

While Winnie was staggering toward the dinghy dock, one arm around Tess Binder, she said, *sotto voce*, 'Hang in there, Win. Warner's walking just ahead of us. Trust me!'

Everyone was wearing leis, and drinking tall tropical drinks with umbrellas in them, and there was much merriment as they boarded the water taxi waiting at the dinghy dock. Winnie was helped into the boat by the older man in the yellow aloha shirt, who said, 'Easy does it. Easy does it.'

The man made sure Winnie was safely aboard, then he seated himself beside Tess on the starboard bench seat.

The shore boat turned out of the cove, cutting right through the silver moonlight on the sapphire water. Winnie kept looking to port, toward Ship Rock, toward the light that said, 'Mariner, beware'.

It only took a few minutes to motor around the jutting cliffs, past the reef and Bird Rock into Isthmus Cove. A cloudband crossed the moon and it was suddenly much darker in the cove. The big custom motor yacht was anchored dead ahead, as white as Bird Rock itself.

Everyone said things like, 'Who designed it?' and 'Why did he have it built in Europe?' and 'Who did the decor?' And so forth.

Then there was more laughter as the shore boat came alongside the motor yacht, and the *Circe* skipper, dressed in whites, assisted the revelers aboard.

The man in the yellow flowered shirt helped Winnie up the ladder through the transom gate, and boarded last. When he was on the deck, he put his hand on Winnie's shoulder and said, 'I'll help you. Just take my arm.'

Tess ran up to them and said, 'Glad to see you and Warner have hit it off. Come on, they say the bidet in the master's quarters is gold plated!'

Winnie stared at the man in the flowered shirt and said, '*You're* Warner Stillwell!'

The older man laughed and said, 'Yes, we met an hour ago.'

Winnie tried to say something, but Tess dragged him

along the aft sun deck, whispering, 'Not now! Not yet. I'll tell you when.'

Winnie was confused. Warner Stillwell was different from what he'd expected. He was more like the handsome healthy man in the photos. Older, but very fit. This man didn't have AIDS. This man was probably more healthy than Winnie himself!

The skipper assembled the visitors in the main salon they entered from the sun deck. The salon was done in pink and aquamarine with 'splashes' of sea-green, as the interior designers say when they're doing a yacht. There was lots of Lalique, which, in high winds, could come crashing down on you and ruin your cruise for sure. But then, the interior designers never made the channel crossing.

A young woman in whites took drink orders from everyone, but Tess declined for herself and Winnie.

'She's eighty-two feet at the waterline,' the skipper explained to the assembly. 'And we're powered by eleven-hundred-horsepower diesels.'

'Never mind all that technical stuff,' an older woman said. 'Tell us how much it cost!'

Everyone laughed uproariously and the skipper said, 'You'll have to ask Mister Bledsoe.' But he took his cue and cut his speech short. 'Belowdeck we can accommodate six guests and three crew. Help yourselves, folks, and any other questions, don't hesitate to ask.'

While the partygoers milled all over the glamorous motor yacht, Tess got caught in a crush of a dozen people in the master's quarters. Winnie decided to make his way topside. He bounced off the mahogany bulkhead a few times and lurched along the teak decks, managing to get back up to the carpeted salon, where he felt brave enough to order a drink like all the other grown-ups.

Warner Stillwell was sitting on a pink leather settee talking to the skipper. He looked up and said, 'Feeling better, Win?'

'Much better,' Winnie lied, because he was only feeling a *little* better. The face of Warner Stillwell was not in focus, but there was only one of him.

'Care for a drink, sir?' the young woman in whites asked, and Winnie hesitated before saying, 'Vodka. Very light.'

The skipper excused himself and went forward, leaving them alone.

Warner Stillwell said, 'So you're a friend of our Tessie. Lucky man.'

'Yeah, I think I'm lucky,' said Winnie. He sipped the vodka. A tall glass. American vodka.

'I understand you accompanied her on the visit to *El Refugio*. Did you like it?'

'Yeah, a lot,' said Winnie. 'You're the lucky man to live in a place like that.'

'I agree,' Warner Stillwell said with enthusiasm. 'There's always something new to see in the desert. The sky's everchanging. Even lovelier than the sky here, I think. Wouldn't want to live anywhere else.'

Winnie was trying to figure out how to begin a clever line of questioning when several people entered the salon, Tess Binder among them. She looked alarmed to see Warner Stillwell and Winnie together, and quickly joined Winnie on the settee.

'I don't think you should be drinking,' she said to him, forcing a smile.

324

'I'm *OK*,' said Winnie and thought he saw Tess shrug, palms up to Warner Stillwell.

Then to Winnie she said, 'Win, go have a look at the engine room. A person could literally eat off those engines. Everything's white and chrome. And have a look at the crew's quarters.'

She nodded at him almost imperceptibly and he took it as a signal. He stumbled his way down below once again, shambling forward until he was standing alone in the crew's quarters. Weaving, actually. The last drink hit him *hard*. Things began to swim and wiggle. He shouldn't drink that lousy American vodka, he thought. *That* was the problem.

Winnie sat down on a crewman's bunk. The anchored yacht bobbed gently. The creaking and groaning in the belly of the luxurious vessel was somehow soothing. *Circe* too had maladies, her groaning seemed to say.

The next thing he knew Tess stood over him saying, 'Come on, old son! Wake up! Come on!'

A stranger was standing behind her. The man said something and laughed. Then there was a woman's laugh from somewhere. And suddenly all those misty balloon-faces with mangled grins hovered over him, their teeth popping like water puffs on the channel. Popcorn teeth! Winnie let himself be partially lifted by Tess Binder and the stranger. Then he was up in the main salon and other people were laughing at him too. *Nothing* was in focus.

Tess said to the skipper, 'Don't bother calling for the shore boat; he's busy over at Cherry Cove. I'm afraid my pal can't wait. We'd better get him to bed as fast as possible. Can we use your launch?'

'It's being repaired, but I'll take you to the dinghy dock in our inflatable,' the skipper said.

'No, no, it's not necessary,' Tess said. 'Stay here and entertain your guests.' Then she turned to Warner Stillwell and said, 'Warner, can you still pilot a dinghy?'

'Of course, Tessie,' he said.

'How about a lift?'

'Love to,' he said.

The skipper of the *Circe* looked doubtful. 'Maybe we should wait for the shore boat. It's dark out there.'

'There's nearly a hundred boats moored in front of us,' Tess said. 'We're not alone in this cove.'

'Yes, but everyone's at the paty, or in Two Harbors having dinner,' the skipper said. 'Maybe we should wait for . . .'

Tess turned to Warner Stillwell and said, 'My boy out there is smashed! I've *got* to get him to bed immediately.'

'Of course.' Warner Stillwell chuckled. Then to the skipper, 'I assure you I'm not too old and feeble to pilot a dinghy eight hundred yards to the dock and back.'

'OK, Mister Stillwell,' the skipper said apologetically, 'but be sure to use the flashlight and watch for mooring lines. There's a *lot* of boats in the cove tonight.'

The black rubber dinghy was large enough to accommodate eight people. It was tied aft, and the skipper climbed down into it to test the five-horsepower Yamaha. The engine fired immediately and the skipper helped Winnie down into the bow. Then he held his hand out for Tess, then for Warner Stillwell, who crawled aft and took the engine control. Then the skipper climbed back on board the yacht while Tess made ready to cast off.

Warner Stillwell said to Tess, 'Remember all the times

we used to go to the club for lunch in one of these, Tessie? Your dad and you and me? They were good days, weren't they?'

'Are you ready, Warner? Are you ready?' she cried, and her voice sounded very shrill to Winnie.

'Of course, dear,' said Warner Stillwell. 'You can cast off.'

While the skipper was waving to them, Tess suddenly yelled, 'Wait a minute!' Then she turned to Warner Stillwell and said, 'I forgot my purse!'

While Tess scrambled out of the dinghy and climbed back up the ladder on to the main deck, Warner Stillwell yelled, 'Comfortable, Mister Farlowe? Everything OK?'

'Sure,' Winnie mumbled. But his head kept falling forward. He felt a sharp pain and realized he'd bitten his tongue when his chin struck his chest. Winnie tasted blood on his mouth.

Then Tess Binder appeared again at the rail on the main deck, but the skipper was no longer with her. She shouted to them, 'I can't find the damn thing! Can you manage to get him into the dock by yourself, Warner?'

'No problem!' Warner Stillwell yelled over the engine noise. 'I'll take good care of your Mister Farlowe!'

Winnie could barely understand what they were hollering at each other. He was drifting far away. Out to sea where it was peaceful.

Warner Stillwell took the dinghy around the *Circe*, on the port side of the big yacht. The dinghy was facing Blue Cavern Point, where, during the Thanksgiving holidays in 1981, actress Natalie Wood fell from a yacht at night while trying to secure a rubber dinghy like this one, down into the dark water she'd reportedly feared all her life. Her body was found near a place they called Perdition Caves.

Warner Stillwell turned the dinghy and they were heading toward shore, away from the red-lighted buoy. And just as the skipper had said, all the boats at mooring seemed deserted except for an occasional dog that ran out on deck to bark at them.

Winnie opened his eyes and looked up. The moon had disappeared behind scudding clouds, the silver light was gone from the sapphire water, and the pier seemed to be getting closer. He thought he saw a bright light under the water, close to starboard.

And then the dinghy *strikes*! They ram something! Or something hits *them*!

And the aft portion dipped and Winnie toppled backward! Then the dinghy took a nose dive, and he tumbled forward, his head cracking into one of the emergency oars.

The water roiled. The dinghy drifted sideways. Winnie heard thrashing water and then a long haunting liquid scream out there in the darkness. Then silence. As the dinghy drifted and turned in the current.

Then Winnie heard his own voice screaming: 'MISTER STILLWELL! MISTER STILLWELL!'

Winnie crawled aft toward the engine. He found it. He turned the inflatable to port. The wrong way! He was heading out to sea in the darkness, totally disoriented. He managed to come about and bumped into a mooring. The dinghy bounced off a mooring can and turned ninety degrees, a blind man at the controls.

It took a full minute to get his bearings and steer back toward the approximate place where Warner Stillwell vanished. The dinghy was making figure eights as Winnie screamed, 'MISTER STILLWEEEEELLLLL!'

Then Winnie, hopelessly drunk, was hopelessly sobbing: 'WHERE ARE YOUUUUU?' Crying like a child under a moon not quite aligned with the earth, now reflecting pale light off dark water.

20: *In Irons*

Two Harbors, at the isthmus of Santa Catalina Island, has the only one-room schoolhouse left in Los Angeles County. Seventeen children of Two Harbors are taught there by a schoolmarm. And Two Harbors also has the last resident deputy sheriff in Los Angeles County, this one a square-shouldered young guy who didn't get island fever or mind living in a mobile home he shared with a K-9 partner.

The deputy was slouched in a chair, watching TV, when the call came in from the Bay Watch, the county lifeguards and paramedics who serve Two Harbors. The deputy quickly got dressed in his green jumpsuit and met the Bay Watch at the pier in Isthmus Cove, and was ferried out to the anchorage of the *Circe*. The Bay Watch, the Harbor Patrol, and the shore boat then began a search among the rocks and caves along Fisherman's Cove, near the University of Southern California's Marine Science Center. The story they had received from the drunk in the dinghy led them all to think that the body of the missing yachtsman would probably turn up near that facility.

All of the guests were gone when the deputy climbed aboard the big motor yacht. The owner, Giles Bledsoe, was aboard, as was the skipper, both crew members and Tess Binder.

The deputy found Winnie Farlowe in the main salon.

He was sitting on the settee he'd shared earlier with the missing man. Everyone had been pouring coffee down Winnie's throat, which did nothing more than insert another drug into an already drugged human being. Winnie had been crying intermittently, and he was still very drunk. The deputy interviewed the skipper as well as the owner. Then he took Tess Binder out on to the sun deck.

When they were alone he asked questions and made notes. Tess had a jacket thrown over her shoulders and seemed to be sobbing. Every once in a while she reached up under her glasses to wipe her eyes.

She said, 'We were going to take Mister Farlowe to the lodge to put him to bed. I forgot my purse and Warner insisted on going without me. He said he could manage alone. Oh, I never should've permitted it!'

The deputy was ten years younger than Tess, who, for the first time, looked every bit her age. He said, 'Ma'am, where was Mister Farlowe seated in the dinghy?'

'In front,' she said. 'In the bow.'

'When he came back what did he say?'

'That Warner had fallen overboard into the water! That he'd looked for him and couldn't find him!'

'Did he say *how* he fell overboard?'

'He couldn't say. He was . . . well, you see how he is.'

'Did he mention they'd traded places in the dinghy? Maybe switched seats?'

'No. He just said the dinghy hit something and Warner tumbled overboard. When he looked around Warner was gone!' Then Tess covered her eyes, and her shoulders shook.

331

The deputy gave her a chance to gain some composure, then asked, 'How much did Mister Farlowe have to drink tonight?'

'A lot,' Tess said. 'I asked him to stop. I think he'll remember I asked him to please stop. He had a *lot*.'

'Those inflatables are very stable,' the deputy said. 'Do you have any idea how Mister Stillwell could've fallen overboard?'

'Well,' she said, wiping her cheeks, her face in deep shadow. 'I imagine Warner stood up in the stern for some reason, maybe to see better. I imagine he struck one of the mooring cans and fell off. Don't you think that's what happened?'

'Maybe,' the deputy said. 'Or maybe Mister Farlowe took the tiller. Maybe he suddenly wanted to drive. People *that* drunk do impulsive things.'

'Deputy,' Tess Binder said evenly. 'Mister Farlowe was too drunk to get up from his seat without someone assisting him. I would swear that he *couldn't* have piloted that boat.'

'How long have you known him?'

'Not long. Just a few weeks, actually.'

'After he realized Mister Stillwell had fallen overboard, what did he do?'

'You can ask him.'

'I will. But what did he *say* he did?'

'He said he was confused and wasn't sure where he'd lost Warner.'

'Where *he'd* lost Warner?'

'No. I mean, where Warner *got* lost. Where he fell overboard.'

'But he said he tried to find him?'

332

'He tried! Do you know that Win Farlowe's a retired policeman? God, he tried! But . . . well, he was *smashed*!'

Tess wasn't given much of a chance to talk to Winnie except to say she'd get a ride back to Avalon, where he was to be driven by the deputy. She told Winnie which hotel she'd be using that night, and that he should meet her there when they released him. Her eyes looked gray as ashes.

Once more, Winnie Farlowe found himself riding in a car over the mountains of Santa Catalina Island, only this time he wasn't remembering the good times with his dad. He was in the deputy's Chevy Blazer, desperately trying to fill in gaps. He remembered dancing with Tess. He *didn't* remember going on the shore boat to the *Circe*! He remembered talking to Warner Stillwell in the main salon. He *didn't* remember being led down to the dinghy. He remembered the dinghy striking something! He remembered a scream! He remembered motoring in circles! He *didn't* remember returning to the big motor yacht.

On the way to Avalon the deputy said, 'I want to advise you that you have the right to remain silent . . .'

Winnie listened quietly, the second time in four months that a policeman had read him his rights. The second time he'd been involved in a bizarre and inexplicable boating incident. The second time he could not remember half of what happened. He'd been lucky last time, but not this time.

He thought of that smiling man in the yellow flowered shirt. He'd smiled kindly when he helped Winnie to board the yacht. Winnie tasted salt in his mouth and realized he was crying again.

The deputies at the Avalon substation gave him a Breathalyzer test. He remembered from last time that the coordination test for boating-under-the-influence is different from driving-under-the-influence. Certain 'stressers' common to yachtsmen may not be alcohol related. Blood-shot eyes could happen as a result of ocean glare. An inability to stand on one foot, or remain stable with one's head thrown back, could happen as a result of experiencing pitch and roll on a boat.

They asked him to count backwards from twenty to zero, but they didn't waste much time with it. Two and a half hours had elapsed since Warner Stillwell was lost, and Winnie Farlowe *still* blew a .28 on the Breathalyzer. The witness Tess Binder was right. He must have been absolutely *smashed* when the accident occurred.

Winnie's signed statement was anything but self-serving. He said, 'I don't know what happened. I was passed out, I think. We rammed something or something rammed us. I fell backwards. I was too drunk to respond effectively. If I hadn't been so drunk, that man would still be alive. I would've saved him if I hadn't been blind helpless stinking drunk. If there isn't a crime you can charge me with, there *should* be.'

There was. Winnie Farlowe was booked for a violation of Section 647(b) of the California penal code, for being drunk in public. After they'd made calls to an assistant district attorney on the mainland, it was decided he couldn't be booked for anything more serious. Winnie had been put into the dinghy by sober people. He hadn't operated the dinghy except when the pilot of the boat fell overboard, and in California there is no penal code violation for failing to act in the rescue of another, even in life-threatening circumstances. Hence, Winston Farlowe was only guilty of being drunk in public.

Saturday morning he was so sick he couldn't get off his bunk in a cell he shared with one other drunk. A decibel of sound was like a mortar round exploding. A kilowatt of light was a laser. He refused food but took water which he promptly vomited the second it hit his belly. Tess Binder did not come to the Avalon substation and did not offer to post bail. The prisoner refused to make any phone calls and said he did not want to be released on his own recognizance.

He was hardly any better on Sunday. Since being locked up, he hadn't slept more than a few minutes at a time, writhing in sickness and horror, too feverish and ill to conjure up his night visitors.

By early Sunday morning, the eighty-two-foot US Coast Guard patrol boat from Long Beach, along with two Coast Guard helicopter teams, called off their search for a floating body. And that night Winnie Farlowe had either a theta dream or an hallucination. He was with his father at Two Harbors, fishing in the kelp beds. Winnie hooked something big. He began reeling it in. His father leaned over the side with a gaff and then . . . His own scream brought him back to reality.

Since the Justice Court in Avalon was only in session on Fridays, Winnie was flown to Long Beach by the Sheriff's

Aero Bureau on Monday morning where the presiding judge gave permission for him to be arraigned by the Catalina judge in the Long Beach Municipal Court.

Winnie was almost doubled over with cramps as he stood before Judge Herman Calloway at arraignment that morning stubbornly *demanding* to be sentenced. The sweat was running down his temples and he was hollow-eyed and clammy, and so shaky that the judge asked if he'd like to see a phsyician. The defendant refused. He also refused to speak to the public defender. He insisted on pleading guilty.

The judge looked nothing like the hanging judge, Jesse Singleton. This judge was sixty-ish and frail, with pitted cheeks and a gray thatch combed back from a diving widow's peak. 'The fact is, Mister Farlowe, Mister Stillwell might be alive today if you had not been in a stupefyingly drunken state on Friday night. Do you agree?'

'I agree, Your Honor,' Winnie said. 'And I deserve all you got.'

'I understand that you have a prior for boating-under-the-influence?'

'Yes, Your Honor,' Winnie said.

'And when was that?'

'Last Christmas.'

'You were no doubt warned about being drunk on a boat or drunk in public?'

'I was, Your Honor.'

'I'm going to set your bail at two hundred and fifty dollars and ask for a probation report, Mister Farlowe. I'm not sure what I want to do with you.'

'I reject a probation report, Your Honor,' Winnie said.

Everyone in the courtroom did a take on *that* one.

The judge said, 'You what?'

'I demand immediate sentencing, Your Honor,' Winnie said. 'I refuse to cooperate with a probation officer, and I reject a probation report.'

'Do you know what you're saying?'

'Yes, Your Honor. I was a policeman for many years.'

'I'm aware of that,' said the judge. 'Very well. You leave me no alternative but to give you the maximum sentence for this misdemeanor.'

'I deserve all you got,' said Winnie Farlowe. 'A man is dead. I should've saved him. I *would've* saved him if I'd been sober.'

The judge studied the defendant. He could see that the prisoner was suffering severe withdrawal pain. Every few seconds Winnie would grimace. The judge figured this guy *had* to confess and be punished. This guy was an alcoholic Saint Augustine.

Finally the judge said, 'I suppose you'll never forgive yourself for this, nor should you. I suppose you might even consider doing something intelligent, like seeking a treatment program. I suppose you *might* stop being stupid. You're only forty years old. You're still a young man, Mister Farlowe.'

'I don't feel young,' Winnie said.

'Do you want some water?' the judge asked.

'I'd just heave it up,' Winnie said.

The judge stared at the wreckage before him and said, 'I'm not going to give you the maximum sentence, regardless of your need to salve your conscience. But a man is missing and undoubtedly dead. I'm sentencing you to ninety days in the county jail. When you come out of there you'll be dry and sober but you *won't* be into a recovery mode. Do you understand the difference between a sober alcoholic and a recovering alcoholic? Only in the AA program can you get yourself into the recovery mode.'

While the judge was still talking, the defendant suddenly grabbed his mouth and began gagging. As the judge watching in horror, the defendant tossed his cookies all over the counsel table.

Winnie was close to fainting when the judge said, 'Get this man to the men's central jail where they can *do* something with him!'

Winnie was not able to recall much about the drowsy drive to downtown L.A. except that something in his chest was trying to break out. Something that kicked like a horse. A buffalo, probably. A Catalina wild buffalo was running amok inside his rib cage.

When he arrived at the men's central jail, he was taken directly to the seventh floor where the hospital unit is located, not because he was suffering from alcohol withdrawal but because he was a retired police officer. There on the seventh floor of the hospital was the high-security wing, referred to as 'the high-power unit', where people like Winnie were housed: law enforcement or former law enforcement officers, most of them unsentenced court prisoners who wouldn't last a week in the general population. Also in high-power were prisoners being held for civil contempt; they weren't criminals and couldn't be housed with the general population.

Along with them there were other special cases on the seventh floor: prisoners into PCP withdrawal, strapped down at the ankles and wrists. There were suicidal prisoners, and diabetics, those needing regular medication. And there were certain court prisoners who needed *ultra* high security. Winnie wasn't there twenty minutes when he saw two deputies walking down the corridor with Richard Ramirez – the notorious Nightstalker who had terrorized the Southland during the bloody spring and summer of 1985, accused of murdering thirteen people and mutilating others.

The first nurse Winnie saw on the seventh floor said to him, 'What's your drug of choice? Booze?'

Winnie nodded, but when he saw her heading for a cabinet he said, 'I don't want any medication. I *refuse* it.'

'Gonna go it cold turkey, huh?'

Winnie nodded again.

'How about just an injection of vitamins?'

He shook his head.

'If you change your mind, call for a deputy,' the nurse said.

That night the spasms were so bad he had to put his blanket in his mouth to keep from crying out. But it was his fourth day of sobriety and he felt a little better when his eyes finally opened. There was no knifing pain. He only ached. He felt like somebody had kicked his guts out.

As far as the ordinary county jail inmates were concerned, Winnie was in 'the playpen'. On this, the hospital floor, there were no cells, only rooms with locked doors guarded by deputies. And the seventh floor was the only place other than the roof that didn't smell like the hold of a slave ship.

In Winnie's room there were five other men. One was a member of the Beverly Hills Police Department, awaiting trial in Superior Court for burglary. Another was a retired probation officer who'd shot his wife. And there was a DEA agent who'd decided that keeping the drugs and releasing the pushers was more lucrative than booking the whole shebang. The latter two were in the middle of their felony trials in Superior Court. The other two roommates were already sentenced misdemeanor prisoners like Winnie. One was a retired corrections officer, convicted for the third time of driving under the influence of alcohol. The last was an LAPD sergeant who'd pleading guilty to a string of indecent exposures, his victims being young schoolgirls. Unlike the general jail population where most prisoners were black or Latino, in Winnie's room they all happened to be white.

There were enough bunks for eight men in the room, four down and four up. There was a toilet, a sink, a metal table and two metal benches, one on each side of the table. The prisoners wore a V-neck dungaree outfit with *L.A. County Jail* stenciled over the shirt pocket. These men were isolated from prisoners in the general population and were allowed to exercise on the roof for one hour twice a week. They could shoot basketball, or jog, or make calls, since there were phones on the roof.

There was another room for active or former law enforcement officers, only this one held four men, one of them black, one Latino. Two of them were members of the L.A. Sheriff's Department, both of whom had worked here at one time. On the proper side of the locked doors.

The most notorious seventh-floor inmates – those awaiting or undergoing trial, like the Nightstalker – lived in private rooms in total isolation, only coming in contact with deputies, or with trustees who used their position to buy and sell and barter.

Winnie was in central jail for five days before he was able to consume a normal portion of food. The DEA agent traded Winnie his lower bunk for the upper when he saw Winnie dry-heaving. He didn't want a sick alky above him. The jail food, the DEA agent warned, was just like they'd served him on Aeroflot on a clandestine government trip to the Black Sea. He told Winnie what to eat and what to avoid.

On Friday, one week after the incident at Isthmus Cove, 547 yachts and 4,000 sailors competed in the forty-second annual Newport to Ensenada International Yacht Race, known as 'The Tequila Derby' for the binge that takes place at the end. For the first time in years, Winnie cared nothing about the race. It was a slow race and, as predicted, Dennis Connor's boat finished first.

That day he'd finally decided to make a phone call. He spoke to his sister and to his mother. He tried to call Tess Binder, but got no answer.

On Saturday, Buster Wiles came to see him. The visiting area for the high-power prisoners was a two-room space divided by a common wall of glass. A prisoner and a visitor could sit and talk by telephone.

Buster shook his head in utter disgust and disbelief and said into the phone, 'You look like shit!'

Winnie nodded.

'You dumb bastard!' Buster said. 'What's wrong with you? Why'd you plead guilty?'

'I *was* guilty,' Winnie said.

'Why'd you turn down a probation report and piss off the judge? You coulda bailed out. Hell, he'd a released you on your own recognizance. A moron coulda defended you and beaten that case. You didn't *have* to go to jail, you asshole!'

Winnie said, 'I did what I had to do, Buster. I killed that man.'

'The guy fell off a boat! It happens all the time. You think that's the first fatality in Catalina this year? It ain't even the first one this month.'

'I coulda saved him,' Winnie said, 'if I'd a been sober. Even if I'd a been just *normally* drunk.'

Buster put down his telephone and shook his head. When he picked it up again, he said, 'Man, you *are* pathetic. You're dumb!'

Winnie didn't say anything.

Buster said, 'The guy'd been drinking too, right? It was his own fault. And he was seventy-two-years old. That's the life expectancy of an American male, for chrissake!'

'That doesn't change anything,' Winnie said.

'OK, if you wanna sit here and suffer for the world's sins like Gandhi or somebody, what can I do for ya?'

'Nothing,' Winnie said.

'Cigarettes?' Buster said. 'You can use them for money.'

'I don't need anything,' said Winnie. 'I had money in my wallet when I was booked. Enough for little stuff. I got all I need.'

'You talk to your mom?'

Winnie nodded.

'You talk to your friend Tess Binder?'

Winnie shook his head and said, 'No answer. I'll try tomorrow. We only get to call out once a day.'

'You shouldn't be in jail. You could be with your little pal, sleeping on peachy sheets,' Buster said.

Winnie could not remember ever having seen Buster Wiles this upset, this agitated, so brimming with frustration. When he got back to his bunk, something Buster had said was troubling him, but he couldn't think clearly, not yet.

He felt like he was in one of the recurring dreams where his sails are luffing, and he's incapable of trimming them. In the dream he's always helplessly drifting out to sea. That's how he felt now. His brain was still in irons.

21: *Peachy Sheets*

On his tenth day in custody at the men's central jail, Winnie Farlowe had a visitor: Martin Scroggins. The old lawyer was waiting nervously in the visiting room when the prisoner entered on the other side of the glass wall. There were two other inmates talking with lawyers, along with the LAPD sergeant – serving six months for indecent exposure – who was talking to his wife. She couldn't stop weeping, and kept touching the glass with her hand.

The lawyer looked shaken. Winnie smiled ironically, the first time he'd smiled in ten days. He said, 'You never been in a jail before, have you, Mister Scroggins?'

The lawyer shook his head.

'Did Tess send you?'

'Yes, she did.'

'I've tried to phone her. Ten times. Once every day. All I get is the answering machine or no answer at all.'

'She's acting on my instructions,' Martin Scroggins said. 'I knew you'd be calling her, but I don't want you two to have any contact whatsoever. Not yet.'

'And why is that?'

'I'm trying to expedite things. I don't want any complications. Any hint. Or innuendo. Not the slightest rumor that because of Tess, *you* could've been having . . . unwholesome thoughts out there on that boat that night.'

'Unwholesome thoughts.'

344

Martin Scroggins seemed unnerved by Winnie's appearance. The prisoner had lost ten pounds. He was already developing a jailhouse pallor. And he spoke in a scary monotone. He looked like the lawyer's mental image of a lifer.

'Look,' the lawyer said, 'when Warner Stillwell fell out of that boat, well . . . some people might think you had certain ideas flash through your mind. Such as: What if I don't diligently rescue him? Then Tess could immediately inherit *El Refugio*. Not years from now. But *now*. It's possible that people could think such a thing if you and Tess were thought to be closely linked.'

'I see.'

'But as it presently appears, you were dating her for a couple of weeks and that's about it. You're not engaged. You're not even lovers.'

'It doesn't appear that we are,' Winnie said.

'So I can expedite things with no complications.'

'What things?'

'Having Warner Stillwell declared dead. I'm prepared to file a petition with the court. In fact, I've brought a stenographer with me today. She's waiting outside. I want an affidavit from you.'

'And what will I say in the affidavit?'

'You'll just describe as briefly as possible the events of Friday night, April twenty-first. You see, when the absence of a person is not satisfactorily explained after diligent search or inquiry, a person can be presumed to be dead. And being the only third-party witness to the tragedy, you, and *only* you, can provide us with an irrefutable presumption. Without any complications, I believe that the remainderman in the trust – sorry, that's

Tess – can automatically receive her inheritance sooner than sixty days. As trustee I can deed the land over to her.'

'And if there were . . . complications, then what?'

'The court would probably decide to wait out the statutory period of five years before declaring Warner Stillwell dead.'

'I see,' Winnie said. 'And I'll still be in jail when he's declared dead, when she gets the property.'

'I don't think so, Mister Farlowe,' Martin Scroggins said. 'This facility is so overcrowded the sheriff is acting under the guidelines of a federal judge with instructions to release. I've learned that the sixty-day prisoners are serving only thirty-four. I expect a ninety-day prisoner like yourself could be out of here a lot sooner than you think. You'll serve less than two months, I should think.'

'Will Tess be willing to talk to me then? Or can you answer that, counsel?'

'Of course!' Martin Scroggins said. 'She wants to see you right *now*! It's just not in her . . .'

'Best interest?'

'Correct.'

'OK,' Winnie said.

Martin Scroggins smiled and said, 'You're doing exactly the right thing. And remember, Warner Stillwell had *also* been drinking that night. He contributed to his own demise. I liked Warner immensely but . . .'

'He *was* seventy-two years old,' said Winnie.

Martin Scroggins stopped smiling because he was seventy himself, and *he* wasn't ready to go over the side. 'I was about to say he should've known better than to be driving that boat with a nearly unconscious man in it, and no-one else to help him. Well, it's over now and I think

Tessie's shown great maturity since the tragedy. I believe she's ready for her inheritance.'

'I imagine she's asked you to take over all her legal affairs?'

'Why not? I was her family's attorney. And I've always hated irrevocable trusts. It's too often used to control others from the grave . . . Vanity. All is vanity.'

'It's a way to take it with you,' Winnie said. 'OK, counsel, send in your stenographer.'

Nineteen days after his incarceration, Winnie Farlowe was sitting on the roof of the jail watching two of his roommates shoot free-throws after they'd gotten tired of playing one-on-one. By this time the DEA agent had been convicted and was awaiting a sentence to a federal prison, and two other ex-lawmen had come into the high-power unit: one a former Secret Service agent, another a police captain from the South Bay.

Winnie noticed that his fellow prisoners weren't much different from all the other lawbreakers he'd arrested in his police career. Each one claimed he was not guilty, or his offense was mitigated by certain factors: a disloyal wife, a jealous superior, an addiction he couldn't control. And so forth. The only inmate who freely admitted his culpability, other than Winnie himself, was Douglas Bracken, the LAPD sergeant who had compulsively exposed himself to schoolgirls many times over an eight-month period before being caught. He was ten years older than Winnie: a lot thinner, a lot grayer.

Even here in high-power there was the inmates' pecking

order. Bracken was ostracized and ignored. They called him 'Short Eyes' behind his back and sometimes to his face. He was the only man on the seventh floor who looked sadder and more miserable than Winnie Farlowe. The man who looked the most content and carefree was the Nightstalker, but when he got into the courtroom he could be irritable and histrionic.

One of the two men shooting baskets missed a dribble pass, and the ball rolled over to Winnie's feet. He picked it up and, without thinking, tried a jump shot. It swished in.

Douglas Bracken was standing behind him. He said, 'Nice shot. I bet you used to play the game.'

'Only in high school,' Winnie answered. 'I warmed the bench mostly.'

Bracken took a few steps closer and said, 'I used to play in high school too. Never got tall enough to be any good.'

When Winnie didn't respond, Bracken dropped his eyes and turned to walk away. Then Winnie said to himself: I'm no better than he is. I'm no better than *anybody*.

Winnie said, 'Wait a minute. Wanna play one-on-one? I'll give it a try if you will.'

Bracken and Winnie exhausted themselves after ten minutes of basketball. When the exercise period was over, Bracken walked back downstairs with him. 'You're looking a lot better than when you first came in,' Bracken said. 'I know about booze. I think it led to my own problem in some ways. The nurse told me you wouldn't even let them give you vitamin shots. You're doing it the hard way. Awful tough to white-knuckle it.'

'Next time you wanna play one-on-one, lemme know,' Winnie said.

Bracken hesitated, then said, 'Instead of spending all

your time thinking about what can't be changed, you ought to think about the future. You'll have a lot of sobriety under your belt when you get out. You can change things.'

'How about you?' Winnie said. 'Can *you* change things?'

Swallowing twice, Bracken said, 'I hope so. I got a wife and three kids. My daughter's gonna have a kid of her own soon. I looked down the barrel more than once. I truly wanted to bite it. Now maybe I wanna live. This place either makes a good man wanna die or it makes him really wanna live.'

Winnie paused. 'Are you a good man, Bracken?'

'I don't know,' Bracken answered. 'But I think *you* are.'

'Oh yeah?'

'There's no secrets here. Everybody knows you wouldn't even *be* here if you hadn't forced the judge to give you time. Only a good man'd do a thing like that. That's what I think.'

That night Winnie started an exercise program. It was very hard to do twenty push-ups. Sit-ups were nearly impossible, but Bracken encouraged him and even held Winnie's ankles so he could do them.

When Winnie had finished, lying exhausted in his bunk, Bracken took out his harmonica. It was one thing about him the others didn't criticize. When they were in their bunks at night, it wasn't unpleasant to hear old Short Eyes blowing a mournful, heart-cracking tune on his harmonica.

There was something Winnie wanted to hear, but he didn't ask for it. He just listened quietly. The others said, yeah, it was the only good thing about Short Eyes. He could really make music, that old wienie wagger.

349

As the weeks passed, on the seventh floor there were some amazing changes taking place in Winnie's little world. It wasn't because of his fellow inmates – some of whom were gone, only to be replaced by other errant lawmen – it was that his body chemistry was being dramatically altered. His cerebral cortex was humming along. The beta brain waves were surging against his skull like the surf at the Wedge. The alpha waves were cresting even while he lay calm and relaxed. It was strangely exciting. He could *think*! He was able to remember things. He could even remember things that had happened when he'd been drinking, many of which he'd just as soon have forgotten. Of course he couldn't remember the real blackouts, but he could remember things around the fringes of those blackout periods and sometimes little moments in the middle of that alcoholic darkness.

Physically, he was healthier than he'd been in a long time. His heart rhythm had smoothed out and the premature contractions were gone. He was able to sleep through the night, except when he had nightmares of screams in dark water. Or when he had a dream about Tess Binder holding him in her arms and calling him 'old son'. Sometimes he'd wake up then. But ordinarily, he was sleeping eight hours every night. Usually though, it was fitful theta sleep. Sometimes it was delta sleep, deep and profound, with tormenting dreams. Of course, in jail, sleep was the ultimate escape. The best and only *real* escape available.

On June first, forty-one days after the incident in

Isthmus Cove, Winnie was lying on his bunk thinking about the past, still unable to visualize a future. Two of his roommates were playing chess. One was writing a letter. Bracken was playing the harmonica. Winnie thought he was brave enough now, or he should be.

'Bracken,' Winnie said, 'can you play "Where or When"?'

Bracken nodded and segued into the song. Winnie had never heard it on the harmonica. It wasn't just more melancholy, it was mournfully sad.

Winnie sang it very quietly to himself:

> *It seems we stood and talked like this before*
> *We looked at each other in the same way then*

Winnie thought of her, how she looked the first time in Spoon's Landing. And how she looked *most* beautiful: in that white linen dress with the gardenia in her hair. On the hilltop overlooking Two Harbors.

> *The clothes you're wearing are the clothes you wore*

Then Winnie stopped thinking of Tess. He had a nagging unpleasant ghost of a memory. It happened when he wasn't well yet, when Buster came to visit him. What was it that had bothered him then, when his brain was in irons? What?

The harmonica wept, the way Bracken played it. It sounded like someone crying.

> *The things that happened for the first time*
> *Seem to be happening again . . .*

Then he struck! Like when the dinghy struck! It was *that* shocking! He remembered now what Buster had said: 'You shouldn't be in jail. You could be with your little pal, sleeping on peachy sheets.'

It wasn't just an expression, *peachy* sheets. Lots of things were peachy, but not sheets. Only Tess Binder's sheets. Only if you'd *seen* them!

And at last, Winnie Farlowe started to grasp something. Partly because of connecting Buster to the peach-colored sheets. Partly because of the song triggering emotions he'd repressed. But mostly because he'd been sober for forty-one days, had stopped hammering his frontal lobes with massive daily doses of alcohol. Winnie Farlowe untangled the dream. The crazed sensation of *déjà vu*. The nymph!

It had happened back in October, months before he'd met Tess Binder in Spoon's Landing, and smelled her jasmine, and become tormented by the words of a song. He'd been drinking a lot that night at Spoon's Halloween party. In fact, he was absolutely fried when he staggered outside searching for the off-duty barmaid who'd come to Spoon's party, dressed as a mermaid with feet, with only green pasties over her nipples.

The night air didn't revive him, and he did something insane. He got into his car and drove twelve blocks to Buster Wiles's apartment, hoping to bring him back to the party.

He couldn't remember parking the car on Balboa Boulevard. He did remember staggering toward Buster's porch. He couldn't remember falling. He did remember lying on the sidewalk and getting up. He couldn't remember crashing against Buster's door, but he did remember falling back on the floor of Buster's porch, flat on his back, with the porch roof spinning above him.

He remembered the door opening and the nymph appearing,

all dressed in white, lipstick like blood. She wasn't wearing her glasses then and her hair was mussed. Buster came out behind her and said something.

The nymph laughed. Like wind chimes. She reached her hand toward Winnie, who was too drunk to lift his head. She held out her hand to pull him up, but he couldn't even take it. Then Buster said something and she laughed again and went back inside, leaving him with Buster.

He couldn't remember what happened next, but he learned the following day that Buster had carried him to his car, drove him home, put him to bed. Buster told Winnie he'd interrupted his opening night with a new squeeze he'd met while on duty. Buster refused to talk about her except to say she was a keeper.

Winnie lay on his bunk tense and rigid. By the time Bracken was finishing with the haunting version of the song, Winnie was as rigid as the nymph.

On his forty-first night of sobriety, Winnie Farlowe wanted out of jail desperately. That was when he began counting the days.

For the ninety-day prisoners the overcrowding had forced the authorities to knock off thirty for good time and work time. Then they took off five days more, pursuant to Section 4024.1 of the California penal code authorizing early releases. Then one day was deducted because of time spent in court. It meant that Winnie would serve only fifty-four days in all. He had thirteen to go.

As he lay on his bunk that evening he had another flash of insight. He realized that for a long time he'd been unable to picture himself in *any* moment of pleasure without imagining a drink in his hand or one close by. Any daydream of himself relaxing on the beach, or listening to jazz, or watching *Masterpiece Theater* – especially any sexual fantasy – all of it included a vivid image of a bucket of booze. That afternoon he'd read in the *Los Angeles Times* about cruising the Mediterranean. He'd visualized himself standing on the aft deck, with Tess Binder who was dressed in white. A drink was in his hand. The drink was the most vivid part of the fantasy.

The only exception was sailing. Winnie could always picture himself in the cockpit of a sloop with the sun at dusk flaring across the sky and a plume of blue water in his face. He didn't need a drink in *that* fantasy. Sailing was enough.

Winnie suddenly jumped down from his bunk and began to do push-ups. Bracken again held his ankles for him while he did sit-ups. Two hundred of them.

22: *The Wedge*

Mid-June could be hot and smoggy and miserable in downtown Los Angeles, but it was usually cool and overcast along the coast. Winnie longed for clouds and cool sea air. In fact, he craved it. He was suppressing thoughts of all the other things he craved.

The early release of Douglas Bracken came rather suddenly, three days before Winnie's. Actually, a misdemeanor prisoner had to be some kind of *bad* not to get an early discharge, given the overcrowding of the facility. The night before Bracken left he played his harmonica for an extra long time. He played every song that Winnie liked, including 'Where or When'.

In the morning, Bracken gathered his things and said goodbye to a few of the others, most of whom still avoided Short Eyes. When Winnie shook hands and wished him luck, Douglas Bracken said, 'I wish I could do something for you like you did for me.'

'What'd I do?'

'Asked me to play basketball.'

Winnie shrugged. 'Well . . .' Then he shrugged again.

Bracken said, 'Remember, about AA, OK? You don't have to believe in God to connect with your higher power. Your higher power can be the AA experience itself. You can't white-knuckle it forever. You'll need some help, right?'

Winnie said, 'I'll keep that in mind. Take care of yourself and your family.'

'Thanks again,' Bracken said, 'for those games of one-on-one.'

Winnie watched when Douglas Bracken was escorted to the elevator. To freedom, where he would once again have to confront his own fierce demons.

Winnie's sister was waiting for him on the street by the jail when it was his turn. She cried and hugged him out there in the shadow of that massive building. Then they got in her car and she drove him to her house in Tustin, where he spent two hours with his mother. She also cried, shocked by his loss of twenty-five pounds, until he convinced her that it had all been booze-saturated, toxic fat. And he made lots of promises to his mother and wondered if he'd keep any of them. Then he drove his ragtop VW out of his sister's garage after vowing to pay her back for doing his mail and cashing his pension check and paying his rent. For keeping his leaky little ship afloat.

He wasn't all that surprised when, after getting home to his apartment, and phoning the Newport Beach Police Department, he learned that Buster Wiles had already put in his resignation papers, stating as his reason that he'd been offered some vague business deal in Hawaii.

Winnie went to his bedroom closet and moved some books on the top shelf. Behind the books was a bundle wrapped in a towel. In that bundle was his stainless-steel, two-inch Smith & Wesson revolver, and half a box of hollow-points. He inspected the cylinder and barrel. He inserted five rounds. He called Buster's house, but got no answer. He changed to a T-shirt, a hooded blue sweatshirt, jeans and deck shoes.

At 3.30 that afternoon Winnie left a note on Buster's door. The note said: 'Am fishing on the jetty by the Wedge. Meet me there at 8.15 tonight. Urgent. Win.'

It was almost 8.30 before Buster arrived at Peninsula Point, parking his Ford on Channel Road, looking for his friend Winnie Farlowe. The thousands of granite rocks making up the jetty weigh ten to fifteen tons each, and are piled about twenty feet above the water at low tide. Buster didn't see Winnie on the beach, so he walked through the soft white sand toward the Wedge, where the waves, crashing against the jetty rocks, exploded off other waves striking the steep beach, thus creating the dangerously huge surf. The body surfers were gone. Even they weren't usually crazy enough to try the Wedge this late, particularly on what promised to be a dark and chilly night.

Buster glanced up at a gull playing on the wind, screaming at him. Out on the ocean was lots of popcorn, little white puffs of water, popping into the darkness. The water looked particularly black now, and the surf was thundering against the jetty. With such an overcast June sky, there had not been a lovely blazing sunset, not tonight. The indigo sky was getting very dark, very quickly.

The last fishermen had gone by now, and he thought maybe Winnie had left too. Then he saw a man sitting fifty yards out on the surf-blackened rocks, gazing out to sea. The figure sat like a statue, his back to Buster, a figure in a dark hooded sweatshirt. It didn't look like Winnie. He wasn't as heavy as Winnie Farlowe.

When he was down below the hooded figure, scrambling up on to the huge blackened rocks, Buster Wiles yelled, 'Win? That you?'

The hooded man suddenly turned and Buster was shocked to be looking into a gun muzzle!

'Win!' Buster cried. 'Are you nuts?'

'Sane,' Winnie said. 'They drove me sane, Buster. You'd be surprised how sane you can get after fifty-four days, locked up with your thoughts. Able to *have* thoughts because you're cold sober.'

'Put that goddamn thing away!' Buster yelled.

But Winnie Farlowe said, 'Keep coming, Buster. Sit down below me on the rocks. That's it. Till you feel the surf spraying your back. And don't think about getting cute. I'm in a lot better shape now.'

Buster's hands were partly raised. He was looking frantically toward the beach. There were two lovers walking along the surf line, heading toward Channel Road, three hundred yards away.

'Put your hands down,' Winnie said, and he dropped the gun down beside his leg. 'They won't notice us, Buster. But if you yell or try to run I'll kill you without a thought.'

'You're crazy!' Buster said. 'You've gone stir crazy!'

'You better consider that,' Winnie said. 'You better if you wanna survive. But on the other hand, I can't guarantee you got any chance at all. Sit down on the rocks, just like the crabs do. Go on, Buster. Sit.'

Buster hesitated, but Winnie's voice persuaded him. He got down on his knees, then sat down on a big rock. The surf was crashing against the rocks six feet below him and Buster was feeling the spray.

He zipped up his windbreaker. 'Goddamnit, it's cold!' Buster said. 'Let's get outta here! Let's go have a drink and talk about whatever . . .'

'No drinks, Buster,' Winnie said. 'It won't be so easy this time.'

'OK, you had your little show. Now what the fuck you want with me? What the . . .'

Winnie extended his arm and fired two rounds past Buster's ear, zinging into the rocks! The rounds ricocheted dangerously. The surf exploded. The shots couldn't have been heard fifty yards away, but there was no-one to hear them anyway.

Buster fell on his knees, yelping when his shin cracked against the edge of a sharp rock. He cowered on the slimy rock in the darkness.

'Goddamnit!' he screamed. 'Goddamnit!'

'I think I might have to kill you,' Winnie said.

'Wait a minute!' Buster cried. 'Wait a minute! Jesus Christ!'

'Tell me how it started,' Winnie said. 'Did you stop Tess Binder for a ticket, or what?'

Buster rolled up the leg of his trousers and dabbed at the blood running down his leg; he was bleeding black in the misty moonlight. Then he looked up at Winnie's face and at the gun muzzle. It was darker now and Winnie's eyes had vanished in shadow. 'How'd you figure it out?'

'Was it a traffic ticket?'

'No,' Buster said. 'I was the one that got sent to bring her to the station when her old man iced himself. I phoned her two weeks later and made a date. I never told nobody about her. She was private stock. I thought she had big bucks.' He paused. 'If you're wearin a wire by any chance, it ain't worth shit. Whatever a man says under duress with a gun in his face ain't worth shit in a court of law. A man might say anything to save his own life.'

'Last August,' Winnie said. 'As long ago as that. Who decided to bring me into your little plot, you or her?'

'Her,' Buster said. 'She saw your picture in the paper when you got sentenced. She said she had a killer idea.'

'A killer idea,' Winnie said. 'To *kill* Warner Stillwell.'

'No! She always talked like a goddamn valley girl. Killer idea. Killer omelet. You musta got one a those goddamn omelets. It's the only thing that bitch can cook.'

'Why me, Buster?'

'I told you. It was *her* idea! She said you were perfect. A guy we could absolutely rely on to be piss-ass drunk when we needed a witness to Stillwell's disappearance. A guy nobody would doubt for one minute.'

'Why so elaborate? Why the gunshots out at the ranch? The seashells? The thing about somebody watching her house? Why not just Tess and me having a little fling, where she destroys what's left of my mind with sex and drugs? And gets me out on the boat with Stillwell? Why not do it a more simple way?'

Buster sat on a rock just as a wave surged in and broke two feet below him. Suddenly he was soaked.

'Goddamnit, Win! I'm freezin!'

Now it was very dark. Winnie scooted to a lower rock, his gun muzzle ten feet from Buster's face. He said, 'Why, Buster? Why all the stuff about how maybe Stillwell killed Conrad Binder and was trying to kill Tess?'

'That was *my* idea, you asshole!' Buster yelled, clutching his arms, teeth chattering. 'I did it for you!'

'You did it for me.'

'Yeah, I know what a mushy bastard you are. I knew how you'd go on a guilt binge when you didn't save a drowning man because you were drunk. I thought up that bullshit, most of it. That part about Hack Starkey, that was *her* dumb idea, and we almost got screwed when you found him and he told you different stuff than *she'd* been feedin you. She was jist supposed to say a tall dark man was watchin her house. Period. She came up with all the rest. The gunshots. The goddamn seashells. She got caught up in it. The lie took on a life of its own! The poor little rich girl was havin *fun*!'

'I still don't see how all that was for *my* sake, Buster.'

'Don't ya see? I thought it'd be easier for you if you thought the guy that got drowned was a murderer. A guy who maybe killed Conrad Binder and *wanted* to kill your lady love. I figured then you'd say he got what he deserved. God settled your problem with a nice clean boating accident. That's what I *thought* you'd say. But no, you gotta put on a hair shirt and beat yourself to death with chains like some fuckin nut case in Tehran! You gotta *demand* to go to jail! Nobody wanted you to get hurt, Win! I didn't want you to get . . .'

Suddenly Winnie cranked off two more rounds past Buster's left ear. The only creature to see the fireballs was a terrified pelican that shrieked and wheeled.

'Goddamn you!' The words got swallowed in a sob. Cowering down on the rock: 'Goddamn you, you bastard!'

'You went to all that trouble to keep *me* from getting hurt? You and your murderous little bitch of a girlfriend?'

Buster looked like he might weep. He said, 'She *wasn't* my girlfriend. She's *nobody's* girlfriend.'

'You were worried about me? You. A guy that murders

a man without a twinge of conscience. What happened out there in Isthmus Cove? Did he fight for his life a lot harder than you planned? Were you forced to cut his throat and swim his body to your boat and weigh him down and drop him in the middle of Catalina Channel on your way home?'

Buster looked at Winnie in astonishment. He said, 'You dumb bastard!'

'How'd you get out to La Quinta so fast to fire those shots at us? You were working with Hadley on the beach patrol that day when Tess and me went to La Quinta.'

A long moment. Then Buster said, 'That was so stupid I still can't believe it happened, those shots. *Her* idea, of course. But then, she's basically a stupid bitch. Cunning but stupid. Wanna know somethin, pardner? I fed her most of her lines. I told her all about you. A soft guy that everybody likes: old Winnie. Watches all those teabag shows on public television. Don't you, *old son*? Likes cool jazz. Even likes to drink at the American Legion, for chrissake. I put it all in her empty head. That bitch thinks of nothin, nothin at all, unless she can live in it, ride in it, wear it or fuck it. I been sittin here believin you had it all worked out. But I shoulda known better. Winnie Farlowe, *ace* detective! You were *never* more than a mediocre cop! Know why? Because you *trust* people!'

Winnie extended his gun hand and said, 'You haven't answered me. How did you get out to La Quinta that evening to fire those shots? Did you leave work early? Did you hire a pilot and a private plane?' He aimed at Buster's left eye.

Buster was livid. He was trembling from the cold, from terror, from rage. He covered his head as though his hands could stop the bullet, but the fury took over. He looked up at Winnie and screamed: 'YOU STUPID SON OF A BITCH! I DIDN'T FIRE THOSE SHOTS! WARNER STILLWELL DID!'

23: *The Club*

Winnie backed up until he was sitting on top of the jetty, then told Buster he could climb up to a drier rock. He kept his gun aimed while Buster dragged himself up higher, until he sat shivering and wet, his arms wrapped around his knees.

Buster said, 'You *don't* have it figured out! It ain't about murder, Win! We didn't want to hurt nobody! You understand about the trust, don't you? It couldn't be broken. That property couldn't be sold till Stillwell died, and he's a very healthy guy with a long life ahead of him. This ain't about murder! It ain't even about theft! It's about fixin a legal technicality!'

'But his life on the ranch was . . .'

'Bullshit! That was bullshit! Get real, Win! Warner Stillwell *hated* the fuckin ranch! Tess's old man was the one who wanted to live on the ranch. Stillwell never had a dime of his own 'cept what Conrad Binder gave him when he was alive, and what was provided for in his trust. Warner Stillwell loves the Riviera, he says. Him and Tess worked out the plan. They needed a guy like me and a guy like you.'

'You're trying to make me believe Warner Stillwell's alive?'

'As you are.'

'Where?'

'Search me,' Buster said. 'He thinks Portofino's gettin too expensive, but he's not too far from there, I imagine. I'd give you the name he used for the passport but I don't know it. Tess does. She'll be sendin serious money soon as she closes escrow on the ranch.'

'You always could think and talk fast,' Winnie said. 'But even for you this is *good*.'

'Jesus Christ, I'm tellin you the truth! Why should I lie?'

'Because *you* murdered Warner Stillwell and let me think I was responsible for his death. And you're trying to save your ass. You still carry your dive knife when you go down?'

'Yeah, I still carry my knife,' Buster said.

'You stuck him because he wouldn't drown peacefully. Then you couldn't leave the body. You swam the corpse out to your boat and . . .'

'I tell ya he's alive! If the goddamn probate and trust laws weren't so strict those two woulda just terminated the trust and divided up the inheritance back when Conrad Binder killed himself! Don't you see, Win? All we did, all three of us, was make the law more workable. More fair. It was *her* money! She wanted to spend it! Warner wanted to spend it! I wanted to spend a little piece of it!'

'Why did you need a fourth?'

'Back in the beginning we were gonna do it *without* a fourth. Without a Winnie Farlowe. I was gonna witness the boat accident where Warner disappears. But the more we learned about probate law the less we liked it. A judge wouldn't declare him dead without an absolutely *convincing* witness. And if the judge had doubts he'd just put it all on hold and declare Warner dead after five years of being missing. Well, we decided we didn't *have* five years to spare, none of us.'

'Then you thought of me.'

'*She* did. After she saw your picture she called me and asked is this the guy that came to my apartment that night so ripped he fell down on my porch. Wait a minute! Is that it? Did you finally *remember* her from my apartment that night?'

Winnie said, 'Keep going, Buster. My patience is limited.'

'Anyways, she said with your history as the boat parade drunk, nobody'd doubt how it happened. Not for one minute. And when I told her what a straight-ahead guy you are, well . . . she said you were jist *perfect*. A perfect . . .'

'Fall guy.'

'Nobody was supposed to get hurt!'

'Fifty-four days in jail, Buster. It *hurts*.'

'That was *your* fault! Nobody wanted that. Not even her. Fact is, I think she got a little soft on you. That ruined my own plans. I was hopin to be her fourth husband when she got rich.'

'Maybe I can spoil *everybody's* plans,' Winnie said.

'It's over!' Buster said. 'Warner Stillwell's been declared dead and Tess has the property. She's in the middle of closin a deal with a developer for almost twenty million. What can you do? You think I'm gonna go into the DA's office and tell him about this? Man, I already got a down payment on a little dive-boat business in Maui. You can go to the DA with a wild story if you want, but people'll jist say your brain's too marinated to come back to normal. You been in the news *twice*. You're a big-time

366

drunk. They'll jist think you got wet-brain.'

'Where's Tess now?'

'You can find Tess livin at her club. She already sold her house and closed escrow on that. I hear she's leased a big yacht for a trip to Mexico. You can go ask if she'll take you along as a deck hand if you want. But if you leave it alone, I bet she'll take care a you. You'll get something for yourself outta this.'

'I got a real problem,' Winnie said. 'If I let you walk away from here I'll never know if I got conned one *more* time, will I? I'll never know if it happened the way you say, or if it always *was* a two-person conspiracy to kill Warner Stillwell. I'll never know for sure whether or not you stuck your dive knife in that old man's guts and dumped him in the Catalina Channel. You always were *real* fast on your feet, Buster.'

'I guess you gotta trust your instincts,' said Buster Wiles. 'You known me a long time. You think I'm a murderer? *You* gotta decide. Either way, there's nothin you could ever prove, is there? Now, I'm freezin to death. So whaddaya gonna do, Win? Shoot me or what?'

Winnie studied Buster Wiles, sitting there on the black rock, teeth chattering, the surf exploding like thunder beneath him in churning foam, then in a swirl of black water. Winnie said, 'I wanna believe you for my own sake. I wanna believe he's still alive. But if his body's *ever* found in that channel, I'll go to the DA whether they listen to me or not. Whether I can *prove* anything or not.'

Then Winnie tucked the gun under the sweatshirt. The last thing he ever said to Buster was, 'Did you get *enough*, Buster? Was it worth it?'

'Enough to start a new life,' Buster said above the shrill hiss of wind. 'I wasn't all that greedy. But then, I'm not a cold-blooded killer. I'm jist your basic nonviolent opportunist, is all I am. And you, you're jist a loser and you always were.'

There was no more to say. Winnie Farlowe stood up then, turned and climbed down to the beach, leaving his friend Buster Wiles shivering and alone while the sea lashed the black granite rocks.

Winnie drove straight to her club. He went to the front desk and asked if they could take a message for Tess Binder who was living in one of the apartments. He wrote out a message and put it in a sealed envelope. It said:

Dear Tess,

I understand you've leased a yacht for a cruise to Mexico. I don't know when you planned to go but you're going *tomorrow*. If you're not out of my town by four p.m. I'm going to the DA whether or not it does any good. Then I'm going to the newspapers whether or not they believe me. Remember, you're leaving here tomorrow and you're not coming back. Not ever.

Yours,
Win

Winnie drove home then. He held the steering wheel in a death grip when he passed Spoon's Landing. He thought about Polish vodka and about a cocktail called The Golden Orange. He wouldn't be having one tonight. That's all he knew for sure. Not tonight.

He slept fitfully. Theta sleep. If he dreamed about the stone nymph he didn't remember it in the morning. He *did* remember a sweet lovely dream about climbing Mount Blackjack with his father, back when he wore Cub Scout blue.

24: *The Seawall*

Winnie cleaned his apartment that morning. When he was finished it was more than shipshape. In fact, he'd never lived in a place as clean and orderly as his was that morning. He phoned his mother to tell her he was going out to look for a job. He told her he was thinking about selling sailboats, and that she shouldn't worry about him; he'd be all right.

Talking to his mother made him feel better. He suddenly craved an omelet with jalapeño chilis, but there wasn't even an egg in his refrigerator. He was preparing to go out for breakfast when the phone rang. It was Sammy Vogel from Newport Beach PD.

'Win,' Vogel said. 'I just wanted to tell you there's an AA meeting tonight at seven-thirty, over on Thirty-second Street. A speaker meeting. I think you'd enjoy it. I'll be there if you wanna come.'

'Thanks,' Winnie said. 'Can't make it tonight. Maybe tomorrow night.'

Before hanging up, the detective said, 'Don't try to do it on your own. A do-it-yourself circumcision'd be easier.'

Winnie was already outside the door when the phone rang again. He went back inside and answered it on the fifth ring.

'Mister Farlowe?' the telephone voice said. 'This is Pete at Boyd Schuyler Yacht Brokerage.'

'Yeah?'

'We've got something I think you'll be interested in, Mister Farlowe. Can you come by this morning?'

He figured it might be a job offer. The day they'd gone sailing, Tess had mentioned to Boyd Schuyler that Winnie was interested in boat sales. So he changed from a T-shirt and jeans to a Reyn Spooner, slacks and his best deck shoes. With socks.

He went straight to the yacht brokerage, where he was met by Pete, who reminded him of himself fifteen years and a thousand drinks ago: a sunburnt sailor who'd take any job that kept him near boats or on the ocean.

The young salesman took Winnie into a private office, where he said, 'I've never been involved in anything like this before!' He opened a drawer and took out a large manila envelope full of manuals and documents, and a set of keys.

He said, 'You've got a boat out there! In *your* name! Paid for. And you'll find in here the location of a boat slip on the peninsula. It's been leased for you for one year. You've got some friend, that Miss Binder! She arranged all this three weeks ago, but I was told you weren't ready for it yet. Today she phoned and said you were ready.'

Pete's grin was wider than the Lido Channel. The kid's nose was peeling from too much sun and ocean glare. He seemed to want Winnie to cheer, or something.

'It's the ultralight, I guess?'

'Oh, yeah! Mister Schuyler said you already took it on a sea trial. She's a sweet boat and she's loaded! Miss Binder wanted everything you could put on it. Wanna take her out now? I got time if you need me to help.'

371

'Not now,' Winnie said. 'I gotta go get a bite to eat. Not now.'

The kid looked disappointed, but he said, 'Well, if you *ever* need someone to crew for you, just call.'

'OK,' Winnie said, standing up and taking his envelope. 'One thing, do you know about her leasing a big powerboat for a run to Mexico?'

'Sure. In fact, there was a panic around here early this morning. She's decided to go today instead of two weeks like she'd been planning. Two of our guys've been working all morning getting the boat ready. It's a seventy-five-foot custom job, called *Windspray*. Wanna see?'

'I don't wanna see,' Winnie said. 'I gotta go get an omelet.'

'I wish I was going on that Manzanillo trip,' Pete said. 'The boss got invited.'

'You mean Boyd Schuyler?'

'Yeah, he's a pretty good friend of hers. He's taking three weeks off, and flying back from there. She's flying on from there to the Bahamas. To *live*, from what I hear. I guess you know all that? Anyway, I sure wish I could go along and bring the boat back, but I don't have enough seniority around here.'

'I gotta go get an omelet,' Winnie said.

'Be sure to buy boat insurance,' the kid said. 'That's a valuable sloop and you're her master now.'

After eating a rubbery omelet at a Balboa Island family restaurant, Winnie didn't know what to do with himself. He had to do something until four o'clock. He knew where he'd be then. He decided to go home and check the mail.

There was nothing but bills. He looked at his watch. He

tried to read but it was no good. He went to his phone and dialed a number a prisoner had given him, the only prisoner more miserable than himself. A young woman answered on the first ring.

'This is Win Farlowe. I'm a friend of Doug Bracken. Can I speak to him, please?'

After a very long silence the young woman said, 'Yes, my dad mentioned you in his letters, Mister Farlowe. I . . . I'm sorry to . . . to say that Daddy shot himself last night, and . . .' There was another pause. 'I want you to know . . . to know how much it meant to all of us that you . . . that you played basketball with him.'

At 3.30 that afternoon Winnie was back on the jetty, only this time on the east side, there by little Corona Del Mar Beach where Conrad Binder had ended his life. Winnie was watching a kid about ten or eleven years old, fishing with his father. They were having a great time, father and son, not caring much if they caught anything. The kid was horsing around, trying to drop an anchovy down his old man's shirt, and the father was pretending to be scared of the dead fish. The 'old man', Winnie noted, was nearly ten years younger than he was.

Finally they got tired of fishing, and the kid snuggled up against his father and they just sat quietly like that. And Winnie sat quietly and watched them, realizing that probably he would never be a father, wondering what kind of father he'd have been, a guy who'd never been much good at anything, maybe not even as a cop.

Four o'clock came and went. So did the father and son.

Other jetty fishermen were calling it a day. Winnie sat and watched the commercial boats coming in, trailing flocks of gulls, the birds hoping for tidbits that might be tossed off the stern.

At five o'clock he thought maybe she wasn't heeding his warning. He was ready to leave when a gleaming white motor yacht came powering down the channel. It was close to his side of the jetty, and he didn't even have to look for *Windspray*. He knew this was it.

Then he saw Tess. She was wearing a white jumpsuit with a white cardigan tossed over her shoulders. She stood on the sun deck, gazing aft toward The Golden Orange. Back to the place she wouldn't be seeing any more. Then Winnie saw a suntanned man in a blue blazer walk out on to the deck, holding a tall glass. He said something to Tess, but she shook her head. He stood behind her and kissed her neck, but she didn't respond. Still she gazed back at The Golden Orange.

Winnie was running along the seawall without realizing it. He was keeping up with the slow-moving motor yacht as it crept out of the harbor, out to the open ocean. Boyd Schuyler put his arms around Tess Binder's waist and kissed her neck again.

Then Winnie yelled: 'NOW I KNOW YOU!'

The couple on the motor yacht looked over at the jetty, at the man in a sweatshirt and jeans running along beside them. 'NOW I KNOW YOU!' Winnie shouted.

Boyd Schuyler said something to Tess Binder, but she shook her head and said something back. He turned away from her and walked reluctantly into the main salon. When she was alone, Tess approached the port rail. She clutched it with both hands, watching Winnie run.

374

'I KNOW YOU!' he yelled, still running. 'NOW I KNOW YOU!'

Tess put her hands to her face, as though to weep. He'd seen her do that before, but he'd seen her *really* cry only once. On that hilltop overlooking Two Harbors, at the isthmus of Santa Catalina Island, when there was magic all around them in the twilight.

Tess dropped her hands back to the rail. She held on to it and shouted something. Winnie wasn't sure what, and he kept running along the seawall, but he was nearing the end. They'd be past the jetty in a moment and the skipper would throttle forward and she'd be gone forever.

Then she shouted: 'ONLY YOU! NOBODY ELSE! NOT EVER!'

He was panting and out of breath when he reached the end of the seawall. Winnie cupped his hands to his mouth, while the skipper was already starting to give the big yacht some speed.

Winnie had to yell it over the rumble of the diesels: 'YOU CAN'T LOVE ANYONE! YOU NEVER WILL! NOT EVERRRR!'

It was like last night. He was standing at land's end seeing someone for the very last time. And not knowing for sure whether or not this one too was a murderer.

The lazy sea lions on the bell buoy weren't even curious when the lustrous white motor-yacht powered past them and turned south-east.

25: *La Venganza*

The yacht brokerage had been closed for hours. He parked his car, got a flashlight from the glove compartment, and ran down the ramp to the docks, carrying with him two five-gallon cans of gasoline. The sailboat was in the same slip where he'd last seen her, only this time there was a name painted on the transom: *La Venganza*.

Winnie climbed aboard and went below to turn on the lights and start the engine. There by the galley, on the mahogany chart table, was a note in Tess Binder's handwriting. The note said: 'Sailing well is the best revenge.'

The harbor was quiet when Winnie hoisted sail. His was the only boat out this late. He wished there was more wind, but even in light air she responded. She was a wonderful light-air boat. He tried not to think of anything until he reached the jetty.

He didn't want to sail her out on the ocean. It seemed a cruel and brutal thing to do. He was already beginning to think of her as a living thing, this quick agile sloop. So he merely pointed her toward the open sea and started the diesel. Then he went back on deck and dropped the inflatable dinghy over the side, letting it trail. He went below again and poured five gallons of gasoline over everything. When he was finished, he poured the other can over the deck, letting it puddle in the cockpit.

He tossed the empty cans into the dinghy, started the dinghy motor, and made sure it was securely tied. Then he climbed back on deck with the flare gun. He glanced down the hatch for only a second or two. He fired once and ran aft. There was a loud PLOOM! and fire burst out of the companionway within seconds. He got the dinghy untied just before the flames spread topside. It was correct what he'd always been told – the resin in a fiberglass boat burns extremely hot and is almost impossible to extinguish.

The burning boat powered out into the bleak infinite ocean, sails alight in the darkness, blazing through sapphire water. The moon had vanished for a while.

When Winnie walked into the office of the Harbor Patrol an hour later, he was greeted with skepticism. An Orange County sheriff's deputy said, 'Your boat caught fire the same *day* you took it from the broker?'

'It was my own fault,' Winnie said. 'I bought a lotta gas for my dinghy and I accidentally dropped a can into the galley. The stove was lit.'

The deputy obviously suspected a torching. He said, 'And how *much* insurance did you have on this new boat, Mister Farlowe?'

'None,' Winnie said. 'Not a dime's worth.'

That stunned the deputy, who said, 'Damn! You should've gotten insurance before taking it out!'

'I've always been a loser,' Winnie Farlowe said.

★

It was after ten o'clock when he arrived at Spoon's Landing. All the regulars hollered his name, and made a fuss, and shook hands with him the moment he entered. Guppy Stover was there and Bilge O'Toole with his turtle, Irma. Carlos Tuna was there with Regis, his stud turtle, who was in a carrying bag on the bar. Tripoli Jones was berating two Vietnam vets who worked at the boatyard next door.

Everyone said how good Winnie looked and how much they'd missed him. But they seemed to sense that he was *much* changed after two months of sobriety. In that they were all alcoholics, they were confused and threatened by such a change. But Spoon understood.

When everyone drifted off and Winnie was alone at the bar, Spoon said, 'You sure look different.'

'Yeah,' Winnie said. 'Gimme a Polish vodka on the rocks. Double.'

Spoon's grin faded. He started to speak. He thought it over, then said, 'Not here, kid. I don't want your business no more. I was hopin I'd never see you again.'

'I read your warning, "Alcohol can harm an unborn fetus." Now *gimme* that drink.'

Spoon started wiping the bar nervously. He said, 'Why'nt ya give AA a try? Ain't ya had enough *misery*?'

'You got a liquor licence on the wall,' Winnie said, a throb in his voice. 'I'm a paying customer! I demand a *drink*!'

'OK,' Spoon said. 'May as well be me makes a few bucks off your corpse.'

While Spoon poured the drink, Winnie went to the old Wurlitzer and dropped in a quarter. The drink was on the bar when he got back, a double shot of Polish vodka on the rocks. In a bucket glass. A sturdy honest bucket. Then Frank Sinatra began to sing.

> *It seems we stood and talked like this before*
> *We looked at each other in the same way then*
> *But I can't remember where or when.*

Winnie Farlowe touched the glass, He left his finger mark in the condensation. A puddle was already forming around the base. He could smell it. American vodka smelled and tasted like nothing, but Eastern Europeans understood that vodka should have flavor and aroma.

> *The clothes you're wearing are the clothes you wore*
> *We smiled at each other in the same way then*
> *But I can't remember where or when.*

Spoon pretended not to look at Winnie. He went to the other end of the bar and talked to Bilge O'Toole. In fact, several of the others tried not to look at him. Winnie didn't notice anybody. He was thirty-eight miles away, on a hill overlooking two lovely harbors, where a zephyr blew gently and he could smell jasmine mingled with the gardenia in her hair.

> *And so it seems that we have met before*
> *And laughed before and loved before*
> *But who knows where or when.*

When Spoon looked up again, Winnie Farlowe was gone. Spoon moved quickly back down the bar. The bucket glass was still full.

The saloonkeeper picked it up, toasted the empty doorway and said, 'OK, kid, you made it through one more day.'

Spoon drank the Polish vodka himself, then said to Tripoli Jones, 'Hey, this ain't too bad. Them Polacks can do something besides go on strike!'

While everyone was watching the big TV, while the Dodgers were rallying from a two-run deficit, Carlos Tuna's stud turtle, Regis, crawled out of his leather carrying sack with a blink of surprise. Bilge O'Toole had left Irma on the bar, dozing in a saucer of beer. Regis eyed the sleeping Irma with a sidelong reptile glance. Then Regis began creeping stealthily along the bartop.

THE END

THE BLOODING
by Joseph Wambaugh

Exceptionally revealing . . . Wambaugh at his most sharp
The Listener

In 1982 a fifteen-year-old schoolgirl was raped and murdered near her home in the quiet Leicestershire village of Narborough. Nearly three years later the police had still not found her murderer when they found the body of another schoolgirl, similarly raped and killed, near the same village.

In the massive murder hunt that followed, a kitchen porter with a history of molesting children confessed to the second murder. Convinced that they'd found their man, the police enlisted the aid of a newly announced scientific discovery: genetic fingerprinting. But the lab report that came back was devastating: the kitchen porter had *not* committed either the first or the second murder. But both *were* committed by the same man. And that man was still loose . . .

And so followed the frenzied and massive blood-sampling exercise that came to be known as 'the blooding', that led at last to the conviction of the rapist and murderer whose callous confession chilled the blood of the most hardened police officers . . .

0 553 17697 8

ECHOES IN THE DARKNESS
by Joseph Wambaugh

'A stark and engrossing tale of crime and punishment'
Los Angeles Times Book Review

'Riveting'
Cosmopolitan

'Don't start it late at night'
George V. Higgins, Chicago Tribune

'Highly atmospheric'
New York Times

'A bizarre, wonderfully sordid story'
USA Today

'The words leap off the page'
Mordecai Richler

'A superior book . . . absolutely compelling'
Chicago Sun-Times

0 553 17555 6

PEOPLE LIKE US
by Dominic Dunne

The new international bestseller by the author of *The Two Mrs Grenvilles*.

Gus Bailey, journalist, divorcé, refugee from Hollywood, and perennial extra man, is the confidant of the New York elité. Gus is perfectly situated to observe the intimate cataclysms that shape and shake Manhattan's ruling class – some ascend, some obstruct those who ascend, others succumb to scandal or relative poverty.

But while he exposes the vanities of the very people with whom he is so intimate, Gus has a dark and painful secret of his own – one that will rise up to haunt him for ever unless he finds some way, violent if necessary, to exorcise it. The beautiful people have their problems too, but Gus is not about to let their Black Mondays deflect him from the path of vengeance – or not if he can help it.

0 553 17676 5

A SELECTION OF FINE NOVELS
AVAILABLE FROM BANTAM BOOKS

THE PRICES SHOWN BELOW WERE CORRECT AT THE TIME OF GOING TO PRESS. HOWEVER TRANSWORLD PUBLISHERS RESERVE THE RIGHT TO SHOW NEW RETAIL PRICES ON COVERS WHICH MAY DIFFER FROM THOSE PREVIOUSLY ADVERTISED IN THE TEXT OR ELSEWHERE.

All Corgi/Bantam Books are available at your bookshop or newsagent, or can be ordered from the following address:

Corgi/Bantam Books,
Cash Sales Department
P.O. Box 11, Falmouth, Cornwall TR10 9EN

Please send a cheque or postal order (no currency) and allow 80p for postage and packing for the first book plus 20p for each additional book ordered up to a maximum charge of £2.00 in UK.

B.F.P.O. customers please allow 80p for the first book and 20p for each additional book.

Overseas customers, including Eire, please allow £1.50 for postage and packing for the first book, £1.00 for the second book, and 30p for each subsequent title ordered.

NAME (Block Letters) ....

ADDRESS ....

....